All For One

All For One

Kathleen Clare

Print information available on the last page.

Rev. date: 10/02/2019

To order additional copies of this book, contact:
Xlibris
1-888-795-4274
www.Xlibris.com
Orders@Xlibris.com
796163

Again, the dedications goes to my friends and family who have had faith in my endeavors to add to the tales of The Three Musketeers, as these are prequels to Alexandre' Dumas masterpieces. Much gratitude and love. Thank you.

"Tous pour un, Un pour to tous"

AUTHOR'S NOTE

As much as I personally would like to continue writing additional adventure of these three famous men, I feel I can't go any further without over stepping literary bounds, therefore, "All for One" is my last.

Many thanks to those that took an interest in my previous ones and hopefully you will enjoy this one as well.

As they would say from their hearts, and I as well, "Merci beaucoup."

As my final contribution to my stories, I decided to draw their true representation of their friendship and camaraderie and what better way then their crossed swords and using my art degree, I did so. It is my wish you enjoy my books as much as I enjoyed writing them. Enjoy!

DISCLAIMER

In my past books, I have stated historical facts regarding the Huguenots and the sieges against Louis XIII, however in this story, I was unable to find any historical significance to support factual events concurrent with this time, therefore this is purely fiction.

The people involved for the most part are historically accurate. Some of the names are fictitious are as the story.

I

"Why do I have ringing in my ears?" Groaned a stout, robust musketeer, whom at the present was lying prone on a chaise lounge with his legs bent to the similarities of a readied trigger of a harquebus, against the head rest.

"Because you, inebriated dolt, we are within four leagues of Notre Dame." Replied a rather portly, hefty musketeer, who stood a head above his fellow companions.

"Alas, it is at such an ungodly hour."

"I beg to differ, all hours of the day belong to God, and therefore not ungodly. How you choose to spend the time can benefit, be of God or a waste, ungodly." Replied the pious musketeer.

"Then, by the bye, what did the clock say?" Queried the one, running his hands through his tangled, disheveled locks.

"BONG, BONG, BONG." Replied the portly musketeer, with a wry smile as he stood afore a warming hearth and kicking a smoldering log, in hopes of bringing it back to life.

The portly musketeer along with his pious companion laughed.

"This might help." Suggested the Pious one, handing the portly musketeer two adequate logs, cut appropriately by a woodsman, to accommodate the hearth.

The three were sharing a bed chamber that was rather small, but it was all the tavern had available.

"Why is it, when one siege ends another begins?" Queried the one lying upon the chaise lounge.

"Men tend to quarrel over the most trivial things."

"Religious freedom is not trivial." Replied the Pious one.

"The king thinks so."

"He is siege mad." Groaned the disheveled musketeer.

"That may be so, alas our given task is not to be taken lightly and he expects to be given accurate information as if he were there himself."

The disheveled one turned his head to the side, "Is it daylight yet?" He queried.

"I know not, the shutters are closed." Replied the portly one, "As your eyes."

"Open or shut they still see the same."

"The hour is late, that I can assure you. No matter, we had best get some rest and in the morn when the sun has at least cleared the horizon we should send for our horses as we make use of the nearest bath house and barber." Suggested the Pious one, "I should think we need to look like we belong to the king and not stable remains."

"Aramis, no matter what we look like, our allegiance is to him." Suggested Porthos.

"We represent our regiment as well, alas no matter how you turn, we represent something or someone and it will not bring harm to look our best as we step in their direction."

The portly one, Porthos sighed, "You are right, *mon ami*. By the bye what condition is our purses in? Are they in want? For breakfast is nigh.'

"Mine has a few sous." Commented the disheveled one, Athos.

"I do believe I as well have a sou or two."

"It does seem we could engage one or two naive cardinals' men in a game of "The Pence in the Pocket."

Aramis reddened with embarrassment as he thought of his first encounter with the game as much to his chagrin, he had lost and as a result was rendered useless as well as inebriated.

Athos chuckled, as he let his legs go lax against the the head rest of the chaise lounge and his breathing became rhythmic indicating he had fallen asleep.

"No point in trying to roust him.", Sighed Porthos.

"He was fully aware of the fact that we need to return to Paris and convey our findings to Louis and Richelieu. Does he not know the importance?"

"He does, but does not find it necessary to break his neck over the haste. The remnants of resistance are not going any where with any kind of haste. The king will be informed and the necessary actions will be taken."

Aramis sighed, "Another siege."

"No doubt."

"Such a waste."

"My suggestion is to follow Athos' example and get some rest while we can. The next day will be hard riding, although truly we are not pressed for time, alas the king and cardinal will want knowledge of the their intent through our investigations."

Aramis took a turn with the hearth and laid another log on, then kicked it into place with his heavily booted foot, sparks danced out of rebellion to the prodding.

"Do you truly want to follow his example?" Queried Aramis, in a serious vein.

"He is a fine upstanding musketeer." Replied Porthos, defending his companion as he would Aramis if the need ever arose.

"When he is up and standing." Commented Aramis.

"Too bad you dismissed the valets this eve. Peste! Could sure use Mousequeton in getting these boots off.", his face reddening with the endeavor.

Aramis smiled, "What did you do afore you acquired him?'

"Slept with them on."

"Then there is your answer."

Porthos then sat on the edge of the bed, that sagged and groaned under his portliness.

With one foot and manipulations thereof, he was able to remove a boot and with that being done, the second foot was freed from the confines of the worn leather.

"Still in need of new boots and stockings. That reminds me, did you ever get the tine of your spur repaired or replaced?" Queried Porthos.

"Ne'. Does not seem to be enough time betwixt assignments to part with it for any great length of time."

"Perchance if you offer the blacksmith a sou or two above his wage will be incentive enough to hasten its repair."

"He moves at his own pace, increase of wage or no, it matters not, unless the directive came from Louis."

"Then it shall come from Louis and his purse." Smiled Porthos.

"In the morn we will have breakfast and the seek a barber and a bath.

"Will our meager purses allow such accommodations, for the common denizen recognizes us not as one of the kings' musketeers?"

"Then collectively meagre or no, we will make the best of our circumstances."

"We always do, do we not?"

"Indeed." Replied Aramis as he sat on the other side of the massive bed, which barely gave as the slight musketeer sat and removed his boots.

They both laid down, turned to a side that was comfortable, covered themselves with their mantles for the room was glowing warm from the hearth.

Aramis extinguished the taper, adjusted himself and promptly fell asleep.

Knowing dawn was nigh, Porthos caught himself breathing in unison with his companions and he too fell asleep.

The sun had barely touched the horizon when Mousequeton and his fellow valets: Bazin and Grimaud, allowed themselves into their masters' chamber and found their prospective master to awaken them.

Mousequeton nudged Porthos roughly on the shoulder and then retreated a pace or two, knowing Porthos had a rough go of it when he was awaken out of a sound sleep.

Bazin lightly touched Aramis and the musketeer immediately sat up and was on the ready.

Grimaud hesitated in rousting Athos, he knew his master did his fair share of counting Anjou bottles, but when morn arrived he knew not whether Athos actually knew how many bottles were laid to rest or if Athos could only guess.

Aramis is glanced over his shoulder to see what state Porthos was in.

Hearing his companion awake with a start, he could not help but smile.

"How many times have you frightened me witless in predawn hours, only to amuse yourself?" Pondered Aramis to himself.

Grimaud touched Athos on the shoulder as the musketeer turned his head and made a feeble attempt of removing his dark hair away from his eyes and out of his mouth.

"Tastes nothing like Anjou.", he muttered, as he exaggerated a shrug.

"Are we stopping at the *Palais Royale* or we going to continue north?" Porthos, "We have only taken in a third of the state."

"We really should continue, considering we have continually send missives to the king with our findings and when we return, he can address any and all situations. Whether he deems it necessary to orchestrate a regiment or two, that remains his decision."

"What I would give to be in my own bed for a fortnight." Sighed Porthos.

"Me as well." agreed Aramis, "Alas we have not the time."

"How can you say that? We have been on the move from most of a year. From our regiment marching south to Montpellier last spring to the siege in August, the truce, Rohan not relenting and as a result, Louis wants us to keep track of the remnants of resistance, thus, I am thoroughly fatigued."

Athos sat himself up.

"Time is all we have, and it seems like it is always the foe and in the end we have to reckon with it and be held accountable."

"We are given the same amount of time every day by the grace of God, squandering it is very much a directive of Satan, spend it well and wisely is that of God." Reminded Aramis.

Sunlight began to filter through the slits of the worn shutters, creating casted silhouettes against the far wall.

Athos chuckled.

"What is so amusing?" Queried Aramis.

Athos pointed in the direction of the wall and replied, "The taper. It looks like a blade on the ready."

"Now gentlemen, if you will, let us take into considerations of what are the contents of our purses. By doing so will either let us feast Iike a king or be the meager findings of a pauper." Reasoned Aramis.

Collectively, they sat around a small table, set afore the hearth, and emptied the contents of their worn purses.

"This sure has seen the wants and needs of many a day." Smile Porthos, as he reached inside his doublet and withdrew the small well worn purse, and untied its strings and cautiously emptied the contents atop the table.

Athos and Aramis did the same.

Aramis, versed in calculations, verified the small pile of coins would allow them a descent meal and no more.

"Then that means, we will have to plead our case to the cardinal whether we like it or not." Conceded Porthos, admitting the cardinal as the minister of finances as well other notable stations considered worthy, by the king.

"Looks that way." Agreed Aramis, sighing.

"Splendid! More dribble from a man who creates policies for the sake of creating policies to say it is good for the state." Added Athos, attempting to stifle a yawn.

Aramis shook his head and glanced toward Porthos, who just rolled his eyes.

"Then, let us have our meal and find, "The Bronze Turtle," in Paris, see if we can secure favored owed, and whether we like it or not. be presented to Richelieu, then secure counsel with Louis."

Gathering their accruements and vestments and other personal effects, made their way to the grand hall which was nigh empty, considering the hour of six.

The innkeep, hearing the commotion they were causing, hastily approached, as they were just sitting down.

"Messieurs, what might I interest you with?" He queried, anxiously as he took note they were part of the newly formed regiment of musketeers under king.

Athos suddenly kicked something that was under the table. He moved it with his foot to bring it closer to his side so that he might be able to reach down to pick it up.

With the dexterity of a court jester, but this time in court entertaining the king and his court was a court jestress, Matherine, he managed to pick it up, he found it to be a goblet.

"I dare say, yes fill this to begin with. Not with that peculiar tasting or odd colored one, Anjou. Drink of choice."

"If your spit has a fowl or two on it and what ever your big kettle contains. Bring it and the appropriate ware for six." Added Aramis.

"Excuse me Monsieur, the kettle contains a mere broth with sparse vegetables with a handful of a wild herb, the kitchen staff found, thrown in and hoped for the best.

The aroma is delightful, alas, I have not tasted it so I can not tell any different."

"Nor should you." Commented Athos.

The valets sat themselves respectfully behind their masters awaiting for the meal to be served so that they may attend their every need.

The plates with nicks and chips, were set afore each musketeer with a roasted fowl upon it and a spoon resting in a worn wooden bowl, and the goblets on the small side, had dents and creases, caused by rather boisterous denizens, celebrating unknown *fetes*.

The Anjou wine was poured and the bottle, obviously from an ancient seldom used vault, was placed in the center of the table, whether by happenstance or intent, afore Athos.

The weary musketeer eyed it with erringly, thought better of it, dismantled the meager fowl, that he could not identify as either goose or duck.

The inn was uncommonly silent, in spite of its proximity from Paris.

The musketeers ate with little conversation, they were fatigued and wanted nothing better than being out of the saddle for a few days to give themselves a rest.

Porthos was about to take a bit of Brie and bread to dip it in his wine, when he heard behind him, "Oh Porthos!"

The giant musketeer clenched his jowl and fist til they ached under the pressure.

Slightly he inclined his head and in *sotto* voc, said, "I thought Pasqual and Tomas fulfilled their reservations at the Bastille, compliments of Louis and Armand."

"I assure you, they did." Replied Aramis.

"Then whom, pray tell is that?"

"That *mon ami,* is Andre'. A lackey if you will of Pasqual."

"He obviously thought himself something of worth in order to obtain a lackey. A valet is another story, but a lackey?"

Again Porthos heard his name, and again he refused to acknowledge the man.

"Perchance if I ignore him, he will go away." Muttered Porthos.

"Not likely. If he is anything like Pasqual, he will be a burr.", Added Athos with a wry smile.

"Peste! Just what I need, another irritant."

"Perchance if you answer his summons, he will leave you be." Reasoned the young prelate, who had left his schooling monastery, found wanting to do something of worth and became a guard of the king.

Serving the king is serving God, for the king was chosen by God to lead the state through all its trials and tribulations.

Finding this king to be rather on the young side, he thought it best to preserve the monarchy until an heir was born, then return to the monastery. God willing.

"There is good in all of us." Theorized Aramis.

"Perchance there is." Replied Porthos, "Although, it might be a bit difficult, fore it would be so minute."

Aramis inclined his head, "Nonetheless…"

Athos drained his goblet, only to refill it, listened to his companions exchange.

Porthos swallowed what he had in his mouth, hastily turned about to face Andre'.

"What is it?"

"Pasqual sends salutations and relay that he bears your no ill will."

"Bears us no ill will, why should he if he did?, Replied the portly musketeer, sternly. "We were not the ones who conspired a treasonous act against the cardinal."

"He sends forgiveness."

"What should I forgive, that he is a dolt? That he created contempt and chaos every time I caught sight of him?"

"He would not be in the situation he is, if he had not been lured away with the vain promises.", Observed Athos.

Aramis slid a couple of souls in the young mans' direction, "Here.. get him a little Brie and broche'. He no doubt is in want." Instructed Aramis, "Porthos, is there something you want to add?"

"Not really."

"Porthos?"

"Aramis?"

Porthos sighed, then suddenly inhaled and held it momentarily, then slowly released it and in *sotto voc,* said, "Send him *bon fate.* May she not snip his thread too soon."

The young man bowed slightly and departed.

Aramis smiled to himself and returned to his breakfast.

"Why did you do that?" Queried Athos.

"Do what?" Replied Aramis.

"Give him some of our sous? Our purses are in want and to settle our debt might be a challenge."

"Pasqual, no doubt is in more want than we will ever be. We have seen our day and more days to come, he? Not likely. Mistakes are made and corrected.", Aramis sighed, "I will never understand what motivates a man, to do the things he does."

"Empty coffers is motivation enough to seek relief in one form or other, a good deed or an evil one, the consequences are the same, the coffers contents were replenished." Smiled Athos, weakly.

Aramis inclined his head in acknowledgment.

"By the bye," Observed Porthos, "How is it he found us?"

"Porthos, may I remind you, we are not that far from Paris. He may have happened in, or no. It matters not. Now, if we may, let us finish. I am so looking forward to my bath and shave.", Commented Aramis.

10 KATHLEEN CLARE

"As you should.", Replied Athos.

On an occasion, the valets attended their masters' whims and needs.

Considering how meager the meal was, they need not rise from their chairs as often as they would were it an elaborate one.

Collectively they counted out fifteen sous and the remaining twelve would be used in preparation for their presentations to the king and cardinal.

Porthos queried if they were going to stay long enough to have an appointment with their beloved captain, de Treville.

"I would be inclined to think he would prorate our wage for our absence due to requests of Richelieu and Louis." Therorized Athos

"It would certainly fill my coffer. It's surplus would be most welcome. Turning a doublet can be turned just so many times afore it looks like it needs to be retired permanently` Lamented Porthos.

"As a Jesuit, my wants and needs are minimal.", Smiled Aramis, "What I have is sufficient".

"Ah, but dear Aramis, you are a musketeer at the moment. Your wants and needs are double that of a priest who has taken the vow of poverty.

"Alas, yes, but nothing added to nothing is still nothing. So what is there to double? Nothing."

Porthos, smiled and shook his head.

"Quite right, but do try to make the most of its benefits. If you care to give it to a charitable cause, so be it, but save a little for yourself for any debts needing to be reconciled."

"Some of us do not voluntarily take the vow of poverty, and yet if we are to survive, we make necessary adjustments to what is available and strive forward." Suggested Athos, as he set his goblet upside down.

"Precisely. Use what you must, tithe what you must, seal the remains in a coffer, but for the moment at hand, I suggest we settle what debt we have and depart. The meal may have been meager and so is our purses, but must not cheat the inn keep out of what he is due." Added Porthos as he picked up the shallow bowl and drained the contents, then using a sleeve, cleared his chin of anything that missed his mouth.

Athos cringed, for he knew it was not proper etiquette for a gentleman, even the least a common man.

Aramis hid a small weak smile behind his hand, stood and replaced his leathered gauntlets upon his hands, scooped up the counted sous and waited til his companions and their valets regained their feet, afore he moved towards the door.

The valets, hastily finished what was on their plate, even if it t'was a heel of bread, it mattered not. Wasting food was not an option.

The inn keep approached and respectfully bowed slightly.

"My apologies Messieurs on the meagerness of your meal, my butcher is ill and the dolt never thought it be a benefit to have an apprentice, but clearly it would have. The cellar, alas is betwixt seasons."

Aramis remained silent as he handed the inn keep what he was due and replaced his cap firmly upon his head and his mantle about his shoulders.

"Jacques," Shouted the inn keep, "Come. Get these gentlemen their horses. Make haste!"

A young boy that reminded Porthos of his young brother, Montaire came scurrying out from a corner by the hearth, clearly trying to keep warm, let the heavy door close loudly behind him as he made his way to the stables to do as his was bid.

It did not take too long afore the boy returned.

As he entered, he inclined his head lightly in the direction of the inn keep and retreated back to his corner, pulling his worn faded mantle tighter about him.

Aramis and Athos, with valets in tow, made for the inns' courtyard to retrieve their horses.

Porthos sought the boy, took his hand and place five sous in his hand and closed it, covered with his maul of a hand and said, "Get yourself a descent mantle, a warm one."

The young boy searched the musketeers, warming eyes as to query, "Why?"

Porthos quietly said, "It is because I have a young brother and you remind me of him. He is not in want and neither should you be."

The young boy let tears of gratitude roll gently down his cheek, afore he wiped them away with a calloused palm and managed a weak smile and nod.

Porthos curtly nodded as well and departed, with his large mantle billowing after him.

They all regained their saddles to begin what they hoped, an unadventful trek toward Paris.

Once the sun had cleared the tops of the trees, it began it daily duty of providing warmth and light to those in need.

"I should think it would take us a fortnight to prepare for our presentation to Louis, Richelieu and De Treville." Commented Porthos, to no one in particular.

"That is a relative short length of time to get a years worth of soil off." Added Aramis.

"They know not when to expect us, therefore we can be at leisure til we deem ourselves worthy." Said Athos.

"Indeed. The last missive forwarded, was just a mere two days back, and we no doubt will arrive afore it does, therefore we can relay its contents with more accuracy than the mere words." Said Porthos, optimistically.

"One thing is for sure," Added Aramis, "We will not be waylaid by antics from Pasqual or Tomas as they try to best Porthos."

Porthos laughed and shook his head, "They never did learn, did they?"

The other two chuckled, "You would think after the first pounding, there would not have been a second." Said Aramis.

"Or a third." Added Athos, with a wry grin, that was toying with the corners of his mouth, under his long unmanicured goatee.

A light breeze caught their plumes in their caps and caused them to waver lightly, although it was a bit cool, it brought no indications of inclement elements.

As they approached their fair city, they caught sight of familiar chimneys with curls of smoke ascending heavenwards brining with it the aromas of whatever was upon the hearths' spitted rotisserie's and kettles that gently simmered its contents.

"Our destination is at hand." Announced Porthos, "If it were not for all the denizens, I so would challenge you to see who would reach its front courtyard first."

"Ah, Dear Porthos,", Reminded Aramis, "Our purses are a collaborative effort, therefore arriving collectively as a whole, is the only sure way. Considering it is still early to some, I suggest we do as we planned. By the time we are coffed and curled, it will be supper time and if we arrive in time afore it is served we could hold audience with all three and not have to divide our time betwixt them."

The denizens of the city, who had begun their day as the sun rose, were about with various errands due to the biddings of others, be it a court courier or a maid in waiting seeking wares and/or attire for her mistress, it all amounted to the same, chaos and confusion.

Some of the horses protested the proximity of other animals and or the denizens.

It mattered not as they carefully picked their way amid the chaos and found the courtyard nigh vacant and they eased their feet.

"I was just pondering if we should have sent the valet ahead to secure us accommodation of such, but it is obvious that was not necessitated, therefore let us make the most of what is at hand." Commented Porthos.

"The hand extended, is rather on the short side." Said Athos.

"That it is, but it is still adequate for all intents and purposes." Smiled Porthos.

As their feet touched the ground, a lackey approached.

"Good gentlemen, what is it you seek?" He queried, chaffing his hands.

"A bit of Anjou, a warm bath, followed by proper preparations for presentation to the king and cardinal." Replied Porthos.

"Why say you, you think you are of the kings' musketeers to request such service?" He queried, somewhat wryly.

Aramis tittered, Athos coughed with annoyance and Porthos pulled himself to his full stature and replied with an arched brow, "I truly am not amused by such a query, alas I find it necessary to forgive such ignorance by saying, since you obviously are aware of such a regiment, yes we are of the kings musketeers. Our tabards are a bit concealed by a years' worth of field work, we will make use of your laundry services as well."

"It did not help that you were knocked down and rolled down the small knoll only to come to rest like an unspent cannon ball, in a trench layered in mire." Suggested Aramis.

"You fail to acknowledge my dear companion, you no less were right behind me in the given matter."

Aramis reddened with embarrassment, lent nothing more to the conversation.

"Then good gentlemen, if you will follow me. There is a small gaming hall you may make use of while your baths are prepared."

At that moment, two of the cardinals men, on horseback, thundered by in pursuit of only they knew what.

Athos only shook his head.

"What?" Queried Porthos, acknowledging the slight movements of Athos.

"They are probably are on a knights errand and leave it to Richelieu to allow such frivolous thoughts to enter that pebble sized brain of his and make more of it than it actually is."

"Or it could be they were summoned by his Eminence and did not want to keep him waiting." Observed Aramis.

"Alas dear Aramis," Replied Athos, "It is he that makes us wait even though we have an appointment. He knows full well that we have other things that could preoccupy our time and mind that would be more productive than idling about his ante-chamber."

"He always has appointments and manages to see to it our appointment is kept. He is a busy man. Seldom idle."

Athos glanced at Aramis, askance, then remained silent.

The valet beckoned them to follow, and were led down a short passage way to a chambers, by their standards a rather small one.

Indeed it was for gambling, but there was no one to counter their wanton purses.

"I sympathize with all stations of the clergy. For the demand is great and trying to answer all in a timely manner remains a constant struggle."

"Indeed. Man and his skepticism concerning his faith in the unseen, though he was taught that there is God, he still wants tangible proof. Richelieu wears many other caps in addition to his clerical skull cap and oversees the functionality of all of them. In addition to that, he mentors the young king. Therefore quite busy, never an idle moment."

"That you know of."

"Athos!"

"Aramis?"

"Oh bother!" Replied Aramis, somewhat exasperated with the conversation.

Porthos sat in silence, amused by his companions, one actually defending the cardinal, or was it the clergy in general, considering, and the other trying to find creative ways to express his contempt with utmost tact and not offend Aramis.

"Are you trying to justify your words?" Queried Aramis.

"Justifying or no, it is all fact." Replied Athos, casually.

Aramis pursed his lips so hard, that his thin mustache vanished amid the sudden in discoloration of his countenance.

Porthos, trying to be inconspicuous, lightly tossed dice upon the table beside him.

Afore the conversation could continue, a valet entered through a small door in the back of the room, followed by a second carrying a large pail.

"What are we waiting for?" Queried Porthos, somewhat piqued by being delayed.

Sensing his companions' agitation, Aramis Replied, "Be at ease old man. They know not that we are here. Therefore there is no appointment to keep."

The first valet retrieved a kettle that hung from the heart of the hearth, poured water from the large bucket into a second kettle, replaced it, added a couple of logs, poked them into place, and then disappeared through a side door with the second valet in tow.

"Apparently our hot water." Replied Aramis, observing the valets actions.

Within a short length of time, the first valet appeared again, with a folded linen draped over a bent arm, held close.

He bowed in greeting, the musketeers returned the greeting with curt nods.

The valet caught Athos attention first and indicated for him to follow.

Athos always on the ready, glanced about him to assure himself he had not forgot nor misplaced anything, followed cautiously.

"Would you like a shave Monsieur?" Queried the valet.

"Bring the implements, then roust my valet. That is what he is for and my purse will not be frequented unnecessarily."

The saloons' valet was unaccustomed to such a request, knew not the appropriate response and knew too, that such a request would mean his establishments coffer would lack, none the less, he complied.

He afforded the musketeer privacy in a small scantly furnished chamber that consisted of a tub, stand with pitcher and basin, linens and crude soap.

The water was murky, which caused Athos to pause in contemplation.

"I assure you Monsieur, no has been here afore you. You are the first."

"This day, at least. No telling of days passed."

The valet wanted to offer a rebuttal but Athos held up his gauntleted hand, "If I had the time, I would be requesting hot previously unused water. I have neither the time or the patience. Now if you will, my valet."

The valet, bowed slightly then departed.

Athos readied himself, closed his eyes, held his breath, then hesitantly stepped in and lowered himself into sitting position with his knees drawn up under his unshaven chin.

There came two sharp raps upon the door as it slowly creaked open. It was Grimaud.

Athos nodded at his valet in greeting.

"Master? Permission to speak."

The musketeer gestured for his valet to continue, permission granted.

"For one Monsieur, you have not removed your gauntlets nor your vestments."

Athos screwed up his countenance and glanced intently at his valet.

"Have you seen this water? I assure you it has seen better days. This tub as it is suppose to be called, is more like a shallow basin without its pitcher. Porthos' goblet is bigger this."

"The hostler valet has not attended the hearth, alas I shall."

With that, he hastened to the hearth and placed two nice sized logs on it and kicked them into place amid the sparks they emitted.

"Now master, if you will, allow me your vestments and I will send them out to be laundered."

The valet glanced about, as Athos queried, "What is it you seek?"

"Your boots, so that they may be resoled and stitched."

Reluctantly Athos regained his feet and stood afore his valet.

Grimaud shook his head, but said nothing, and went to see if the water in the kettle in the hearth was faring better, which was no more than five paces away.

"Boots too."

After Athos replaced himself in the tub, Grimaud wrung out the excessive water from each vestment through an open window, then gathered them up to take them to the establishments' laundress.

When he returned, he began his regiment of assisting his master return to the recognizable musketeer that had been absent for almost a year.

He began by adding more hot water then wetting a small square of linen and soap and made use of them.

As Grimaud rinsed Athos' hair, a rap came upon the door.

It was the innkeep with a straight razor and a comb.

"Your masters' vestments are nigh dry. It is fortunate that there is a good steady breeze this day and no indications of inclement elements."

Grimaud accepted the items and returned his attentions to his master.

"Splendid. I was beginning to think you would have had to use my poniard."

The session ended with Grimaud changing the water, adding additional hot water then awaited for the return of Athos' vestments and boots.

Another rap on the door, found Mousequeton inquiring if they had any soap that did not smell like the royal stables on an off day.

"Upon the faith of a gentleman, those were my masters' exact words.", Mousequeton was heard to say.

Athos hid his a wry smile.

"Yes, Porthos would say something like that."

From within the next chamber, they heard a loud thud and mild oaths uttered in a loud boisterous voice.

"Shall I?" Inquired Grimaud.

Athos nodded his consent as Grimaud made for the door.

Mousequeton met Grimaud at the door as he was about to knock.

"Fear not my fellow valet, it is my master, his tub is about the size of a tea cup served at court. Finds it extremely uncomfortable but alas, under the circumstances it is the best we can do and he may not like it, but it is the best we can do for the moment."

"If your master has the tea cup, than my master has the tea urn. He most definitely found it most appalling and has never seen water of that color afore. With much hesitation and trepidation he reluctantly accomplished his feat. I recently changed the water and added essentials and he can be at ease til his clothes are dry, they were laundered an hour or so ago."

"I am guessing that is what it means to be a part of civilization."

"Not always appealing. When we were betwixt villages and a river let flowed, it certainly was a whole lot cleaner than this."

"…And colder." Added Mousequeton, with a wry smile, "that would certainly mean they would not linger any longer than they had to."

Both valets chuckled at the image their conversations had created.

As they were about to part company, Bazin was making his way down the passage way with an armful of vestments and boots, barely able to peer over the mound he beheld.

Mousequeton and Grimaud went to assist him as the prelates valet subsequently dropped the boots.

Gingerly, the valets were able to identify their masters' vestments amongst the jumbled heap.

"One moment if you please." Said Mousequeton, as he held up a pair of pantaloons,

"I do not think my master will be able to squeeze into something this slight. He might be slight in some ares, but certainly not his girth."

"I do believe this boot belongs to my master. See? There is a tine missing from this spur." Said Bazin, identifying Aramis' boot.

Grimaud sighed.

"What gives?" Queried Bazin.

"I should think the water has cooled off and thus not be as comfortable as once requested, therefore our masters are in of our assistance and their vestments."

"Oh bother!" Exclaimed Bazin, suddenly.

The other two valets glanced in his direction with inquiry.

"My master had requested to be shaved and shorn. He wants to be able to attend a high mass. His appearance is his utmost concern."

"It always has been." Commented Grimaud.

"Indeed. Bye the by, it is Sunday after all. All the more reason to attend mass. Now if you gentlemen will excuse me, my master awaits."

Mousequeton chuckled more to himself than to Grimaud.

"What gives?" Queried Grimaud.

"This is the most we have heard you. Mind you it is not a bad thing, it is just we enjoy your presence and would like you opinion now and again."

"It was given direction of my master that I remain dumb and mute and only respond minimally when the occasion arises. He as well, speaks little. That is his choice."

"That makes him a man of intrigue and caution."

"It is what he wishes. Query of me not, further, I may be a key to my masters' lock, I can not nor will I turn it. Alas, I must query of you, what was that loud noise coming from within your given chamber?"

Mousequeton whole heartily laughed, then sighed.

"That was indeed my master. Frustrated over the size of his tub as well condition of the water. Far too cold for his liking and in the stead of milky white caused by the warmth of added essentials, it was very murky and uninviting."

"Seems to be the consensus. I remedied it to the best of my abilities and limited available resources, as well, I should think Bazin and yourself did the same."

"To spare us from our ears being accosted in the future, I recommend that we remind them of their current situation and avoid this hostler at all cost."

They both laughed at the mild oaths they would hear if they did not continue with their tasks and it was best if they made haste.

""Take good care, my good man. Athos is a man of honor and his silence is and will be respected. Although, caution, in due time all secrets, will be exposed for what they are worth. Whether you turn the key, or someone else, it all will be revealed."

In parting, Grimaud suspiciously queried, "Are you a sooth sayer?"

Mousequeton smiled, "Ne." He replied, "Just silently and casually observed many a situation. Everyone has a story to be read. Even if it is old, dusty and forgotten, the book will be found and read. If some of the pages are misplaced or missing, the gaps will be filled in by fact or fiction, no matter, the reader will improvise and then book will end."

Grimaud then lifted the latch, sighed and allowed himself in and quietly closed the heavy oak door.

II

Porthos was the first one to re-enter the gaming room to await his companions.

He again picked up the dice to toss them, but paused as he glanced about in search of cards.

He wanted to practice at Lansquenet. Although he was a master at the game and was known to empty many unaware gentlemen's purses, he just wanted to pass some time in a semi-constructive manner.

At the far end of the hall, a door clicked open.

It was Athos.

The musketeer shuddered and drew his mantle closer and sat next Porthos.

The hefty musketeer heaved himself out of his chair and strode to the hearth, threw a couple of logs into the fire to stoke it and using his spurred heel, moved the logs into place, sending sparks heavenward.

"Move closer, if you so choose."

"It is a given that Aramis may be particular about his countenance and he should make his appearance sooner than not, what say you we find dinner. It is close to twelve, I would so imagine."

"Perchance did your stomach sound an alarm that it is empty?" Smiled Athos.

Porthos chuckled.

"It does now and then, yes now is one of those times."

Athos sighed.

"Alas my dear companion, we have to wait for Aramis. Most peculiar young man, if I do say so."

"Why say you?"

"Have you not noticed how he pinches his earlobes, or that his hands are rarely touching his sides. One is resting on his sheathed swords' pummel and the other tucked un his doublet?"

"Perchance his hands bother him." Reasoned Porthos.

"At such a young age? I doubt that. He is a fine musketeer and efforts are flawless."

"Then perchance his ears are cold and he wants to make sure they have not froze off." Theorized the hefty musketeer, "Do you find it bothersome?"

"Only when we are to be silent and unobserved by those that oppose us, of which is often these days."

"I should think he knows the difference when to remain still and when to move without notice. Then I would think, it is one of those inexplicable things and pay no mind to it."

Athos smiled weakly, "Indeed. Alas it is seldom done as it is said."

The door at the end of the hall once again creaked open and in strode Aramis, with Bazin respectfully two paces to the right, behind.

"Since it indeed is the Sabbath, a day of rest, yes, I will use that as an excuse, and the fact remains, we did not relay the fact we were arriving, I suggest we utilize the time as we see fit. I for one would like to attend mass. Would like to revisit my proclaimed oaths, lest I should forget."

"Like you ever could. You have it so ingrained in the recesses of your mind, You probably could recite mass while at repose." Commented Athos.

Aramis smiled, "The benefits of being pious. Repetition has its merits."

"Then," suggested Porthos to Athos, "What say you, we frequent our favorite establishment and lay waste to some purses?"

"It would not cause harm for you two to attend a service as well."

"Mass is held at various times through this day, we will pick a time and go." Said Athos, in hopes of appeasing his companion.

"Then collectively as Norte Dame strikes the hour of six on the morrows morn, we will descend on De Treville and have him join us at court for breakfast with the king and the cardinal."

"The king is not an early riser and does not like to be disturbed." Observed Aramis.

"Ah, but we have credence and justification for our actions." Replied Porthos as he inclined his head.

"Mind you, anything that walks like a siege, acts like a siege, smells like a siege, it no doubt is a siege and he will pay attention to what is to be said, no matter the time." Added Athos.

"He would rather be impostioned and have the given knowledge of intent than be considered ignorant and clueless." Observed Porthos.

"As with most people." Added Athos, in agreement.

"Quite right." Added Aramis, "But the fact remains, I am going to attend mass to atone for any misgivings. As for now if you will excuse me, Bazin?"

"Master?"

"Aramis?" Porthos called, "What of breakfast?"

The young prelate turned, "My flesh is not hungry, alas my soul is."

"Can not say the same for myself." Murmured Porthos to himself, but was loud enough for Athos to hear but not the retreating Aramis.

Athos smiled, "His professed station in life, keeps his soul in perpetual want. Deny the flesh, though its due is given now and then."

"Is your soul never in want?" Queried Porthos.

"God has forsaken me." Sighed Athos, in *sotto voc.*

"Surely..." said Porthos, but Athos held up his hand to halt him in mid-sentence.

"We will feed our souls afore the sun rests upon the horizon this eve."

The musketeers with valets in tow sought the comforts of familiarity, "The Sword and The Pendulum."

Upon exiting the establishment, Porthos was accosted by a young man, whom he had never seen afore.

"Monsieur Musketeer?"

Porthos as well as Athos turned, not certain who he was making references to.

"Are you Monsieur Porthos?" He queried, glancing from one musketeer to the other awaiting a response of acknowledgement from one or the other.

"Aye." Replied Porthos.

"I was requested to give you this."

"Who is it from?" Queried Athos.

"I know not, there is no scripting on it." The hefty musketeer replied, turning it over in search of a familiar hand.

Retrieving his poniard, he broke the seal, hastily read it and immediately blushed.

The musketeer tucked it inside his doublet.

"It is nothing." Said Porthos.

"Must be something of worth, a common response, would not cause a stir, this caused a disturbance in your soul, therefore noted and therefore something of worth."

"Later."

Porthos turned to resume his search for the, "Sword and the Pendulum."

"As you wish. I will not pursue it."

They did not get more than fifty paces away when again they were accosted by someone unfamiliar to them.

"Monsieur?"

They paused their pace and glared at the young man, who boldly tried to block their progression.

"What is it? It had better be important. I am rather famished and appointments to keep."

"I request that you accompany to a local magistrate."

Porthos arched his brow in query.

"Why for? I have done nothing warranting such a comment such as yours."

"You are refusing?"

"Indeed I am, unless you produce something of worth."

"Insidious solicitations. You took something from that courier at the point of your poniard. You threatened him."

"Peste! Is that what you have, unsubstantiated claims of an untrue act. I threatened him not. If anyone is to be threatened, it shall not be the likes of I. I do not take kindly to be accused of something I did not do, justice is then settled by Balizarde it is swift and just. I then, give you a chance to reconsider your accusations and withdraw it."

"Can you prove otherwise?

Porthos' countenance reddened, and muttered, "It is personal."

"What is it you are saying? Are you challenging me?"

"Indeed, upon the faith of a gentleman to be preserved as such, I am."

"Granted this conversation did not yield the results I was after." Sighed the young man, "It is much far more than I bargained for."

"I suggest you arrive at the musketeer gymnasium when the Luxembourgs' clock strikes the hour of one. Take heed, do not make me seek you." Cautioned Porthos, visibly agitated by the inconvenience.

"Be on your way young man afore Monsieur changes the hour to sooner than later." Suggested Athos.

The young man took a deep breath, held it as he spun around and hastily departed, exhaling and muttering to himself as he went.

"Foolish dolt how could you.....?" He was heard to say as he vanished into a crowd of denizens.

"I truly hope he was referring to himself as the dolt and not I, I need not another excuse to poke another hole into him."

"As it is dear Porthos, we have not much time to waste afore you are to hear his concession. Now if we may, the "The Sword and the Pendulum," awaits."

Arriving at their favored establishment, they paused long enough to establish the current elements. Nothing gave inclinations of inclemency or forebodance.

Upon entering, they were immediately greeted by fellow musketeers and denizens alike.

"Porthos, Athos..when did you return? You look like you have been for quite sometime." Said one fellow musketeer.

Another hooked arms with Porthos and hastily turned the hefty musketeer in the direction of the table of were he sat in hopes that Porthos would relay tales of his whereabouts during his absence from the city.

Another musketeer with a bottle in one hand and a half filled goblet in the other, beckoned Athos to join him and his companions.

Athos shrugged and complied.

"Just keep one bottle in your hand." Instructed Porthos as he was led away.

Athos, for his part just smiled mischievously. He always added to the definitions set afore him by his companions and always had a ready explanation as to his error in judgments, though he did not readily see it as a misjudgment just a lapse in constant thoughts.

The din and chaos was the norm much to the chagrin of the church, for their view everybody needed to attend church and yes while there, tithe.

The church could and did wield its power in an attempt to keep its denizens from being too outspoken against them or the state.

For the main part, through fear of severe repercussions, the denizens kept quiet and abided, but some, with thoughts of their own, made use of their local hostlers, no matter the day, including the Sabbath.

Suddenly there was something that sounded alike cannon fire, followed by extreme laughter, amid Porthos' booming voice.

"As I took careful aim and fired my harquebus, at the keg of powder by a door that led to to the courtyard, there was a cloud of smoke, as it cleared, two Huguenots stood afore me. As I was contemplating whether it was my harquebus misfiring or if I had actually hit my mark, the keg, another explosion sounded. I had not the chance to fear anything, but did flinch a might. When that cloud dissipated, I realized it was Aramis above and behind me who had hit his mark."

"What of the Huguenots?" Queried a fellow musketeer.

"What of them? They were seized and taken into custody, naturally. Do you honestly think I would let them go about their merry way?"

"The mighty Porthos, flinching?...Tsk, tsk, tsk. I should think this was not the first time." Chided another companion.

"Ah, dear Ta'bay...I have seen you flinch at mere rain drops and we all know Paris sees its fair share of rain, sometimes on a daily basis, more than once."

More sounds of laughter.

In the far corner, the sounds of a bottle shattering was heard over the sounds of a chair being made into kindling.

Porthos shook his head.

"That is probably Athos reintegrating a few fact among the fiction."

Porthos seated himself at a table where the meal had already been laid and served and heap an empty plate what the spread had to offer and no one seem to pay mind to him being in the midst of it and cleared the plate with minimal effort.

As the Luxembourgs' clock struck twelve, he thought it best to round up Athos and seek Aramis.

"Athos my good man, it is time we continued on our self proclaimed adventure. I see that your wick is wet."

"Aye my good companion,". Hiccoughed Athos, "But alas not throughly doused. You have not allowed enough time for that."

"I suggested you make do with one bottle." Added Porthos, sternly.

"I tried, but the others were under the threat of being split and I wanted to prevent any mishap or waste. Noble me." Smiled the inebriated musketeer.

"Noble you! Peste! If that is all it took to become a nobleman, I too surely would have been one, a long time afore this."

As they exited the establishment, Athos was hit square in the back by a dark cloaked man, nearly knocking the musketeer to his knees.

As Athos regained his composure, he spun around hastily, to access and address the situation.

"What gives? What is the cause that hastily hurries you along that you recklessly and blindly knock denizens about?" Queried Athos as he hiccoughed.

The young man untangled himself from the folds of his mantle turned to face the musketeers.

Porthos immediately recognized him.

"My dear Athos, it is he who accosted me earlier. Apparently he deems to think it is your turn."

The young man reddened with ire and embarrassment.

"I should think you should pay no mind to what I am about." Stated the young man.

"I pay mind when I am brought unexpectedly to my knees for no apparent reason."

"You Monsieur, are inebriated."

"What has that got to do with you accosting me?"

"If you were not in such a state, you would have avoided me."

"Then you are accusing me of willful intoxication in public and am a hazard to current denizens?"

"That being said, yes. Therefore, you need to come with me to a magistrate."

"I think not." Hiccoughed Athos.

"Then I suggest the Cardinal." Claimed the young man.

"What is that going to do? Surely you do think he has a say." Scoffed Athos, then said, "He does not have jurisdiction over me, fore I am not one of his musketeers. I am one of Louis'". Then adding a hic-cough to accentuate the statement.

"Are you being a self proclaimed representative of the governor of the Bastille?" Queried Porthos, arching his brow.

The young man retreated a pace or two and looked up and again his face reddened as he too recognized the portly musketeer.

"I do not take kindly to be insulted by the likes of an insolent youth that has no etiquette and you need to be taught etiquette. The youths these days." He said as he shook his head.

"By the likes of you?" Queried the young man boldly, trying posturing for the first time.

"If you have not learned anything from me, then you can receive further education immediately after with Monsieur Athos. I will allow you an hour with me, then Monsieur will have his say. One o'clock behind the our barrack."

"Dear Porthos, I have an appointment with him at one, at our gymnasium. Jussac has it in mind that if we are caught dueling we would be in violation of the issued edit against it. Therefore we will not be at open domain, a closed sector belonging to the musketeers."

Athos hiccoughed.

"Then young man, since you will already be accounted for, I make my appointment with you at two. At our gymnasium."

The young man, gathered his mantle about him and made haste around the nearest corner, madly tapping his temple as he went.

"Dolt" he was heard telling himself, "dolt, you are going to get yourself dispatched. If not by one but by both. Dolt,.. dolt... dolt."

The musketeers chuckled and shook their heads.

"Do you think he will keep his appointment with us?" Athos managed to query.

"Well, my dear Athos, he was cautioned that he had better and not make me seek him Bye the by at the minute, I should think we should seek Aramis. But, what church? This city has so many churches, cathedrals and chapels."

Athos paused, causing Porthos to pause as well.

"He is one not for extravagances, just look at his vestments." Observed Athos.

"Then take a look when he thinks we are not looking at his time away from us is lace and silk, though he claims poverty."

Athos staggered his pace as he shifted his weight from one foot to the other.

"What say you, we try Norte Dame? St.Eustache, holds mass even though it is still under construction. The nave will hold a few of the devote if they arrive afore dawn. He mentioned it once the Monseigneur reminder him of his task master at his monastery of which he was so fond of."

"How can one be fond of a task master?" Queried Athos.

Porthos shrugged, "Anything is possible."

"Indeed. Take Jussac for example." Winked Athos.

"Why him, he is a dolt?"

"For some unknown reason, he his fond of Richelieu."

Porthos turned his companion about as Athos hic-coughed again.

As they strode towards Norte Dame, the bells tolled the hour and acted as a beacon and beckon.

"What is it with these young people these days? They are so presumption and pretentious."

"Might I kindly remind you, you are young." Replied Athos.

"So are you." Smiled Porthos.

Athos inclined his head, "Aye, but still older than you. Respect your elders." He added trying to sound serious.

"If you insist."

Athos tried to laugh, but was seized with a fit of hiccoughs.

When they got within one hundred paces of Norte Dame, then paused, in order to get a glimpse of the their companion and hailed him.

As Aramis descended the neatly manicured steps, free from winters' debris, a man in tattered vestments approached the young prelate with an extended arm, palm up.

"Does Monsieur have a sou or two to spare so that I may survive another day?"

As Aramis reached into his doublet to retrieve his purse, the young man that accosted his companions earlier came from around the corner.

Porthos nudged Athos into observance.

Aramis carefully untied the binding cords, withdrew a couple of souls, retired it and replaced it inside his doublet.

As he took the paupers' dirty well worn hand in his and placing the sous within and closed the fingers around his new found wealth, to secure it the young man, brandishing his ponaird, hastily approached the musketeer.

"Hold!" He shouted.

Aramis took a step back, said something of a blessing and encouraged the pauper to make himself scarce.

"Hold I say. What gives you the right to take from those who have very little or nothing?"

Aramis scowled and glared at the young man.

Aramis crossed his arms over his chest and queried, "What gives you the right to question my charity?"

"It was a pure act of thievery." The young man stated boldly, "Therefore I hereby order you to come with me to the the governor of the Bastille."

"Who are you to judge my integrity, and question my intent? A self proclaimed vigilante? Do you not know who I am?"

The young man let his arm drop to his side, but still kept up his façade.

"I am Aramis, a musketeer."

It was then Porthos and Athos took their position behind their companion.

"Remember us?" Queried Porthos.

"I am Porthos, one of three."

"I am Athos. Two of three."

"...And I am Aramis three of three. I do not take kindly being falsely accused of despicable acts against humanity, such as thievery."

"Aramis my good man, I see you have made the acquaintance of our young man who readily made himself look like a dolt for our sake and it is quite apparent he has managed to do it again."

The young man hung his head.

"If I were not such a forgiving man, I would pardon your etiquette, rather the lack there of, of such."

"You would?" Queried the young man, hopeful.

"I never said I was as forgiving as I should be."

"Aramis, we already have an appointment shortly with him." Said Athos.

"Then, might I join the counsel?"

"By all means." Smiled Porthos, wryly.

"Where is the rendezvous point?"

"Behind your barrack." Replied the young man.

"Do you need a reminding, it is at one at our gymnasium at one and two?" Corrected Porthos.

Aramis inclined his head.

"I suggest you go and ready yourself, for I assure you it will be a rather short appointment. My appointment then is at three. I will allow my companions to impart their lesson on etiquette then I will impart mine."

Athos hic-coughed and said, "Now young man be on your way."

The young man, not needing to be told twice, hastily departed.

"Peste!" Exclaimed Porthos, suddenly.

"What is it?" Queried Aramis.

"I so dislike dueling with some one I know not."

"If he has any sort of etiquette, he will allow us to know his name. Short lived if nothing else." Sighed Aramis.

"By Jove, I think that he knows not what etiquette is. If he had he surely he would know not to make accusatory remarks concerning a gentleman's personal affairs. He truly needs to take heed in this matter and yield." Remarked Athos, piqued by the present situation, and tried in vain to stifle a hiccough.

"In any event, I do believe Athos, you had better find a way to regain your wits so that you may adequately hold your blade." Observed Aramis.

"Whether I be inebriated or other, I still can hold my blade."

Porthos smiled wryly.

"Alas, do you know which end is proper?"

They all laughed as they turned and began their way to their gymnasium.

As they entered they noticed a couple of the companions practicing parries and thrust with their buttoned foils.

Others made use of mannequins, while still, a rider was sitting upon a wooden horse on wheels, as two pushed it along as the rider tried to make contact with a target.

Loud oaths were uttered as the harquebus misfired in a cloud of smoke.

"Corbleu! Hold! Let me reload, retreat and let me have a go again." They heard.

"By the bye..", Commented Porthos, "There is a way I learned while we were away, on how to quickly and efficiently remove a sword from a foe."

"Do tell." Smiled Athos.

"I do have to act as an advocate," interjected Aramis, eyeing Porthos askance, "By chance, what if Jussac or his men show?"

"Let them. This is our barrack and gymnasium and it is where we practice and when our little dolt makes his appearance we tell Jussac he is a companion and we are practicing, and if by chance he already has a few holes poked in him we say he has not learned how to parry fast enough. If it gets to the point he is already lying on the planking, his recent parry failed him."

In the distance, they heard the Luxembourg strike the current hour of one and a door at the far end of the grand chamber opened suddenly, causing them to turn about, the door closed.

Porthos sighed in disappointment.

It was another companion, who had recently joined the regiment, a fledgling.

He was there to hone his skills in sword exchange, fencing and attend a given lesson in ballet as part of the prerequisite of becoming a musketeer.

"Do you think you will see the likes of your opponent?" Queried Aramis.

"I know not, alas I should think so." Replied Porthos sternly, "he obviously needs some educating in the art of etiquette and wing held accountable

Aramis drew his foil, buttoned it and took a stance.

"*En Gard!*"

Porthos drew his as well and buttoned it.

"*En Gard!*" He replied, as he touched the foible of Aramis' foil and stomped an advance pace.

Aramis retaliated by parrying and deflecting the thrust.

"He may not have the humor to be educated on this day on such a topic."

Aramis advanced and thrusted.

Porthos in turn retreated a pace, parried the thrust, then suddenly advanced a pace, slid his blade hastily down Aramis blade and with the tip of the foil under the bell guard, he suddenly snapped his wrist upwards, causing Aramis to loose his grip on the handle and sent the foil in the direction of Porthos who was able to catch it in mid-air.

"You disarmed me!" Exclaimed Aramis, surprised by sudden maneuver as he dropped his arms to his sides.

"I did not." Countered Porthos, "You still have two arms." He said, smiling wryly, as he touched his companion on each of his shoulders as a sovereign would a new knight.

Aramis glared at him in mock seriousness but soon found himself laughing in spite of the circumstance.

"May I have my foil back?" Queried Aramis, "So you can show me the maneuvers you had learnt while we were absent from Paris. Your move was a mere fluke and nothing more."

Porthos arched his brow and replied, "Fluke or no, it indeed will be beneficial if we by chance are backed into a corner. By the bye, who said I learnt it?" He replied winking, *"En Gard!"*

Aramis held out his empty hands.

"My apologies. It is not customary to argue with an a gentleman who has no means of defending himself with his wits or otherwise."

Porthos returned his companions' foil and again took his stance.

Aramis readied himself as well and took his stance.

They touched their buttoned foil tips and in unison said, *"En Gard!"*

Without being forewarned, Porthos again stomped his heavily booted foot, lunged forward and thrusted.

In response, Aramis parried and successfully deflected it and retreated a pace.

The hefty musketeer again advanced and used the new maneuver and again with the desired success, Porthos caught his companions' sword.

Aramis again let his arms rest against his side.

"Then are you going to give me a lesson in the new maneuver or are you going to let me configure it on my own?"

"I just did. As you feign an advance, hold up your foil,"

Aramis did as he was instructed.

"You hastily slide your blade down your adversary's like so." Porthos demonstrated as he spoke, "Then when they are fortunate enough to deflect yours with a parry, as you lunge, get the tip of your sword under their bell guard and snap your wrist upwards. The surprise move will startle them into releasing the handle in your favor. *Voile!*"

The slight musketeer seemed to approve of the new maneuver and genuinely smiled.

"When Athos has his wits once again about him, we can demonstrate that to him."

Porthos unbuttoned his foil and resheathed it as the door once again opened and closed but did not allow admittance of his adversary.

"My stomach has commented that we missed dinner. Peste! If the little man does make his appearance, it will be a rather short lesson." Scowled the hefty musketeer.

Behind them came an explosion and a cloud of smoke from a spent harquebus, followed by uttered oaths of frustrations.

"Hold! Stop moving the target!"

"I did no such thing!" Came a reply, "You need to be steady minded and steady handed and keep your wits about you."

Athos erstwhile was using his kerchief and wiping the smudge marks from his blade.

"By Jove!" He commented, "What is that on the bell guard and pummel?"

He tried buffing it harder but the stain remained.

He tucked his kerchief inside his doublet then picked up the corner of his tabard and began rubbing it with that.

The stain slowly dissipated til it was nearly unnoticed.

As the Luxembourg announced the hour of seven, it took the three men by surprise.

Once again the door at the far end of the grand room opened and closed as it allowed admittance of the brazier keep as he went about his given task of lighting the lantroons and sconces that were about the chamber.

"My apologies old man," Said Aramis, "It is quite apparent your little adversary is not going to make an appearance this eve."

"Perchance he felt overwhelmed and intimidated." Suggested Athos, shrugging.

"Consider the fact there is three of us and one of him." Aramis added.

"The Luxembourg recently announced seven. What say you about supper, considering this appointment was not kept and a disappointment? Queried Porthos, as he resheathed his blade then queried, "What are his chances of getting waylaid by an insulted Jussac?"

The three laughed knowing the young man could not hold his tongue still for very long.

"Then since we missed the opportunity in joining Louis at supper we might as well scrounge and find something we can afford." Suggested Aramis.

"Pshaw!" Said Porthos, "Choose and I will meet you there. If I may supplement any given thoughts, I would say something obscure and out of the ordinary, for if we are known to have returned, then the summons from various quarters will not cease and we be inundated with requests for our presence. By the bye, we have ample opportunities coming forthwith that will allow us to join Louis, Richelieu and De Treville."

"I have heard of a hostler. "The Purple Peacock", it is quite obscure indeed. It's a half a league from, The Sword and the Pendulum." Interjected Athos, "West."

"Do you agree Aramis?" Queried Porthos, "For I care not, just as long as the spit contain fowl and the kettle brims, I shall find contentment."

"...And I will find contentment with a bottle or two of Anjou within my reach as well." Smiled Athos.

"Now if I may beg my leave, I shall rejoin you in an hour. Mousequeton my good man, if you will."

Athos and Aramis with their valets turned about and began to make their way towards, "The Purple Peacock."

"Master?" Queried Mousequeton as they walked.

"Hmm?" Replied Porthos.

"Why is it you do not want them to know about Madame? It is not an uncommon situation. Surely if the king were older and perchance wiser he too would have taken on a mistress."

"They need not know she is my benefactress, if they were aware of the fact of her existence they would naturally assume many things including funds for campaigns."

"She does, does she not supplement your musketeer wage?"

"Indeed she does. At times. Although I am fond of my companions, and they, me, alas I see no need at the moment to share such a luxury unless it is dire. For the moment, I will tell them I frequented my apartments and pilfered my coffer."

"Will they believe that?" Queried Mousequeton, somewhat skeptical.

"Why would they doubt me? I do leave some in reserve for such an occasion. For the time being they do not need to know the difference."

Rue aux Ours came into view as they rounded the corner.

The brazier keep still about his task, shuffled by.

The tile announcing Monsieur Coquenard's professional practice and that was of a lawyer, ornately adorned the thick heavy oak door.

Polished frequently to a proud sheen, it signified Monsieur still took on cases and adamantly argued for his denizen or the state, it mattered not, he represented any and all who came to him for assistance.

He was known for being practical, tactful and fair, alas time had taken its toll and his wits were not what they once were and on several occasion of late, he would pause too long it was mistakenly though he had fallen into repose and the magistrate would suspend the proceedings til the following day, then commence where they left off.

Porthos decided not to use that door and casually slipped quietly unnoticed to the side of the establishment where a small step beheld an inconspicuous door aside a mass of vines that climbed carelessly but deliberately towards the heavens.

In the past, after knocking to announce his presence, he was gently chastised and was instructed to allow himself in and if confronted by a valet or other, it would be then to explain himself he was there to run an errand for either the Madame or Monsieur, preferable the Madame, for Monsieur was frequently absent due to his profession.

He instructed Mousequeton to stay behind, he did not anticipate being preoccupied for any great length of time for his stomach was constantly reminding him of his missed meal.

Quietly he lifted the latch and allowed himself admittance, then just as quietly closed it behind him and cautiously ascended the steps, using care of not letting the spurs on his heavy boots scuff the highly polished patina wood step or make any sound, thinking of how it must be a burden to his benefactress and Monsieur as their aged legs struggled with the incline.

Knowingly though, they had each a personal attendant for various duties that eased what time had taken from them and would never be returned.

As the musketeer, with his cap in hand, topped the stair, Madames' hand maiden rounded the corner and nigh collided with him, almost spilling the contents of a basin.

"Oh Monsieur Musketeer, I knew not you were here, no one announced you. Are you in need of counsel with Monsieur Coquenard? He is not present, he is frequenting a young man in need of his profession."

A slight almost unnoticeable smile played on the corners of his mouth.

"Ne, it is not he whom I seek, it is the Madame. Is she available? Is she not well?" He queried, somewhat alarmed at the sight of the used basin.

"Ah, Monsieur, she indeed is well. She just felt she needed a cool cloth, the hearth is a bit too warming. Is she expecting you?'

"Ne, she knows not that I am back for a brief layover in our expedition. Will you please announce me?"

"Yes Monsieur. Allow me to dispose of this and I shall."

She slightly curtsied and hastily disappeared only to reappear with a lit taper with the flame slightly dancing against the movements.

She motioned him to follow her and he kept his pace slow and deliberate so as to not tread on her small dainty heels.

At the entrance to the drawing chamber she paused and indicated for him to wait.

She quietly slipped through the half opened door.

He heard his benefactress gasped and say, "Yes, please."

As she reappeared, she beckoned him follow.

He took a deep breath, held it then slowly released it.

His heart, beating nervously strong, pounded wildly within his chest.

She was standing afore the hearth, her back to him.

"Madame? Monsieur Musketeer." Informed her hand maiden.

Silently she turned and with a slight gesture, dismissed her maid.

"Porthos?" She said, in *sotto voc.*

"Oui Madame. 'Tis I."

He opened his arms and to fill the void, she fell against his chest as he closed his arms about her, she sighed.

"'Tis been too long." She said.

"Hmm." Was all he could manage to utter for the moment.

"When did you return?" She queried.

"This morn."

"Does all of Paris know of your return or just a select few?"

"If you mean, Louis, De Treville and Richelieu, ne,' they know not. Soon enough though."

She tittered.

He gently removed her from his chest and reached inside his doublet to retrieve his purse.

"I so dislike being a pauper pleading for alms, but the truth be told, my purse is empty and my coffers are in want. I know not whether we will be compensated for our absence or no. If it be a loan, then so be it, it shall be returned...."

"If it t'were a gift, it need not be repaid as it was given." She interjected and a slight smile and a twinkle in her aged eyes appeared on her countenance.

"Good Madame, I have little to no time to spare this eve and a pending debt has to be settled."

She pouted, "Is that all I am good for?"

Porthos was ready to laugh when she said, "How you repay me is how you see fit."

The musketeer arched his brow and inclined his head, "Is that all I am good for?"

As she opened the immense coffers lid, untied the purse strings and filled if and retied it, she again smiled wryly and replied, "Perchance."

He replaced his cap and tugged on the brim to bring it down over his brow.

Madame Coquenard tittered.

"What gives?" He queried.

"As if you do not want to be recognized, to draw your cap close, it is eve, rather late at that."

"My mantle even closer."

They both laughed at the thought of trying to conceal their identity.

He hastily embraced her.

"Your kindness knows no bounds." He smiled again.

"Come back." She replied in *sotto voc.*

"Soon. Promise."

He turned to take his leave, but found himself turning about in spite of himself and took hold of her and the embrace was fond and genuine.

"Leave me not." She said, still *sotto voc.*

"I must." As his chest heaved and then settled with a soft barely audible sigh, "If it t'were not for the fact I am being waited upon, I would make better use of my time. Alas my companions know not the true circumstances of my absence, but they are counting on my return."

He again removed her from his broad chest and looked into her eyes that were moist with emotion.

"I must beg your leave, they await."

"Do I know them?" She queried.

"Ne, alas does it matter?"

"Ne." She replied, "Just wanting to be assured the outcome of your rendezvous will be favorable."

"Rest assured Madame, it will be."

"Then they are not like those two treasonous dolts, your burrs as you called them?"

Porthos laughed.

"On the contrary. Very honorable and trustworthy."

"Av Revoir."

He once again turned and then made his way to the steps that lead to the avenue below.

At the door, he paused, replaced is purse within his doublet, lifted the latch and allowed himself exit.

Once out of doors and his eye became accustom to his surrounding, he glanced about to locate Mousequeton.

He was standing next to a brazier, observing the comings and goings of the common denizen, unaware that his master, keeper of his mortal fate, stood directly behind him.

Porthos suddenly clasp him on the shoulder, catching him off guard, startled him.

"OH!", He exclaimed, "What gives?"

He sighed with relief when he saw it to be his master.

The portly musketeer, chuckled.

"You make a splendid guard." Said Porthos, wryly.

"Oh," He said again, "Beg your pardon master. Just observing the denizens..their habits are different at this hour compared to those during the hours of light. How amusing."

The braziers' flamed flickered and danced, causing shadows to move awkwardly about on the rue afore them.

"May I inquire if Madame was accommodating?" Queried Mousequeton.

"Ne, you may not inquire, but yes she was and then some. Alas my good man, time dictates to be elsewhere. Let us rejoin my companions afore Athos make a nuisance of himself."

Mousequeton's smile was lost to the dark.

"Do we need our horses?" Queried the attentive valet.

"Ne, 'tis clear this eve, nary a cloud to obscure the moon and the way is debris free."

As they set upon their way, less denizens were about, causing the musketeer to query if something were amiss.

This tavern they chose was not within the protection of the city walls and when things that caused political and civil unrest were still occurring, it would still cause a man to be wary of his surroundings no matter how many or how few traversed to their favored establishments.

Because of Porthos' size, he was left be, for any man that considered him to be their adversary, was considered foolish and suicidal.

The warm glow from that taverns' windows emitted, beckoned in a most welcoming manner as the musketeer and his valet hastened their pace.

As opened the door, above the loud din came a familiar loud voice, that of Athos.

"Where is the rope?" He called out, "She is a criminal of the state, can not you see that? Good, now throw that end over that bough. I am judge and jury, proceed."

Porthos sighed, "'Tis too late, his wits have left him and he has turned into a nuisance and a dolt at the same time, only he can manage that in the same breath."

The musketeer and his valet sought the origin of the loud query and it to yes indeed it was, Athos, standing upon a table with loitering gentlemen about observing his antics as if it t'were a stage production.

One man was leaning upon his musket, with the barrel resting haphazardly upon the mans' foot.

Porthos, in the mans' ear with *sotto voc*, said, "Monsieur, I would not be doing that if I t'were you."

"Do what?" He queried, surprised.

"Some dolt in a foolish manner with you preoccupied, cocked your musket and lit the fuse."

As the man was attempting in vain to disarm his musket, it fired, leaving a flattened musket ball in the indent it left on the man's heavy boot.

With the cloud of smoke dissipating, they heard, "The bough broke, run. Find your saddles, make haste! Make haste!" Shouted Athos as he pitched forward and tumbled off the table and fell to the planking in a heap.

Yelling oaths, the man with the discharged musket, stumbled away amid the laughter to evaluate any injury his foot may have sustained.

Porthos and Aramis rushed to Athos' assistance and aided him to a chair and set him upon it.

They allowed him to slowly sink forward and bury his head amid his crossed arms and mantle upon the table.

The two musketeers sat down themselves, and queried what the kettles and spit beheld.

Porthos gestured, "In reality, it matters not, bring what you have and you will be well compensated for your efforts."

The inn keep, bowed slightly and as he went towards the kitchens, he summoned his lackeys to give instructions.

Aramis shook his head.

"The minute he walked in, he queried after a bottle, I suggested to wait for you and rather than query after a bottle, a kettle of stew would suit him better. He did not like that suggestion too well, rather annoyed actually, so he set about with a bottle. Thinking his goblet was not big enough, he threw the goblet towards the hearth and proceeded to relieve the bottle of its contents. Then with a dialogue with only himself, proceeded and there my dear Porthos is the result."

The portly musketeer laughed.

"What do you find so amusing?" Queried Aramis, thinking his companion was making light of the situation.

Wiping a tear from the corner of his eye, he replied, "Just thankful that we were not afore Richelieu and he let the Cardinal know his thoughts about the activities he has heard about and how unjust he feels they are and how unbelievable and unbending and unbeneficial they are as well."

Afore their conversation could continue a gentleman with an attire completely unfamiliar to them inquired, "Dear gentlemen Is your companion mad?"

"Ne, although on an occasion we are inclined to think that." Replied Porthos.

"He is actually quite engaging when his wits are about him." Added Aramis, with a weak smile, then muttered, "when he does speak."

"Since we are with out the citys' protective walls and thinking the gates from all sides are guarded and locked at this time, I suggest we seek lodging nigh and make our attempt to seek counsel with the; cardinal, the king and our beloved captain." Suggested Aramis.

Porthos nodded his ascent as he drained his goblet.

III

The tavern was quiet and secluded which appealed to the musketeers, alas it offered no accommodations for those desiring repose.

"Within a league is Cre'teil, we can take refuge there. If I am not mistaken there is a small inn with minimal accommodations, but to us it will be well equipped."

"What of him?" Queried Aramis, in reference to Athos.

"What of him? He weighs no more then a keg of powder and that is no effort? I assure you I have a hefted a keg or two."

Aramis chuckled and shook his head.

"That you have and whether they as in the Huguenots realized it or no you assisted them in their own destruction and defeat."

"It is a wonder they have gained anything with their sieges if they are at a loss as to correctly identify their adversaries."

They both laughed as a roasted goose was set afore them as well as other edibles they found amusing.'

Bazin and Mousequeton were engaged in a conversation much like what their masters would talk of, religion and affairs of the state.

Laughter would erupt when Bazin mocked the young king and Mousequeton would try to mimic the cardinal, erstwhile Grimaud stayed somber and silent.

On an occasion, they would prod Grimaud in hopes of soliciting a response, alas nothing was offered.

If it t'were not for the sworn oath of silence instilled upon him by his master, he would have happily contributed to the conversation, alas, he was forbidden to to speak unless spoken to by his master, if anyone else spoke and expected a response it would be minimal in return.

Porthos turned in his chair to glance behind him, making sure the valets were looked after as well.

He reasoned, a well fed valet was more compliant and accommodating then one that was not.

He would not tolerate insolence from a beast or man.

Over time, a few weary denizens shuffled in to find accommodations and solace in the warmth and companionship of fellow denizens, though the hour was late and the moon low.

The inn keep reluctantly approached and inquired if they required further assistance from he or his assistance.

Declining any further needs, he withdrew leaving his lackeys to settle the musketeers' debt, he yawned, and silently and cautiously made his way to his bed chamber, afore his true absence was detected.

Porthos stood, retrieved his purse from the inside his doublet, untied it, picked out two coins and placed them upon the table, retied his purse and secured it from whence it came.

Nudging Aramis, he sighed.

The two then stood on either side of their inebriated unconscious companion and hefted him to his feet.

Grimaud hastily moved his masters chair out of the way and waited for his fellow valets to come about, retrieving his masters' fallen cap, followed closely.

Once out of doors, Porthos turned and with the assistance of Aramis, situated Athos over his shoulder and with a firm grip on a leg and arm, the began their short trek to Cre'teil.

The well trodden path, skirted a forest with evidence of mans' intervention.

Felled trees in various stages of decay lay about and spent fires as well.

Porthos just shook his head and muttered, "In the name of progress? Peste! I should think not! Waste."

Aramis turned about once or twice to validate the well being of the valets.

Satisfied on seeing that they were able to proceed, continued.

With hints of daylight, they approached Cre'teils' gates.

Two guards propped against the wall, immediately stood to make it look as if they were at continuous attention.

Aramis took note and just shook his head.

"What would Louis say if he knew how lax you are? He considers the Huguenots to be vermin and wants to eradicate France of them. You have to be vigilant and mindful. Pay mind like you mean it." He cautioned.

"We were." Commented one.

"Care to retract that statement? You are talking to a prelate."

Both shuffled their feet out of embarrassment and tried to avoid the musketeers' stern gaze.

"Pardon Monsieur."

The second cleared his throat, "State your business.", avoiding further confrontations from the musketeer.

"Need lodging for the remainder." Commented Porthos.

"Oh Monsieur, is your companion ill?" Queried the guard, concerned.

"If you consider being melancholy, then surely he is."

"Nothing like a good bottle to cure what ail you." Added the first guard, jesting.

"Jest not. He already does that, but it seems whatever has caused him to be so crestfallen, continues to annoy whether he speaks to us or a bottle, it matters not, he allows his wits to leave him as we patiently, admittedly at times impatiently as we pause to permit the passage of time to rectify his doltish humour." Replied Porthos.

"In seriousness, we are in need of rest. My companion here can not shoulder his burden much longer, for he does not favor few stone."

Porthos shifted Athos to retain his grasp on a leg as the inebriated musketeer let a low groan escape him.

"The Speckled Boar", is forward on and is always accommodating no matter the hour. It is in the midst of the village. I dare say, can not pass by without notice, for its façade resembles that of an extravagant chateau."

The light breeze caused the torches flame, that were in the wall sconces, to dance, casting unfamiliar shadows on the cobblestone foretelling of an impending storm.

At this point, the two musketeers could have cared less about the appearances of the establishment, just as long it suited their current need for rest and warmth.

Porthos turned and queried, "Do have to prove a point of how uncomfortable it is to convey my companion? If he t'were a stone or two, then so be it, alas he is not and I at present am in no humour to try to persuade you to comply in our request that you step aside and let us proceed."

One guard glanced towards the hefty musketeer then to his own companion and shrugged.

"I do not Monsieur, necessarily wish to find out your method of persuasions..."

Afore he could finish his sentence, Aramis hastily brushed passed him and in the wake of his following dark mantle, Porthos regained composure and readily followed.

As much as Porthos wanted to pause, he knew that with every step he took, it brought him closer to their destination.

The guard was right, there was no possible way to miss the establishment, the façade did indeed look like an extravagant chateau, so extreme that it looked gaudy.

Porthos was well acquainted with the refinements life had to offer, but rather flaunt the availability of such, he chose to live on a level that befit his station, although indeed he had a few choice pieces of jewelry that was purchased with the gifts from his benefactress, he wore them discreetly.

He found the appearance of the establishment excessive and tasteless.

Too many gargoyles, even though, initially they were in place to ward off evil. The evil was in the mind of the architect that designed it, for he did not consider the effect of the appearance would have and would boast being macabre and sinister.

That kind of humour would not sit well with the local denizens and the establishment would be doomed to failure.

Too many columns upholding a rather small portico making it look out of architectural balance, lacking harmony with the rest of the establishment.

The windows were too narrow. They might be used as in defense with a crossbow, although that initially was not the intent of such, but the error was then explained, certainly, yes, it was the intent.

The steps, too many, too steep.

As Porthos took on the steps, he staggered slightly under his burden, his knees slightly sagged but he refused to allow himself to succumb to his overwhelming desire to relieve himself of the weight he bore, he continued.

Aramis, a pace or two ahead of him held the heavy door open for him and allowed him to pass.

Porthos paused in the small foyer and glanced about.

It was well light as the richly decorated surroundings gave the illusion that the proprietor was stately and proper.

As a lackey tried to scurry by, Aramis was able to get his attention.

"Ah Monsieur Lackey, you happened by at the right time. We are in need of securing a chamber for the remainder of the eve and possible for the morrow as well. Is the Keep available?"

The lackey appeared witless and as Aramis readied himself to repeat his request the lackey rapidly blinked his eyes as if adjusting them to a sudden brightness, disappeared down a passageway.

Upon hearing a distant door open and close, a pause then the door opened and closed sharply.

Muffled heavy footfalls followed as a slight aged man appeared from the shadows.

"I was informed you are need of a chamber." He stated gruffly.

Aramis cleared his throat.

"Come now, I have not the patience nor the strength to be afore you long!"

"Aye, Monsieur, we are, and a request for a bottle of Anjou and some bread."

"Umph!" Grumbled the elder.

With a curt nod at his lackey, he returned to the shadows.

The lackey beckoned them to follow in which they did.

Down a dimly lit passageway one of the doors stood slightly ajar.

The lackey pushed it open and proceeded them into the darkened chamber.

He lit a couple of lantroons and set up the hearth and with minimal effort had heat emanating from it, then he quickly withdrew to fulfill Aramis' request of the wine and cheese.

Glancing about, they noticed a rather large pallet on the floor and a couple of crude chairs.

Porthos chose the chair closet to unburden himself from Athos, who slightly moaned again as he was plopped into a chair.

The hefty musketeer took a deep breath held it momentarily, then slowly released it.

As Porthos himself sat down afore a small table, Aramis strode over to Athos and gingerly replaced his cap.

"As if that matters." Commented Porthos with a wry grin.

"He is the epitome of fashion."

Porthos chuckled as he shook his head.

"To think when we began this past morn, we were on the ready to seek counsel with our necessary officials and relay the latest. By the bye, we even extended ourselves and took it upon ourselves to make use of a laundress and a barber."

Aramis sighed, "Yes indeed only to be lead in another direction by some dolt and challenge our identity and integrity."

"Very foolish indeed."

Aramis kicked the smoldering log to expose a vulnerable tender old seasoned side, which readily caught, producing the well welcomed desired warmth.

A light rap came upon the door and Mousequeton took it upon himself to open it without prompts from his master.

It was the lackey with the requested wine and bread.

Mousequeton in turn handed it to the musketeers and withdrew.

Aramis handed the bottles to Porthos, who thus proceeded to relieve the bottles of their given stoppers and as he tore pieces of bread from the loaves and distributed to the valets.

"Here. It is not much I admit, alas for the moment it will have to be enough til morn. Get some rest for I assure you there will be much to do. Unfortunately there is no beds to rest upon, make use of your mantles and each other as bolsters. Some of you are more bolstery then the other, alas all will be well."

"Peste!" Commented Porthos, "There truly are no beds."

"May I remind you, this is not *Palais Royale.*" Replied Aramis, casually.

"Ne, you need not."

"Shall we roust him?" Queried Porthos, in reference to an incoherent Athos.

"Ne. It will only add to his present state. He need not have his wits further away from his grasp than they already are."

"I do believe though that he would be far more at ease if he were reclined." Observed Porthos, as Aramis sat opposite him at the small table, afore the hearth.

"He will end up looking like a crumpled spent parchment if that be the case. Leave him be, he will be no worse for the wear. At the moment, he can not protest. Should he resist, he at times listens to reason and will not pursue it further."

"Shh!" Instructed Porthos suddenly as he gestured for silence, "Listen."

"Where?" Queried Aramis, in *sotto voc.*

Porthos pointed to the wall upon a very worn mural depicting "The Garden of Eden."

A deep gruff voice said, "La Rochelle will have to be refortified, time and again. It is a stronghold that we will not readily give up. Louis ought to know that by now. He can not be that stupid."

"Or not that informed." Replied another voice.

"That sounds like Rohan. Has he not taken up residency in the Bastille?" Suggested Porthos.

"I thought that as well." Replied Aramis, quietly.

"No matter," Added the first voice, "there is a very little establishment in the bend of the river. Only two small windows, word has it when both are lit in the eve, munitions have arrived from Montpellier, Nemes and Uzes and need to be sent on to La Rochelle."

"I thought that the king had them deconstructed, dismantled."

"I am sure he had thought as much as he claimed victory. Ah but the siege mechanism moves forward as does time."

"Then what are we to do?" Returned the second voice.

"Escort them to La Rochelle. All munitions will be accumulated there, then covertly distributed."

"When are we to do this?"

"On the morrows' eve. The first parcels will be arriving by ten, then within the hour, they will leave for La Rochelle. Subsequent arrivals will arrive and depart bi- weekly." Wednesdays and Saturdays."

"Is Rohan taking the lead?"

"I know not, but where ever he is, he sent word for a formation and to proceed hastily and as covert as possible."

"Aye. As for now, I will by my leave and relay on. Time has slipped quietly by, hardly noticed the hour, alas I know it is late, but if I do not relay it now, it will not be relayed at all."

"I beg you, the way is treacherous, leave in the morn when you can thus see any obstacles whether it be an act of God, or human. I surely would not welcome a courier with word that you have fallen prey to some heedless scoundrel who is trying to make good on a bet."

"For a traitor, you are quite hospital."

The gruff voice chuckled.

"It is a necessary illusion. Gullibility of the common denizen with the belief of benefits of well being and of a sustainable existence adds and they in turn add to our cause."

The two musketeers heard a door open and close followed by silence.

Aramis wanted to speak, but Porthos held up his hand, indicating wait, be still a moment longer.

Again the door was heard to open and close.

"How did…?" Began Aramis.

Porthos inclined his head and raised his brow, "Just a casual foregone conclusion to a conversation betwixt two dolts who presumed it was covert and truly it certainly was on the contrary."

"How do you figure?"

"We heard it, so just how covert was it?" Wryly grinned the portly musketeer.

Aramis chuckled.

"So, dear Porthos how do we proceed from here?"

"I think an ambush is in the making. First we find out where Rohan truly is, re-route the munitions to a stronghold held by the crown and continually do that, 'til a siege erupts, which is bound to occurs. The Huguenots do not have patience when they are in want of what they feel they are entitled to."

"What is close in proximity to a remnant of resistance to determine their intent as well as a deposit for the munitions."

"We will have to consult a chart, I know not at the present. Surely there is something we can make use of. We rounded up Rohan once, we certainly could do it again."

"Alas my good man, we have to definitively locate him and his lackeys and halt his transfer of munitions and short fuse what he already has, thus make any siege short lived."

"Why can not Louis uphold the edict?" Sighed Aramis.

"He is an obstinate young man. Many people around him, often have strong persuasive opinions and to avoid confrontations, he gives. When he feels it is the right thing, he refuses to budge as in the edict."

"He upheld it."

"Then he reconsidered, causing continued conflicts. It is quite fatiguing."

"Then we will do our part in prevention of transference."

"Indeed. As for now, I suggest some rest. We will need to be attentive on the morrow to locate their little establishment and find place for an adequate munition holdings."

Porthos emptied his goblet and inverted it as he set it on the table.

Aramis stared for a moment at the contents of his goblet afore he emptied it, stood and kicked the log again.

Without assistance from their valets, they removed their boots, laid down and got as comfortable as the circumstance would allow, used their heavy mantles as a counterpane, and their folded arms as a bolster, then fell asleep.

With no preset time to be awake, they slept til the early morning light filtered through the smudged panes of glass and warmed their countenances.

Athos awoke with a start.

"Hold! What gives?" He queried to no one specific.

"Hmm? What is your concern?" Queried Porthos, as he sat up, then nudging Aramis.

"Where are we? Last I knew, we were in a hostler."

"Indeed we were, but we are here, relocated for the necessary need for rest. Alas, Aramis and I overheard a conversation concerning the Huguenots moving munitions and continuing their fortifications of some of their stronghold. La Rochelle is one of the prime locations."

Athos stood and after odd contortions to relieve stiffness that settled about his joints during the chill of the eve afore, queried, "You overheard a conversation stating such?"

"Yes." Interrupted Aramis, "T'was not the intent to hear such for they said it was covert that is why they were here."

"Not very covert, if you query me of it, since you two dolts heard it." Smiled Athos.

"That is what Porthos said."

"So, he did? Now what do you purpose we do? The king, cardinal and De Treville still do not know we are about?"

"That might be to our advantage." Replied Porthos.

"Oh, how so?"

"We were going to intercept their caravans and reroute them to a general depository in the name of the crown. Enough collected, dismantle their own strongholds with them with regiments and orders from the king and we will set off our own fireworks." Explained Porthos.

"Alas my good man, we have to first locate the Duc. He most likely is the one with all the thoughts behind this scheme." Added Aramis.

"Did we not make his acquaintance once?" Queried Athos.

"Indeed."

"Then we can reacquaint ourselves."

"Would it be worth an encounter with Pasqual and Tomas?" Queried Aramis.

Porthos cringed involuntarily at the mere mention of them.

"Why so?" Returned Athos.

"Perchance they know the whereabouts of Rohan."

"I do not have thoughts that he is anywhere near here. If he has any sense at all, he would do his manipulations from afar."

"He no doubt already does. Still, conversing with them might reveal an overlooked fact or two." Replied Aramis, off handedly.

"Tsk, tsk, tsk." Interjected Porthos, "I should leave that task to the likes of you two."

"I should think not!" Retorted Athos, "We need to be a unified force, if they think they think they have the best of you, they will continue to prey upon your weakness."

"I am not weak willed." Replied Porthos sternly.

"His mere words affect you."

"Ne, I beg to differ, it is his mere being. Constantly finding ways to annoy me. You would think there would be better ways to spend his off time. Alas, with he and his co-hort lodged in the Bastille, it has made life a bit more tolerable." Porthos waved his hand as if annoyed, "Life has enough trouble of its own, they need not contribute to it."

"They only contribute to it if you allow it." Reflected Aramis.

"Peste!"

"Aside from that, we need to locate a suitable munitions depository. Converse with some of our other companions to have them pose as suitable Huguenot sympathizers to command the route. Find Rohan. Again! In the name of the crown, conveniently convince him to relinquish his hold on given fortresses and dismantle them afore they can pose any real threat to Louis and or to any and all denizens of France."

"May I query as to where you would like quartered?" Queried Aramis, causally.

"I give thought as to be away from Paris. For far too many are familiar with our countenances and would lend an ear as to our activities. Far be it that it should relate to mischief," ginned Porthos wryly, "but no doubt be misconstrued and misinterpreted therefore it is best we escaped any prying ears and eyes and go beyond the city walls. Any missives received or relayed can and should be done through our valets."

Athos and Aramis nodded in agreement.

"Where to, from here?" Queried Athos.

"Send forth a valet or two, seek him, and upon location bring word and we will set in motion the rerouted munitions, assist in a siege or two," Porthos shrugged his massive shoulders, "and make good with Louis."

"Ne," Smiled Athos, wryly, "Louis will need to make good with us and our purses."

"I suggest we make our presence known, alas do not disclose our intent 'til we have it in place and functional." Added Aramis.

"So much for anonymity." Sighed Athos.

"It is early enough that if we sought Richelieu, we might be able to join him at breakfast, then if he deems it, we will be informed of his and Louis' attempts to subdue the Huguenots."

"They are so taxing." Said Porthos, with an edge of contempt in his voice.

"Easy, my good man. In due time. As it is said, this too shall pass." Replied Aramis.

"Now, let our saga begin. Mousequeton and Bazin, you possess the tact of a church mouse. Go forth and seek he who opposes our church and state."

Mousequeton with a determined glance, queried, "Whom might that be?"

Bazin roughly nudged him, "It is Duc Henri de Rohan." Replied the valet, curtly.

"Bear in mind my dear valet, temper your razor sharp wit, for swing the blade one way and it is countered by the other." Cautioned Aramis.

Porthos produced a Louis d'or and pressed into the palm of his valet, "Godspeed my good man. Garner what you can and return, we will utilize the given information the best we can, acquire what assistance we can and give the Huguenots the chastising that they will not soon forget. On your way now."

Aramis chuckled softly.

It still never ceased to amaze the three of them how Rohan managed to escape being charged with treason and was granted a pension in lieu of a view from a small window that the Bastille beheld amongst it architectural integrity and façade.

Granted, they accepted the fact he was Henri's cousin, but since when, as history had dictated being related to the crown, directly or indirectly meant nothing. You could still manage to be removed from society or any memory of you, on a permanent basis.

As the door closed behind the two valets, Aramis turned.

"What say you, we make the most of what time we have wisely, for we have plenty, see one at a time? It would be far more beneficial to spend quality time with each rather than quantity with another."

"Quantity is a good thing." Replied Porthos.

"Depends on what you are referring to." Interjected Athos, "The quantity of words pales in comparison to the quality."

"Do we cast lots to see who is the first to grace with our presence?" Wryly grinned Porthos.

"It is not necessary to cast lots." Replied Aramis, as he inclined his head, slightly.

"Then who do we bestow ourselves on first?" Queried Athos.

"Richelieu." Suggested Aramis.

"You must have an ulterior motive. Why else? You know full well he is our least favored." Replied Athos.

"Least favored? Indeed. Alas, my soul is in want and what better that to see the man that is more capable of restoring the health and well being of such, than that of one with similar attributes? Aside from that, he has great concern with the movements of the Huguenots."

"As it is, the only reason Louis has any part in this, is for the fact they took up arms against him. If it were for any other fact, he would not have bothered. He would have followed the Edict his father had set forth in their behalf." Replied Athos.

"Taking up arms was to emphasize their want of freedom." Observed Aramis.

"If they had presented in such a manner, their intent and requested recognition there of in a non-threatening manner, surely Louis would have conceded and supported them. Taking up arms as they did, he perceived it as a threat to the stability of the state and to prevent collapse upon which it sits, he saw the only way to preserve it in such a manner was to defend it the way he saw fit. Sieges and the shear force it produces is enough to convince even the brave hearted to step down and concede to the state. The kings' and what he stands for." Replied Athos, philosophically, "Unity."

"I must query of you Aramis," Inquired Porthos, turning to his companion, "Do you think a man such as yourself, a man of God is closer to God if he were a cardinal or bishop, than you a mere prelate?"

"I believe that a man no matter the tint of their vestments, be it black, purple or red to distinguish their rank amoung the church's official clergymen, they have equal access to God and his teachings. Vestments do not make the man, man makes the vestments." Replied Aramis, with a slight curt nod, to emphasize his statement.

"Then how is it that the church wields such force and be allowed to do so?" Queried Porthos with an arched brow?

"They instill fear, reverence, and obedience, all in the name of God. The common man fears Gods' wrath and will abide by what the clergy dictates in order not to be oppressed by the seen and unseen. This is all man made, not of God. Man will fall well short of the glory that could await him if he continues to follow what man has produced. Follow God's word and succeed."

"Alas every man has his own interpretation of what His words mean, that is why there now is the Huguenots and Catholics. Each faction believes he is right in their interpretation and will argue their point." Observed Porthos.

"True." Agreed Aramis, "But my good man, it all comes down to the fact we must abide by the fact, Jesus wants and that is to acknowledge His father and his teachings, no matter what you call yourself, be it Catholic or Huguenot. And!," continued Aramis, "To accept the fact he is the true Christ and accept Him as your personal savior, for He and

He alone died for your sins. Imploring forgiveness of your sins as well. Then acknowledging this, He will allow you admittance."

"Our Sundays' sermon, the only thing missing is communion." Wryly smile Athos.

"Me," Wryly grinned Porthos, "We just heard it."

"I assure you my good Athos, when this is all said and done, we will attend a mass befitting the king and court. Assured Aramis.

"So," Said Porthos, "Let me get this in a correct manner. We go seek counsel with Richelieu, give report on what we have observed but do not divulge our intent to way lay the munitions conveyance from one fort to the next. Find Rohan and persuade him to quietly give up arms and fortifying their remaining strongholds."

Aramis nodded.

Athos tried to unsuccessfully stifle a yawn.

"You realize, do you not that Rohan is a breath away from treason?" Queried Porthos.

"Indeed. Alas, it is for the king to decide his mortal fate. What he favors one day he may not favor the next."

Porthos chuckled at the thought of the disdain of his two nemesis who currently have taken up residency in the Bastille for duration undetermined.

Aramis kicked a charred smoldering log in the hearth.

"It looks as if our stay here is over. No need not to renew our request for our lodgings. The warmth from the fire is spent, the day is wearing on and my stomach is summoning. Pay mind Richelieu is no doubt readying himself for the day, pay our respects and we will be fed." Smiled Porthos.

As they entered the passageway, a young valet de chamber rounded the corner and hastily became part of the shadows and vanished into the darkness.

The musketeers side stepped to avoid a collision and possible catastrophic upset.

Athos muttered something about the lack of etiquette as he recovered he stature, Porthos refrained himself from snatching the valet up by the nape of his neck to give him a verbal chastising and Aramis, crossed himself and sighed.

They managed to locate the proprietor and settle their debt.

Tying their purses' closed, they made their way out of doors, located their horses and returned to Paris.

As the sun was just barely clearing the tops of the trees in the Tuileries, they entered the courtyard off of Rue du Rivoili.

A stable lackey, curtly bowed in acknowledgment, received the reins and departed to provide comfort to the weary animals.

They knew where they could find the cardinal and that being his private apartments, readying himself for the day.

The passageways were like a hive disturbed in the search of honey.

Pages, valets, retreating kitchen attendants retrieving the remains of meals served to those who chose not to attend a meal in the grand hall with their sovereign with the excuse the wording of a current writ needing additional words of persuasion and lackeys, all running to and fro from various chambers with various errands to accomplish.

Just as Aramis was going to bestow knock upon the heavy door, it opened.

There stood Jussac, somewhat preoccupied, glancing downward, tying and adjusting his mantle and baldric.

Finally glancing upward, he was taken aback as the three stood afore him.

Touching the pummel on his sword, still in its sheath, queried sharply, "What is it you request?"

"That is not necessary." Stated Porthos, in reference to the sword, "...And it is not what, rather who." Replied Porthos, as politely as he could.

"So be it, whom do you request?"

"An audience with Richelieu." Replied Aramis.

"He does not want to be bothered. He is readying himself for the day."

"Precisely. We are aware of what time it is and what his daily habits are, therefore afore much is interjected onto his agenda, we reserve the right to postpone anything that interferes with our current counsel with him." Boldly stated Porthos.

As the three stepped over the threshold, Jussac hastily stepped aside and reluctantly allowed admittance.

The cardinal had his back to them, still in his nightshirt and dressing gown, chaffing his stiff, chilled hands, as he stood afore the hearth, it's embers restored and adding warmth to the chamber.

Upon turning to face them, with a gesture dismissed his captain, Porthos and Aramis doffed their caps and bowed.

Aramis roughly nudged Athos as a reminder of necessary etiquette and in turn grudgingly and curtly bowed.

Athos' gestures did not escape the attention of the cardinal.

"I see you still hold animosity towards myself. Does that animosity include the church as well?" He queried, with a furrowed brow.

Aramis again nudged him to induce him to remove his cap in which the musketeer did so in such a rancorous manner that it continued to irritate the cardinal.

"Whether you resent me or no, it matters not, we have a common goal and that is to achieve victory over the Huguenots. The king may not have grown weary from the continued strife, for he is an ambitious young man with my ideals, but I have. I would like to have seen it resolved as in the day afore this. Alas, since that did not occur, we need to do what is necessary and put an end to it all." He sighed and continued, "I am elated to see that you have returned safely. Now what is it you are about?"

Aramis stepped forward.

"To let it be known what we have obtained in our observations and our current status and our intents."

Cardinal Richelieu then moved to the window that overlooked a small garden befitting a humble man and sighed.

"I admit my good gentlemen, I am well beyond fatigued by it all, alas we must persevere."

Then he turned to face the musketeers.

"We may not have always been equal on thoughts of how to deal effectively with current or past affairs, but the conclusions will be the same."

Athos shuffled his feet in irritation, but said nothing.

The cardinal picked up a small bell that sat upon the corner of his desk, and rang it lightly.

Vitray suddenly appeared from behind a tapestry with the haste of a scared fox, pursued by the royal hounds, that led the musketeers to believe that he had been there all the while.

"Monsieur?" He queried.

"Send word to the kitchen that we are seeking breakfast and would like that in an hour, and when you return, I would like to be readied for the day. Would like ordinary pantaloons, a colorless linen shirt and my well worn shoes. Those new ones certainly know how to irritate my ankles and toes and I certainly do not have the humour to wear them today to allow them the luxury of becoming familiar with my feet."

Vitray bowed and departed from whence he came.

It was not long til the tapestry parted and allowed the admittance of Vitray who bowed again curtly to his master, the cardinal.

In a silent manner, with Cardinal Richelieu leading the way, quit the chamber, with Vitray close behind.

The three then strode over to the window that was the previous vantage point of the cardinal, and glanced up and down the avenue in observance of the common denizens as they went about their day with given duties.

Be it their own or those given them by a higher station, no matter, the activity brought the city to life, signifying the previous eve had drawn to a close and was over and done.

As the mantle clock intruded on their reveries, the Cardinal re-entered the chamber, tugging on a pair of riding gauntlets as well as parts of his pantaloons.

"'Tis well we are using horses." Said Porthos, smiling.

"Think again my good musketeer." Replied the Cardinal, inclining his head ever so slightly.

"We are not YOUR good musketeers." Mumbled Athos, "We are Louis'."

"Pardon?" Queried Richelieu.

"Ne, 'tis nothing." Replied Athos as he shuffled his feet in annoyance.

"I thought as much. Now, if you will, the Tuileries does not adequately accommodate a rider on horseback very well with all the hedges, and such, therefore I have chosen on foot. It is more beneficial for a brisk stroll."

"A brisk stroll? How is that when we will be aside for conversation and at the risk of repeating our statements I assure you it will not be "brisk"." Commented Porthos.

"On the contrary. You will not dawdle, I have not the time nor the stamina in prolonging my daily habit. Once through the Tuileries and back afore breakfast will be sufficient. Whatever is not said nor missed in translation, will indeed need to be re-thought."

"Do you not fear eavesdropping, for that leads to intrigue and treason?" Queried the Portly musketeer.

"Indeed it does lead to such. But you should know, I am immune to that, I assure you."

"Pity." Murmured Athos.

Aramis concealed a wry grin, in-spite of himself as he silently queried if the Cardinal heard his companion.

Whether he had or no, he continued, "Any one who double crosses me will find I have made reservations at the Bastille, and only I will turn the key one way or t'other."

The cardinal glanced about as Vitray approached.

"Monsieur le Cardinal, are you needing assistance with something?" He queried.

"Aye! My satchel, mantle and cap."

"What of your ponaird?"

The Cardinal sighed, "You know how I dislike violence."

"Indeed I do your Eminence, but in this age, you need protection."

Richelieu glanced about.

"I have that."

The valet cleared his throat.

"Alas dear Eminence, they are the kings."

"Forsooth they are, but surely you do no think when it matters they would scatter themselves like autumn leaves to the wind and leave me to my own defenses?"

"I would…" Mumbled Athos.

The Cardinal turned to face Athos.

"I realize YOU would, but short of treason, your companions would not."

"What they lack in judgement, they adequately make up in character." Replied Athos, calmly.

The Cardinal hastily made for the balcony door afore he said something that would cause strife with the young sovereign, but paused to await his valet.

The valet curtly bowed and withdrew momentarily from the chamber.

"'Tis a fine looking morn." Observed the Cardinal as he tried to maintain a level of civility towards the insubordinate musketeer. He opened a door to the balcony to allow the light breeze, freedom about the room.

As the draught rustled the sheaves of parchment upon his desk, he decided to close the door rather than chase after the unpublished writs and circumstances.

The valet allowed himself back into the chamber with the requested items in hand.

The Cardinal placed the satchel over his shoulder as he would a baldric, with Vitrays' assistance he accepted his mantle and then firmly placed his cap upon his head.

"Would you be requesting Jussac?"

"Ne. 'Tis well and good, but it is not as if I were wandering aimlessly about the city. It is that it will be the Tuileries."

"Indeed Master, but there is the small market with its establishments and those in want."

"No matter where one is, there is always the likes of that."

Turning about and glancing about, he slightly inclined his head.

"You seems to be searching for something, what is it you are searching for?" Queried Aramis.

"Not so much as what…" paused the Cardinal, as he rounded his desk to put readied documents aside and re-cap the ink and free the quill of any current debris, "It seems two of your valets are misplaced."

"My dear Cardinal, I have it on the best authority, you are known for your keen observations, how is it that something as obvious as two absent valets whom are our apparent shadows escaped your acknowledgment?" Inquired Athos, with an ever so slight almost undetectable wry grin.

The Cardinals' countenance instantaneously went red with ire and suddenly slammed a closed first upon his desk, and shouted, "Monsieur la Musketeer, I will not stand for this insolence!!!"

"Then dear Cardinal, I offer you my chair." Athos replied casually, as he regained his feet, and slightly pushed the chair towards the Cardinal, then turned and strode towards the door.

Using a mantle brooch, the Cardinal adjusted the vestment and satchel, took a deep breath and slowly released it.

Vitray touched his masters' arm in an attempt to reassure him that Athos' words will not bear weight, for they are hollow and meaningless.

The Cardinal glared at his valet with a furrowed brow and narrowed eyes.

"The man thinks he is beyond reproach.", he commented in *sotto voc.*

"Ah, Monsieur la Cardinal, he is." The glancing about, Vitray added, "They all are."

Richelieu's countenance reddened again at the mere consideration of being ignored or being played for a dolt and having a musketeer, one of the kings' no less, speak to him in a such a demeaning manner, angered him.

He knew if he brought up their insolent manner to the king, he would ignore his pleas for discipline.

"If they have not committed anything short of treason, then bother me not. Alas if you insist I reprimand them, I will speak with them. But, my good Cardinal, bear in mind, YOUR musketeers are YOUR responsibility and mine under De Treville, are mine." Is the conversation they had afore and will again.

As long as there were musketeers, there was always a chance they would cause havoc with words or with actions, no matter.

Vitray opened the door leading to the passageway and allowed his master to pass, then nodding to the musketeer and the remaining, silent valet, they in turn, followed.

Porthos, managed to get his companion, Athos' attention, winked at him and smiled.

Athos inclined his head slightly as he pulled on his gauntlets as well.

Not so much as in preparations to ride, but out of habit.

Once out of doors and down the few steps that lead to the gardens, they paused in observations of the elements.

The slight breeze that stirred the documents from the opened door in Richelieus' apartments, rustled the leaves in the trees and caused the bees to find difficulties in their daily given task in their collection of pollen.

It annoyed the musketeers as well, it caused their plumes in their caps to obscure their sight and if they removed their caps, it would cause their locks to tangle about their countenances and cause additional annoyances and frustration.

"Ah, what a morn! Not any inclinations of anything foreboding of impending inclement elements." Exclaimed the Cardinal.

"Except for this nuisance of a draught." Complained Porthos.

"Then to make the most of our morn and not let anything annoy you further, the Tuileries are vast as the sea. There is no set way that we must abide by, therefore, head into it as a caravelle would to make progress, and it will thus remove any obstacles, be it a plume or other."

Porthos and Aramis placed themselves on the sides of the cardinal as Athos and his valet lagged slightly behind.

Athos knew one way t'other he would be informed of the contents of the conversation and it mattered not where he heard it from.

Be it directly from the cardinal or his companions, it was all the same to him.

"Now, good musketeers, what precisely is it you need to relate? I have no time for embellishments or embarrassments."

"We had decided it best to send on Mousequeton and Bazin…"

"…And they are?" Inquired the Cardinal, already showing signs of annoyance.

"Oh, pardon Monsieur." Replied Aramis, "They are our two valets."

The Cardinal nodded, "Continue.", he instructed, as they turned to walk along the Seine.

The little rue was lined by small establishments, making up a market on one side and on t'other was the river itself.

Denizens found this little market more accessible and easier to move about than the larger market in the center of the city and the cost of the vendors' wares were more appreciated and accepted.

"We sent them to seek Monsieur Rohan, locate where he originates from and glean what information they can, then return. It was to be then we relay what we have been informed to you, Louis and De Treville."

"I would think your return is a bit premature." Replied the Cardinal.

"Ne. I, pardon, we think not. While away, our souls had become thirsty and the only way to quench their thirst was to seek the font of wisdom from an authority."

"Surely there were, are others who could have satisfied your want."

"Not as well as you. You do have very persuasive words in this regard." Smiled Aramis.

"Only in this regard. None else. So many words with so little meaning." Muttered Athos.

Grimaud hid his wry grin as he turned his attention to a butterfly that had alighted upon flowers' upturned blossom to catch the morns' sunlight.

"I have it that he originates from Castres and returns there now and again when he is tween two differences."

"Ah, we have heard that too." Commented Aramis in agreement, "We think it best to verify it and seek a place for a place to secure ammunition that we obtain."

"…And how are you obtaining the ammunition, from the state?"

Porthos chuckled softly.

"If you think that, then it must be so."

Aramis cleared his throat and with a grin, said, "Ah dear Cardinal Richelieu…why must we have to wait til' Louis deems it fit to send munitions to various forts, hence or thence, when we can conveniently re-route them under the guise it is for their benefit, within a league or two from a rogue regiment, and use them when we have enough stock piled?"

Richelieu paused in mid stride, turned to face Aramis.

"In in other words, your ambushing them."

Aramis inclined his head and replied, "Call it what you will, but we prefer calling it profiteering."

"Profiting who? Certainly not them."

"Precisely." Laughed Porthos.

As they rounded a hedge, they were accosted by Matherine, the court jestress.

"Ho! Is the court buffoons rostered out this morn?" She jested, as she danced and pranced about them.

The Cardinal arched his brow, "Whom do you consider buffoons?", he queried.

She positioned her bauble upon her shoulder as a sentry would his musket.

"Your Eminence, surely you do not think I am implying you."

"With you, I never know what you are implying, for you are inconsistent with your thoughts and words."

"Forget not, deeds as well." She added mockingly as she resumed her prancing.

"Do be on your way. We are in need of completing our conversation without additional ears in attendance."

"Dear Matherine, I do not consider myself a buffoon." Said Porthos, adding to the conversation just for the sake of hearing himself.

"YOU may not consider yourself a buffoon, but that does not necessarily reflect the opinions of the others." She grinned coquettishly.

"Madame, if you will…" said the Cardinal.

"Oh very well. But I assure you, we will continue this conversation." She sang as she danced away with the bells on her slippers, merrily jingling.

The Cardinal sighed.

"I am certain we will, for there will be no avoiding it."

The path they were using, led them to small establishments along the Seine river.

Rounding a small establishment, Aramis nearly collided with a young lady exiting it.

"Pardon my lady…" He said, doffing his cap, "It is quite apparent you are in haste. I assuredly request nothing of you other than to be allowed to continue on my way."

She glared at him and remained silent.

Aramis tried to step around her, but she obstructed his way.

"Excuse me, if you will…"

"What?" She scoffed, "Am I not good enough?" She queried, placing her arms securely across her bosom.

"Surely you are worth what you are worth, I shall not dicker over triviality of it, but we must pass on and continue."

"Are you now saying I am trivial?" She queried, her countenance reddening with ire.

Aramis' countenance reddened as well, not with ire but with embarrassment.

"To lessen the burden of this conversation, allow me to offer you a sou or two to compensate."

"Now am I a sous purchase?" She shrieked, drawing many unwarranted stares from the denizens. "I so am worth more than a mere sou."

"Indeed you are, your soul is far exceeds any earthly value…." Began Aramis.

"Monsieur, do not lecture me on such, needless to say, that value has no monetary earthly value. It does not allow me to frequent a market or Milner, a seamstress or any other whim I may want to satisfy."

Another young lady exited the establishment, causing the Cardinal to sigh.

"Such immorality." He muttered.

The Cardinal reached into his satchel and withdrew a Louis d'or and gave it to the young lady.

"I know this will not make an honest woman out of you, take it in faith and make the best of it."

"I can not be bought." She scoffed.

The Cardinal narrowed his eyes in sternness, "Surely you do not think of me as such an oldster, though I truly am not *that* old that I know not the difference. If I do not buy your time, I will not, for my station forbids it, some other will."

She glanced from one man to the next.

"It is the only thing I know." She finally said, *in sotto voc,* eyes lowered.

"I assure you, my child there is other things to preoccupy yourself. Allow yourself to honestly wander about and listen to others talk. You are bound to find some one that will need your assistance. Now be on your way so we may be on ours."

She took the cardinals' hand took his hand and embraced his ring.

"May your sins be forgiven." The Cardinal said in *sotto voc* as well.

"Merci Monsieur." She said and disappeared in to the crowd of denizens.

The Cardinal once again reached into his satchel, but this time he withdrew a bottle of holy water that was recently blessed during a mass in which he officiated.

He unstopped it, dribbled a little on some fingers and as he was about to place the sign of the cross upon the black painted door, Porthos spoke.

"Monsieur La Cardinal, do you not know that this is a *Maison d destin malady?"*

"Indeed I do."

"Then I would not do that if I were you." Replied the portly musketeer.

"Pray tell, why would you not?" Queried the Cardinal with an arched brow.

"It might explode."

The Cardinal shook his head.

As they rounded their third and last corner, the palaces' small courtyard leading to the cardinals' narrow enclosed stairs came into view.

The three musketeers and valet stood back and allowed the Cardinal to enter first, followed by his valet, Vitray, then they in no particular order.

Once in the passageway, Vitray took the liberty to precede them as to allow himself to open the door and hold it for his master and his guests.

Once inside, the small group of men strode to a small anti chamber that served as a small hall in which the Cardinal utilization of it was for meals and appointed counseling.

Pre-lit sconces illuminated an adequate sized table, laden with a desirable breakfast and an abundance of wine.

Athos scowled.

"Athos, what is amiss?" Queried Porthos.

"'Tis not Anjou." He replied as he recognized the bottled heralding from another accompanying region and not that of Anjou.

"I should think that if the Cardinal had expected us, the drink of choice would have been more accommodating."

Erstwhile, the Cardinal exited the main chamber by the way of behind the large tapestry that hung on the wall, that concealed a small, private narrow passage way that lead to a larger secluded dressing chamber. Vitray silently followed to offer his assistance.

The three amused themselves with a self made game with the chess pieces the were upon a small table.

"It looks as if there was a game in process. Who ever had this king within reach of the rook, is about to succeed in securing a victory." Observed Aramis.

"Indeed there is a game in progress." Grinned Porthos, "By us."

Athos sat down betwixt Porthos and Aramis as the portly musketeer picked up a handful of random pieces and surrounded the king on the center of the board.

Then a second handful of pieces he placed a line of afore and behind the king, with two vacant rows that marked boundaries in betwixt.

"Now,". Instructed Porthos, using your line of defense with the given movement of the piece, free the king in fifteen moves or less."

Athos picked up a pawn and with it he readily removed a knight that was directly in front of the king.

Porthos inclined his head towards Aramis.

The young prelate found it befitting that a bishop was at his disposal and thus moved it til it over took the queen that was befittingly next to the king.

For what ever the event, it struck Porthos, amusing him.

Athos moved the rook til another pawn obstructed his path to an accompanying knight.

Aramis moved a pawn and took the helpless bishop.

Athos took the opposing queen and removed the queen that stood next to the king.

Aramis moved a knight to within striking distance but it was too late Athos took the king.

The Cardinal re-entered the room, pausing. He took a deep breath and held it momentarily and slowly released it.

"Good gentleman, join me if you will at breakfast. As you can see, there is plenty and you shall not want. Vitray?"

The valet took the prompt and served his master that was seated at the head of the table with Aramis on one side and Porthos on t'other, with Athos next to Porthos and Grimaud across from his master, next to Aramis.

With food upon their plates and the wine poured Richelieu inquired if Aramis cared to give a blessing.

"Ne, good Cardinal, it is your house, I, a mere guest have not got such eloquent befitting words to match this occasion."

The cardinal bowed his head as did his guests.

His blessing was brief and to the point which pleased the portly musketeer for his stomach beckoned numerous times and went unheeded.

Murmurs of, "Praise be to God and His ultimate goodness and mercy. Amen." We're heard around the table.

Now at last, his stomach would be filled momentarily and he would be satiated til dinner.

"Now gentlemen, what can you tell me of the situation at hand?" He queried, as he glanced about the table to see if anyone would offer up any useful information.

After swallowing what he had in his mouth, Aramis said, "We know that Monsieur la Rohan has taken up residence in Castres, and makes frequent sojourns to the south."

The cardinal interrupted, "It is my understanding, Rohan is being given a pension and that was on the contingent he was to dismantle his forts at Utes, Nimes and Montpellier."

"Indeed. As we had observed shortly after the siege, it was in the progress of being deconstructed and all munitions surrendered in the prevention of further conflictions tween the state and the unamused denizens."

"Has the fire been put out at Montpellier?" Queried the Cardinal, with an arched concerned brow.

"My apologies, your Eminence, but it is still smoldering." Replied Porthos, as he cut off a wedge of cheese from the small Brie wheel that was within arms reach of him.

"As soon as a caravan of contraband was removed and made it way to the mutual collection spot, under the guise of compliance, another caravan would bring in current supplies and be readily concealed. For all intense and purposes, it would appear he is not defying the king."

The Cardinal's countenance reddened with ire, making it difficult to distinguish his countenance and his robes, save for his aging goatee to which he meticulously manicured daily with the assistance of his *valet de chamber.*

He suddenly slammed his closed fist upon the table, taking his guests off guard.

"Oh! Bother, he is!" He exclaimed. "Do I dare inquire of Nimes and Uzes?"

"There is no denying the fact your Eminence, they too have accepted contraband munitions and are concealing it." Replied Aramis.

"Alas, our current concern is La Rochelle. They are putting forth much effort in this and will not at what ever the cost, let the fort fall back to the king."

Through clenched jowls and barely audible, the cardinal queried, "Where are they concealing the diverted munitions?"

"Malamort. It is within a league of Castres. It consists of a valley and caverns and a waterfall." Added Porthos.

"We have sent Bazin and Mousequeton forth to seek Rohan's whereabouts, observe his movements then implement our own ways of creating a diversion that would be the most beneficial." Commented Aramis.

"One of the ways we thought of was to recruit a number of our fellow musketeers, position them along the way to La Rochelle, Nimes and Uzes...." Began Porthos.

"Do not omit Montpellier." Prompted Aramis, dipping a morsel of bread in his wine, drank the wine and poured himself some more.

"There too..and inform the caravan master there is an obstruction and to get around it divert them to ! Then once there, they will be relieved of their duties and the burden of munitions and secure both in a manner that is in compliance with our sovereigns wishes."

"When do you expect your valets to return?" Queried the Cardinal.

"They just left." Murmured Athos, shaking his head.

The Cardinal glanced at Athos, but said nothing, then returned his attentions to Aramis and Porthos.

"Your Eminence, pardon your lack of knowledge of such, they just left afore daybreak." Replied Porthos.

"Then erstwhile, would it be beneficial to employ Jussac and his regiment?"

Athos cleared his throat, annoyed at thought of dealing with not only the Cardinal, but with his captain whom he deemed to be a dolt and as inept as his master.

"As much as we would like to say, we will prevail and subdue the insubordinates and constituents belonging to Monsieur la Rohan with minimal efforts, his determination has proven to have taken on a life of its own with a swiftness of a determined donkey." Replied Porthos.

"Alas, nonetheless the longevity of such determinations need to be curtailed and the kings' regiments as well as your, your Eminence, has just so many men, as a suggestion we should combine our efforts and put an end to such foolishness." Added Aramis.

Athos shifted his posture while pouring more wine into his nigh empty goblet, with one hand and spearing a poached pear with his poniard, with the other.

"If we employ the ineptness of Jussac, we might as well say the Huguenots will have an advantage that we do not." Commented Athos, off handedly.

"….Dare I inquire what that advantage is?" Queried the Cardinal, clenching and unclenching a fist.

"Have ranked officers that know what is what and how to maintain a healthy balance betwixt their regiments and munitions and not short on either."

The Cardinals' countenance immediately changed in hue and indicated a forth coming barrage of oaths.

"Monsieur Athos, I find your insolence most bothersome, alas I must inquire of you, are you always this insolent?"

"Ne, your Eminence." Replied Athos with a wry grin, "Sometimes it is worse."

Aramis managed to conceal a slight smile and Porthos just shook his head, his smile concealed behind his raised goblet.

Athos inclined his head and resumed his consumption of various tidbits of food that was setting afore him.

The Cardinal took a deep breath and reminded himself it is not worth an effort of forcing an issue over hollow words.

"Messieurs, what are your designs on the remainder of the day, it is nigh spent." Queried the Cardinal

"It is just that, nigh spent. It no doubt be worth finding a chamber and make use of either a pallet or bed. It matters not, we are thoroughly fatigued." Suggested Porthos.

Vitray, who had been silently standing behind the cardinals' right should, stepped forward as they heard the as they heard the Luxembourg' clock strike the hour of three, and in *sotto voc,* reminded the cardinal of something.

"Then assure him, I will take care of it as soon as I am available, which by the by will be momentarily."

Vitray bowed slightly and withdrew from the chamber.

"It seems, my good gentlemen, the day has progressed so much as to the point that other things need my attention and I must attend to them. Erstwhile, let us make it a point to adjourn for now, then as the sun arrives in the morn, so shall you and we will finalize our discussion."

"Your Eminence, begging your pardon, we were in hopes of obtaining counsel with the king and relay our finding with him as well." Replied Aramis.

"Is he aware of your return?" Inquired the Cardinal, with an arched brow.

"Ne."

"Then if he is unaware, so be it and we can finish, then collectively inform the king."

The Cardinal regained his feet as the three did also.

Richelieu took a pace or two then turned about to face Athos who had his gauntleted hands on the back of his chair.

"I do have one other query of you my dear Monsieur Athos...."

The musketeer inclined his head.

"Do you cause this much anguish for the king?"

"Ne."

"Perchance telling me why not?"

"It is because, your Eminence, I like him.", came the reply as he slowly slid his chair in the direction of the cardinal, as he turned and made for the door.

Cardinal Richelieu took a deep breath, "See yourselves out," he said, as he too turned to make for the concealed panel behind the tapestry, with his robes sailing behind him.

Athos bowed deeply as he doffed his cap.

Once in the passageway, Porthos commented.

"It indeed is later than we expected, but alas, there is the need again to refill our stomachs and what better way then to find a suitable hostler."

"We were not able to refill our coffers." Reminded Aramis.

"Has that ever deterred us in the past?" Queried Athos, "We have always managed to make the best of our situations and this is no different, except we are smartly dressed for an occasion."

"Precisely." Smiled Porthos, "It could be assumed that we are employed by the king and therefore carrying out our duties."

"Then they can settle the debt incurred with the king." Suggested Athos.

"The Silver Pigeon", "awaits." Replied Porthos.

"Indeed it does." Added Aramis.

Upon arriving at their decided location, they found it nigh vacant and much to their liking.

Their desired corner was occupied by a rather hefty man and a very slight woman, so slight as to query if she were an invalid.

"Do we dare approach and request them to vacate?" Queried Porthos.

"We do not need to cause grief from something so trivial. Mind you, there is one other back corner, rather obscure at best." Observed Aramis, "Let us make use of it afore someone else has the same idea."

The men obtained the corner with Porthos and his back against the wall and his companions on either side.

The valets were allowed a small table just a pace or two away.

"Now,..." Began Porthos, "We have a slight difference of opinion."

"That being what?" Queried Athos.

"My opinion is that we seek the covert munitions that Rohan has accumulated thus far and either set a keg or two to it or assist them in kegging La Rochelle, unbeknownst to them. Let them think they are aiming it towards the kings men when in actuality they will be kegging one of their very own forts."

"So much for security." Laughed Aramis.

"Indeed." Smiled Porthos, "The difference of opinion is, do we wait for Bazin and Mousequeton to return within the fortnight or do we silently go forth and leave word for the to join us?"

"It will not do us any harm if we waited for them." Observed Aramis, "By doing so, we can get much needed rest and a chance to replenish our purses."

Porthos inclined his head slightly.

"What say you Athos?" Queried Aramis.

"We need some Anjou."

IV

As if knowing the musketeers intent, the innkeep approached and slightly bowed.

"Messieurs, what is it you request?"

"Anjou, Brie, broth and bread." Replied Aramis, knowing how slight and in want their purses were.

Subsequently, two rather oddly dressed men sat next to the musketeers, continuing an apparent on going conversation.

"I must request something of you." Said one, whose doublet was tied in a most obscure way and the shirt did not resemble the common linen.

"That being?" Replied the other, who by no means had anything to indicate his station.

Straight boots, unlike the musketeers who were known to wear bucket boots with spurs, his shirt bore no ruff nor seam and if closely observed, no ties.

The inn keep approached them cautiously, for he too recognized the fact their origins might be a matter of concern.

"The spit goose, Brie, wine and a small kettle of soup." Instructed the one with his doublet being obscure.

The inn keep bowed slightly and withdrew.

"The query is, have you ever been shot by a musket?"

The other laughed.

"What do you find so amusing? I am serious with my inquery."

"As I am sure you are. First, the musket is very inaccurate when it comes to their target, you have to over compensate, by that time your target will have escaped your grasp and will have made haste to whence it came. Then to answer your query, no but would like to."

"What?" Queried his companion, aghast at such a thought of being grievously wounded, if not something far more serious. "Why would you want that?"

"It would have to be a gold musket ball."

"Why gold?"

"For compensation of course."

"Then my dear companion, what if t'were mere silver and not gold?"

"It would mean they would be a shovel shy of a total burial."

"Then *mon ami,* what if it rendered you incapable of relaying your tale?"

"Then it would take care of my burial expenses."

The three musketeers just shook their heads.

"So reminds me of Pasqual and Tomas." Commented Porthos as he drained the contents of his goblet only to refill his and Athos' as he noticed his companions was nigh empty.

"Fine thing that their name should surface in our conversation," interjected Aramis, "If we decide to await the the return of our valets, we can pay counsel with them."

"We need to garner all the information we can concerning his whereabouts." Added Athos, as he too drained the contents of his goblet, only to have Porthos to hastily refill it.

Porthos shuddered.

"Dear Porthos, fret not, they can not cause you anguish from there. I assure you, not many if any common denizen will pay heed to anything they speak of." Assured Aramis.

"Then I take it, we will await their return?" Queried Porthos as he swallowed what he just took a bite of.

"No use going blind. If we can ascertain as to his whereabouts, it will make it easier to point the governing regiments in the right direction. Misdirections, mind you could have disastrous consequences and effects." Replied Aramis.

Porthos silently refilled his unsuspecting companions' goblet again and covertly nudged it towards him.

Aramis aware of his actions, furrowed his brow and inclined his head inquiry.

Porthos raised a brow in response, indicating he had an ulterior motive for the application of the wine to their unwary companion.

Porthos happened to glance down at the contents of his shallow bowl.

"My how pale this broth is..it would cause a pauper to be more in want."

"Alas our attempt to refill our purses failed this day, it does not mean we can not try again on the morrow." Hic-coughed Athos.

"True enough. By the bye, Richelieu wants to continue the conversation on the morrow, therefore we stand a good chance of accomplishing just that. Considering he is the queens' almoner." Observed Aramis.

"Surely we should be compensated…." Commented Porthos.

"Bah! He will probably wait 'til we are bringing Rohan with us at the end of a siege as proof we accomplished our set task. He is such a dolt!" Added Athos, "He has so many locks on the kings' coffers, he forgets what key goes to what lock."

Aramis poked at a piece of bread with his ponaird and proceeded to dip it in the remains of his goblet, then in his mouth.

Once again Athos drained his goblet and Porthos drained the last contents of the bottle into it, then summoned the inn keep for another bottle.

Obligingly the inn keep did as he was bid and departed.

"Easy old man, he is not that bad that we have to be at odds with him every time we are in counsel with him." Aramis said, trying to make the conversation lighter.

"As you should think." Scowled Athos.

The inn keep approached with a platter of roasted fowls from the hearths' spit and set it in the center of the small worn table.

Porthos glanced at the inn keep, who just shrugged and walked away.

"Bother! An added expense, unaccounted for."

"Ah Porthos, fret not, do not discredit the gesture. He obviously meant no harm."

"What?" Hic-coughed Athos, "Does he consider us a charity case?", querying sarcastically.

"Never hurts to be on the receiving end of a good gesture." Sighed Aramis as he slightly inclined his head.

Porthos glancing askance at Athos' goblet, and seeing it was nigh empty again, retrieved it.

"Ah my dear companion, allow me this gesture and refill your goblet."

"Dear Porthos, your gesture is accepted. It is not charity, it is a necessity." He grinned.

"How do you know it is not charity?" Replied Porthos.

"It comes from you." Laughed Athos as he drained his goblet.

"Ply me again dear man, with your trade." Hic-coughed the now inebriated musketeer.

"Apparently, my good man, you are a man of many talents." Smiled Aramis.

"Let us just say, adaptable." Replied Porthos as he again filled his companions' goblet and slid it towards him.

Aramis used his ponaird to spear a generous portion of roasted goose.

"What say you Athos we make use of the gymnasium on the morrow to hone our use of swords. Perchance we will find a new way to utilize them and relieve a given opponent his burden of carrying his sword. That can be cumbersome." Laughed Aramis.

Athos did not reply which caused his companions to glance at him to see what was amiss if anything.

They noticed the vacantness in his eyes as his head slightly bobbed.

The telltale signs that their companion has been rendered senseless in a common way.

Then suddenly without warning Athos pitched forward with is brow hitting the table and then allowing his head to roll to a side.

"Athos?" Gently called Aramis.

Porthos nudged him.

Suddenly, Athos sat up quickly as if he were struck by a lightening bolt.

The portly musketeer nudged him again and he too gently called, "Athos?"

Athos blinked twice and turned to face his companion who had called to him.

"Hmmm. You said something?" Queried Athos.

"Indeed I did. I must query something of you." Replied Porthos, warily, as he slid another filled goblet in the direction of his companion.

Athos hic-coughed, "You know you can always query of me anything your big generous heart wants."

Porthos anxiously glanced at Aramis.

The young prelate inclined his head and raised his brow as he gently dabbed the perspiration from it with his kerchief.

"Dear Athos, why is it, when we are at counsel with Richelieu, you proceed to mock his chosen station?"

Athos leaned back in his chair, arms crossed over his chest as if pondering an adequate response.

Porthos, adequately refraining himself from laughing aloud, glanced at Aramis, who could only raise his brow in amusement.

"Pray, tell my dear companion, why do you hold such contempt towards Cardinal Richelieu and as I previously queried, mock his station?"

"Hmmm....why you query I do such?" Replied Athos, who had picked up his goblet and gingerly sipped at its fullness, cautious not to spill the contents.

Aramis dabbed his brow again, then leaned in to listen to Athos' chosen words.

"'Tis, not so much the man, I presume, it is what he represents."

"That being?" Prompted Porthos.

"He represents the church and the church represents God."

"What difference does that make?" Queried Aramis, somewhat crossly.

Porthos gestured to Aramis to keep his ire under control and let their companion speak his peace.

"It is that I feel very betrayed, by life itself and hold God personally responsible."

"How can you hold God responsible when man has free will to make the choices he does and if something falls short of his expectations, he has only himself to find fault with, not God." Replied Aramis.

"In theory only." Hic-coughed Athos, "God, when he answers prayer the way He deems fit, and when things go awry that is when I want to hold Him accountable. He holds us accountable for our actions, so reciprocation is only fair."

"May I inquire whom you believe God betrayed you with?"

"Who said it was it is a person?" Inquired Athos sarcastically.

"It only stands to reason." Replied the young prelate.

"So be it." Replied the inebriated musketeer.

Porthos and Aramis, gave pause and waited for an answer that never came.

As soon as Athos set his goblet back upon the table, he pitched forward and his brow again hit the table.

"I do believe we got a little more insight as to the makings of Athos." Sighed Porthos.

"That may be so, but he still is enigmatic. He has contributed more towards the continuation of the problem of secrecy and intrigue than to the conclusion."

"We know that it is a person…"

"Seriously? We do not know that to be fact."

"What else could it be?" Returned Porthos, he shrugged, "By the bye dear Aramis how is one to hold God accountable as Athos seems to think one can?"

"You can not. We were given free will and how we choose to use our free will is a variable and with many variables and varied outcomes, it sometimes is difficult to conclude if it was Gods' will or ours, as man. We pray, yes and at times when He is silent, that is our answer, but as impetuous as we are, we randomly pursue our whims and when we experience a shortcoming we tend to blame Him. Use Him as a scape goat, if you will. His answers are not always what *we* want. We want Him to make our life perfect. Alas, as perfect as it would be if that were the case, something would befall us and thus again blame God for not protecting us. It is just not logical to even try and hold Him accountable."

"But He holds us accountable."

"Of course He does. That is what He does best."

"What about predestination?"

"I tend to believe it is a mixture of free will and Gods' intervention. He gives us choices and we with our limited intellect should choose right, but,…". Sighed Aramis, "alas, we do not always heed what is directly set afore us. We falter. We do not see our destination as predetermined, just something we want to do, rather than have to do."

Somewhere in the distance, a bell tower told the hour of one.

Athos again turned his head, and let out a rather loud sigh.

"I tend to agree with him." Smile Aramis, "It is rather late and the Cardinal wants to see us again. In the morn I might add."

"YOU might but what say we do?" Jested Porthos.

"I do. Need I remind you, we still need to see the king and De Treville and relay it all over again."

"Practice makes perfect." Again Porthos smiled, although it was concealed by his raised goblet and slightly inclined his head.

Aramis sighed lightly.

"What gives?" Porthos queried.

"Knowing we have to frequent the Cardinal, Athos will not have the humor to do so. In any event, we still need to and he will just have to bear up."

"You know as well as I, he will not keep his tongue still. We will be hard pressed to know what he is going to say." Laughed Aramis, "Poor Richelieu to be at the sharp end of Athos' tongue."

"Poor Richelieu nothing!" Replied Porthos, "I agree with Athos on the point he needs to implement tact. He so lacks that attribute."

"I so suppose it is better to have tact in certain circumstances and then there is a time a subject should be approached with out caution."

"He seems to not know the difference."

"It is just as well he does not. What is said, is said and what is done is done. Be it for the state or the church, he cares not."

"Does he even care?" Queried Porthos, doubtful.

"Of course he does."

"Peste! Only if it concerns him."

"Now, my good man, what are we to do with Athos?" Queried Aramis, with a glimmer of mischief in his dark eyes.

"Since we were partially successful in obtaining some information, perchance when our purses are replenished we can set about and draw more information from an inebriated Athos." Suggested Porthos.

"As for now, beckon Grimaund. Since we are within shouting distance of our apartments, I suggest we deposit him in the care of his valet and collect him early in the morn."

Aramis gestured to the anxious valet to come forth.

"My dear valet, I leave your master in your care. See to it if you will, let him get adequate rest and we will be around to collect him. We have counsel once again with Richelieu."

"As he has sworn you to his secrets, we must add one of our own." Suggested Porthos.

Grimaud raised his eyebrows in query, then furrowed them in worry.

"Say nothing of our intent to ply him with drink to obtain information. Even though he is a dear companion to which we value, we know very little of whence he came or what he is about. At times it seems he is hiding. From someone or something we know not."

"Hiding in plain sight." Nodded Aramis, murmuring.

Porthos regained his feet, sat Athos upright and with minimal effort adjusted the inebriated companion across his shoulders to wear him as a mantle, snug and secure.

Aramis stood to regain his feet as well, he retrieved his companions' cap that had fallen from his head to the well worn planked floor and carefully removed the sheathed sword and baldric and handed them to Grimaud, for safe keeping til his master needed them in the morn.

Once out of doors, Porthos adjusted the added weight and paused.

In the dim light the moon emitted Aramis mistook the pause for an issue.

"Porthos?"

"Hmmm?"

"Are you right, has he caused you imbalance?"

"Ne, just getting him adjusted."

"That is good. So as long as you do not drop him."

"If I did," Porthos tittered, "He would not feel it.

"Yet." Interjected Aramis, "When he becomes coherent, he would feel it and his curiosity would cause him to query the nature of his aches."

"He weighs no more than a keg of powder. Fret not. I as of yet, have not misappropriated the use of a keg of powder."

"When his fuse has been lit, he is just as explosive as a lit keg."

"Again, fret not my good man, his returnment to his apartments will go without incident. Now if you will, retrieve our horses and let us be on our way.

"You never cease to amaze me." Said Aramis.

"Is that a good thing or a bad thing?" Inquired Porthos.

"I know not. I have not had the opportunity to decide that." Replied Aramis, smiling.

V

The avenue in which Athos resided, Rue du Ferou, was adequately lit by well maintained braziers, in spite of some that had been reduced to shouldering embers.

The brazier keep had made his rounds prior and no doubt had just began his rounds again as the Luxembourg clock criticized the hour of three.

Athos let out a sigh, that startled the horses.

With *a sotto voc,* Aramis soothed the anxious animals.

Porthos paused.

"My good man, are you right?"

"Why would I not be?"

"You paused."

"Of course I would, if I were at your door."

Aramis tittered.

"Grimaud my good man, take your masters' horse to the stable and have the valet attend him, return. Now, make haste, then return hence." Instructed Porthos.

The valet accepted the reins to his masters' horse from Aramis and scurried hastily away only to return moments later.

"Good man. Now allow us admittance to deposit Athos into the care of who knows him best, you." Suggested Aramis.

Porthos carefully manipulated himself and his parcel without incident, as he entered his companions' apartment, behind the weary valet.

Grimaud without delay set flame to lantroons that were about the chamber and soon the warm glow created dancing silhouettes against the walls.

A chair close to the unlit caught Porthos' attention.

"This will suffice nicely." Smiled Porthos, "In fact anything will have been sufficient."

The gentle giant of a musketeer, unshouldered his inebriated companion and sat him up in the chair.

"If we did not know any different, we would say he is at rest." Mused Aramis.

Athos' unshaven chin resting on his chest, moved rhythmically with the breathing. Even and steady, indicating he was more at slumber than inebriated.

"Grimaud, my good man, is this where you would like him? Say now if there is a difference, for I will move him again. I so doubt that you could move him by yourself."

The slight valet just shrugged, as he indicated to bring his master to his bed chamber and lay him down and he would tend to his master.

Porthos, with no effort, picked up his companion and proceeded to follow the valet to Athos' bed chamber.

It's furnishing were scant, but accommodating and comfortable.

Grimaud set the lit taper on a small table next to the bed and stepped aside to allow Porthos access.

As Porthos laid his unconscious companion down, a barely audible groan emitted from him, followed by soft snoring.

"When dawn breaks, give him an hour to collect his wits and bring him to me." Instructed Aramis, "Then we will seek counsel again with the Cardinal and if time permits, Louis."

"We really should not keep our good captain til last." Suggested Porthos.

"Just think of it this way, we are saving the best for last. Surely he will be told the same as the others and therefore it really matters not in what order we seek them. For do remember, they know not that we are here, save Richelieu and he may be too preoccupied and much to do to send a courier to Louis to inform him otherwise."

Somewhere in the distance, a rooster crowed.

"Dawn is not far off, Since we do not have our valets, we will just have to make the best of it. If you awake afore I, seek me and I shall do likewise. Collectively we will see the Cardinal as he requests." Suggested Aramis.

"Do you think Athos will be in any condition to sufficiently answer what the Cardinal queries of him without letting lose on his tongue?"

Aramis chuckled softly.

"Need you query such a thing? I doubt it."

Porthos just shook his head.

Vieux Columbier was nigh vacant, but within a matter of a few short hours it again would be bustling with denizens making their daily visits to their favorite establishments for their desired refinements that their purses would accommodate.

"Ah, my home!" Exclaimed Porthos, "I have not seen you in a very long time."

"My dear Porthos, we basically have a half a fortnight to culminate all task we set out to do and then we must return out there to find Rohan and assist in putting an end to these little sieges.

The hefty musketeer made no attempt to stifle his yawn.

"I suspect though, good Aramis, all these little ones are leading up to something big. We already know La Rochelle is causing grief."

"Alas, we have to find out just how much grief and if we can remove the fuse afore it is even lit, we stand a good chance of settling all the Huguenot differences with one treaty, for then they will see that Louis is serious and he is not toying with them. He wants peace just like all the commoners."

"He also like his sieges." Prompted Porthos.

"That he does, indeed. In order to maintain peace throughout, he has to have put out all the fires and proceed."

"If it t'were not the Huguenots causing grief, it would be some other faction."

"True. Let us deal with one issue at a time."

"I certainly shall likes of my bed. There is none other like it." Smiled Porthos.

"Same. As for now my fellow musketeer, allow yourself admittance, find your night shirt, don it and lay down.

"Rather fall down. I am so fatigue, I feel as if I could fall. By the by, I so doubt it will take very long afore I am asleep. Mind you, it might take cannon fire to awake me since I do not have Mousequeton. I am sincerely and thoroughly fatigued."

"Fret not, you will make do as you always do and I too are in agreement in being fatigued. I assure you our valets will return afore too long and things will be set right once again. More so out of habit rather than convenience."

"'Til later then?" Suggested Porthos.

"Yes. Later." Agreed Aramis.

They respectfully pressed each other's palm.

As Aramis brushed a lock of hair out of his eyes, tucked it under his cap, he strode down the avenue, seeking his own quiet apartment.

Porthos found his hidden key, unlocked the door and stepped in, but paused long enough to follow his companion with his eyes in the very early light of dawn, til he disappeared around a corner.

The musketeer, being very well acquainted with his surroundings, made his way to his bed chamber and sat heavily down on the edge of his bed.

He found his night shirt, where he had left it, laid out across the end. He picked it up and vigorously shook it off, lest anything had settled in it or on it in his absence.

He briefly struggled with his boots and spurs, but once removed he tittered to himself.

"How I envy Mousequetons' persistence in getting these off. I suppose I could make it easier on him if I did not curl my toes. Now for the rest of me."

He hastily changed vestments, pulled back the counterpane, laid down covered himself up, briefly thought he should have laid a fire in the still hearth, but thought again he did not want to make the effort, and promptly fell asleep.

After what seemed like only a matter of a mere hour if that, a rap came upon Porthos' door.

"Mousequeton!" He called out, "You do not have to prove you are a lazy valet on your good days…MOUSEQUETON!"

The rapping again sounded, persistent and rapid.

As Porthos regained his wits, he remembered his valets' absence, and murmured an apology, for he knew his valets' true worth.

"*Mon Dieu!* 'Tis too early. If it truly is Aramis or Grimaud…" His thoughts faded as he opened the door to find a very young boy afore him dressed in a court pages attire.

"Monsieur Porthos?" He said, sounding more like a query rather than a statement.

"What if I said, "no", 'tis not I?" Replied the giant.

"Then I again inquire, if I received the same reply I would inquire where I would be fortunate enough to locate him. For I have a message from his majesty to he and his companions."

Porthos yawned.

"I bore you?" Inquired the young man eyeing the musketeer

"In a sense, yes. Alas admittedly I have had very little rest. Presuming that I am the one you seek, how is it you came here?"

The young man took a stance with his hands on his hips and squarely glared at Porthos.

"I am a page and courier of the king, he knows everything he needs to know and no doubt, more. He discreetly knows where his guards live beyond the *Palais Royale's* walls, he makes it his personal interests to keep things in order. You, Monsieur are a personal interest as well as you companions. So, again I query of you, are you Monsieur Porthos?"

"It would make no sense to deny the fact."

"Indeed it it would not."

"I admit *mon petite Monsieur,* I am he whom you seek with such ardent enthusiasm."

"Then the message is by days' end, you are to seek a Monsieur Jean Percerin. He is the kings' tailor. His establishment is Rue St. Honore. Honorably labeled. It is in the proximity of Rue de l'Arbre, sec."

"I have a query of you."

"That being?…."

"How did you know I would be here and not elsewhere?"

"I did not in truth. The king suspected you had been absent long enough and for the last fortnight has sent me forth to seek you and I was to continue and til the message has been delivered, now that it has, I can enjoy an extra hour of leisure afore I am formally summoned by the king for the day."

"Very well. I shall inform my companions as soon as I see them. Return the message to the king that his message has been duly acknowledged and will be complied with in accordance to the time we are allocated, as we have other unfinished business we must attend to as well."

"*Oui* Monsieur." Replied the young man as he hastily departed to relay what the musketeers' response had been.

The fatigued musketeer softly shut his door, heard the latch catch then retreated once again to his bed chamber.

He pulled the heavy drape close to shut out the suns' early morns' beckoning.

The musketeer turned his back to his shuttered window and tried to get comfortable as he lay down, alas it seemed as soon as he was about to finally doze off an unfamiliar sounds jostled him awake.

Uttering a mild oath, he turned himself to his other side and tried again to sleep.

Erstwhile, Aramis had rousted himself, found some breakfast and a half a bottle of Anjou wine to accompany his findings.

He decided to attend mass after he recited his daily ritualistic prayers. He knew that the mass would be quite lengthy, alas it mattered not, it was something he was accustomed to.

The city was starting to come to life with the daily activities of the denizens as the sun had cleared the tops of the distant tree. Morn had arrived.

Once inside St. Eustache church, Aramis removed his gauntlets, tucked them into his sash, dipped his finger tips into the shallow font that beheld the holy water that was recently blessed, and crossed himself.

He found a pew relatively close to the front alter, reverently genuflected and sat down and sighed.

"With so many souls in want, why are so many homeless have not found refuge from the raging storm the world imparts, here within the safety of these walls. Nourishment for the soul is so close, yet so far. Mercy has no bounds."

Aramis knew he and Porthos were to meet with the Cardinal, and assured himself that His Eminence would understand this need.

As the mass was ended, he decided afore to hastened to Porthos' apartment to see if his companion managed to get himself ready for the day but then decided Athos was a more pressing situation.

He rapped upon his companions' door.

As his summons went unanswered, he thought he would try again, knowing Athos had been in no condition to fend for himself and no doubt reeling from the aftermath of imbibement, unequivocally had the need to locate his companion.

Not only for the satisfaction in knowing he would be right, he still had to accompany he and Porthos to their appointed counsel with the Cardinal.

He so hoped he would hold his tongue and not be irritable.

Alas his hope turned to apprehension when the door creaked open and Grimaud stood afore him chaffing his hands.

"Grimaud, my good man, what gives, is your master right?"

The valet stepped outside and closed the door behind him so that Athos could not hear him speak.

"What is bothering you?" Queried Aramis.

"Masters' formality."

"Pardon? Formality? How so?"

"He got himself up, dressed himself afore his cheval, adjusted his baldric, polished his spurs, put on his boots and spurs, sat himself afore his hearth and summoned me and requested breakfast and acknowledged that he will be awaiting you and Monsieur Porthos."

Aramis furrowed his brow.

"My dear Grimaud, I tend to agree. That is not the usual way Athos progresses through a day after a night of imbibing. Hmmm."

Grimaud lifted the latch and allowed the young prelate to proceed afore him.

The musketeer did not know what to anticipate, for currently Athos was not in proper character, alas curiosity took a firm hold which motivated Aramis to cautiously step forward.

Standing afore his companion, the lifeless hearth, offered no comfort nor consolation.

Aramis gestured for a chair to be set afore his companion in which Grimaud readily complied.

Rounding the chair he sat upon the thread bare brocaded chair opposite of his dear companion and leaned forward to take in Athos' countenance and his attire.

Athos indeed was particular about his appearance and with Grimaud daily grooming allowed him to have an air of confidence and persuasion. Even after a eve of frequenting his favorite establishment, "The Sword and the Pendulum", he still maintained.

With a glance, Aramis was able to conclude his observation of Athos.

His eyes were vacant and hollow, with a pallid tint to his skin which Aramis deduced Athos was at the mercy of aches and pains that were the residual repercussions of too much wine.

"Athos?", Aramis called, in *sotto voc.*

The afflicted musketeer, turned his head to look at Aramis, his eyes almost look like they were pleading.

"Is there anything I can do for you?" Queried Aramis, continuing in the *sotto voc.*

"Seek the apothecary, ask for willow. When he queries of you the quantity, reply, "A whole Coppice.""

"We can remedy your situation as we keep our appointment with the Cardinal."

Athos let out a moan that more sounded like a a wounded dog whining, than a man in agony.

A slight grinned toyed about Aramis' mouth, but alas Athos was too preoccupied with his situation to have noticed.

Clearing his throat, Aramis queried, "My good man, are you willing to take breakfast?"

Athos held up his hand in suggestion for Aramis to lower his voice, for he ached too much to bear a heavy voice, therefore as mild as Aramis' were, he dread Porthos' who was considered in operatic terms, a baritone.

"Send Grimaud around to the apothecary as we traverse towards the *Palais* and round up Porthos as we do so. Once we are settled in Richelieu's' presents, complete our narratives, it would no doubt be supper time for we got a rather late beginning this morn. Perchance Richelieu forgo our tardiness."

"Like he will overlook a multitude of sinners in desperate need of absolution." Mumbled Athos.

The young prelate chose to overlook the comment as he stood up.

Athos took the clue and regained his feet as well and began for the door.

"Grimaud my good man, you heard the suggestion from Monsieur Aramis. Seek the apothecary and request some willow. If you do not have a sou or to for purchase, inquire after an extension on my credit. My purse is due to be re-filled by weeks' end and I will settle any and all my debts with him then. Then we will be with the Cardinal til only the Lord knows, for when he begins his narratives whether be in his chambers or Gods', it matters not, he prattles on and on."

"Athos!" Exclaimed Aramis.

"Aramis! You know he does. I only speak the truth."

"So you do. Alas, must you be so blatant?"

"Would you rather have to phantom what constitutes and preoccupies my mind or having it said and be done?" replied Athos, with a twisted wry grin.

Aramis just shook his head as he accompanied his companion out of doors, where they parted with Grimaud.

"Will Grimaud be able to negotiate with the apothecary?" Queried Aramis.

"The apothecary is a reasonable man and rest assured Grimaud will be able to procure some willow."

The brightness of the sun on the clear mid-day caused Athos to flinch and shield his eyes.

"'Ods' bodikin…need the likes of a cloud."

"Just think of it as a gentle reminder the elements will soon be in our constant favor. Yes occasionally we will have a difference of opinion but fair elements none the less. Take joy with what you have."

As they rounded to corner to Porthos' apartments, Aramis caught sight of Jussac strolling casually with no obvious intent.

The young prelate took advantage of that, and ushered Athos hastily towards Porthos' apartments, afore Jussac or Athos could exchange their thoughts for action.

As Athos was taking the liberty of rapping on their companions' door, it suddenly opened.

Instinctively, Athos grabbed for the handle of his sword and it was half out of its sheath when he heard the familiar voice of Porthos.

"Steady old man. I am not willing to partake of you poking holes into me for the sake of you being an anxious soul."

"When I poke holes into an antagonist, it is with a deliberate intent. With you, consider it a reminder, do not vex me. I should think you would be thankful for my agility."

Porthos sighed loudly.

"Believe you, me, I am. For your agility has caused no grief thus far, to yourself or Aramis nor myself, therefore I will vex you not and cause you to reconsider."

"My dear companions, we have kept the Cardinal waiting long enough and he no doubt has other things on his agenda in addition to us and better things to do with his time." Reminded Aramis.

"Playing chess or *Lansquenet* with Vitray?" Queried Porthos, to no one in particular.

"I should be inclined to agree." Replied Athos.

Aramis said nothing, kept his thoughts, "This counsel will prove futile. Athos will see to it. I agree with him, war is a waste but it also serves its purpose of proving a point with a given adversary.", to himself.

Upon entering the *Palais Royals,* the usual activity was less, for it was dinner time and no doubt those that usually attended the king and his needs were doing just that, any courier sent with missives, where out and about delivering them to the prospective denizen, court pages were predisposed by orders of the king, queen, regent and cardinal.

"Where might he be?" Queried Porthos, glancing hastily about, as the grand clock reverberated the hour of two.

"I am inclined to believe he is either in the grand hall, with the king, or in his chambers up to his chin in parchment and ink." Replied Aramis.

"If I t'were to choose," Replied Porthos, "I would choose the grand hall."

"Of course you would." Smiled Aramis.

"By the by," Interjected Porthos, "If we are to have a spare moment or so, we are to pay a visit to Monsieur Jean Percerin."

"Whom might that be? That name does not sound familiar." Queried Aramis.

"He is the kings' tailor."

"What does he want with us?" Queried Athos, always skeptical of unfamiliar people that could possibly lead to intrigue and deception even in the mildest forms.

"I know not. A courier came round this morn with the message from Louis."

"How did he know we were about?" Queried Aramis.

"I inquired that as well from him how he knew the difference and he said Louis suspected we had been gone long enough and sent him round for the last fortnight with the message and do not, not deliver the message. See to it that it is received, and thus he did and I pass on the message to you, lest I forget." Replied Porthos as he touched the rim of his cap.

"Shall we try the grand hall?" Queried Aramis.

"Lead the way." Smiled Porthos.

Athos bit his lip with contempt, but remained silent.

Collectively, their brass spurs clinked rhythmically on the marble floor as they made their way to the grand hall.

The grand hall was on the east side of a wide corridor thus allowing the sun to illuminate it and eliminating the need for tapers at certain times of the year, looking glasses paneled the room to allow reflected light to assist in the lighting of the room as well.

The tall heavy ornate oak doors were opposite the king and his court, thus allowing him to observe who came and went, were opened to allow admittance of couriers, pages, guards from both regiments, various attendants and valets.

Around the perimeter of the grand hall were long tables set with finer linen embroidered with the royal coat of arms, the serviettes were embroidered with gold thread and with the sovereigns' monogram, the tableware and serving platters were silver, the tureens, porringers were made of finely crafted porcelain and the goblets were simple but elegant, were made by a glass blower in the Tuileries.

"I would rather have been received in his chambers than here." Commented Porthos, in *sotto voc,* "My wits are dulled by chaos."

Aramis glanced at him askance, smiled and said nothing.

Peering over through the plumes on his companions' caps, Porthos scanned the hall in search of the cardinal.

"I see him not." Observed the friendly giant who was clearly a head above his companions and had the advantage of perceiving things that others could not, "His Eminence is not present."

"What of De Treville? We still need to allot some time with him as well as Louis." Queried Aramis.

"Nothing like being in demand.", Chuckled Porthos.

"I realize we initially intended to be here for a brief time, only long enough to consult with Louis, Richelieu, and De Treville. Now we have our agenda added to." Added Aramis.

"Alas, sometimes the best laid plans go awry." Replied Athos.

Porthos inclined his head.

"I tend to agree with that. So basically we should just go as a draught, be consistent and deliberate afore we wane off. A given draught does not deviate its path unless an obstacle presents itself. At times, when it happens upon an obstacle, it will over over or aside to continue, but it does continue. Therefore, perseverance will not allow us the chance to go awry. We just have to keep progressing no matter the cost." Theorized Aramis.

"We will accomplish what we set out to do, we always do, and we will continue, even though we will be slightly delayed. Just means we will have more time to prevent anything from going awry." Added Porthos.

"What do you propose we do?" Queried Athos, silently hoping Porthos' stomach would dictate, even though he no doubt would pick and choose 'til supper where then he would make use of his empty stomach at the kings' expense.

Porthos did not hesitate in replying.

"I suggest while we are here to make the best of it and make use of our continually open invitation to sit at the kings' table."

"Since when has it been an open invitation?" Queried Aramis.

"Right about now." Replied the hefty musketeer, smiling wryly as he removed his gauntlets.

"Do we need to sit close to the king, then?" Inquired Aramis.

"I think not. If we do, he will assume that it is his turn to have us join him in counsel. Far be it for me to deny his request, alas we still need to bring our counsel with Richelieu to a conclusion. Then we will seek him. Ah! We still need to pay heed and frequent Monsieur Percerin afore days end."

Porthos once again surveyed the Grand Hall as a peregrine would in search of prey upon tilled soil.

"My good companions' rarer things have occurred than this I assure you, alas I see not the king, nor De Treville nor the Cardinal."

"So much the better." Sighed Athos.

"Hate to be bearer of bad news, we still have to seek him. He expects us."

"You do remember, do you not dear Porthos, what happened to individual who bore bad news?" Inquired Athos, a most wry grin upon his countenance.

The three strode forth and found three empty well upholstered chairs conveniently grouped together.

It mattered not whom they set next to, be it a comte' or a duchess, their etiquette dictated the three should follow their example, lest they would bring unwarranted attention and be removed for truly they were not formally part of a courts' entourage, even though they beg to differ.

The din from the crowd did not allow them to talk to one another as they would have liked, so therefore they ate their fill and quietly and hastily departed.

No one would be none the wiser as to their identity. So much the better.

The Cardinals chambers' were beyond the courtyard, on the north side.

Cardinal Richelieu was not overly fond of the chambers even though they afforded him the seclusion he desired, the vastness of the chambers, the well manicured courtyard that allowed quiet reflective moments in a chaotic day, a small secretive door allowing him admittance or hasty departures, as he liked, undetected, alas the cold winter months wreaked havoc with his mind as well as his joints.

The marble stair case, garnered by statuettes of notable saints, particularly Joan of Arc adorned the small hewn grottos in the wall.

Small offerings were left in hopes the saints would smile favorably upon them and with Gods' mercy, grant their various petitions.

The wide passageway was nigh empty as well.

Porthos thought it was just as well and that meant their requested audience with the Cardinal would be granted post haste.

Even though their heavy boots echoed, it caused them to smile.

The echoes made it sound as if a whole regiment were storming the palace and not a select few that could do very little damage, although Porthos could work his way through a regiment if provoked and he himself would be left unscathed.

At the end of the corridor were two guards dressed with white tabards with red embroidered trim, even their plumes were red, their tabards denoted small red crosses in favor of Richelieu.

As Porthos was about to rap upon the door, Grimaud came scurrying down the hall in search of his master.

"If I did know any different, I would query as to why you are so tardy." Athos inclined his head slightly, "Alas, knowing the apothecary is within the vicinity of the Tuileries as well as other means of commerce, and many denizens frequent that location. As I am almost positive there are other apothecaries, this one is I am most acquainted with and will continue to frequent Monsieur. This day is no exception, denizens fall ill and seek relief from his remedies and in search of his establishment others were doing that as well. I do, however commend you in locating myself, therefore my relief is at hand.

Aramis took the liberty and stepped forward and rapped sharply upon the door.

Vitray opened the door and stepped aside and allowed them to enter.

The Cardinal had been debating whether to step out of doors to his narrow balcony or return to the still hearth.

Closing the door, he turned about, remaining silent.

He gestured for them to sit opposite of him as he rounded his desk.

Porthos and Aramis accepted, as Athos received the small vial from Grimaud he strode over to a silver gilt tray that beheld an ornate decanter with just as ornate goblets.

The musketeer emptied the contents of vial into a goblet, followed by some wine.

The powder slightly caused minute bubbles, but quickly dissolved as the liquid came into contact with it.

He turned to face his companions and raised the decanter slightly as if querying if they too would like him to share it with him.

With an inconspicuous shake of their heads, they declined.

Athos again inclined his head with a raised brow as if to say, "Then be you content."

Bringing the decanter with him, he sat down aside Porthos.

He refilled his goblet and then set the decanter upon the planked parqueted, floor under his chair in prevention of accidentally knocking it over.

Richelieu scowled, but still remained silent.

The sullen musketeer slumped in his chair and pulled his cap over his eyes to shut out the light, for he still ached for the moment, his arms crossed over his chest.

The Cardinal leaned forward and tented his fingers, with an arched brow.

Porthos stifled a yawn with a gauntlet hand.

"As we were saying, Rohan is at Castres and we know he frequents Montpelier and Montauban

"They were supposed to be dismantled under the directions of the king. Erstwhile, while he preoccupied himself, they made the most of the diversions and began to refortify those two as well as Utes, and Nimes." Added Aramis.

"My patience is wearing rather thin." Said the Cardinal.

"I imagine it would. For when he strikes, it is with haste and accuracy and most deliberate." Replied Aramis.

"Not to mention debilitating." Commented Porthos.

Athos mumbled, "…And frustrating."

The Cardinal turned his attention to Aramis, who seemed to know the most of the situation and queried, "Monsieur Aramis, I realize a day is a day and may not seem to make that much of a difference, but truly it does, I must query if you have seen the likes of your two absent valets?"

"Ne. I should seriously think by weeks end we will learn more of Rohan. When we do you will be the third to know."

"Third?" Mused the Cardinal.

"We all conclusively are second, for the valets will be first."

Athos chuckled lightly.

"I do not know what you find so amusing."

"Nor should you." Mumbled Athos.

The Cardinal returned his attention to Aramis, letting his ire subside.

"We do know he is continually fortifying La Rochelle. Once we confirm that, we will set up obstacles and divert the munitions elsewhere, but letting a lesser amount to proceed thus allowing Rohan to believe his has the upper hand, and then we will assist them in destruction of their own fort."

"He is not easily deceived, for he is an intelligent man. He calculates all things mathematically with alarming accuracy. Including anything that deals with sieges." Commented the Cardinal.

"Even the strongest, most intelligent of men, have a weakness." Added Porthos.

"Indeed. Rest assured afore this is all said and done, we will exploit his weak points and turn them to our favor."

As fluid as a rivulet flows to a tributary into the Seine, Athos reached under his chair to retrieve the decanter.

Not caring to move his cap aside, he removed the stopper and readily drained the contents.

The mild healthy coloring of the Cardinals' countenance drained as the contents of the decanter were, with ire rising hastily was replaced by a darker almost red hue.

The Cardinal managed to keep his wits and managed to say, "Then I shall await word from you as to when your valets have returned. 'Til then, my suggestion is seek the king and give him the information he requests, to the best of your ability. Then of course your Captain will need the information as well so he can formulate and implement plans. Draw the battle lines and move them accordingly. By your summations, he will recruit the necessary regiments and munitions."

As Porthos and Aramis regained their feet, they collectively nudged Athos.

He pushed his cap up and away from his eyes and he too regained his feet.

Aramis and Porthos bowed, "Your Eminence.", they said in unison, turned to take their leave.

Athos placed the decanter whence he was seated, and silently rounded the chair and gently pushed it towards the Cardinal, straightened his cap, touched its brim and joined his companions in departure.

"Either of you have a thought as to what time it is getting to be?" Queried Porthos as they returned out of doors and the sun was now once again beginning to touch the tops of the trees.

This time opposite of what they had observed earlier.

"How amusing is that?" Smiled Athos weakly.

"Perchance, why is it you say that?" Inquired Porthos.

"Your stomach is a good indicator when it is meal time. Has it spoke lately?" Returned Athos.

"Ne, can not say that it has. Perchance by being preoccupied with the given counsel, I had inconveniently turned a deaf ear."

Aramis inclined his head, but said nothing.

"Do have the time to spare to keep our appointment with Monsieur Percerin?" Queried Porthos, "For it is a formal request we do so."

"Indeed it is. If your stomach is silent, then so be it, we have time to spare. For it looks like the the Cardinal was severely distracted and because of that, he paid no mind to being an accommodating host and request we stay for supper. Ah, alas we did have dinner so all is not lost." Commented Athos.

Afore they got a steady pace in sync with one another, Grimaud took the liberty to tug lightly on his masters' loose sleeve.

The musketeer turned and carefully leaned towards his valet to listen to his *sotto voc-ed* request.

"My good valet, how genuine your concern is for my well being. At present I can honestly say, I am in need not of such. Rest assured, if the occasion arises, you will be sent on an errand of mercy. "Til then…"

The valet bowed respectfully to his master, then resumed his position five paces to the right, rear of his master.

Upon entering Monsieur Percerins' establishment, many mannequins were about up holding various forms of vestments that he and his apprentice had assembled according to various thoughts of design and what he thought the denizens would find appealing and fashionable.

While too, some mannequins beheld garments at various stages of their constructions. Be it the material draped and pinned in place with desired effect or to the completion of a hem to added ornamentation.

Porthos was admiring his bulk of a narrow cheval, and when he took a pace backward, he bumped into a mannequin.

He hastily had the grip of his blade in his fist, "Hold denizen, what say you?" He queried as he turned to face a possible adversary.

To his chagrin, his face reddened as he replaced his blade back in its sheath and sought Monsieur Percerin and his companions.

A local Milner had his wearables on consignment to accent what the tailor had on display. The chosen plumes, were of various colors, sizes and textures. All in accordance with the intended purpose of a purchaser had in thoughts.

A lot of the gowns, pantaloons, mantles, and tunics that had been created did not resemble every day wear, rather it would be better worn by nobility.

The rich embroidery and more vibrant colorings due to the discovery of various means of dye, allowed it to be admired by many, alas worn by few.

There were of course, vestments that were worn by the commons denizen towards the back of the establishment with a narrow margin of choice and less obvious.

"Ah Messieurs," Exclaimed the Proprietor, "I have been expecting you."

"You have, have you?" Inquired Porthos, brow arched, though he knew it to be true.

"Indeed. The King requested you receive tabards."

"We have. See?" Replied Aramis, making references to the plainness of the single color of an overlay.

"True. Alas dear *mon amis,* they do not represent his coat of arms. May I inquire, how did the common denizen perceive you wearing as such compared to the not wearing one at all?"

"Not much of a difference. Some thought it as a statement of fashion rather than an assigned station." Conceded Porthos.

"That will change I assure you. The king has chosen this blue." Showing them a bolt of cloth, obviously unused, laying upon a large table with various marks of measurement carved into its top and sides. "Be it deeper and richer in hue, then wants gold embroidered symbols of his choice upon the front, back and shoulders as well as the seams. No one hence forth will you be mistaken as subservient to the common man, and you are a representation of the king. An official musketeer, chosen by the king."

"…And not the Cardinal." Muttered Athos.

Monsieur Percerin beckoned a younger man and conveyed to him to log each mans' measurements so on the next day they could proceed to bring the kings' thoughts from speculations to reality and if approved, each man in the subsequent regiments would be issued such and become the set forth that as standard.

The young man ended with Grimaud.

"Nice thoughts though." Commented Athos, "Alas, he 'tis not a Musketeer, therefore his measurements would all be for naught."

The young apprentice blushed with embarrassment, not realizing the valet was a valet and not a musketeer. But truly how could he, for he was with the three, how could he assume the difference and not the norm?

As Porthos' final measurements were being finalized, his stomach spoke, and it took a lot for the hefty musketeer to maintain his wits.

Aramis and Athos were each stepping off of a very short precarious podium.

As the last of the sunlight was fading, a young apprentice was going to set about to light the in ornate chandeliers and various lantroons.

"Bother with them not." Instructed Percerin, "They are the last on the roster. Time to lock the doors, shutter the windows and seek supper. By the bye, give me a fortnight to complete them."

"Singly or collectively?" Queried Aramis.

"Collectively. I shall send a courier."

The young apprentice chuckled and set about shuttering the windows, save one so that the occupants could see and allow themselves to return to the out of doors.

Once out of doors, the brazier keep had begun his rounds with the din of the waning day fading into the subsequent twilight.

"It is apparent that it is supper time. Even though my stomach had made that announcement not long ago." Said Porthos.

"Why did you not say something?" Queried Aramis.

"I did not want the tailor think me rude." Smiled Porthos.

"Since when would that have made a difference?" Inquired Athos.

"I want him not to think ill of me."

"What is the opinion of one compared to that of many?" Queried Aramis, softly chuckling.

"Alas, gentlemen, however it is perceived, let it be so. Now I query, do we seek the kings' table and company there of or fend for ourselves as we so often do?"

"Salt is good tender." Smiled Athos, wryly. "If a purse is tossed at the right time to the inn keep, he will be none the wiser 'til much later."

"Athos!" Exclaimed Aramis.

Athos just shrugged, as Porthos rounded the corner and began for their establishment of choice, "The Sword and the Pendulum."

"If the proprietor seeks us, he will be compensated when we are." Theorized Athos, "We always make good."

VI

The morn found Porthos still in his night shirt, trying in vain to lay a fire.

"How does Mousequeton manage with success to preform such a trivial feat with expertise. Peste! I do wish he would return. I can only hope I can dressed hastily enough so that the chill in this morns' air does not adversely affect myself.", He said to himself, as regained his feet.

Out of frustration, he threw the two logs he had in his hand, into the health, stirring up the cold lifeless spent charcoal and ash.

Waving it away, he made haste to his bed chamber to dress.

Aramis was regaining his feet after saying his ritualistic morning rosary and crossing himself with holy water from small vial, he too was wishing his valet was about.

Though he could and would do things for himself, he had grown accustomed to the presence of his valet and mild chaos he created in each morn as he set about preparing his beloved master for the day. Thus he was sorely missed when he was absent.

Athos was being rousted by his valet who was proffering him a goblet of weakened wine.

Although he did not like the wine in its current state, he still drank it, knowing once his purse and coffer were replenished, he in turn would replenish his wine chest.

With Grimauds' assistance, he hastily dressed and took it upon himself to recruit his companions for breakfast, for he was the one with the valet who could and was instructed to get him about as the dawned came about and not let it slip away as the day afore had.

He suddenly shuddered as he slipped his tunic over his head.

"Thankfully, these chilly morns' will soon come to pass. Alas my good man, then we will have to accommodate ourselves to the hotter elements that the coming months will be bring. Corbleu! No matter what the elements produce, someone always has something to say."

Once out of doors, and his wits were not shrouded under the influence of wine, he found the chill quite invigorating.

His pace quickened as Grimaud tried to keep in stride with his master, alas his legs became fatigued and soon lagged.

He, however knew where his master was going and therefore was not concerned if he momentarily lost sight of him in a mass wave of denizens.

To their advantage it was early and the city was just beginning to stir, and very few denizens were about.

As he rounded the corner, his master was already at Porthos' door poised to rap upon it.

"Oh! There you are! Nice of you to join me." Chided Athos, as his weary valet tried desperately to catch his breath.

Grimaud bowed his head and in *sotto voc* said, "I am sorry Master. I will do better at your next request."

Grimaud knew Athos was a complicated man to understand, had many facets and thus, at times the dutiful valet knew not how or when his master would respond.

"Humph!" Was all Athos said, then proceeded to rap upon the door.

The opening door revealed that Porthos had dressed and was ready for what the day had to offer.

"Salut my good Athos." Exclaimed Porthos, enthusiastically, "My you look as if you caught a fresh wind."

"I did indeed." Replied Athos, inhaling deeply, taking in the freshness of a brand new day.

Porthos pinned his mantle in place and shut the door behind him as he stepped into the bright morn.

Pausing for a moment, Porthos queried, "Where might we query as to the whereabouts of Aramis?"

"Given it is early, he is probably at home reciting his rosary."

"Then he will not like to be interrupted."

"Like it or no, no matter, we have to continue our mission and see it through to completion and if that means a few brief interruptions, then so be it. He will see the necessity behind it, all will be well." Reasoned Athos.

"Shall we send Grimaud ahead to request counsel with Louis?" Queried Porthos.

"Indeed! Then he can be a most accepting and accommodating host and have a well laid table." Athos chuckled softly, "As if he does not always."

The two musketeers sought their companion at his apartments and as suspected he was reciting his rosary and preforming his ritualistic service for himself.

"I so want to be a cleric." Aramis would lament and sigh, but either Athos or Porthos would then say, "Then when you say that and momentarily practice the given, you then say you long to be a soldier."

"Is there no way to make the ends justify the means?" He would query.

His two companions would just shake their heads.

"If it t'were that simple, I would take up another task as well and justify my need of being a soldier as well." Smiled Porthos.

As Aramis opened his door, he was putting aside his bible, rosary and extinguishing a taper.

"Where is Grimaud?" Queried Aramis, out of concern for the absent valet.

"He has gone ahead to secure us an audience with Louis." Replied Athos.

"Too bad we do not have our new tabards to show Louis that his current thoughts of conformity have come to pass." Porthos said.

"True." Replied Aramis, "For remember Percerin said they will not become available for a fortnight. Pity."

"So much the better." Added Athos.

"Why do you say that?" Queried Porthos, inclining his head out of curiosity.

"Do we really want the Huguenots to know we favor the king? Surely if they knew that they would hastily set a fuse. Truly, it is to our benefit they know not our identity, but we know them simply by their actions. All you need to do is silently observe, then act."

"When our valets return and then get a better idea as to what Rohan is about, we can set about defusing his munitions and hopefully make short his activities and put an end to all this nonsense." Commented Aramis, "Even though he has a right to his opinion."

"Surely. Alas his opinion has to coincide with Louis'."

As they entered the *Palais*, they found it beginning to come to life as the day did about the city.

The chill in the air did not seem to deter many from their given agendas and proceeded as they normally would.

The varying elements were never a concern for the common denizen, for they had grown accustom to the unpredictability of such. The only thing that would cause concern would be a storm and the potential hazards that accompanied them.

Aramis inquired of a page where might they locate the king and the reply was in his small drawing room adjacent his bed chamber.

Although the chamber was small according to the kings' standards, it was overly sufficient for the common man. Just a matter of whose opinion you heeded.

In the corridor, on either side of the heavy door leading to the chamber were two musketeers who chose to display their large cumbersome muskets in hopes of deterring any vagrants wanting the sympathies of the king, in case they did not accept, "no" as an answer.

"Praytell, was it your choice to brandish such a cumbersome harquebus?" Queried Porthos, "For if in fact it was, that surely means you know not how to wield a blade."

The young guard that was of slight stature, coughed lightly and shuffled his spurred foot on the highly polished marble floor.

"It would a harquebus to you, but to me it means a way of defense." He replied sternly, trying to sound more confident than he was.

"Defense?" Mocked the musketeer, "Hardly worth carrying. By the time you retrieve your tinder box, reload it, re-fuse it and get your fuse lit, your adversary would possibly have already taken advantage of you, much to your chagrin. That musket is an oversized, inaccurate, cumbersome harquebus as I said. It could not hit the broad side of a slight man, even on your best day. The best thing for defense is a blade. Our blades are forged at the Quai de Feraille And maintained there as well. They are accurate as you are."

Afore Porthos could continue, Athos stepped forward.

"We have counsel with Louis. My valet preceded us in securing our request, now if you would be so kind."

The second guard stepped aside and gestured to his companion to do the same.

Aramis then took the liberty and he too stepped forward and rapped upon the door.

Much to their amazement, Vitray opened it and stood afore them.

"There is rain on the horizon." Muttered Athos, then aloud "His Majesty is expecting us." He stated, "My valet preceded us to secure an audience with him."

"So he has, he is here."

Vitray led them to a well laid table, much to Porthos' delight.

The table was large and round so that the king could view all who were in attendance without having to over extend himself.

They heard laughter come from the young kings' direction and Athos deducted it was Grimaud.

Athos' smile was weak, alas genuine as he realized his valet who appeared meek and somber, was content.

There was a vacant seat next to the king that was soon filled as the large tapestry behind him parted and allowed admittance of Richelieu.

"It is about to storm." Mumbled Athos as Aramis glared at him.

The Cardinal remained standing and requested everyone bow their heads in acceptance of grace and mercy as he asked a blessing of the food the were to partake in.

As the Cardinal paused afore he sat down, the young king, with a gesture of annoyance, exclaimed, "*Mon Dieu*! Richelieu do sit and stop hovering over me. I am grown and can think for myself."

The Cardinal, muttered, "Of course you are grown and can govern yourself, but not of age for the state." Then not knowing a proper response in reply to the young king, kept silent and sat down.

Young Louis nodded at his valet, Bompar, who in turn took his goblet and tapped lightly upon it causing it to sound alike that of a small bell that summoned couriers, pages and valets or any other at the kings request.

Richelieu regained his feet, turned and bowed respectfully to the king then turned to face the small group.

"If it pleases your majesty, I humbly request Monsieur Aramis to give detail as to what is about concerning Rohan."

Aramis swallowed his morsel of roasted duck, followed by the remains of his wine, then he too regained his feet and bowed to the king.

"Your Majesty, less than a week hence, two of our valets were sent to Castres' to seek the whereabouts of Monsieur la Rohan. It is suspected that he has been diverting and concealing munitions towards Malamort. Malamort is situated about a valley with numerous caverns that could be used as storage 'til they are filled to capacity. Then utilize it in defense of; Uzes, Nimes and Montebaun. La Rochelle is a grave concern. It has been for quite sometime. The fuse has not been lit but someones' tinder box is being readied I assure you."

"They were suppose to be dismantled under the direction of the king!" Exclaimed Richelieu.

"Indeed they were, alas his word bears no weight and Rohan has taken it upon himself to direct to them and turn a deaf ear and blind eye to what was instructed by the monarchy."

Porthos then regained his feet as well and slightly bowed in the direction of the king, then said, "There is a waterfall as well and behind it is a vast cavern and they no doubt are using that to their advantage."

"How is it you know this without actually speaking to your absent valets?" Queried Louis, "Is this then speculation?"

"*Oui* your Majesty, pure speculations. Rohan is an intelligent man, but again, he must have a weak spot and we will find it."

"When we were beyond Paris seeking remnants of resistance, we happened upon it. We sat in observance for half a fortnight to establish consistencies of activities and *voila!* It is viable and thus a suggestion your Majesty, have some regiments placed close at hand so if a fire is sparked they can immediately extinguished it afore it spreads. Once we culminate our given tasks, we again will set forth and continue seeking any and all factions caused by Rohan and subsequently subdue them and with the assistance of field regiments, convey them back here to have them dealt with accordingly." Concluded Porthos.

"Have you much to accomplish afore you set out again?" Queried the king with a raised brow..

"Our fair share." Replied Aramis, then added, "We still have to seek our Captain for he too probably thinks we have been gone long enough, speak to Tomas and Pasqual and then when our tabards are completed, retrieve them from your tailor."

"Why praytell are you seeking Pasqual and Tomas, are they not an installation in the Bastille?" Queried Louis.

Porthos again cringed at the mere mention of their names and slightly shuddered.

"Indeed! They were previously with Rohan and perchance the Duc let it be known what and where he is about and possibly because of that, they know what is to come so that we may be prepared." Replied Aramis.

The Cardinal took a deep breath afore he turned towards Athos and queried of him, "Is there anything Monsieur Athos you would like to add?

Athos nonchalantly glanced in the Cardinals' direction and replied, "Oh! The pawn speaks."

The Cardinals' ire began to rise as his countenance slowly changed hue.

"I, Monsieur Musketeer, am no ones pawn."

"I then, am no one's dolt, and not easily fooled." He replied, smiling wryly.

The Cardinal suddenly regained his feet, opened his mouth to respond then hastily shut it and sat down, breathing heavily with ire.

Vitray, who had been standing behind his master, quietly placed his hand on his masters' shoulder.

Louis repeated the Cardinals' query, "Is there anything else that needs to be added?"

All three shook their heads, for their mouths were full of the last of their meal.

"Very well then, I shall wait upon the return of your valets to meet again. A thought just occurred, when you receive your new tabards, were them not, forth. You need not cause unnecessary confusion, for there is enough of that already, we will address the situation as needed. Your vestments are just that, vestments. Yes you represent me and France as a whole I assure you, and when the time comes to confront Rohan, he will not have the chance to mistake your identity and what and whom you represent. You shall be in front of him, behind him and on his flanks and he will have no choice other than to concede."

The young king drained his goblet, regained his feet and hastily retreated behind the large tapestry from whence the Cardinal arrived, with the Cardinal, Vitray and Bompar directly behind him.

"I dare say, this counsel has drawn to a close." Stated Porthos as he tried to stifle a yawn.

Somewhere deep in the midst of the *Palais Royals,* a clock, with deep resonating tones, chimed the hour of six.

Athos counted along with it to clarify the time if queried.

"Since we have been eating enough all day and the day has waned, what do you propose we do to preoccupy ourselves with?" Queried Athos.

Porthos arched his brow mischievously.

"If it t'were not for the fact that I am thoroughly fatigued, I would suggest we go to "The Sword and the Pendulum" and find some gullible dolt and play, "Whose got the Pence in their Pocket?" Said Athos.

"Indeed!" Added Aramis, "It escaped our thoughts to query of the king at what point will our coffers be replenished, for mine is more than nigh empty."

"The only true dolts that I am aware of, are instilled in the Bastille where they will reside to their end days. Unless the king is seized with a sudden fit of mercy." Replied Porthos.

"They can not vex you any more." Soothed Aramis.

"Alas the mere sight of them cause a case of vapors. For they caused me enough grief to last me."

"My dear Porthos, we do have a day or two to be about the city and collect debts owed and they happen to owe us an explanation as to what and when, when it comes to Rohan."

"You know perfectly well as I they, they will not see it from that point of view." Replied Porthos, "Alas, if I must, I shall prove a point again as I did when Rohan signed the first treaty presented to him."

"Apparently it does not make a difference to him, he still sets fuses alit then vanishes only to resurface in another *arrondissement* and not to mention other locales."

"I would imagine afore too long, we will again catch up to him." Mused Athos, yawning, then pushing himself away from the table so that he may regain his feet.

As he stood, a young chamber valet entered carefully carrying a lit lantroon from which he was to set a flame to sconces and chandeliers. He would return within the hour and if he found the room vacant he would extinguish what he had previously lit so as to not waste valuable tallow. If the room was occupied, he would see to it the tapers were trimmed or replaced as what the need warranted.

"Oh pardon Messieurs." He said, taken by surprise that the chamber beheld the musketeers.

"Mind us not. We were just taking our leave."

Porthos chuckled, "….And I might add, to see what kind of mischief we can immerse ourselves in yet come away as the implications arise and have it look as if we had nothing to do with the chaos that ensues."

"Yes indeed agreed." Athos, "In the short time we had become musketeers for the crown, we have found the necessity to amuse ourselves when any opportunity arises."

Aramis shook his head.

"Pity though it has to be at some dolts expense."

"Rather at their expense and not ours." Replied Porthos, "For Pasquel and Tomas made it their mission to antagonize me and cause me much grief, therefore proper expenditure is warranted and I am more than happy to oblige."

The young valets' face blushed with embarrassment at the confessions of the musketeers activities, then hastily finished his task and departed.

Aramis regained his feet as well.

"Do we have a unanimous decision?" He queried.

"I opt for finding my own chamber, sitting in someone else's, depending on whose, is one thing and then being at counsel to hear and repeat the same information and take better part of a day to accomplish, that is quite over taxing." Added Athos.

"Be that as it may, we still have to repeat ourselves again on the morrow, for we need to see De Treville." Replied Porthos, reminding them of their fore gone obligation to their Captain.

Athos let out a low moan out of annoyance.

"Enough already! Does it have to be on the morrow, can it not wait til we see our valets with new additional information, then gather them together one more time to relate all?"

"That certainly makes sense." Agreed Aramis, "Considering he still knows not we are about. The two that would have preceded us can not tell him unless he himself went to see them and I for the life of me can not see that occurring any time now or in the future, much to their disappointment."

"I might also add, our anominity still remains in the balance, bordering on obscurity, infamous and well received and known." Grinned Porthos, with a glint of mischief in his smiling eyes. "Then perchance our valets will return betwixt now and then, then all will be well." He suggested, as he too regained his feet.

As he did so, he emitted a rather loud belch.

"Is it any wonder why I could not eat another morsel? Can now." Smiled Porthos.

"Too late, the damage has been done." Smile Aramis, as he began for the door, with Athos following and grabbing the nigh empty decanter as went past as small cart that beheld the various wants of the kings' small audience.

Once out of doors again in the cool air, they crossed the courtyard and entered onto the quai.

The brazier keep had begun his usual rounds, making his way in and around denizens, carts, oxen and carriages.

"Then on the morrow as will no doubt still be in waiting for our valets to return, I suggest we make good use of their absence and seek the residents of the Bastille." Suggested Aramis.

"While you are at it, throw holy water on them and watch them disintegrate." Added Porthos, with a wry contorted grin upon his countenance.

"They are not evil." Replied Aramis, calmly.

"If a person causes grief to another, is that an evil intent and character?"

The young prelate inclined his head as he pondered the inquiry.

"I see your point, alas I shall not have holy water with me."

"Then just the same my good man, praytell why not? They no doubt have not seen the likes of a religious service since being incarcerated. Perchance they would like to make amends with God and his fellow man." Suggested Porthos.

"If that be the case, then I will need to find my small vials of sacramental wine and yes holy water, missal and a couple of hosts. If you two care to join in I can do a scaled down version of a mass that would be befitting under the circumstances. Then we can try and extract information concerning Rohan from them."

"Such is the life of a traitor. It is a wonder they still have their heads still intact." Commented Athos.

"True enough." Sighed Aramis, "The king can still change his mindset at any given whim."

"It does not help matters when he has so many offering counsel as to the dealing with criminals of the state." Offered Porthos.

"That is why is was left up to the noblemen of their self contained estates to be judge and jury and preside over the activities of such. The noble man had no one to persuade him on how hard his gavel should hit his podium." Suggested Athos.

Porthos with an arched brow glanced at Aramis, who in turn seem quite amused by the comment, but remained silent.

"Pardon?" Queried Porthos.

"Said too much already." Mumble Athos.

"Athos?" Queried Aramis, in hopes that his companion will become less enigmatic.

"An acquaintance, if you must know, held in confidence, a situation. A nobleman that. He took it upon himself to be judge and jury of his estate and his attempt at implementing justice failed or so he was informed."

"What became of him?" cautiously queried Porthos.

"He fled."

VII

The full clear moon had just touched the zenith on that late night as they rounded the corner and strode towards Porthos' apartment.

"How are you fairing with the absence of your valet?" Queried Porthos to Aramis.

"Far better than you." Aramis replied, with a grin, "I have always been self reliant. Having Bazin surely adds, alas I have made the best of his absence and regret him not being about. When he has returned, so much the better. 'Til then, I shall go about the day as if I never had a valet to begin with. I then can only hold myself accountable for the day if it t'was well spent or well wasted."

"Indeed. It t'would be so much better I assure you to begin then day as I have grown accustomed to, rather than left to my own devices. It is so complicated. I so do wonder how he manages so many tasks in a such a short length of time and done to completion as well. I still have frayed ends in the morn I have to tie in place afore I can even begin to ponder what my day might hold." Sighed Porthos.

"How is it you faired as you did when you first arrived in the city without the likes of a valet?" Queried Athos, in mock seriousness.

"I immediately set about to seek a valet. Have not ever been without and I assure you I was not nor am I going to lack such. At present, it is temporary. It is difficult to find the same resources Mousequeton does with such ease and fluidity makes it seem so effortless."

"Then you have trained him well." Commented Athos.

"So I have." Mused Porthos, "Makes me want to go and seek him and return. The anticipations of his and Bazins' return it quite maddening. Alas, there is nothing I can do to hasten their return. Is not patience a virtue?" Queried Porthos to Aramis.

"Indeed it is." Assented Aramis, with a curt nod.

"Are you saying you lack such?" Queried Athos.

"Ne, I am not completely virtuous-less. If I lack in patience, than you must surely see that I am charitable."

Aramis chuckled loudly.

"What, praytell, do you find so amusing?" Queried Porthos.

"You, you big dolt. You truly are the epitome of being not only charitable but being a true illustration of charity."

"Why so do you think that?"

Aramis glanced at him askance, knowing that his companion had a benefactor somewhere and when his coffer and purse were nigh depleted, somehow he managed to have them mysteriously replenished, thus when Porthos claimed he was nearly a pauper, Aramis knew the difference, but said nothing to the contrary.

The friendly giant never offered an explanation, thus none given, for he did not want his source exposed nor exploited.

As they approached Athos' door to his apartments, Grimaud came from behind to lead the small procession.

"Praytell, what does our agenda have on it for the morrow?" Queried Porthos, in hopes of diverting the conversation.

"As I run the risk of repeating myself, after breakfast, I suggest we frequent the governor of the Bastille, and gain admittance to Pasquàl and Tomas, query of them the likes of Rohan and offer mass, but not necessarily in that order." Smiled Aramis, "We need to garner as much information as we can afore we accost. De Treville. No need to repeat ourselves a second time for having left some details to the way side."

"True enough. For I am quite sure he would appreciate that, then he can summon the necessary regiments, armaments and a cartographer and formulate his thoughts and put them to use." Suggested Athos.

"Are we in agreement then?"

"Aye." Replied Porthos.

"Aye as well." Added Athos.

"One last thing…when morn arrives, Athos send Grimaud around and we will go to breakfast and from there to the Bastille."

"We should have him gather our horses, considering the distance." Suggested Porthos.

"It is nothing a little foot effort can not harm." Replied Aramis.

"Alas these boots can."

"Then so be it. Add the task of the need for our horses. If Bazin and Mousequeton were about, the task would befall them as well."

Athos nodded and would instruct Grimaud of such.

"Now my good man, here you are, safe in the comforts of your own apartments." Jested Aramis.

"…And sober." He replied with a half hearted smile.

"Bon Soir, mon ami." Said Porthos as he stepped past the small group, in order to proceed towards his apartments.

Aramis pressed his companions' hand and he too bid him a, *"Bon Soir."*

Athos stepped over the threshold, Grimaud had already preceded him, and quietly shut the door.

Porthos let out a sudden loud sigh.

"Problem?" Queried Aramis.

"Ne, not really."

"Then?"

"Do you honestly think by going to the Bastille and addressing Pasqual and Tomas, that they would set straight their involvement? For truly they are gullible and easily led astray."

"Are you now defending them? A change of heart perchance?"

"Ne, just a causal observation. You may not obtain what you are after." Suggested Porthos, with a shrug.

"That remains to be seen." Returned Aramis.

"Indeed it does."

As they approached Aramis' apartment, they young prelate said, "If by chance we do not get the necessary information we are after, yes it would delay things but clearly it means we have more to put an end to, rather than begin new. Either way, we will accomplish what is set afore us, finish what we began, sooner the better, yes. Delayed? It still will be completed."

"Indeed. Alas, to be perfectly honest with you, I grow quite fatigued by all the insignificant details."

"Ah, my dear Porthos, but they aid in the understandings and the completion of our task."

"So they do. Just not wanting so many to clutter the ponderings of a common man."

"Good gentle Porthos, you are not common."

"Neither are you."

With a fond, *"Bon Soir,"* betwixt them, they went their separate ways.

Aramis continued to walk up the quiet rue with a many a query he wanted Pasqual and Tomas to answer and wording it correctly would make a difference of acceptance or rejection of the answer.

Although they would ultimately leave it to De Treville to decipher and differentiate fact from pure fabrication

Porthos leaned heavily upon his closed door for a moment, then slowly opened it to see if he could get a glimpse of his departing companions' whereabouts.

Not seeing him or a even a silhouette, he slipped out and shut the door. He then stealthily returned whence he came, but rounded a corner to Rue aux Ours.

"Just a few coins to erase the appearance of being a pauper. Only 'til our coffers are restored to their former glory." He smiled at the jest, "What glory? Soon as they are filled they are in want. Never ends."

He rapped lightly on a concealed, ivy covered door just as the moon slid behind a cloud.

In the morn, Porthos awoke with a start.

Something had hit his heavily paned window, for he had not took the precautions the eve before to shutter them.

He hastily sat up and glanced about his chamber to get his wits about him, then sat on the edge of his bed in deliberations.

Without the assistance of a lit taper, the room was dim in the predawn hour, thus giving the musketeer the option of laying back down and let the likes of Grimaud roust him and assist him in readying for the day or have himself to rely on, including shaving.

Afore he left the comfort of his fathers' estate of Vallon, he had his beloved valet of many years assist with all his needs and wants. Although being privileged and having a personal valet, subsequently left him at a disadvantage of not knowing the proper procedures of daily toilet. Such as a clean shave, meticulously manicured hands, and his hair given a distinctive appearance of someone of prestige.

Yes it was difficult the first couple of months within the confines of Paris, to acclimate himself to his new surroundings. Yet he was determined to find a valet and make a descent wage when he heard about a small group of men who frequently met in a gymnasium to practice using various weaponry including a foil.

Fascinated by the activity more out of curiosity than necessity, he decided it might a difference in his ability to survive the rigors of city life, compared to that of a self sufficient, self contained estate.

After frequenting the gymnasium, he became very proficient with a blade, seemingly knew how to use it without proper instructions, and thus virtually impossible to defeat.

As fate plays tricks on leery men, she also claims those who pride themselves of having vast knowledge and nothing could escape their finely tuned minds, and this fine young man, naïve about the ways of the city, claiming not to be leery nor haughty, by accident or coincidence, depends on who was telling the tale, came across a worthy opponent as in Athos.

Their first encounter lasted hours, his pride would not allow him to relent.

As next few hours wore on, obviously becoming fatigued, and spectators were gathering to see the grand clashing of blade to blade, they called truce.

"Then my good man, I can truly say, I have not ever come across such a worthy opponent as you." Athos was heard to say.

"I, nor you. It is with pleasure to meet one as competent, not merely one that thinks using a blade is for display only, or sport."

"Where did you learn such dexterity, agility, and boldness?" Queried Athos, dabbing the beads of sweat from his brow.

"Necessity is a great pedagogue." Smiled Porthos, although is given name was Pierre.

Then within a fortnight, fate intervened again and allowed them to become friends with a young prelate, who laid claims of only wanting to be a guard for a short period of time and wanted to learn the art of defense as he was preparing to set out to educate others on the holy word of God.

He was Aramis and already had a valet in his employment, Bazin.

Athos, had silent Grimaud, who was instructed not to talk unless necessary and then say little as possible.

"How is one to go about and obtain a valet?" Queried Pierre.

"There is always a small group of denizens loitering about the guards barracks and gymnasium, in hopes of attracting a gentleman's attention and gain employment."

"Are they honest and loyal?'

"Depends on who you ask." Chuckled Athos.

Aramis too, knew how to use a blade and had the stamina to procure a victory in a duel when an event warranted it.

The three had become fast companions and was rarely seen without one another and with the assistance of his new found companions Pierre obtained a new name, Porthos and a valet, Mousequeton.

Their first two years brought many changes to their lives and to their environment.

By August of 1622, they collectively had been summoned by the young king, Louis, for counsel.

He related to them that he had heard about their restless souls and skirmishes and their undefeatable techniques in utilizing their blades and proposed orchestrating a group of elite men to represent him as his emissaries and be his guards and call them, "musketeers".

Porthos again sighed and returned his ponderings to the current situation of being without Mousequeton as again something hit his heavily paned window.

"Musketeers, indeed. We do not even carry the weapon. Ah but let the king think as he chooses as we choose ours." Thought Porthos as he released Balizarde' from the confines of its scabbard and went to his window.

As he opened it, he was met with a chilly draught that almost caused him to drop his blade and hastily raised the hairs on the back of his neck and arms.

"Peste! I was not expecting that." He exclaimed as he hastily retreated a step.

Leaning forward, he glanced to the south, then east, then north, he saw nothing that would cause harm and as he was closing the window another draught caught a shutter and slammed it harshly against the windows' casing.

Propping his sword against the wall, he caught both shutters, closed them then the heavily paned windows and latched them against further draughts and catching him completely and unexpectedly off kilter.

"Now let me catch you doing that again." Said Porthos, scolding the wayward shutter and chuckling softly.

He retrieved his sword that had been leaning against the wall and went back to sit on the edge of his bed.

He decided to ready himself for the day for he knew not how long it would take Grimaud to come for him and his stomach began to protest against its lack of contents.

It had grown lighter out of doors so he was able to see the small table with the pitcher and basin under a highly polished looking glass. The razor lie next to it neatly atop a folded linen.

The musketeer glanced into the looking glass and smiled.

"Let me see if I managed not to slit my own throat. That certainly would not be a good way to start the day."

To his amusement and amazement he managed to shave himself, leaving his goatee intact, he again smiled at his reflection.

Wiping his countenance with the linen, he stepped away to go in search of his pantaloons, tunic, doublet, stockings and his boots.

Once dressed, he picked up his purse tied it again and tucked in his doublet.

"Peste! How does Mousequeton do that?" He smiled to himself, "He so manages to get the ties on this doublet straight and makes the doublet look almost new although it has been turned a few times."

Just as he was adjusting his cap, he heard his horse and a rap upon his door.

"'Tis that time."

Sheathing Balizarde' he opened the door to greet Grimaud.

"Salut my good man. All is well I would imagine."

Grimaud shrugged, then nodded.

"I gather we need to seek Aramis next. He no doubt is ready. He has long grown accustom to rising early and doing what is necessary to begin his day, valet or no, he is rather self sufficient. Is Athos like that?" Porthos queried, askance.

Grimaud slightly inclined his head and shyly, barely noticeable shook it, almost embarrassed that the musketeer relied on another for assistance.

He knew, no one would think ill of Athos for it nor chide him, alas Grimaud found it awkward, but would never admit it, so he left it be and discussed it with no one.

If a man could keep a valet for what ever his reasoning it was to no one to query as to any motives and discussed it not. It was all too common.

Once they arrived at Aramis' apartment, Grimaud took the liberty to rap upon the young prelates' door.

Aramis stepped forward and shut the door behind him and gladly accepted the reins to his horse.

Once in the saddle, they turned and picked their way cautiously towards Athos' apartment and had hopes that Grimaud saw to it that his master took the care in obtaining the assistance of him, afore he set about with his given errands.

Although they had no time frame to abide by, they had always liked to accomplish what they needed to early on so they had plenty of time to seek their own amusements, whether it be loitering about the *Palais* or playing *Lansquenet* at the, "The Sword and the Pendulum" they found it to be fond way of being at ease and carefree and worry not about where the Huguenots were causing anguish or how much of a rise in taxes might occur so that the monarchy could continue to transcend through time without disruption or transference of titles.

Arriving at Athos' apartments, they were rather surprised to see their companion already out of doors awaiting them.

As alike the previous day, he had the appearance of having frequented a barber, which delighted Porthos and Aramis. Now they had to forage for breakfast and pay a visit to the Bastille to visit two of their favorite residents.

The day had a slight chill in the air as Porthos could attest to that fact, but with the sun already making its daily sojourn across the heavens, brought a promise of it being warmer as the day progressed.

"Is this an absolute must?" Lamented Porthos.

"Indeed it is, if we are to gain an advantage over the Huguenots. Rohan may be clever, but there is always a way to out wit even the cleverest of the clever." Replied Aramis.

As they were about to pass a small courtyard that belonged to the *Palais,* Porthos slightly pulled back on the reins, causing his horse to halt abruptly.

"What gives?" Queried Athos.

"My stomach does not want us to pass up the chance of having breakfast. The door leads to a lower level that has a hearth and no doubt has remains of supper last in its kettles and perchance a roast fowl or two. I would think the king would not want his prime guards to be in want, for he takes care of us and we take care of him. It is all fair." Reasoned Porthos.

"Then we need not bother him with the formalities, we will find our own accommodations and then proceed with our day." Suggested Aramis.

Tethering their horses to the wrought iron rings that inconspicuously lay in the small recessives of the wall, they sought the door.

Athos gestured for Grimaud to follow as they paused afore it.

Porthos stepped forward and cautiously opened it, they were warmly greeted by the generous delicious aromas of the dinner that was being prepared.

Roast venison, fowls of choice, breads, cheeses, broths and soups and various vegetables, all blending together and creating a want within their souls.

A pastry assistant was just beginning his task of combining some his basic ingredients afore he added the clarified butter and the remaining spices and the finely diced dried fruits, as they entered the chamber.

"Salut!" Greeted Porthos, as he caught sight of the assistant with the large wooded ladle.

"Ah Monsieur Porthos, what brings you? Do not tell me, let me guess, is it your empty stomachs?" He queried as he chuckled.

"Yes, and not to mention empty purses."

"My good gentlemen, you certainly are resourceful."

"When necessity dictates, we are adaptable." Replied Porthos, "By the by, is there anything you can spare from last eves' supper for three hungry musketeers?"

"Fate always interferes, excuse me, I meant to say intervenes, when you least expect, truly. Yes there is a kettle of poached fish, roasted fowl and bread. There is a table you may set in the far corner, make use of it as I gather what there is. Corbleu! At the kings' expense no less."

"Better his than ours. He will not know the difference." Replied Athos.

"He just might. Consider Monsieur." Replied the assistant, in reference to Porthos.

The three sought the table and sat as a few idle assistants brought the kettle and roasted fowls.

As an after thought, another brought a loaf or two of bread and then hastily departed.

The three then proceeded to wage a small siege on the remains of a roasted wild boar, and waste not their impromptu meal and little time was wasted on leisure.

Much to do to ensure dinner was served on time and not make the king wait any longer than he had to, for on this day he had a prior engagement for a resounding round of lawn chess with pages and couriers acting as the chess pieces. He was anxious to see who was appointed to act as king and queen afore the game commenced, and offer a bit of sage advice.

As it was customary to prolong the meal for it was a time of conversations and laughter, intermingled with the likes of state affairs, they decided to suspend with the custom and hastily consume what they had so they may begin with their prior arrangements.

When the activities in the chamber subsided, it was an indication that dinner was about to be served.

Thus various attendants, servants, valets, pages and couriers were put to use in serving the bountiful meal, carrying pots, kettles, tureen and platters of food to the grand hall.

The shuffling of feet sounding over their heads, reminded them of the rats that they had come across in an abandoned turret while looking for rogue Huguenots.

Not overly fond of them scurrying across the tops of their boots, they hastily drew a conclusion that nary a man would be wise enough to seclude themselves amongst such persistent and bothersome vermin, Huguenots or no it was not worthwhile.

By the time they had each regained their feet, nothing but a pile of bones tossed in an empty tureen, a heel of bread and a few drops of wine was all that remained. None too sorry to see it had gradually ceased to exist.

"Too bad we can not delay our trek to the Bastille, forsooth I would so enjoy seeing the progression of that chess game on the lawn." Observed Porthos.

"Not I." Countered Athos, "'Tis a bit too cold for my liking."

As they were leaving, they had not noticed that the passageway was unlit, but successfully navigated their way through the darkness to reach the tethered horses in the courtyard.

Gaining their saddles, they turned their horses about and made their way to the Bastille.

As they entered the courtyard to the Bastille, they each could not refrain from shuddering, for it was quite foreboding with its looming turrets and high walls.

The gates were closed and closely monitored by guards that Pere Joseph personally selected. The distant keep gave the illusions of a disgruntled peasant in search of relief of his daily burdens, alas no relief and was in store, thus he was bound by obligations to continue his servitude to the nobleman that acquired him, in a card game no less.

Dark, cold and filled with tortured souls screaming and pleading relentlessly to any one with a sympathetic ear, had hopes of one day they would be liberated due to the mercy of the king or God, whom ever was the first to reconsider their pardon.

Pere Joseph was a personal friend of Cardinal Richelieu and appointed him as governor.

Some speculated Richelieu owed him a favor while others thought perchance Pere Joseph owed Richelieu and accepted the position to alleviate the desperate position Richelieu was in to fill the vacancy the previous governor created when he stepped away from his responsibilities and the Bastille.

Coming upon an expressionless guard, they pulled up rein and halted.

"Pardon Monsieur, but we are in search of the Governor, may we gain admittance?" Inquired Athos.

The guard looked them over, looking for anything familiar about them.

"Is he expecting you?", Inquired the guard, suspiciously.

"I should think not, for he knows us not." Replied Aramis, appearing to refrain from laughter.

"Then why should I allow you admittance?"

"There are two dolts foolish enough to commit treason and Louis has not decided one way or t'other what to do with them. Alas, while he deliberates and ponders his choices, we need to speak to them."

"Whom might you be to request such an impromptu audience?"

"Some of the kings' guards."

The guard beckoned to a companion to join him for a small conference.

With their backs to the musketeers, the first spoke and queried, "What is it do you think we ought to pursue? They want an audience with the Friar and yet he knows of them not."

"Do you have thoughts that it might be a conspiracy inclining towards assassination?" Queried the second.

"Why would anyone want to assassinate a mild mannered Capuchin Friar?"

"Consider for a moment who his connections are in relation to the crown. He is the grey eminence, he is a close confidant and agent of Richelieu and the Cardinal has the kings' ear."

"....And?"

"....And if the wrong thing is said or done, you would yourself in here like so many who has irritated the king."

"I suggest, one of us go and inquire of the good friar if he is aware of these gentlemen and if he answers, "no" query of him how he would like us to proceed with this situation, if he says, "yes" then we will accompany them to his chambers and see that no harm comes to him.'

The second curtly nodded his head in affirmation of their plan and returned their attention to the three.

The first gained his saddled as he urged it into a hasty gait and disappeared through a gate.

"He shall momentarily return and you shall proceed accordingly to the Friars' answer. Might I inquire how you know of it is you have come to know *Pere* Joseph?"

"Is it not true his given name is Francois?" Inquired Athos.

The guard taken by surprise, glared at Athos.

"What difference does that make what he chose at his ordination, whether it be Joseph or other? By the by, how is it you know this?"

"I have my ear to the ground." Returned Athos, managing a weak smile.

"You are speaking to someone who truly literally has his ear to the ground more times than naught." Laughed Porthos.

Erstwhile, the guard on horse back returned.

"*Pere* Joseph is not familiar with the likes of you, alas since you have piqued his interest, he has granted you an audience. If you will gentlemen, this way."

He again turned his horse and cantered off towards the gate whence he came, with the three close behind.

The heavy iron gate slammed ominously behind them and simultaneously, locked, startling the horses.

To the rear, in the far right corner, away from where the prisoners were secluded, of what was a fortress then converted to a prison, was the Friars' private living apartments.

One of the chambers' were specially suited for the clerical aspect of the prison. Keeping records of who were released, which were very few if any, the date of liberation, what they were incarcerated for, again the date, their sentence bound by the king and sealed, if executed and the date it occurred, all kept by the hand of Pere Joseph.

He had a small bed chamber he called a cell, leftover from his monastery days', a small hall for dining, but large enough to accommodate any sojourning official and a drawing chamber. Although it lacked in splendor as it ought considering it was a prison, he found it suitable since he was a capuchin monk that had taken the oath of poverty. Finally, in a secluded chamber adjoining the drawing chamber, was a chamber with a few crude uncomfortable chairs, a small table and a hearth with the remains of a spent fire.

The guard tethered his horse and indicated the musketeers ought to do the same.

Once they regained their feet, they followed him through another gate to a heavy door shrouded by trees that offered relief from a glaring sun in the warmer months of the year.

He allowed himself admittance and indicated to them pause as he went to acquire whom they sought.

A young page went scurrying past them and into aged looking tower that had archery slits for windows that allowed very little light to penetrate and illuminate the interior of the structure, the door had a solemn observing sentry guard on either side that was to scrutinize any and all activity within and without that particular tower. Other guards, with sets routines, paced about the structures.

The three observed two guards exit a small barrack in the back of the courtyard, stoically march forward to replace the two currently on duty.

The two former guards hastily retreated to the barrack and disappeared into the shadows of the structure.

As they heard a heavy door rattle and slam shut, they turned to see Pasqual and Tomas laden with heavy shackles, shuffle unsteadily towards them. They were in tattered clothes that hung on them as they would in the wind during laundry day at court, barely recognizable with their gaunt countenances, hollow cheeks and vacant, lifeless eyes, with a guard behind them occasionally reminding them to keep moving forward.

Porthos managed to find levity in the situation and chuckled softly.

"What is it you find so amusing?" queried Aramis in *sotto voc,* with all the seriousness of a cleric hearing the confessions of a heretic, with a dismal future.

"Those shackles they have bound them with are of no use. They can not escape, their present condition was rendered them incapable and unless a brave gale lifted them aloft and made off with them."

As they reached the door, it was opened by their escort.

He stepped aside and as he did so the young page had returned and hurried past the to return to his duties.

The three stepped cautiously over the threshold, not knowing what to expect.

Their escort lead them down a dimly lit passageway to the small room where a fresh laid fire awaited them, to take the chill from the damp still room that seldom saw sunlight, even on the best of days.

Athos and Porthos seated themselves by the fire, while Aramis sat at the table across from Pasqual and Tomas, his back against the wall and empty chair aside him.

The guard stood motionless at the door.

"Out of extreme curiosity, does this room have a name?" Queried Porthos of the guard.

"Indeed. It is the interrogation room, where the prisoners are ritualistically queried and they in turn are given the chance to confess, desiring a diminished period of time spent here, if they said what the king wanted to hear."

"As if it would matter." Mumbled Pasqual.

"Silence!" Ordered the guard, "Need I remind you, you respond only when and if necessary. 'Til then…"

"All this for the likes of taunting of a musketeer?" Jested Athos.

"Aye, all this."

Porthos regained his feet and strode towards the small roughly hewn table. He paused in front of Pasqual, sarcastically queried, "How are you finding your accommodations, satisfactory I trust?"

Pasquels' unshaven lip curled in contempt as he prepared to comment, but kept silent, fearing repercussions from the guard.

The door opened once again as *Pere* Joseph entered and closed the door behind him.

He sat next to Aramis and glanced about.

"Now, what do we have here?" He queried as he tucked his arms into the oversized sleeves of his capuchin robe and leaned forward.

Aramis was the first to speak.

"We represent the king and we are here to seek information from these two concerning a person whom opposes the crown and state."

"How would they know?"

"They rode with him and campaigned with him as well and was readily found guilty on both accounts. We need information, anything that will lead us to him and thus curtail his activities and right his erroneous ways."

"Are you then implicating treason?" Inquired the Friar.

"Yes."

"The man has a fault." Stated Porthos.

"What man are you making references to, if not these two?"

"Duke du Rohan. He has lead multiple campaigns against the crown in the name of Huguenot Reform. His weakness is, he is indecisive. He is like a pendulum that swings. One way for the crown t'other for the Huguenots. What ever his humor he is in for the day, is how he determines what strategy to implement."

"Is he not a cousin to the king?" Queried *Pere* Joseph.

"Indeed he is, but that is not enough to make him commit to one cause."

"That is why my good Friar, we are here to gain insight if we can as to what kind of strategic moves he has thought of and rendezvous with he and his troops, defuse the situation and bring him back with us so he can join the king in counsel and come to admirable terms of agreement."

The Friar leaned back, this time his arms were folded across his aged chest.

"How do I know you truly represent the king and not the Cardinal, are you not associated with him as well?"

Athos chuckled, "Not if I can help it." He chuckled softly again.

Pere Joseph glanced in his direction.

"You have something to add?" He inquired.

Athos cleared his throat, "We are not that dull-witted enough to acknowledge the likes of him."

"Surely you must acknowledge that he too represents the state and has the kings ear."

"I acknowledge nothing when it comes to him."

"Is that the general consensus of all three of you, or just your general opinion?"

Athos inclined his head slightly and then kept the remainder of his thoughts to himself.

"Good gentle Friar, in Athos' defense," began Aramis, "everyone is entitled to their own opinion even if it differs with the majority around him."

The Friars' countenances' reddened, for he was not accustom to anyone opposing himself or his brothers in Christ, be they a friend or foe, it mattered not.

Armand a friend and confidant of the Cardinal may not have been a Capuchin, but he represented the church in a most reverent and official way.

Pere Joseph acknowledged the comment and replied, "With that said, let us continue. What is it you wish to know?"

Aramis turned to Pasqual, for he knew Pasqual was more outspoken than the meek Tomas.

"Monsieur Pasqual, are you aware of any regimental movements of Rohan?"

"How am I to know anything for being confined in here, we have everything restricted and are less likely to hear anything worth our while." He replied wryly.

"Then allow me to re-phrase, do you know of any of his for thoughts concerning what his strategic plans are? You know Louis does not like surprises."

"Neither do I."

Aramis paused as Porthos regained his feet and strode in their direction.

He loomed above the incarcerated waif in an ominous way that caused Pasqual to shudder.

Tomas leaned towards Pasqual and in *sotto voc,* "Did he not say something about the small hamlets about Uzes, Nimes, Montebaun and Montpellier?"

Pasqual suddenly straightened his posture as if prodded by a ponaird and sternly glared at his companion.

Porthos leaned forward at the waist, so far that he was almost touching his nemesis nose with his own, and arched a brow.

Pasqual fidgeted with the frayed end of a shirt sleeve, avoiding Porthos' glance.

The giant leaned even closer.

"If I were you, I would let it be known or your stay here can be a lot more uncomfortable. You see, he is for the church and not the Huguenots, he sympathizes with them not. You two are obviously in favor of Rohan, who favors the Huguenots."

"What of La Rochelle?" Queried Athos, who at the moment was standing afore the hearth, chaffing his chilled hands.

"He had his confidants." Replied Pasqual.

"So has everyone, and no doubt when he said something it quickly transcended through the ranks and even lowly sentries were aware of what he had said." Suggested Aramis.

Pasqual sighed as he realized, no matter what he said in Rohans' defense, it was countered and returned.

"Yes he did say he wanted to strike out at the little hamlets surrounding those towns as a suggestion to them to assist in the repression of the crown, for being a Huguenot was a way of gaining Louis' attention and gaining religious freedom."

"You got his attention. Now that you have it, we need to turn the tide back in favor of the crown and not this little religious fiasco. Which towns was he making references to?" Queried Aramis.

"Nimes, Uzes, Montebaun, Montpellier and La Rochelle."

"Those were to be de-constructed on the kings order and because of the treaty he signed." Said Aramis, quite surprised that Rohan had the audacity to go against the king after giving his word.

"When you want something that you can not have, it makes you strive even harder no matter the cost to obtain it, even if it means going against what was said previously or even who said it."

Athos turned, "Are you aware of where he is to begin?"

Both Pasquel and Tomas, shook their head.

"He did comment that he was going to make it as difficult as possible to catch him, for he knows where to hide." Commented Tomas, quietly, then pitched suddenly forward, "Aie", He exclaimed as if in pain as they heard a dull thud, emanating from beneath the table.

Every one in the room turned to glance in Pasquels' direction as he shrugged with his head slightly inclined.

"Is there anything you would like to comment on or inquire?" Queried Aramis, directing the query to *Pere* Joseph.

The Friar too, shook his head.

"Then my good man, we appreciate the time you allowed us and it will be put to good use, I assure you."

All three with Grimaud immediately behind Athos, gather as the Friar rose to regain his feet and allowed himself out of the room as the guard stepped aside.

The door shut heavy and loud behind them as they followed *Pere* Joseph from whence they came.

Once they reached the courtyard Porthos queried, "What is to come of Tomas and Pasquel?"

"Whatever the king sees fit."

"When is that?'

"Whenever he sees fit."

"*Pere* Joseph, we thank you for your time and the allowance of conveyed information. We as you would like to see an end to this Huguenot insurrection. For it is quite taxing, alas we are for the king and once we are able to bring Rohan to him, hopefully it will put an end to all this foolishness and once again be a whole state that can stand in support of its monarch as one and not divided." Sighed Aramis.

"So well said. Godspeed good gentlemen."

VIII

They found their horses dozing where they were left and startled them slightly as they grabbed the reins and a stirrup and alighted into their saddles.

"Whoa girl." Porthos was heard to say as he prevented himself from loosing his hold on the reins. He knew if she would have her head she would have her feet and there would be slim chance of getting the situation under control 'til they reached the musketeers' stables and by then due to fatigue, she would submit.

As she turned she tried to toss her head, Porthos not having any part of her ill humour, pulled hard back so her lower lip touched her chest and she abruptly ceased her outburst.

They all began their trek back to, "The Sword and the Pendulum."

"Were you seized with a fit of compassion?" Queried Athos, "When you queried the Father of them?" As he jested with Porthos.

"Ah, ne." Replied Porthos, readily to admit his naivety when it came to the Bastille, but decided not to for he knew Athos would chid him mercilessly any chance he got.

"Why are we here?" Queried Athos, as he brought his horse to a halt alike his companions.

"It is supper time." Replied Porthos with a wry smile.

"No use querying of him how he knows." Added Aramis with en equally wry smile.

"I suppose not." Commented Athos.

Upon entering, they noticed it was nigh vacant again, which as much as they liked it noises and chaotic, they too enjoyed the quietness.

They knew by weeks' end, it would be a collecting place of many from various stations including them not only would there be gambling and carousing but many a covert in- scrupulous, insidious denizens would lurk to take advantage of the unwary.

To their silent delight, their favor corner was unoccupied.

Once seated coincidentally within earshot of a couple of gentlemen, who apparently weary from their travels, decided to use the accommodations and be at ease.

The innkeep who was well familiar with the three, need not inquire of them what their requests were for they were not one to pick and choose from the kettles remains. If the kettles were nigh empty it meant whatever they beheld earlier, the denizens found it palatable and worth filling their plates and bowls.

As he was bringing the wine, bread and cheese, Athos was heard suggesting to Porthos in *sotto voc,* "Porthos my good man, way not engage them in a game of *Lansquenet* and relieve them of a few souls. You are a master at playing the game, if left to me, I would end up owing them two months worth of wage."

"Indeed, it appears they know us not and that *mon ami* is to our advantage." Added Aramis.

Porthos furrowed his brow.

"Is something amiss?" Queried Aramis, concerned over Porthos' apprehension.

"I should say, there is. If I am to undertake your suggestions, my stomach will protest in the most unruly manner, which will be most embarrassing to us all."

Aramis chuckled softly, "Then by all means, satisfy your whim."

"Most assuredly, I shall."

As if being prodded by unseen forces, the innkeep followed by an assistant brought forth the abundant meal."

"I have a thought." Said Porthos, exclaimed suddenly.

"You do?" jested Athos.

Porthos arched a brow

"Why not engage them, inquire if they would like to join us and when we clear the table of spent kettles, we can request the cards and the dice and have a few hardy rounds. If fate should happen to smile on us this eve, their purses will be nigh to completely empty." He smiled wryly, as he so often did.

"Leave them some to live on." Suggested Athos, "Their might be a slight pause in availability of sous."

"'Tis a splendid thought." Replied Aramis.

As the innkeep stood aside Aramis to place a tureen in front of him, he relayed Porthos' suggestion.

The innkeep nodded in acknowledgement and retreated towards the weary travelers, and conveyed the extended hospitality of the musketeers and paused then waited patiently for their reply.

The innkeep returned to the young prelates side.

"Gentlemen, they acknowledged your intent, but wholly decline, for they know not how the game is played."

Porthos with a glint of mischief in his eyes, replied, "The game is learnable and they can do that by observation."

Athos nodded understanding Porthos' objective.

Again the innkeep withdrew.

"Is that not thievery?" With *sotto voc,* Aramis Queried, while arching a brow and now being moralistic.

"Not if they voluntarily capitulate and once the game is explained, you then can not fault us if they do not grasp the concept of it.", Replied Porthos.

"Messieurs," Said the innkeep, "The corpulent one, the one closet to the smudged window, has relayed that they will join you as soon as they finish off the contents of their bottle which for appearance sake is only a matter of raising their elbows once or twice."

"*Merci,* my good man. Now if you will, may we make a request for additional wine for us and some more bread and Brie?" Requested Aramis.

The innkeep gathered a lot of the empty vessels and made towards the kitchen and the cellar to fulfill the musketeers request.

As he returned, the travelers were just sitting down at table with the three and he heard them introduce themselves to each other.

He smiled, for he knew them quite well and how they at times took advantage of unsuspecting travelers, not to mention himself, as they, coming from a distance had not the chance to hear of them and be aware of the chaos they could create, and mind you did.

Setting the wine and bread down, he again, cleared off more of the empty vessels and retreated towards the kitchen.

"So, you have not heard of, *"Lansquenet"* afore?" Queried Porthos.

"Ne, can not say that I have. Is it a court game, like chess?" Inquired the corpulent one, known as Jean-Tems.

The three chuckled, "'Tis nothing like chess, Porthos, set the tableau and we will begin."

The cards were dealt accordingly and Porthos held the remainders in his maul of a hand.

"It is to bet as you would think of what card is next, after everyone wagers whether or not you are correct. If you are, you acquire the pile of sous, if not, we continue etc."

The two had the look of being thoroughly vexed upon their countenances as they heavily bet on the first round.

"Go easy gentlemen, you do not want the game to cease afore it even begins do you?" Queried Porthos.

The two tittered almost coquettishly.

"What do you find so amusing?" inquired Athos as he drained the last of his goblets' contentment's only to find it refilled by Grimaud who immediately remedied the want.

"Messieurs, forgive us, for a few sous or Louis d'ors, have no bearing on the minimal or maximum bet. For we have plenty"

"Indeed. The Duc we serve has a pension that he shares amoung his regiments. Needless to say, it is sufficient and our wants are nominal."

Porthos silently tapped Aramis' foot beneath the table.

Aramis understood and said, "How convenient to have such a benefactor. Is he close at hand?"

"Ne." Replied Jean-Tems, unaware of the need to cautiously monitor their words, for they did not know the three represented the King and to an extent the Cardinal, although they would not readily admit that to any one.

Jean-Tems continued, "He traverses frequently to many outposts to observe if they are in want of anything to see if things are progressing as he would like."

"Praytell,". Said Athos aware of the ruse, "How does he know where to find you so that he can share his pension and you are not left in want?"

"He has couriers at his beck and call and no matter day or eve they do his bidding and we fore tell him of our intended location as we never traverse very far from Pontivy, which is his family seat.

Porthos tapped the table with a finger three times afore a card laying face down.

"Do you mean this one?" Queried Aramis as he tapped the same card.

"Yes that one." He tapped it but thrice. It was his turn to bet and guess.

He tossed a sou towards the small pile.

"It is to you to guess, *mon ami.*" Said Porthos.

"….And so it is. Hmmm." Replied Aramis, going through the motions as if in a contemplative state.

"I do think it is three *tre'fles.*

Porthos turned the card and low and behold, it was just as Aramis relayed, causing the two travelers to gasp in amazement.

"Do you play often?" Queried Jean-Tems companion.

The gentle giant leaned back in his chair, its joints groaned as an oldster would if he had to regain his feet.

Porthos just shook his head.

"They certainly do not make furniture like they used to and by the by we play when time allows."

Jean-Tems, whom was sitting next to Aramis, tossed in another Louis d'or, "Is it to me to make a guess?"

"Indeed it is your turn." Nodded Athos.

"My wager is placed on the card having four *carreaux.*"

Porthos deliberately paused to add suspense to the anticipation.

He flipped it and to the disappointment of the travelers, he laid it aside so as to discard it.

Porthos glanced at Athos, "'Tis your turn *mon ami*. This is the card." He said as he tapped it once.

"This one?" Queried Athos, knowingly pointing to an off center one.

"Ne, my good man, this one." He said as he tapped the card rapidly five times, as if impatient with his companions' inability to concentrate on the game.

Athos drained his goblet and as he was setting it upon the table, he said, "This one has five *coeurs*."

Porthos turned it and it was as Athos' predicted.

Porthos took his turn, placed a nominal wager and purposely lost it so as to not cause concern with the travelers.

They each had multiple turns til the deck was spent

The game finished as Porthos was able to add the pile of coins to his purse, he suggested another round, they accepted and Porthos once again set the *tableau*

As he gave Jean-Tem a chance to proceed ahead of the others, Athos poured himself more wine, then offered some to the travelers who respectfully declined.

Slowly, without much concern, their purses' contents were nigh depleted and the second game ended.

Porthos queried of them if they cared to join them in a third round. They declined that as well, with the excuse they were well fatigued and needed to be well rested for their trek to Castres, to meet with the Duc to get acquainted with their new assignment.

"I must query something of you Monsieur, does your companions not add to to their purse as well?" Inquired Jean-Tems.

"One purse, one cause, one dispersement, three acknowledgements."

All five men regained their feet at the same time and strode towards the door.

Porthos paused and gave the innkeep one of the newly acquired Louis d'or.

"This is for your generous hospitality." He said as he pressed it into the proprietor palm, "*Merci.*"

Jean-Tem too, was going to offer the proprietor a few sous for his companion and himself.

"Ne, re-purse it, your generous benefactor here has seen to it that your debt to me has been settled. God-speed gentlemen."

"Messieurs, we want to thank you. What a most interesting and enjoyable way to spend an eve."

The three collectively bowed.

"Perchance we shall meet again and if by chance we do then another couple rounds of *Lansquenet* if you choose." Replied Athos.

"Splendid thought." Added Jean-Tems companion, "'Til then."

"'Til then."

The two alighted into their saddles, turned their horses in the direction of the north gate and hastily departed for the citys' gates, for they close in the eve at the Luxembourg's prompting at the stroke of twelve.

The three stood momentarily in the meager shadows of a lit brazier, conversing lightly.

"My do you not think their stature got a might slighter?" Queried Athos.

"Most assuredly looks as if they did. Although they were sufficiently weighted, loosing excessive bulk can be beneficial." Added Aramis.

"Alas, good gentlemen, it did not benefit them." Commented Porthos.

"Ah Porthos, I stated not who it would find it beneficial, did I? Indeed it was beneficial....for us."

The three laughed and Grimaud smiled at the thought of his masters' soul being enlightened.

"Consider the fact, it was and is to our advantage, we know how to play the game correctly." Said Athos.

"It certainly was to our advantage as well, someone afore us, who frequents the tavern used a quill and ink and minutely marked them and we thus in time we became accustomed to what those little ink blots meant. To the commoner, they look like they were a part of the intended design, ah but my good gentlemen, we are not commoners." Observed Porthos.

Again they laughed. This time hard enough to cause tears to spring from their eyes and then had to be wiped away with the back of a hand.

"Do you think we will see the likes of them again?" Queried Porthos, after he collected his wits.

"I doubt under these circumstances." Replied Aramis.

"Pity." Said Athos.

"In all seriousness, what is on our agenda for the morrow?" Queried Porthos, "For we still have not seen De Treville."

"Hopefully the fates will find favor with us and deliver our two absent valets."

"Indeed that would be so beneficial." Agreed Porthos.

"Can not imagine what it would be like without Grimaud. How fortunate I am to have a valet that knows my worth."

Grimaud bowed slightly as the gesture did not go unnoticed by Athos, they both smiled.

"Now *mon amis* the morn is approaching and what better way to greet it than being in our own familiar chambers?" Queried Porthos yawning.

Then as the clock struck the hour, the four men regained their vacant saddles and turned about and began down the rue.

"Is it agreed upon, that we *rendezvous* at dawn and seek breakfast. It would be a fine time to solidify our agenda and what better way to do that than with a full stomach?" Said Porthos, as his two companions laughed softly.

"It is agreeable." Said Athos.

"Most definitely. What a splendid way to begin the day. I agree as well." Replied Aramis.

The eve was nigh still save for the sounds of the shod horses feet on the cobblestone, some denizens in search of something to amuse them, an occasional early seasonal chirping of a cricket and in the distance a screech of an owl, descending upon an unwary prey.

One by one, each man left the company of one another as their avenue was obtained and they turned in search of their apartments.

Porthos by passed his apartments to return his horse to the stables as believed his companions would do as well.

The stable lackey heartily greeted him as he entered the courtyard and received the reins to the fatigued animal.

"Will you be needing her in the morn? Queried the lackey.

"I will seek her if I do, as for now, a little leather to the cobblestone now and then, does no harm."

"Aye Monsieur. *Bon Soir* Monsieur."

Porthos touch the brim of his well plumed hat, turned and disappeared into the darkness.

Although it was a chilly moonless eve, Porthos was quite familiar with the route and knew how to navigate his way without hesitation.

When he arrived at his door, he paused and listened.

Nothing out of the ordinary attracted his attention, all was well and he allowed himself admittance.

"I so wished you would return Mousequeton." Lamented Porthos half aloud, as he made his way to his chamber and readied himself for repose as he had for almost half a fortnight.

He paused in front of the still cold hearth, the fire had long ago had been spent, and he deliberated if it would be worth the effort of laying another fire and have a goblet of wine or just make his way quietly to his bed chamber.

As he paused, he again listened.

"Peste! I hear not my clock. 'Tis another reason to have Mousequeton about. To tend to the minute details of every day living so I in my preoccupations of life, so often forget, such as something as simple as winding the clock on a daily basis."

He removed his hat, mantle, baldric and doublet and laid them across a heavy, oak upholstered chair and strode to the window.

The heavenly bodies twinkled a greeting and gave him meager lighting, enough to see that the shutters were closed and latched as well as the window.

Rounding his bed, he sat down and pried off his boots, donned his night shirt, removed his stockings and pantaloons, found his counter pane, lie down and covered up and promptly fell asleep.

When the morns' light arrived, it tried to peer through the shuttered windows to summon the slumbering giant, alas to no avail.

Within a short while, he turned to his side and eased his eyes open and regained his wits.

He got himself up and ready for the day, paused in front of his chevel and theorized, "If I lack, then so be it, I lack. Can not be an image of perfection all the time, but I can be as close as one gets."

Tying his mantle in place and firmly placing his cap on his head, he made his way towards, "The Sword and the Pendulum."

As he absorbed the day, once or twice, he thought he got a glimpse of what he had hope would be his valet, alas when the denizen turned about, with grave disappointment, the resemblance quickly faded and dissolved.

Entering his favorite establishment, he glanced about as his eyes adjusted to the dimly lit chamber.

A kitchen valet, whom Porthos did not recognize, approached and queried, "May I assist you with something Monsieur?"

"Young man, probably not for I have never seen the likes of you afore and to say that you no doubt do not the know the likes of me is fair therefore since that has been established, you will not know my two companions that I seek for you will know them not."

"Would Monsieur care to have breakfast while waiting for their arrival?"

Porthos hesitated but conceded, "T'would be best. Never could ponder things of interest on an empty stomach, or make sense of common things. Aye, breakfast is a splendid way to waste time waiting for my companions."

The musketeer then made his way to his favorite corner as he did, he tried to peer out the window that faced the rue to see if Athos and/ or Aramis were about.

The young valet reappeared with a goblet, wine, bread and some Brie.

"Ah splendid. You must have been instructed by a mentor of such to know these things."

The young man laughed, "Only if you would consider my uncle a mentor, for he knows the likes of you and your companions and by the by half of Paris. He saw you and informed me of such, Ah, 'tis well he has a favored establishment so well liked by so many."

Porthos poured himself a goblet of wine as the door opened.

He was so hoping it was his companions, but the silhouetted stature indicated otherwise.

The musketeer then resumed to tear off the heel of the bread and dip it into his wine and as he put it in his mouth, the form appeared at his table.

It was Jussac, the Cardinals' captain.

"Have you seen the likes of your companions?" Queried the guard.

"Ne' can not say that I have. What gives, why do you need to see the likes of them?"

"Ones of my officers claim, your Monsieur Athos insulted him and wants to settle the insult in the proper manner."

"Sounds about right." Murmured Porthos with a slight slanted grin, then aloud, "….And praytell, when did this occur?" Queried the hefty musketeer in his companions' defense.

"Last eve."

"That can not be so."

"Are you insinuating that he is not telling the truth? How do you know Monsieur Athos did not utter such nonsense?"

"He was with myself and Monsieur Aramis. We were attending business in this very establishment. Mainly supper." Chuckled Porthos.

"What of after your supper?"

"We were preoccupied with business as I said. Forsooth, he had not the opportunity to utter much of anything against anyone."

"Was he in his cups?" Queried Jussac with all the seriousness he could collect within himself.

"What is with the interrogations? It matters not if he t'were in his cups or not, he was here with Monsieur Aramis and myself and there were two others. He had not the opportunity, alas if the opportunity had arisen, then no doubt that should have transpired, but ne'. He said nothing of the nature. He kept his tongue even. For he was not in the presence of the Cardinal."

Jussac cleared his throat in annoyance and his countenance changed hue.

"Is something amiss? Your countenance has the color of his Eminences' vestments."

Jussac clenched his jaw tight and managed to query, "What of these gentlemen, who were they?"

"We know not. Once we had completed our transactions, they made for the north gate afore it closed for the eve and they did not want to be detained within the city. Afore you query, where were they headed, that information I can not provide. If I knew, I still would not divulge it. I prefer they stay anonymous and leave it at that. Now afore you spoil my appetite, I request that you depart."

"No one can spoil your appetite I assure you." Replied Jussac.

Porthos arched his brow.

"Reveal my secrets not." Instructed Porthos, "By the by, tell your officer that if he is to accuse a musketeer, correctly identify him afore you think it be one of us. If we were in error, we would not be above reproach, alas in this instance have him keep his false accusations to himself. When Athos learns of this, expect repercussions for he does not like to be falsely accused. See to it that an apology is forthcoming."

Jussac rested his hand on the pummel of his sheathed blade.

"There is no need for that alas, if my request goes unheeded then there might be a cause to unsheathe it."

"Then I would have to arrest you for there is an edict in place against dueling."

"Like it ever mattered and you know that as well I as do."

Jussac suddenly spun around and hastily withdrew and as the door closed, Porthos could not refrain himself from laughing heartily aloud.

As he was ready to cut into the small block of Brie, the door opened again and he heard a familiar voice query, "Would you mind very much if we sat down? Mind you, we do not want to be inconsiderate."

"You dolts, of course I would and by the by, you already are."

All three laughed.

His companions the sat down.

"You were expecting us, were you not?" Queried Athos.

"Indeed I was, why do you think other?"

Athos poured wine into the goblet and drained the contents.

"There is only one goblet, now *that* is inconsiderate." He replied as he refilled the goblet.

Porthos caught the young valets' attention and summoned him.

He hastened to Porthos, followed covertly by his uncle, his mentor.

"Ah, my good man, these are the companions I was waiting for, and since they are in attendance, we should like some breakfast afore the kettles and pots are empty and our little visit here would be all for naught."

"What is then Monsieur are you requesting?"

"A couple of roasted fowls from the spit, make the wine pour like a fountain, a couple of loaves of bread, this should be plenty of cheese, and a tureen of that soup that your uncle makes all the time. I might add, two more goblets. Etiquette dictates proper usage of wares and so very uncouth to ignore the use of such."

Athos slightly smiled, he knew that if it were eve and they were there for supper, it would matter not if they had goblets or no, the wine would flow like the Seine, would be consumed just the same in vast amounts, no matter if a vessel was available or no. A goblet made things a little easier to manipulate when inebriated, rather than a cumbersome stopped bottle.

When the young man departed for the kitchen, the proprietor stepped forward to greet the three.

"Salut gentlemen, how are you faring these days? Far be it for me to judge, but from the looks of things, better."

"Correct my good proprietor. Although there is still a lot to be done, it will all transpire and when it is all said and done, it will be beneficial for all." Replied Aramis.

"Care to elaborate?"

"Not really." Shrugged Porthos.

"Although gentlemen, when you are here, you cause curiosities and at time atrocities, you cause vermin to hasten for the door, alas, always welcome."

"You mean Jussac and his regiment?" Queried Aramis, as they laughed.

"Exactly." Replied the innkeep as he winked and he too withdrew and made for the kitchen.

Porthos chortled softly as his companions glanced in his direction.

"Care to share what you find so amusing?" Queried Athos.

"If you had arrived a bit earlier you would have found yourself having a conversation with the likes of Jussac."

Athos' countenance changed in expression and hue.

"You find that amusing?"

"Ne', can not say that I do." Replied Porthos.

"Are you going to tell us what he said or do we have to guess?" Inquired Aramis.

"Guess." Smiled Porthos.

Athos and Aramis glared at him, for it was apparent they were not ready to be toyed with.

"He queried as to your whereabouts Athos, last eve."

"Why would he want to know that?"

"He said one of his officer's had accused you of insulting him and he was taking the matter into his custody and to rectify it."

"I was no where near any of his men. That scoundrel!" Exclaimed Athos, thoroughly vexed.

"Easy old man." Soothed Porthos, "I made it quite clear he ought not accuse a man of anything 'til he is certain he has the facts. His officer had a case of mistaken identity for you were here with us, conducting business. You are due an apology."

Athos drained Porthos' goblet as their meal arrived.

Once their plates were filled and the innkeep and his attendants had departed the men decided to solidify their agenda and try to make the most of what information they beheld concerning the current situation.

"What no Grimaud?" Queried Porthos.

"Ne' not this morn. I have him posted in front of Aramis' apartments with anticipation of the return of Mousequeton and Bazin and bring them directly here if that should occur."

"Then aside from that, what is it we are to do with our day?" Queried Aramis.

"We still have not seen our good Captain and since we have been back a little over a half a fortnight, I am certain he has had word we have been seen and wonders why we have not requested counsel with him." Replied Athos.

"If that be the case that he knows we are about, then why has he not sent for us and tell us the hourglass has been turned?" Reasoned Porthos.

"True enough." Interjected Aramis, "It is a certainty that he has had counsel with Louis and Richelieu, why have they not said something?"

"Perchance it is a misguided oversight." Suggested Porthos

"So, oversight or no, since we have not been summoned by him, consider it good fate and we can prepare our strategic maneuvers in capturing Rohan."

Athos with drew his ponaird from the top of his boot and made use of it and cut off a leg of a roasted fowl.

"You were not going to need it anyway." He said to the bird as he put it upon his nigh empty plate.

"What is it we know thus far?" Queried Athos, with a mouthful of bread, recently dipped in wine.

"We know Pontivy is his family seat, the chateau overlooks the River Blavet, he also has made use of Castres and with Malamort within reach has utilized its caves and caverns." Replied Aramis.

"Basically, we still need to await the arrival of our valets to locate him and seize the opportunity to surround him and bring him to Louis.", Agreed Porthos.

"When we do speak with the captain, we need to make a request to draw on a regiment or two to be obstacles and divert his caravans to mutual location and then other regiments guard it so as to not let him by to reclaim them and use them against the crown."

"Is he not the kings' cousin?" Queried Athos.

"He is, but it matters one time and the next it does not." Replied Aramis, "That is his only weakness that I am aware of, his indecisiveness."

"Have to find a way to exploit it if we can." Added Porthos, with hopefulness.

"Are we still in agreement to wait for our valets to return?" Inquired Porthos.

"Technically, we have no choice. For they are the key factor with knowledge that needs to be shared. 'Til then, patience."

"'Tis that not a virtue?" Queried Porthos, as they laughed and continued to clear the table of its contents.

"Would it not be beneficial to seek counsel then with Louis?" Queried Aramis.

"Why so? I find the throne room quite over crowded as certain individuals jostle about for the throne." Commented Porthos.

"It is just him." Replied Aramis as he inclined his head ever so slightly.

"Ne. Richelieu is on one side forever moving closer." Said Athos, in agreement with Porthos, "You also have Madame de Medici with her over bearing, over protectiveness, and relentless pursuit to influence Louis' thoughts and sway him in her favor."

"She is regent, considering he is minority." Commented Aramis.

"Then too, there are too many to name. All want a piece of France and a say what goes. There are far too many for him to keep in constant contact. 'Tis too taxing for such a young inexperienced monarch." Said Porthos.

"Richelieu silently hopes Louis will find it too daunting and forfeit his right of succession." Added Athos.

"Give Louis credit. His is educated in the way of the state. Unfortunately he does not have Henri to lead him and encourage him. Alas he still has a few honorable, honest nobles who want the best for him and want him to succeed." Said Aramis.

"'Tis true." Nodded Porthos.

"Too bad his mother is too self-serving." Sighed Athos.

"We do have some time available afore we seek De Treville, so what say you, since we would have access to the king, make use of our privilege and seek his counsel?" Suggested Aramis.

"I can think of better things that I would rather occupy my time with." Said Athos.

"I am sure you can." Muttered Aramis.

"Alas, we have naught to report at this time considering our valets have not thus returned." Added Athos.

Porthos and Aramis nodded.

"He can counsel us on strategies and make useful suggestions as how to effectively utilize regiments." Suggested Porthos.

IX

The three finished their meal and it was decided that since day beheld favorable elements, they would stroll through the Tuileries, with no intent, trying not to fret about their impending encounter with Rohan.

Minor regiments of Trevilles' were out practicing maneuvers about the gardens as a couple of fledglings approached and tried to order halt.

Porthos towered over them with an imposing manner and they submitted, realizing it would be futile arguing with such a large man.

He could and would pummel them with minimal effort if he deemed them nuisances, they left them be to continue unobstructed.

The market was always the busiest part of the city with denizen coming and going, seeking wares, selling precessions for a few sous to make a purchase that would contribute towards a supper and denizens finding solace of the springtime warming sun.

The three were always amused at how the city thrived at such diversity of commerce and the difference of opinions the denizens had, but they had one common thread that caused the cohesiveness of all, the common understanding in the preservation of the monarchy through defending it against any scandal or intrigue that would jeopardize its stability or undermining its worth.

Pausing on the edge of the Seine, Porthos said, "I still would think we should seek our good captain. Not so much for counsel, but for acknowledgement of our presence."

"What? So that we make roster?" Queried Athos. "I relish the brief solace from our responsibilities we have. I fear not the responsibilities, just want to be able to have my wits about me now and again without the interference of others."

Aramis and Porthos slightly inclined their heads in agreement.

Porthos stooped to pick up a adequate sized stone and hefted it towards the opposite bank.

Watching the ripples expand then dissipate, said, "That sums it up nicely."

"What sums what up nicely?" Queried Aramis.

"The effects of that stone. The center is intense and deliberate, but the more the ripples expand the less likely it will cause damage. Same with Rohan. When he stages a siege, it is intense and deliberate but as it wears on, it is less effective."

"What happens if he lobs a larger stone?" Queried Athos.

"Then we use one too large for him to match and return the volley."

Two young children ran by, trying to catch a dog that had somehow managed to seize a loaf of bread and escaped their grasp.

Guards that had been rostered, strolled past and they too seemed to have no set intent, seemingly oblivious to the activities of the denizens, they continued, speechless.

As twilight was descending upon the city, the brazier keep had begun his rounds.

The three always seen the same keeper and thus deducted, he was only one that attended the current needs of the braziers.

His cart and horse were in want, alas his wage reflected that it was insufficient and obtaining a more reliable means of earning his keep, was clearly just a mere passing fancy.

Slowly and methodically, the rues, avenues and quais became less congested as the denizens made their way to their chateaux or apartments or other means of shelter in search of supper.

"Would it be worth a visit to, "The Sword and the Pendulum" or some other establishment?" Queried Porthos as the brazier keep attended the brazier next to them afore moving on to the next.

Athos had been staring intently in the direction of the Bastille, therefore his thoughts were not entertaining thoughts of food, while Aramis quietly sat on a bench close to edge of the river watching the various water fowls make a nuisance of themselves as the river navigators moored their vessels to piers and pilings.

"'Tis a mere thought. As much as it is that, it is something we need to address." Said Aramis.

"Aside from the fact, "The Sword and the Pendulum" are on the other side of this fair city, we are closer to, "The Yellow Rooster." Replied Athos.

"Indeed it is, alas "The Sword" is within walking distance." Reasoned Porthos.

"Think about it you dolt, everything is within walking distance." Chided Athos.

Porthos glowered in return at his companion.

"No matter to me." Said Aramis.

"It would matter if the food was not prepared correctly and it crawls off your plate." Replied Porthos, trying in vain not to smile

"Let us just begin walking and wherever we end up should be just as substantial." Concluded Athos.

The three then turned about and began walking away from the heart of the city with the intent of finding a small hostler to accommodate their immediate need.

If it were secluded, so much the better. They could converse with the less likelihood of being eavesdropped upon or recognized and strategize the remainder of their week and into the next.

They shortly found themselves in front of an establishment unfamiliar to them.

During the light of day and if on rounds, this part of the *arrondissement* was overlooked for they were rostered to other parts of the city. In the eve's darkness it lurked quickly in the recessed shadowed, unobserved by the common denizen.

The three paused.

"Why the hesitation?" Queried Aramis, in *sotto voc.*

"Why the *sotto voc?*" Queried Porthos.

Once inside, they found it lacked ornamentation, décor and patronization.

"Perchance it will be to our benefit." Suggested Porthos, thinking the pots would still be filled enough to accommodate them.

"On the contrary, they may have never been filled in the first place for the lack of denizens in want." Said Athos.

"Or it crawled off the plate." Smiled Aramis.

As Porthos' hand touched the latch to lift it, they heard, "Gentlemen, gentlemen, gentlemen. Do not leave. I have plenty to share with you. If you please, allow me."

They reconsidered their circumstance, dismissed their ill at ease feeling and followed as he provided an adequate sized table by their hearth that gave off a comforting warmth.

"What I would not give to have this when I reach my apartments." Sighed Porthos.

"What? Do you not know how to lay a fire?" Queried Athos, glanced at his companion, askance.

"Indeed I do, alas, I do not lay one in the morn, for it would be wasted by the time I return in the eve, I do not lay one in the eve, for when I return, I make use of my bed almost immediately."

"You miss Mousequeton, then?" Queried Aramis.

"Most definitely. That valet has the where with all to have everything in place as I desire it as I return, no what what time morn, day or eve. Fine man, he." The musketeer sighed.

"Fear not my good man, the familiar will become familiar again." Suggested Aramis, who would never admit his reliance on Bazin, but the residual effect were just not as obvious.

The innkeep approached and queried of them their desires.

"Were your spits put to use this day?" Queried Aramis.

"Pardon Monsieur, alas ne', they are cold and still at the moment. My huntsman returned not, therefore had to improvise with what was available."

"….And just what is available?" Inquired Porthos with grave concern for his empty stomach.

"Mirepoix. In the cellar, I have reason to believe there are the remains of the seasonal sausage that was made just afore January and smoked to preserve and retain it. I can not say for sure if my wife was able to make bread this morn or no. Oh! And come to think of it, there is a small smoked ham."

Porthos arched his brow, "Just how "small" are you making a reference to?"

"'Tis about the size of both of your fists."

The others were in disbelief.

"How is it that it is so small?" Aramis wondered.

"He was butchered by accident."

"The yield was not sufficient I assure you. Therefore my huntsman has to be engaged almost on a daily basis and need to depend on what he is able to procure. As to why he did not return this morn, I can not say."

"Why are your spits cold, have you no reserve?"

"He too was responsible to oversee the spits and the hearth and supplies are as scant as my purse."

"Then my good man, we shall make use of your sausages, the ham and mirepoix. If there is bread, that is good add that as well?" Suggested Porthos.

"Have you a wine cellar?" Queried Athos.

"Yes, Monsieur."

"Is it Anjou?"

"Ne', it is from my own grape yard in the north. Processed and bottled in mid-summer to catch the benefits of the sun for a week, then stored 'til autumn in a cool cellar beneath my chateau and the culmination of its cycle, it is transported here and stored."

"Do you drink from your bounty often?" Queried Athos.

"Ne', I have saved it for denizens such as yourselves, and serve it then as requested with their meal."

Athos arched a brow in skepticism, Aramis slightly nodded as Porthos suggested, "Why then, do you not bring us what you have suggested? It should be adequate."

"Very well." Replied the innkeep as he withdrew.

"Never trust an innkeep that will not willing to taste the likes of his own wine." Smile Athos, in the most satirical way.

"...And for that matter," Added Porthos, "his stature was on the slight side and his countenance, quite pale and drawn."

As they were sitting, toying with the ends of their poniards, the door once again opened and closed.

Four men allowed themselves admittance without the assistance of the innkeep and chose chairs within the hearths' reaching warmth but at a distance in which they foolishly thought their conversations would not be over heard.

Each of the musketeers' favored the ability to single out a single mans' voice out of many a skill developed out of necessity of preventing and discouraging differences as they arose against the crown.

Their meal arrived and place afore them and as the innkeep placed the last platter atop the table in which their sausages rested, he took note of his new arrivals and hastily attended them.

The three began to help themselves to their now available meal and feigned too much preoccupation with their meal to pay head what they were saying.

"The munitions were successfully place within reach of La Rochelle." Said the first.

"Rohan was made aware of that, I would image?" Queried a stocky man, resembling Porthos' stature, but on a much smaller stouter scale.

"Indeed he was."

"Where is he now?" Queried the stocky man.

"He has made his way south."

"Do you know exactly where and what of his planned strategies?"

"Not precisely, but we do know he has enlisted Soubise." Added the fourth man, as the third one sat quiet.

"What does Benjamin have to do with it?"

"He thinks alike of Henri and believes in the cause just as much."

"Rohan is still diverting munitions to La Rochelle, but as he receives them, he divides them. Sends some to the south and some to remain at La Rochelle."

"Do not forget to include Pontivy. He believes that having them on his estates they will less likely be confiscated and used against him."

The three silently chuckled and continued eating, as Aramis gestured for them to keep their voices on the quieter side so they may garner necessary information.

The innkeep approached and queried if they would like some wine as well.

"I think not." Replied Athos, "It might be best to keep our wits about so that we will be able to navigate our way to our apartments and make sound judgements if the need arises."

The innkeep scowled in response, and withdrew.

When the tables' top was littered with nothing but the empty vessels, Porthos leaned back in his chair and glanced about.

It was then another couple of denizens made an entrance and joined the previous ones.

"My how infamous can one get in one eve?" Said Porthos as he picked up the end of a discarded sausage with his ponaird, scrutinized it afore he put it in his mouth.

Aramis again gestured for him to keep quieter.

They did so with their conversations and still able to hear what was said on the opposite of the chamber.

The first of the new arrivals was heard to sigh heavily and say, "I swear if I did not know the difference, I would think Rohan has gone mad."

"Why do you say that?" Queried the stocky one.

"Why would you begin at the farthest point, spend regiments and munitions as you go and by the time you return to the point of origin, victory in plain sight, you have naught. Nary a thing to conclude your quest." He replied, shaking his head.

"I am sure he has his reasons. Query of him not, it might scatter his concentration."

"Only thing, Monsieur, I surely would like to have known where his first strike would be so that subsequent and supportive regiments could be set." Suggested the fourth one of the first group.

"Do not be in such a haste to light the fuse. The Catholics are not going anywhere soon." Smirked the second one of the second group.

As the three regained their feet, found the innkeep and settled their debt.

"….I might add, neither are you." Said Porthos, in *sotto voc.*

Once out of doors and with the cool air about them, they drew their mantles close and began walking back towards the city.

"Truly those gentlemen seem to think Rohan can single handedly subdue all the Catholics of this state." Began Porthos.

"How arrogant can one get?" Queried Aramis.

"You are inquiring that of the wrong person." Replied Athos. "By the by" he added, "...I know not of you two, but I am thoroughly thirsty and as I would not trust something the innkeep himself would not. Therefore, I suggest we quench our thirst from the familiar, "The Sword and the Pendulum."

"So agreeable idea." Confirmed Porthos.

"Aramis, what say you?"

"I am in agreement too. Alas, I am needing to remind you, the establishment is on the other side of the Seine and closer to the *Palais* then where we stand now, therefore we are within the city, and having no fear of the gates closing and omitting us, we have and early morn."

"Why for? We did not make anything definite that we had to attend to. We were just hoping our valets would return and then we would see to it the frayed ends would be hemmed and sewn." Interjected Porthos.

"Do you realize do you not that we seriously do not know the names of those involved in this little tit for tat skirmish. It would be much more beneficial when making references to them rather than trying to describe them." Observed Athos.

"We do know that Rohan is one of the master key players and has involved his brother, I believe his name is Benjamin. Beyond that we might need to employ the likes of an honest soothsayer in extracting names and locations." Smiled Porthos.

Aramis laughed aloud.

"What is so amusing to you now?" Queried Athos.

"As if there is such a thing as an honest soothsayer." Replied Aramis, ridding his cheek of a tear streaking down it.

"At least when the Huguenots believed they had the upper hand when they abducted you, we were fortunate enough that you were able to leave hints along they way. We are going into this blind and have very little facts to rely on." Said Porthos.

"Their activities seem to be more frequent and intense. If they are trying to draw our attention, they certainly have accomplished that." Interjected Athos.

"We need to sit back and listen." Said Aramis.

"Alas, we can not sit for too long and I do believe the longer we sit, the more difficult it will be to roust them."

"I do suppose that we should seek Louis and convey to him what we just heard and then let him decide how he would like us to proceed. Once we have completed our counsel with him, we can make use of our favored establishment." Suggested Porthos.

"Can we make do and share a bottle of Anjou?" Queried Athos.

"Ne'. Once one is unstopped, and emptied, you will request a second and thus it will render you witless and insensible. Thus Louis will not be able to convey his thoughts and have them adequately enacted upon. It will be maddening for him to think his words will go is words will go unheeded and uncomprehended." Said Aramis.

Athos silently sighed and submitted to his companions' request as the turned a corner and began to make their way to the *Palais Royale*.

Upon entering the side courtyard they regularly utilized, they found it full of activity.

Some guards were changing their posted positions and others that were already rostered, they were making their rounds.

One of the Cardinals' guards was loitering in the door jamb of his ante chamber, trying to appear inconspicuous, alas to no avail.

"Why is it, when things seem to be as they ought, a misintended writ falls on the planking, then it is retrieved by an unsuspecting dolt, misread and discarded for the lack of comprehension."

Athos, paused, clearly agitated.

"Monsieur, are you insinuating we are misguided?"

"Indeed. For you are of the king are you not and not the cardinal?" He queried with a sneer.

"Take ease my good man," Cautioned Porthos, "You most certainly do not want him to get his ire up."

"Why for not? Rumour has it, he would rather keep company with his bottle than with his companions."

Porthos and Aramis stepped forward to usher him out into the courtyard and away from Athos.

"Hold!" Instructed Athos, "I will settle his insolence towards us. I may crawl into my cups now and then for the view through the bottom, is much more appealing than it is now, my reasons are my own. Alas, you dolt, your comments are unwarranted. A new lesson for you to learn is at hand."

The guard inclined his head.

"I shall be more that obliging to give you a lesson in defense for you will need it."

"As if...", Said the guard.

"As if you think you will not need the lesson? I assure you will."

"When are you and where are you making that a reference point?" He queried.

"Our barracks is where we practice our maneuvers, be it there."

"As if I need to step one foot into the likes of your domain." He retorted.

"I caution you, do not make me seek you." Warned Athos, clenching his jowl and removing his gauntlets, one finger at a time, then tucking them in his sash that was about his waist.

"Your present humour is in desperate want." Said Porthos.

"I so inquire how it could be in want when it is in attendance."

"Enough bantering. Nothing will get settled here." Said Aramis, quite sternly, "Now if are finished bickering, for we wasted more than enough time listening to your provocations, that is so as we have said, unwarranted. Query, what are trying to prove by engaging a musketeer in a duel? Do you have a death wish, for do you not know we three are known for our aptness and dexterity?"

"I am not trying to prove anything to anyone, lest of all to myself."

"If you are seeking approval from Richelieu, need I remind you, there is an edict in place that prohibits dueling?" Queried Porthos, "Issued by the king."

"Dead men tells no secrets." Replied the guard, with a *sotto voc.*

"Indeed they do not!" Commented Athos.

The three in unison inclined their heads.

Erstwhile, during the exchange of words, curious denizen gathered to witness the outcome.

Porthos took an imposing step forward, with Aramis following.

As they brushed by Athos, they each grasped an arm and lead him away from their antagonizer.

As they did so, Athos called out, "The day after the morrow, at one, musketeer barrack. Best bring a second. A by thought, be I on the morrow at one. The sooner you have learned your lesson, the better."

"Where do you believe we shall find Louis at this hour?" Queried Porthos, trying to lighten his companions humour, as they rounded a corner.

"At this time of day…by the by what time is it?" Inquired Aramis.

Somewhere in the *Palais* a clock began its hourly chime.

"One…two…three…four…five..six…seven.", Counted Athos.

"Inquire and ye shall reap the benefits of an answer." Smile Porthos.

"Who is it you are quoting?" Queried Aramis.

"None other than myself." Replied Porthos

"Since it is officially the hour of seven, I would think he is in counsel with Madame de Medici then on to supper an then he will join his advisors in his gaming salon and try his hand at the various games of chance." Said Aramis.

"Unless two things are apt to occur. One, get waylaid by the Cardinal and with that inflicted counsel it can last 'til who knows when or he will feign an illness to escape it all." Observed Athos.

"I doubt if he will feign an illness." Commented Porthos.

"Why for not?" Queried Aramis.

"His surgeon, Heroard takes every little complaint uttered by the king serious and thus, Louis will be in for a blood letting and that in the end will leave him in want of stamina and perseverance and at this time, the Huguenot insurrections, needs him to devote as much time as he can spare to see it to their submission." Replied Porthos.

"Then will come to his aid and liberate him from the monotony of it all." Suggested Aramis, with a raised brow in anticipation.

As they approached a rather short set of stairs, Bompar, the king favored personal valet appeared, descending the steps cautiously, for the steps were narrower than the grand staircase that was constantly in use.

"Hold!" Said Aramis, "May we inquire where Louis, pardon his Majesty is at the moment?"

"Oh Messieurs, he is in his chambers readying himself for supper and to escort *Madame le regent* and Madame de Medici."

"So much the better." Said Aramis, "He will be easy to locate than. Gentlemen?"

"Alas Messieurs, he is going to be in counsel with his mother." Stammered Bompar.

"Since when did it ever prevent us from seeking him or us from seeking his Majesty or his approval or counsel?" Queried Porthos, with a wry smile toying with the mere corners of his mouth.

"Then it is to me to announce you." Said Bompar, "Protocol."

"Fie! Since when does protocol ever pertain to us?" Queried Athos, feigning disdain.

"We three have own protocol of etiquette and ethics we adhere to. Go about your errand of mercy and we will secure our well being with his Majesty." Gestured Porthos.

"Alas…" Said Bompar.

"Alas? Ne' my good man, on your way. Whoever you were seeking will no doubt be impatient over your slight delay." Prompted Aramis.

Bompar hastily and curtly bowed and hastened away.

"All those formalities in the name of being of high regard." Sighed Athos.

"Those, "high regards", keep your coffer from want." Said Aramis, "Some of us." He Mumbled incoherently.

As Porthos was going to rap upon the door, it opened.

It was the young king attempting to adjust his mantle.

"Oh! Messieurs!" He exclaimed, "Pardon."

"We humbly implore you, will you spare us a moment of your time?" Queried Aramis.

"I am seeking my mother, Madame de Medici, it is time for our daily counsel and supper to follow." Said he Louis as he rubbed his temple.

"Your Majesty?" Queried Porthos, as he touched Louis' elbow, concerned.

Louis slowly shook his head.

"'Tis nothing, I assure you. My head always begins to ache at this time, every day."

"Then what say you, you spare us some of your time, beckon your chamber valets and have them serve your supper within the confines of your own domains?" Queried Porthos.

The young king pondered a moment then said, "My mother expects me."

"She expects a lot of things from you." Added Athos, *in sotto voc.*

Louis then turned about, re-opened his door and stepped in and invited the three of them to join him as well.

He lead them to a small chamber that contain a hearth, an accommodating table with a side board of decorative decanters.

"How unfortunate and a pity," Mused Athos, "Some are empty or nighly so."

Porthos picked up a adequate sized log and tossed it into the hearth, sending sparks and embers in every direction.

The few that landed at Porthos' feet, were immediately stepped on by the heavy non-assuming, foot and extinguished.

Louis seat himself at the head of the table and gestured for them to sit as well.

"Afore I inquire as to why you are requesting an audience with me, fear not about supper. Bompar will be sent around momentarily after Madame notices my absence. Any sojourning dignitary will have to accept my apologies and readjust a requested counsel in which I might oblige to accept."

Momentarily, Louis' wine steward rapped lightly and let himself into the chamber.

"Begging your pardon, your Majesty.", he said, bowing respectively to the king, "I did not realize you were present. The cellar master suggested I replenish the decanters for he said they were high empty.

Louis inclined his head in appreciation and acknowledgement.

The steward gathered the decanters from the side board and utilized a small delicately carved cart. "Your Majesty." He said as he again bowed, turned and withdrew.

As soon as the door closed, it was opened again.

As predicted, it was Bompar in search of him.

"Your Majesty,". He said, breathless, and bowing, "Mother, Madame de Medici awaits."

"Tell her if you will please, that I have a last minute appointment that needs my attention." Replied Louis.

"To add your Majesty, she is already impatient and agitated."

Louis slammed his clenched fist upon the table in front of him.

"Should be left to me to decide as to where I want my whereabouts to be and this eve I choose to be here in valid counsel. Now, if you please, go round to the grand hall and see that I have my supper served here."

Bompar fidgeted, alas withdrew.

Louis chuckled lightly.

"May I be so bold and inquire what is so amusing?" Queried Athos, raising a brow.

"Bompar does not like to be in the vicinity of my mother, let alone speak to her. Now he has to."

"You would think he would obligingly comply." Suggested Aramis.

"True." Replied Louis, "alas I do not consider it insolent, it is just a matter of opinion in which I concur."

"What?" Queried Porthos, "Does she strike that much of an intimidating, imposing presence?"

"Not really." Replied Louis, "She talks a lot. My father was a man of words followed by appropriate action. No one ever doubted his intent."

"He was beginning to understand the Huguenots and their wants. Then some quite mad religious dolt, Ravaillac assassinated him, over a difference of opinion." Sighed he young king. He then queried, "What brings you? Certainly is not for nostalgic reasons."

"Why say you that? Perchance that is the sole reason." Replied Aramis.

The king sighed again, "Alas there is not much to be nostalgic over."

Afore anyone could reply, a light rap upon the door and it opened allowing Bompar, followed by the wine steward and various carts of food to enter.

The valets served the food and wine, then stepped aside in anticipation of a want or need.

"Well, your Majesty what brings us, is we wanted to discuss your cousin." Said Athos.

"Which? Fore I have many." Replied Louis, as he nudged something that he did not recognize, to the edge of decorative, porcelain plate, with his fork.

"Henri, Duc de Rohan." Said Porthos.

Louis laid his tableware aside, folded his hands and leaned forward.

Aramis drained his goblet, then said, "Rumour has it that he has gone through the south to do some recruiting of regiments."

"He certainly can not do it here in Paris." Mumbled Porthos as he refilled his goblet, from a bottle that was very close.

"I have dispatched many a regiments with the intent of curtailing his current activities. They always seem to lack and are always five paces behind." Said Louis as he rose from the table to regain his feet.

He then strode overtook the glass, panel doors that gave him a panoramic view of the Tuileries and his current courtyard.

The distant denizens that strolled about the Seine in the dusk appeared as mere marionettes being manipulated by a hidden puppeteer. Their intent in life, unclear and uncertain.

Louis mused silently at the thought as he turned about.

"Then what is it you propose?" Inquired the young King, "I may be majority, but my mother still maintains I am a minority and need to consult her."

"Nothing gets passed her?" Inquired Athos, with a raised brow.

Louis chuckled, "So she thinks." He replied.

"We are awaiting for two of our valets to return. We had them discreetly as possible, follow Rohan and bring back information as to what he is about. Upon their arrival we will be seeking a second counsel with you, one with Richelieu and De Treville."

"Then, what is it you are requesting of me now?" Queried Louis.

"Send a half a dozen regiments to La Rochelle in an effort to intercept him afore he reaches Calais."

"Good as done. I shall summon De Treville and inform of this. He will have them assembled and on the move afore the first light of day and Mother will be none the wiser."

"Another suggestion?" Queried Aramis.

"That being?" replied Louis as he reseated himself at the table.

"You have not seen the likes of us as if we were never here."

"What would it matter? You are my guards and my responsibility."

"…And our responsibility is to protect you. The less said the better. I assure you." Smiled Aramis.

With all the goblets filled, a tray of lemon custard filled tarts made their rounds.

When the tray held nothing but crumbs and their goblets were empty save a drop or two, the musketeers allowed the king to regain his feet first, then they and bowed respectfully to him with doffed caps as he silently disappeared behind a large mural paneled door. Bompar and other valets cleared the table and they too withdrew, leaving the three to their own devices.

"Since there is not even a drop of wine to confer over, what say you we seek, "The Sword and the Pendulum?" We can make the best of it til the morn and prayfully by then, our absent valets will be absent no more." Suggested Athos.

"Confer over wine and dice?" Queried Porthos, "'Tis a splendid idea, considering the moon is just touching the tops of the trees now."

"'Tis a good a time as any." Agreed Aramis

They all regained their feet, paused a moment to decide to leave the way the king did, or the door which opened to the passageway.

They chose the door, for they knew not where the other might lead and to their chagrin it might prove to be unpopular with whom it lead them to.

X

The three concurred with their thoughts as they rounded the corner and their favorite establishment was a mere twenty paces.

Upon entering, they found it well lit and lively.

Betting games of sorts were being played.

The winners rejoiced and the losers cursed and accused the host of the game of being a master of deception.

"Let us not indulge ourselves in such frivolous attempt to restore our purse this eve." Suggested Aramis, "We have had enough deception to last us."

"How is it you feel deceived?" Queried Porthos.

"I have an inclination that the conversation we heard earlier this eve was meant for us to believe that is how Rohan intends on manipulating things, but I do not believe that. Granted he is an intelligent man and cunning I might add. How do you think he escape our grasp prior to this? Yes a treaty was signed but he has managed not to grasp the concept of it and has departed."

"Still causing Louis anguish and leaving him to questions his motives are true and sound as well." Added Athos.

"We shall see if the truth was spoken or no just as soon as Bazin and Mousequeton return." Suggested Porthos, "Then I should think there will be another grand time to play, "The Pence in the Pocket." Even though truly it is not a true pocket, just a mere fold in the vestment of extra material."

Finding their favorite corner occupied, it mattered not, they chose another table closer to the kitchen. It was not much more secluded or quiet, for the activity about was quite stirring.

As the proprietor happened by, he had two bottles of Anjou, three goblets, bread and Brie.

"He knows us." Smile Athos.

"Is that a good thing or a bad thing?" Queried Porthos.

"I know not, I have had not the chance to decide." Smiled Aramis, pouring the wine.

Porthos smiled slightly, then inclined his head the remark, for it sounded familiar.

"Since our agenda is not anyone else's that we are aware of, why not use of it and frequent our gymnasium again and put the mannequins through their paces and see how well they can defend themselves from wayward blades." Suggested Porthos.

"Sounds reasonable, since we have not seen the likes of it recently. Wayward, indeed!" Laughed Athos.

"The only way the blades will be wayward is if they had the goblet filled one too many times and knew not when to put a stop to it." Suggested Aramis.

"Does not altar wine have what it takes to alter or make one loose oneself in reverie good or bad?" Queried Porthos, to Aramis.

"I know not. Never imbibed enough as I served mass." Smiled Aramis, "T'would not be the proper way to remember our Lord and His sacrifices He made for us."

Athos' countenance reddened slightly as he dipped a piece of bread he had spread Brie on into his wine, then into his mouth, saying nothing.

"Any other time than that?" Inquired Athos, out of curiosity, coughing lightly.

"Perchance, once or twice when in the company of loving dolts." He smiled.

They laughed for they as companions for the same cause had grown quite familiar and fond of each other. Each allowing the short comings of another.

Brothers in arms in favor of the king and crown, that they be.

As the tapers in the chandeliers above their heads, extinguished themselves, one by one, no one bothered to replace them for it was getting late and the proprietor had long since closed the offerings from the spit and kettles to denizens coming in at such a late hour.

He wanted sleep like any other fatigued denizens, alas as the sun cleared the trees, each day, he would be putting his key in the lock once again to ready his establishment for breakfast, dinner and supper.

Being favored by so many, the musketeers knew so very well his pantries and cellars were well stocked and would not go without.

With a drip of tallow from an overhead taper, it dimmed their surroundings.

Fortunately for them, it did not cause total darkness, thus they took the hint that it was time to put an end to their day.

"Is their a set time? If there is, I can send Grimaud 'round for you. Better still gentlemen, I WILL send him round to gather you at seven. You can join me at breakfast. Grimaud does a splendid preparation. Even when my small pantry is in want. What say you? If nothing else, we can take it with us to the barrack as we await the little insolent dolt."

"So early?" Lamented Porthos. "I have as of yet to get decent sleep for someone wanting my attention one way or t'other well afore I have even had the chance to open my eyes."

"Our days are so often filled by the wants of others, why then can we not take a small slice of the day and make it ours? I can almost guarantee you, something will arise that will summons us away. Be it our valets, the king, even the cardinal has and no doubt will again. Considering the ineptness of his guards, is it no wonder why he summons us?"

"It is agreeable that our lives and this state are in a chaotic predicament as of late, we can afford a bit of off time for reflection. It will do us good." Added Aramis, "I would think sitting amoung companions rather than an unscrupulous lot, will be most beneficial and I might add our conversation will not be overheard by prying ears."

"There will plenty of time for rest and other forms of amusements that capture your fascinations and thus, there you be. You will be able to spend times with your whims and fancies." Replied Athos, "What say you, will you join me?"

"Yes, I agree. Send Grimaud around. I shall be ready."

"Porthos?"

"Athos?"

"Porthos?"

"Aramis?"

"Yes, I agree. I deny not food. I need not waste away due to neglect."

"Far be it that you would waste away. It would have to be a grand lapse of time in order for you to do that." Commented Athos, chiding his companion, trying to conceal his wry smile behind his raised goblet as he finished the contents remains.

As they regained their feet, Porthos reached inside his doublet to retrieve his purse.

His large fingers fumbled with a knot he inadvertently created in haste the last time he withdrew money from it.

"Here, allow me." Offered Athos, as he withdrew his ponaird from the top of his boot.

"I think not, but thank you just the same." Replied Porthos.

Aramis extended his slight hand.

"May I offer you my assistance? I assure you I will not use my ponaird."

"Very well."

Aramis reseated himself, scrutinized it from various perceptions, sat it on the table afore him.

In a matter of a short time, he managed to un-do the knot and hand it back to Porthos, who then withdrew a couple of coins and laid them in the center of the table, then retired it, but this time not as tight as afore.

"'Tis well Aramis, thank you."

"Next time my dear gentleman, do not be in such haste."

As the three then strolled towards the door, a man, brandishing his blade, clearly and totally inebriated jumped out from the shadows and proceeded to block their way.

"Peste! What gives?" Exclaimed Porthos.

Athos and Aramis had the blades half out of their sheaths when Porthos said, "Fret not my good gentlemen. I should make this duel if one would like to make references to it as such, a short one, forsooth it certainly will not a lengthy one."

"Indeed." Agreed Athos, ""For you have an advantage the common man does not. Height, weight, reach and stamina."

"Then withdraw so I conclude what he has began."

Porthos' companions cleared the planking of debris, not wanting their companion to stumble and have his adversary hold the upper hand.

The musketeer took his stance, with his blade and gaze steady, he queried, "What argument have you with me, to cause me delay and my departure?"

"This state has caused me to become a pauper in my own time. Anyone who carries a sword must be for the crown and defends its taxation. Taxed for this and that so much, I can not see straight."

Athos turned to Aramis and in *sotto voc* queried, "Did he say he was a pauper in his own mind?"

Aramis furrowed his brow as he slightly inclined his head.

"If we are for the crown, what does it matter? We do not decide the finances of the state. There is the minister of finances who oversees that and it is not Louis."

"No wonder why my purse is always empty." Mumbled Athos.

"Then who ever it is that has controls the coffers still make references to the disbursements." Replied the adversary, making a hasty lunge at Porthos, blade wavering in the dim lighting.

Porthos just as quickly stepped aside and turned to face his opponent again.

His opponent now had his back to the wall, tried in vain to make his lunges count.

Porthos gestured for Athos to toss his ponaird to him so he could use it in a non conventional way.

Athos did as Porthos suggested and Porthos was able to obtain it by the handle and not the blade.

The hefty musketeers' adversary readied himself as if in a jousting tournament and steadied himself the best he could.

Porthos resheathed his sword and changed the ponaird from his left hand to his right and waited.

As he shook his head in disbelief, his adversary charged forward.

Porthos stepped aside and from the gathered momentum, he could not stop in time and tumbled over a table.

Getting to regain his feet, he shouted, "I still would hold you accountable. Go then, talk to the king and have him leave hold of our purses and coffers and then something will be able to trickle into them without disappearing into nothingness."

"Our words mean nothing to the king when it comes to running the state. Defending it, is an entirely different matter. It is then we have a say, for then our words bear weight."

His adversary again took the stance of a tilting knight and readied himself again for a charge.

As he ran past, Porthos was able to catch hold of his collar and lift him off the floor by several finger widths.

"Put me down!" He shrieked, in dismay.

"I promise I will." Smiled the giant.

Stepping forward just enough that he could not advance further, he took Athos' ponaird and jabbed it through many layers of cloth still it stuck fast into the wooden paneled wall. His toes barely touching the planked floor.

"I would not squirm too much if I were you. The cost of a tailor these days could cost far more than what you have in your purse."

Porthos gathered his belongings, put on his mantle and tied it in place and again made his way towards the door.

"I will see that you pay for this." His adversary shrieked again.

"I am sure you will." Replied Porthos as he touched the brim of his cap, bowed, turned and followed his companions out of doors, back into the coolness of the eve.

"My dear gentleman, I can not recollect if the Luxembourg sounded the current hour or no, but having a rather fascinating day or as it is, eve, I should be inclined to think it best if we went in search of our beds, for I believe on the morrow without a doubt we will again have a day filled with various amusements. Although we have claim the day ours, surely someone somewhere has already laid bets on it." Said Aramis.

They all laughed knowing how true that was.

The minute they paused and wanted to own a few minutes, as they wanted to call theirs, they were summoned by someone else, be the king, their captain or the cardinal.

The brazier that casted short stout shadows, flickered and struggled in vain to stay lit, illuminated the corner well enough that turned to Rue de Vaugiard, it was there they bid each other a *bon soir,* and Aramis doffed his cap and bowed.

"Good gentlemen, it is here I must say, *bon soir* and bid you a fond *Av Revoir.*" Said Aramis.

"If you must." Jested Athos.

"I must as you and Porthos."

Athos chuckled, "So be it then. My avenue is up a bit and yours Porthos is just beyond. I dare say, no one will toy with you. They would be quite foolish if they did as that fellow just found that to be fact."

"Indeed I say." Began Porthos, "I am far too fatigued and agitate easy and if I am to be toyed with I assure you it will not end on agreeable terms." Then to Aramis, "My dear companion is it your way lit enough to guard against any obstacles to see your way clear to your door?"

"I should think, even if it were not adequately lit, I would fumble not, for I am quite familiar with the way."

"Good gentlemen, forget not the morn. Breakfast and hoping the fates show us kindness, we will have the day to ourselves." Concluded Athos.

"Shhh!" Suggested Porthos, "Do not tempt the fates in thinking other."

"Do remember, dear Athos, your score you want to settle with that young inexperienced guard. That my dear companion, is later, as for now, be on your way and we will see you at one at our barrack. Grimaud, if you would be so kind to see to it that your master is well rested and fit. Need not some insolent dolt get the best of him."

"Never!" Mumbled Athos.

The three parted and went their separate ways in search of the comforts of their own apartments.

Porthos reached for the latch of his apartments' door, paused and listened as was a ritual of his to catch anything amiss if there were.

Hearing nothing, he allowed himself admittance and went straight to his bed chamber.

Sitting as he did customarily on the side of his bed, he removed his spurs, although the day did not warrant their use, he still applied them to be on the ready if the occasion arose, then he retrieved his ponaird from the top of a boot to prevent an accidental injury, then relieved his fatigued legs of his bucket boots.

Then realizing his sword was still in place, he hastily stood to remove that and his baldric and placed them inside his armoire as well as his other implements, and quietly shut the doors.

His pantaloons, tunic, and stockings were placed over a chair that sat beside his bed and as he found his nightshirt and donned it and laid down.

His weight causing a comfortable indentation, he quietly drifted off to sleep.

In the predawn hours as he shifted from his comfortable supine position to prone, he thought he heard something creak, he hastily dismissed it because the age of his establishment, for all old establishments creak and groan at some point.

Alas the sound of glass rattling against metal stirred him.

He silently lay and listened for further indications as to what was causing such.

It happened again and as he swung his legs about to sit on the side of his bed, a slight illuminating glow filtered into his chamber and he heard his mantle clock ticking with a louder click indicating it was readying itself to strike the hour.

As silently as he could, he crept to his armoire to retrieve his blade and then proceeded to investigate the strange yet familiar sound.

As he approached his grand room, it got warmer and brighter, he discovered there was a disheveled figure kneeling afore the still hearth, placing small pieces of kindling beneath heavier logs and using his tinder box, set sparks to it, to light it.

Once lit and was evident it was going to catch and continue, the figure stood and turned.

"Oh Monsieur, if you please, please put your blade aside, for 'tis I"

Porthos chaffed his eyes and countenance and peered more intently at the figure afore him.

"Mousequeton?"

"None other I assure you."

Porthos let his sword fall to the planking and heartily embraced his valet as a father would a wayward son.

Setting him a pace or two back he queried, "What are you doing?"

"Is it not time to lay a fire to begin the day."

"How befitting. Indeed it is, alas I would think you need to rest up. How is it with Bazin?"

"He no doubt has given Aramis the start of his life." He chuckled at the thought, then added, "Forsooth we knew not when you would return and tried to make the best of it."

"Is that why the hearth was cold and lifeless?"

"Again, I say, I tried to make the best of it."

They both laughed.

"Then you missed me? It has been just short of a fortnight."

"I did not say that."

"You did not have to."

XI

With Porthos' assistance Mousequeton once again turned into a recognizable denizen and valet of Porthos.

The musketeer then encouraged him to find his familiar nightshirt and make use of it, thankfully morn was still a few hours and getting the chance at repose, was heavily endorsed.

"For in the morn, your counterpart, Grimaud will be round to remind us of breakfast with his master. Mind you 'tis well and good that you returned when you did, for that will be most beneficial. You can relate everything you saw and did as it corresponds to Rohan. To fore warn you, you need not relay lay it now, for you will wasting both your breath and time. Tell it once afore all and be done."

"Alas, Master..."

"Aye, Mousequeton...I assure you, it will keep and all will be said in done in the morn. Rest now, no doubt there is plenty to tell. I dare say, my companions have a barrage of queries as you have answers. Omit naught, we need to content ourselves with the knowledge we obtain will be sufficient and it will cause a culmination of any and all events."

"As you desire Master, all to the benefit of the state."

"Indeed. Now throw another piece or two on to the back, bank it, then retire."

"*Bon Soir* Master."

"*Bon Soir* Mousequeton." Smiled Porthos, elated that his valet had returned.

Mousequeton, as was his daily ritual arose afore his master and set about rekindling the fire and stirring it back to life. As the wine he was mulling warmed in the small kettle, he was able to retrieve Porthos' vestments and made them readily available to his master when he rousted him, opened the heavy curtains, then the shutters.

The valet smiled as he heard Porthos snoring loudly, indicating sound sleep. He really did not want to wake his master, alas he knew Porthos had an engagement this morn with his companions and he too had to accompany him for he and Bazin had to recount their journey.

With the wine mulled and poured he went to roust his master.

Of all the duties Porthos held him accountable for, this was his least liked one.

Caring for Porthos' wants and needs was simple, for the musketeer did not have a demanding demeanor.

That being said, he might be vain, but his vanity did not equal demanding as Mousequeton reasoned.

Athos' attitude towards some things were daunting and challenging and found himself thankful that he was not Grimaud. Although Athos had at times a harsh exterior, Grimaud found he was grateful for a master as such and had grown fond of him.

There was simply something not so common about Athos that he found endearing and worth defending.

He and Bazin had many a conversations while they were absent and Bazin always alluded to the fact as much as Aramis had his strict rituals, he also had a calming non-demanding demeanor and actually was quite thankful for the strict religious regulations the young prelate had imposed on him since entering Aramis' employ. It allowed him to realize how little he really wanted things and how little his needs were. Both easily met with minimal effort.

Porthos groaned in protest as the sun filtered into the chamber and illuminated literally everything it touched.

"I know…", Mumbled Porthos as he returned to his comfortable supine position, with his eyes closed to avoid the mornings' beckoning.

"Your vestments are nigh, the wine has been mulled and given Grimaud will no doubt be rapping on your door within the hour."

Again Porthos groaned.

"'Tis well I rise although I would rather not budge, but our allegiance to the crown dictates otherwise. Peste! 'Tis too early."

Mousequeton who had already had dressed, went about his duties til Porthos was needing his assistance.

The hefty musketeer was adjusting his pantaloons when Mousequeton reappeared with a goblet of the warm mulled wine.

Setting the goblet down upon the small table beside the bed, he handed his master his doublet.

"Oh Mousequeton, that one no longer fits well. It is too snug. Turn it and you wear it. I have purchased a new one that is more befitting. The color is suitable and will not cause a stir with the common denizen and have them thinking I am extravagant or eccentric. For I am neither."

Porthos again went to his armoire and retrieved his new doublet and put it on then picked up the goblet for a sip of the still warm mulled wine and grimaced.

"Master?"

"You were a touch heavy handed with that new spice that was imported."

"My apologies."

"Accepted."

Mousequeton with his nimble fingers, tied the binding ties neat and straight as Porthos had tried in his absence but never quite mastered it, leaving the musketeer vexed.

The dutiful valet turned the proffered doublet and donned it and tied his own ties while peering at his reflected image from the cheval.

As he was tying the last one, a rapping sounded at the door.

"Just finished." Said Porthos, "There is no cause for delaying Grimaud or Athos. Let us step lively. Sure as I know Athos he will either grow weary or impatient, depending the time of day. Considering it is early morn, he will be impatient. Let us be on our way."

Upon opening the door, to Porthos delight Bazin was with Grimaud.

"Bazin my good man, how delightful to see you as well. Did you think Grimaud would not find his way?" Jested Porthos, he glanced about, "What? No Monsieur Aramis?"

Bazin slightly blushed.

"Ne' Monsieur Porthos, 'tis been awhile since I have seen him and my master knows the importance of being able to communicate with a colleague of the same station, thus allowed me to accompany him. My master is with Monsieur Athos."

The valets, including Grimaud enjoined in a light conversations concerning the issues of the state. Including the Huguenot conflicts.

"Some how," He mused, "they have managed to stay current of the states activities, even in their absence. Yes they have been away and aware of Rohan but the Peste! To have connection unbeknownst to us? How beneficial."

Reaching Athos' apartments, he lifted the latch, opened the door and stepped in and aside.

He had prepare the small table afore he gathered the valets and musketeers and he found his master conversing with his companion afore the fire.

"'Tis well and good they have returned. Now perchance we can put together a couple of strategies ourselves and then present them to De Treville and with his expertise on the playing field he can assist in suggest maneuvers that will out flank him." Aramis was heard to say.

"Remember, we too have to verify his whereabouts, acknowledge that and covertly send for additional regiments." Added Athos.

"It is too bad that we can go in three separate directions and close in." Said Porthos as he stepped up to join his companions afore the fire.

"That would cause delays. By the time he is located in one place he will have moved on. If we send missives amongst ourselves, by the time we get it, it will be too late, the event will already have taken place, and if we can have a way of relaying missives hastily to De Treville and either incepting him afore he strikes or just after. He needs to surrender all intent and make nice with the king." Theorized Aramis.

"The king was fair and equitable when he was offered the treaty last year but Rohan chose to walk through it and not abide. Louis does not have to play nice if chooses not to."

"Louis has far too many people trying to get close enough to borrow his ear long enough with their opinions to make a difference." Sighed Athos.

"It really is sad when there are so many opinions and all think their opinion matters more than the next. If they all could be combined and have one logical conclusion…", Offered Aramis.

"Even his most trusted advisors find it hard to borrow his ear, the multitude is too suffocating to get near enough to matter." Said Porthos as he poured some wine into a goblet.

"It is a pity really, alas what can one do?" Queried Aramis, expressing concern for the minor king, whom was at the mercy of his mother, Madame de Medici, regent.

"My dear brother in arms," Said Porthos, "Once again we find we are in each other company, we have decided to congregate at Athos' establishment as he has requested so that we might propose some strategies to present to the king in his efforts to locate Rohan and return with him and put an end to this Huguenot insurrection. Generous, kind Athos, we thank you as our companion and host as we now put forth our suggestions. Alas in order to do that we need to consult our valets who recently took on the role of sentry to pursue information in an effort to assist De Treville our dear captain and Louis. What say you Bazin?"

"Mousequeton and I set out for Castres, for that is where we heard he was aiming at.

Once in Castres we we able to obtain information that he was on the move to various sights, to oversee any, all refortifications and fortify those needing it."

Porthos sipped some wine and and queried, "From Castres, where was he going then?"

"He gathered two regiments and marched off towards Malamort. He stayed long enough to surmise the area, being somewhat secluded in the valley, still needed more defense. He left part of a regiment at Malamort, sent a missive to Castres and Pontivy requesting additional regiments then set off for Montpellier."

"We know what Pontivy is." Said Aramis, "that is where his family originates. It seems not likely he would besiege them."

"Perchance no. Alas I do not think he would not hesitate if it meant defying the king. Family that Louis is or no." Reasoned Athos.

"Montpellier has a treaty in place." Observed Porthos.

"That may be so, but it matters not to him, for he wants to get his point across that he like many other Huguenots want their freedom and they will get it, no matter the cost,". Replied Aramis, "Ignatius Loyale would agree that the freedom to observe a chosen religion comes second after honoring our Lord and Saviour and defending that right goes without being said, it just has to happen."

"With so many aspects of mankind, how do we know which aspect to conform to? So many conflict arise from that." Queried Mousequeton, for on this occasion the valets were treated as an equal and their opinions and concerns mattered.

Aramis sighed.

"Precisely. For they all struggle and endure and conflicts are a product of a someones' over active imagination and their conquest over the meek and mild then on to glory and earthly material things. Louis wants to have the state one religion in order to control all of it with one stroke of his quill, one edict, not a multitude."

"Montebaun is in the vicinity and we would image that is next on his agenda." Suggested Mousequeton.

"There is also Bressols, Le'ojac and Villemade." Said Bazin.

"So true. By Montpellier Collioure', Pe'zenas and Se'te will be within his reach."

"Any mention of Nimes?" Queried Athos, "For that too is not that far off.", as he drained his goblet then refilled it.

"A vague off handed mention yes." Replied Bazin.

"Master?" Queried Mousequeton.

"Mousequeton?" Replied Porthos.

"We must not forget Uzes and Uze'ge. The ones we have mentioned are ones he mentioned and use them to drive home is opinion of the current opposition to Catholicism."

Porthos found a croissant and put the whole thing in with mouth and as he began to chew he drained his goblet as well.

Grimaud served some quiche that he was able to prepare in the pre-dawn hours in the anticipation of his masters' companions arrival, as well as poached pears, and a couple of fowls on the spit.

"The biggest concern is La Rochelle. Has been for quite some time and no doubt he will do what he can to keep control over it and to him there will be no such thing as over fortifying it. It may look formidable but rest assured, like everything else there is a weak spot, hit that a few times and it will crumble like the walls of Jericho." Said Aramis.

"If memory serves, did they not walk around Jericho sounding horns numerous times and with the assistance of God was able to succeed as the walls crumbled." Queried Athos.

"Yes Monsieur Athos your memory has served you well. Even with our faith in God, it will not do us any harm in having supplemental armaments to hasten things." Smiled Bazin.

"Indeed." Said Aramis, in agreement with his valet.

"I have a concern." Said Porthos.

"What is your concern?" Queried Athos.

"Even with the knowledge that our valets have thus provided, how do we know where to begin? We not squander our time chasing after him. Is there a way of knowing where to begin and lo and behold there he is too and beat a hasty retreat and show up at Louis' breakfast table with Rohan in tow? He never lets the dust settle, he is in constant motion and knowing that the crown opposes his thoughts he will move twice as fast and twice as far."

Bazin shook his head.

"Bazin?" Queried Aramis of his valet, "What is it?"

"Monsieur Porthos has a point with his concerns. We were given knowledge as to where he was, made haste to that location and by the time we had arrived, he had long since departed departed. Thankfully we obtained the knowledge as to the locations as to what his plans include. As for actually knowing his whereabouts, it will be a hit or miss situation."

"Must not forget that we heard rumors, his last location is to frequent La Rochelle in regards that it is close to Calais and he wants to escape to England to invite George Villiers to assist him in his endeavors in defending the fort."

"That means we have to see Louis again AND the Cardinal." Observed Aramis, "..and as of yet we still have not seen De Treville."

Athos shuffled his feet in annoyance at the thought of having to have another counsel with Richelieu.

"So much the calling this days ours." Interjected Athos.

"When this is all said and thoroughly done, we will call many days ours." Promised Aramis.

"Perchance. Alas, I think not for there will something more pressing that will need our attention. If not the Huguenots, then surely something. There always will be. Can not have a monarchy without intrigue and deception." Said Porthos.

Slowly empty vessels started to clutter the small table.

Grimaud kept pace and removed them as soon as he was able in addition to accommodate them with wine and what ever else they may have requested.

"Then what do you propose we do?" Queried Athos, to no one in particular.

"Since the hour has struck twelve, I dare say we make use of our appointment and repair to our barrack and prepare him for a chastising he shall not soon forget." Suggested Porthos, "Then, when that is finished our time will be our own."

"Ah, yes. We will see De Treville and relay what we now know shortly thereafter. Seek his advice on how to proceed so that we may end with a positive out come." Suggested Aramis.

"That is why he is called, "captain"." Smiled Porthos.

"Amoung other things." Chuckled Athos.

As their goblets were being refilled, a rap came upon the door, they all turned in the direction of the door to get a glimpse at the visitant as Grimaud opened it.

"Is Monsieur Musketeer present?" Came a query, the voice sounding unfamiliar.

Grimaud nodded slightly and stepped aside and gestured for Athos to come towards him.

"What is it, my good man?" He queried.

Again, Grimaud gestured, this time towards the courier.

Athos stiffened and cautiously approached with curiosity.

"First and foremost, your identity has presented a mystery, please clarify that and whom you represent. Then I will inquire who is it you seek?" Queried Athos.

The young courier replied, "I represent Monsieur Percerin, the court tailor and I am Mateau and Monsieur I am seeking; Messieurs, Porthos, Athos and or Aramis. Am I speaking to one of the three?"

Athos slackened his composer and replied, "Indeed you are. May I inquire why we are a target in your quest?"

"Monsieur Percerin has sent me to to inform you at his request, frequent his establishment either some time this day or on the morrow, for the commissioned work has been completed in compliance with the king and would like you to wear them for the his benefit. You Messieurs will set the standard and use you as a measure as mentioned afore. Monsieur await you."

The courier curtly bowed and departed.

Athos arched his brow as he turned to his companions as he shut the door.

"What say you?" He queried.

"Finish what we began, then the choice is do we see De Treville or Percerin. For we really have not the time to waste, considering we need to find Rohan as soon as possible, for while he is about, he will cause havoc." Suggested Porthos as he finished off the quiche and picked up his goblet and another croissant.

"In all seriousness, the frequenting of Percerin should be rather short and brisk. If the tabards fit and appear well, we should conclude our visit afore the next hours strikes." Suggested Aramis.

"Perchance we ought to conclude this at the barracks, for surely we have dawdled much." Suggested Athos.

Porthos and Athos nodded in agreement and managed to mumble, "Mmhmm".

Arriving at the barracks, they were nigh empty, save for a musketeer or two making use of pallets in a secluded corner by the hearth, for they had just finished their nightly rounds and were exhausted, a third one was propped precariously in a chair.

The three sat at a small table in front of the hearth as their valet set the remains of breakfast afore them, for better part of two hours, waiting.

"What is it with youths these days, do they not know how to uphold honor?" Queried Athos.

"Apparently not." Replied Aramis, "By the by, if the next denizen that comes in, is not the little dolt, I say we continue on to Percerin and finish the day like would have without further interruptions."

The large door opened and closed allowing no one familiar to enter.

"It seems you are going to have go and seek him." Said Porthos.

"I pity him." Said Athos.

"Indeed." Added Aramis.

Grimaud poured the last of the wine into his masters' goblet and he turned to go retrieve more, Athos stopped him.

"My dear valet, hold! I do think we have had our fill on all accounts and it is time we departed to pay our respects to Monsieur Percerin and gather our commissioned vestments."

"My good Athos, truly your valet is quite versed." Said Aramis.

Both Grimaud and Athos genuinely smiled at the compliment.

"Are we deciding then to frequent Monsieur Percerin?" Queried Aramis.

"I do believe so." Replied Porthos as he tried to retrieve what he thought had the last couple of drops of wine from his goblet, then turned it upside down and nary a drop escaped from the empty vessel, "Peste!" He muttered, incoherently.

Aramis had speared a poached pear with his ponaird and tried in vain to eat it without letting any of the sticky, honey laden juices drip down his clean linen shirt.

"*Mon Dieu!* Why is it so difficult to eat a simple fruit as this?"

"Even a French nobleman would have sat it upon a plate and discreetly diced it into more manageable pieces." Said Athos, with a *sotto voc,* with a melancholy smile.

Aramis furrowed his brow and said nothing more and managed to eat it after the advice from his companion.

Finishing off the contents of a tureen or clearing a platter of a roast fowl, was did so with minimal effort and thus when the last morsel was disposed of and the last drop of wine was swallowed, they each gathered their mantles, caps and their sheathed blades that hung suspended comfortably from their baldric.

Porthos wiped the blade of his ponaird on a sleeve to relieve it of any debris and then re-placed in the top of a boot.

"I do believe that having the valets with us will be most beneficial considering De Treville should hear the narrative from them, since ours would only be an interpretation there of. Considering we were not there, we might omit something crucial, by accident and it could be key." Suggested Porthos.

"Can not argue with that reasoning for indeed they saw him and heard him." Agreed Aramis.

"At the present the only thing that bothers me about this whole thing, is we really do not know where he intends to strike first so as we could be waiting for him." Added Athos.

"I realize Aramis, you are skeptical with the conversation we overheard at that secluded tavern, alas it would stand to reason to begin in the south at Montpellier where he left off last year and move north. It is a shame we can not ambush him as he goes through Calais." Said Porthos.

Aramis sighed.

"Truly that would be best, alas we must try to get to him afore he gets to any city or town and lay siege to it. The less destruction the better. Certainly do not want a repeat of the Siege of Negre'plessis, from 1622."

"I should think not." Agreed Athos.

Grimaud proceeded them and held the door and with the last man to step over the threshold, he closed and latched the door.

Rounding a corner, Athos caught sight of a red mantle or tabard, it mattered not.

"Hold!" He called out, without success.

"What gives?" Queried Porthos.

"I do believe that I caught a glimpse of the *petit* dolt. I should catch up to his pitiful self for he is due his chastising."

"Do not bother with him. Cowards create their own demise." Said Porthos, as he was able to get a purchase on the back of Athos' baldric and hold him fast.

As the hefty musketeer released his hold on his companion, after he had Athos promised no further pursuit at the moment, Athos then adjusted himself and his implements.

"By jove!" He uttered.

Strolling through the avenues, rues and quais was congested and made maneuvering about difficult but managed to find themselves at the tailors' establishment.

Allowing themselves in, they found tailor scurrying about, attending to the details of a denizen who had chosen a heavy woolen material for a mantle and doublet to keep her aged husband warm during the colder months of the year, alas she felt that the fabric was out of fashion for it was early spring, and he should reduce the cost.

"Alas Madame, staying warm at any given time of the year is never out of fashion therefore I must beg to differ over the cost and construction of said vestments."

"The cost is exorbitant, therefore I shall consider consulting another tailor." She said trying to sound as if money was no object and she was a part of court.

"So be it Madame, but I assure you, I shall not starve if you do seek services elsewhere. As you can plainly see, I am not in want, for the king certainly keeps my pins and needles from rusting. I might add, other tailors may deplete your purse even further, and more hastily than I, so I say to you, *caveat emptor.*"

"Humph!" She retorted and departed hastily with a timid young handmaiden in tow.

Aramis chuckled at the same moment Porthos queried as to what the tailors' statement meant for he recognized it not.

"It means, my dear companion, "let the buyer beware"."

"What is it gentlemen you are seeking?" Queried the tailor as he set the heavy bolt of woolen fabric aside.

"It is you who seek us." Replied Aramis casually, "We are the three you fitted with tabards about a fortnight ago, the kings musketeers."

"Oh! Quite right Messieurs. Excuse me, I shall get them."

As he departed he called for his assistant, "Mateau, if you please.", then disappeared and they heard a door close.

"More than one station.", Mused Porthos, "A man of many verses."

The three began glancing about to see what else the tailor had to offer.

Porthos accidentally backed into a mannequin and said, "Pardon," and as he turned about, "I did not see you there." Than realizing it was a mannequin, he laughed aloud.

Athos picked a doublet off a stout mannequin and held it up.

It was a simple weave of dark color with a simple blue stitch around the hems.

"Perchance this will do me well." He mused, as he laid it next to the bolt of cloth.

Percerin returned with Mateau and betwixt the two gentlemen, they carried all three and dispersed them.

"This obviously is not measured correctly." Said Aramis as the one he had donned, laid easily against his knees.

Porthos chuckled has he struggled to remove the one that barely covered his sash covered girth.

"Athos, my good man, does yours do well by you?" Queried Aramis.

"I know not, for I have not tried, I am too amused by the likes of you. Clearly you are in error as to whose you possess."

With ease Athos was able to slip it over his head and adjust it afore Percerin assisted Porthos.

"Monsieur I beg of you, do not struggle so. I do not want the seams to give and have to reconstruct the garment. Settle Monsieur, settle." He cautioned.

With the vestment finally removed, Percerin turned the tabard correct side out so that the large golden *fleur de lis* on the front was clearly evident.

Aramis had less issues in removing the one he had donned and replacing it with the correct one.

Once removed he gave it to Porthos and Porthos had the tailor exchanged the one he beheld with his companion.

The hefty musketeer found the exchanged tabard much more to his benefit and with Percerins' expert hands helping adjust it and the large oversized sleeves of his linen shirt beneath, he went to the nearest cheval glass turned this way and that as to get a view of the splendid tabard that was now the standard by which all musketeers were to wear in honor of their king.

When all three stood next to one another, Percerin took a stance as he was ready to pray as he said, "Oh Messieurs! Splendid, simply splendid!"

"Indeed they look magnificent." Said Athos.

"Aie!" Exclaimed Porthos, suddenly.

"Monsieur?" Queried Monsieur Percerin.

"Here!" Replied Porthos as he offered the tailor a hem from the back of his tabard.

Carefully the tailor felt along the hem.

"Here is the source of your discomfort, Monsieur." He said as he removed one of his pins. "My apologies for an oversight. Is there anything else I can do for you gentlemen, eve is as nigh as my supper."

"Forsooth there is." Exclaimed Porthos, "I have taken a liking to this mantle here." Which was a celestial blue, and was large enough and heavy enough to comfortably cover the oversized musketeer, "...And this doublet. The one I have given my valet has been turned so many times that it is thread bare and any subsequent sneeze or cough from him will send it to the planking."

The tailor shook his head as he smiled at the comment.

"Very well Monsieur, collectively it is a double doubloon."

"Send your courier to collect it from the kings' coffers."

Athos boldly added, as he showed the tailor his intended purchase, "This too my good tailor. The king will not miss a few pieces of coinage."

"Do you not think Monsieur de Schomberg would?" Queried Percerin.

"Who is he? Can not say that, that name has has any sounds of familiarity to it." Commented Porthos.

"It should. He is the Superintendent of finances."

"Is it not Richelieu?" Inquired Aramis.

"He too is, as well as the head of the church as he silently oversees many things."

"Submit your request to him and tell him it is a business expense. It is for the business end of being a guard for the king."

The tailor furrowed his brow in disbelief, but said nothing.

"You will submit your request for these tabards, will you not?" Queried Porthos.

"Most definitely." Replied Percerin.

"Then just less noticeable, add these."

XII

Collectively the six men strode casually towards Captain De Treville's chambers for they were in no hurry. No hour glass had been turned to cause them to make haste, so the men found an obscure quay by the mighty Seine River to pause.

Carriages carrying nobility and common denizens alike were traversing towards destinations of choice, be it supper or beyond the city's gate, it mattered not, the impending eve was pleasant enough to make their jaunt enjoyable.

The brazier keep was beginning his rounds as they entered the Musketeer Hotels' courtyard.

Captain De Treville was an admired man, held in high regard by the king as well as his regiment that he orchestrated and the denizens of their fair city.

His passion was seeing to it that the city was safe and secure from any stray threatening marauders, alas found it difficult when the threat came from within the city.

The latest strife, he understood their want for freedom of religion, but could not comprehend how the factions could want for communication. He always found the young king compliant and accommodating.

Alas, at the continuous prompting from his mother, Louis stood a firm stand against Huguenotism for they had taken up arms against him with the intent of doing harm to those that opposed them.

The good captain was just closing the door to his establishment as they happened upon him and taking him completely unawares.

"*Mon Dieu!*" He exclaimed as he recognized them, "I heard you had returned."

"Indeed. Alas good Captain, our presence had been predetermined by Louis and Armand." Said Athos

"Armand?"

Athos grimaced and with clenched jowls, replied, "Richelieu."

De Treville nodded slightly in acknowledgement.

"We have already have spoken to them and we did not wish, no offense please, to speak with you 'til our valets returned. Which they just did, the day afore. We mistakenly thought we had another day or two afore their return."

"What are you about at present?" Queried the Captain.

"To seek you and relay their findings and seek advice as to how we can proceed with a favorable outcome in name of the king and France." Replied Athos.

"Then care to accompany me to the, "Bronze Pig", for it is supper time."

The three immediately agreed, even though, "The Bronze Pig was not their first choice.

"By the by", Commented De Treville, "Your tabards are magnificent. Has the king seen them yet?"

"Ne'.," Replied Aramis, "We just finished with the tailor afore you and we were going to go in search of him after. As it is, it might be on the morrow when we finally see him again."

As they walked, they talked.

"What of Richelieu?" Inquired the Captain.

"What of him?" Queried Porthos.

"He does not like to be kept waiting."

"Indeed he does not, but we did not intentionally delay our valets return. Surely he will understand that." Added Porthos.

"You should hope."

"He sometimes seems to forget, we are the kings' musketeers and not his. We are not Jussac. By the by, how many times has he kept us waiting on those rare occasions that he has summoned us and forgot he did so?" Queried Athos.

"It matters not." Quietly, replied De Treville.

"Ah my dear Captain, indeed it does. For there are times when we are embroiled in something the kings has ordered and his summons comes through. We can not leave Louis hanging by a ribbon. We can not just tie the loose end, do Richelieu's bidding then come back, untie it and complete the task. Louis would not understand that. Sometimes it seems he seems to forget who governs this country." Added Aramis.

"He seems to think he does." Said Athos.

"Or who governs whom." Added Porthos.

"May we inquire as to why you chose this tavern and not our usual?" Queried Porthos, upon seeing the establishment resemble a small chateau rather than a grand sized tavern.

"It is quiet here. I can actually recollect my wits at days end, rather than leave them scattered 'til the next day."

As they entered the entrepreneur lead them to a small chamber behind the hearth. If by design or coincidence, it mattered not for there were two adequate size tables that would comfortably accommodate them all.

"Is anyone else here?" Queried De Treville.

"Ne', my good man, tis just you."

"Just as well. I do have a request, see to it that if anyone requires services this eve, turn them back and I will see to it that you are well compensated."

"Aye Monsieur. What is it Messieurs desire for supper? There is plenty of mirepoix, roasted wild boar, stewed apples, Brie and wine. Bread, yes bread, have plenty. This establishment may be small, alas it is sufficient."

"Very well then, bring it forth."

The tavern keep bowed and as he retreated he closed the door.

The musketeers knew De Treville would like to face who he speaks to, thus they took upon themselves to place the table aside each other so that in an essence they resembled the long tables in the grand hall in the *Palais*.

Their captain then seated himself with his back against the wall so as to see who entered the small chamber and not catch him unawares.

Porthos sat to his right and Aramis to his left. Athos sat with his back to the door amoung the valets. Grimaud sat quietly aside his master and listened.

Once the wine had been poured and the tavern keep retreated to retrieve their supper, closing the door, he took a sip of wine then said, "Dear valets, it certainly is a great relief to have you back. You no doubt seen and heard many things and we must align all the information, have it make sense, then proceed to formulate a solution. We really do need to find Rohan and bring him back so that he may have a conversation with his cousin, the king."

"Dear Captain, we respectfully firmly believe that is not likely to happen. When it is merely mentioned, another town of Catholics goes up in flames." Replied Bazin.

"Praytell, what did you observe while you were away?" Queried De Treville of the two valets that were dubbed their unofficial temporary emissaries.

Bazin glanced at Mousqueton who said, "If you please, begin for you are so well versed with words. More so than I."

"Ah but consider you have a master who is fond of so many words." Said Athos, in agreement with Bazin, "and one would think, so are you."

"I assure you, not as many." Smiled Mousequeton, "Alas you are more versed than I. I will contribute when and if necessary."

The young prelates' valet took a deep breath in preparation for his narrative for he knew it was going to be lengthy and would do his best not to omit anything intentionally.

"Too begin with when we began, we learned that he was very unaware that we were following him as closely as we were for if he knew or even suspected it, he would have been far more elusive."

"Perchance even if he did know, he would have thrown caution to the wind." Said De Treville.

Bazin slightly inclined his head, then continued.

"Castres was his destination for it is from there he mainly sends missives to his officers and subordinates. Once in Castres, we approached him and gave him the impression we are in opposition to the crown, in short of treason, and would assist in his resistance. He then relayed to us his coveted covert munitions depot in Malamort and that is where he was leading a regiment in order to preserve it. It is well preserved I assure you. A very large cavern behind a waterfall in the valley is well stocked and very over looked from the road."

"Is it locateable if given proper instructions?" Queried De Treville.

"It is indeed." Replied Mousequeton, "He showed us certain trees that were marked surrounding the perimeter and the cavern was within."

De Treville nodded, "Any sentries?"

Mousequeton nodded.

"They are the peasants that tend the neighboring crops and herds, with an intricate communication system if a need arises."

"Continue." Gestured De Treville.

"Upon seeing everything in place, we proceeded to Pontivy."

"Is that not where he heralds from?" Queried De Treville, taking a sip from his goblet.

"Indeed yes. He is concerned with three small towns that surrounding it. There is *Maison de Trois Pilliers*. He has regular scheduled counsel with officials."

"The towns of concern?"

"Right. There is Dijon, Lyon and further south Montpellier."

As Bazin was about to sip his wine, the door opened and the tavern keep, laden with a large tray, an assemblage of palatable delights stepped in and set it upon the table, dispersed the plates and bowls and withdrew.

"I so would imagine that he would, if he were clever, bypass Paris." Suggested Athos, as he cut a wedge of Brie and adequate size piece of wild boar.

Bazin continued, "Nimes, Toulouse, Bordeaux, La Rochelle, Nantes, Angers and Rouen."

"Do not forget Calais." Prompted Mousequeton.

"What is so important about Calais?" Queried De Treville, "What is so important there that he is culminating his trek there."

"Not so much as what, to make it his final destination for rather who is on the other side of the channel. Rumour has it, he wants to enlist the aid of George Villiers in taking ultimate control of La Rochelle."

"The Duke Of Buckingham?"

"None other."

"Monsieur Captain?"

"Mousequeton?" Replied De Treville.

"He also plans on recruiting a regiment or two from every stop over so that he has enough so when it comes to the point of laying siege he will not be short handed on men or armaments."

"What is it you would like us to proceed with?" Queried Porthos, after helping himself to the tureen that sat afore him.

"Do you know precisely when and where he is to begin this so call rampage?"

"Unfortunately Monsieur he did not disclose that, therefore it will be a hit and miss affair. I doubt if he will stay in one place for too long, for specifically he will not want to suffer the consequences to his actions if he is actually apprehended." Replied Bazin.

Captain De Treville leaned back in his chair and closed his eyes.

"Such trying times." He sighed, "Allow me a day to deliberate and consult the king and Richelieu as to how they would like us to proceed. Surely a day will not make much of a difference. I am grateful for this knowledge for it should be beneficial."

Leaning forward, "Let us just hope we get to him afore he crosses into England. If he manages that, all will be lost."

"Begging your pardon, good captain, a day will make a difference. Alas I will not undermine your decisions as how to go about this. I would like to query though, what is not to say to instill a blockade to prevent his passage at Calais." Suggested Aramis.

De Treville inclined his head slightly and tugged gently on his goatee, as if in thought.

The tavern keep again allowed himself into the chamber and queried, "Monsieur is there any requests?"

"I think not, for we will finish what we began and depart. All is well."

"Very well, as you wish."

"When would you like a *rendezvous?*" Queried Athos, pouring more wine, from the now empty bottle.

"The day after the morrow. That should give me plenty of time to address the situation with his Majesty. Meet me in the main courtyard at ten, better yet at seven then we can join Richelieu and the king at breakfast. They might have further instruction as to how to handle this."

Murmurs of agreement were heard, for they too wanted to have an end the conflicts Rohan incurs.

Captain de Treville yawned and the others tried in vain not to, thus they had to reconcile their over anxious ponderings with the fact they were thoroughly fatigued.

For they knew not the morrow had to offer other than it will dawn anew.

"What day is this?" Queried the captain, "My days are so over full they spill one into the next without being so obvious, thus my days run together non-stop, unless someone puts their foot in it."

"Dear Captain, it is Tuesday, the twenty-sixth of March." Prompted Aramis.

"Then is it agreed to meet again in the main courtyard of the *Palais royals?* It could be then, we collectively relay all this to Louis and the cardinal again. Erstwhile, I will speak with them and garner their thoughts and formulate a few of my own to relay. 'Til then, I suggest we make adequate use of our chambers, for it is getting quite late."

"I whole heartily agree that we should make use of our beds, stay there til' the sun has well cleared the tops of the trees, and let the rooster contract laryngitis from crowing too much in his efforts to roust us." Replied Porthos, smiling, as he relished his chance at repose and made the most of it when given the opportunity.

Mousequeton pried the last bit of meat from a bone then tossed the bare bone onto the platter afore him that already had a small mound of discarded debris.

Athos dipped the heel of the loaf into wine, then into his mouth, drained his goblet, some may consider it an act discontentment and disparagement alas, Athos had always done it with no malice intent, he turned the goblet upside down.

Aramis used his ponaird to jab at a small leek that was in the mirepoix and chuckled lightly when it glanced off and rolled away.

Bazin and Grimaud finished off a small tureen and they too chuckled at the thoughts of what they possibly could be eating, for it did not looked nor tasted familiar and was far too embarrassed to query of the tavern keep as to the identity of the mystery within the tureen.

De Treville, with the assistance of the table, hoisted himself to regain his feet.

Betwixt being fatigued and satiated, it was an effort to stand.

"My good host," Said De Treville to the tavern keep, "Seek Monsieur Schomberg at the *Palais* for payment, tell him it is in the name of the king that his guards were compensated."

"See,?" Said Porthos, in *sotto voc,* to Athos, "We are not the only ones that are under the recompensations of the king?"

The others too regained their feet and followed their captain as the valets followed their masters.

Once out of doors, the men strolled back towards their apartments and their beds, their conversations were light and held no merit.

As the parted was at their rues, the were each bid a fond, *"Bon Soir",* from their captain and remaining companions 'til all that remained were De Treville and Porthos.

"My dear good captain, do you believe you will be needing an escort this eve?"

"I appreciate the consideration, alas, ne. I do think one would want to toy with a crotchety old man, who has many years and much experience about him. Laying siege 'tis not mere child's play and knowing such to my benefit makes finding a worthy adversary a bit difficult. My apartment is not much more up this rue by the large oak. Surely the shadows are a grave distraction in the middle of the eve and they could conceal much, only a witless wonder would attempt a doltish desperate feat. Mind you, there are plenty, alas, they like everyone needs rest at some point."

Porthos softly chuckled as his captain concluded his soliloquy as he and his captain parted ways as the *Palais Royale* loomed large in the background.

The morn found each man well rested and set for the day, alas with the dawn came inauspicious signs of an impending storm.

When that happened the storm usually arrived afore dinner. Some carried on their wrath for the better part of a day while others went as soon as the arrived.

Unfortunately there were no given signs to show the men what to expect, so the dressed accordingly.

As it was customary, the valets had breakfast prepared and ready for when their masters' rousted themselves and since they had no specific plans orchestrated, they were at ease all day, staying in and making use of their idle time.

At one point, Porthos has contemplated writing a missive to his family and thought better of it when he realized how stale the information would be by the time they got it.

"An heir to the throne could have been born and taken the throne by the time it reached them…I would be better off seeing them. Perchance in the near future a moment might present it self so that I might." He smiled as he mulled over his ponderings.

Athos with Grimauds' assistance set about rearranging what few pieces of furniture he had.

When he finished and was satisfied the way they had done it, it closely resembled what it was afore they began.

Aramis and Bazin had arisen at dawn and attended daily mass at *St. Eustache* and had breakfast with a sojourning bishop, which lasted most of the day.

"What a fond way of wiling away a day." He thought as the expected storm heralded the dinner hour of two.

At one point the bishop as well as other clerics had queried of him why he did not establish more time towards the church and he always replied, "I am only a musketeer 'til an heir to the throne is born."

They in turn would add, "Knowing the state of the young king, that might take years."

To that he would reply, "I know."

Although they regularly sought each others' companionship, on an occasion they each would withdraw and stay within the confines of their apartments and if they were in want of something they would send their valets.

The next day was spent at leisure as well and they did little to venture forth, for the elements did not want to cooperate in allowing them to move about as the would have liked.

Athos reasoned, if the king had sent for them, he had hoped he had the decency to send a carriage, for catching a bothersome cough from a cold damp drizzle of the spring did not appeal to him, nor the others.

When Thursday dawn broke it came with clear skies and a warming sun and very much to their liking.

Bazin had rousted Aramis and once he was dressed and groomed they went to seek Porthos and Mousequeton.

There was a slight delay at Porthos' apartment, for the musketeer could not find one of his gauntlets til he was assisted in putting on his boots.

"Peste! How did that manage to find its way there, of all places?" To which Mousequeton could only shrug in his defense.

Aramis and Porthos had the same thought in wearing their new tabards so the king could see his thoughts become a reality, and they hoped Athos would have the same thought as well.

Grimaud wore one of Athos' recently turned doublets, and since the musketeer covertly knew about the refinements of what life had to offer, the doublet although extensively worn, still looked worthy of any man, Mousequeton was given the doublet his master had acquired and was a splendid fit and Bazin worn a simple linen shirt, a wide red sash and a weighted mantle.

As agreed they met in the courtyard as the Luxembourgs' clock indicated seven, the appointed hour.

"Splendid!" Exclaimed the captain, smiling wryly. "I need not have to turn the hourglass."

"I should think not, a meal is involved." Replied Porthos.

Everyone chuckled heartily and used the heavy oak doors that opened into a large wide passage way that lead to the grand hall.

They were intercepted by a young valet and queried of them if they were expected by the king.

"My young courier, you obviously have met our acquaintance yet. For I am the captain of his guards, Captain De Treville and these are three of his guards. Porthos, Athos and Aramis."

As he mentioned their names, they one by one stepped forward at their introduction and bowed slightly.

"We have access to the king day or night for we at times have information to pass on to him from surreptitious sources and he and only he needs to hear it. If he decides to share the information, so be it that is entirely his choice."

The young courier inclined his head in confusion, "Is there not more than the four of you"? How do you expect to defeat any adversaries when there is only four of you?"

De Treville shook his head.

"Dear young courier, there are many, but these three are the best, for their skills are notably impressively splendid. The king personally chose them. Now if you will, we are to have breakfast with him. This counsel was predetermined a couple days back."

"No one has informed me and I am informed of all."

"Obviously not." Muttered Athos.

The young courier turned to retreat and seek approval from a more experienced member of court.

"Hold young man. May I inquire as to where you intend to go?" Queried De Treville.

"I intended to seek approval from a more experienced member court, for surely they would know who frequents the king or no."

"Young man, you are delaying our appointed counsel. I assure you the king is expecting us therefore let us pass and be on our way."

Porthos took a a large lunging step forward and as a result the young courier immediately recoiled.

De Treville paused and turned, "One thing more…"

"Monsieur?"

"Is he in the grand hall or his own drawing chamber?"

"From what I gather, he is in the drawing room."

"*Merci.* I will send him your regards." He replied, smiling sincerely, as he turned and continued in the direction of the kings' private quarters with his small entourage following close behind.

The recessed chamber door was guarded by two fledgling musketeers.

Neither one of them recognized who stood afore them wanting access to the king.

"Gentlemen, do you not recognize your own captain?" Queried Athos as he stepped towards them.

"Beg your pardon Monsieur, and who might you be?" Queried a fair haired young man, trying to maintain his grip on his musket that was clearly taller than he.

"Again, I query of you, do you not recognize your captain as he stands afore you?"

"It is quite apparent he does not." Replied Aramis, "Forsooth, I should think you need to. Praytell, if you were to go on a campaign and you were instructed to seek Captain De Treville to receive additional information relevant to the occurrences and a timely response was needed, how are you to acknowledge such without a mortal consequence?"

"Recognition of your superior officers is of the utmost importance." Added De Treville, "I can not stress that enough. No matter where you are or what you are assigned to do, you respond to me when summoned, for I am your captain they are making references to."

The young mans' face reddened as the second one shuffled his feet.

"If I may add additional information?" Queried Porthos.

De Treville consented.

"When the captain sends for you and the courier tells you, "the hour glass has been turned,". It means two things. One, an hour glass has been turned and you need to be standing afore him afore the stream of sand ends. If that happens, you will be assigned extra duties beyond your wage and two, by the courier saying it, that means it has come directly from the captain, no chance of a fraudulent summons to send you on a knights errand."

"Now I presume you will recognize me well after this brief encounter, I so request you step aside and let us commence with our given counsel, we have been delayed too many times in the short time of our arrival." Said De Treville, "It so seems these fledglings care not to recognize their officers. This is not the first offense. There has to be a way of remedying this in short of each spending more than a day with me, assisting with errands and counsels I attend. It is not like I have vanished and not seekable for truly I am."

The second fledgling immediately stepped aside, the first, eyeing the captain, cautiously and slowly did the same.

Bompar met them as they entered, muttering something about possibility of sending for the courts' physician, Monsieur Jean Heroard.

He seated them around the warming hearth as the table was being laid in an adjacent room and offered them a goblet of wine.

Athos was going to cordially decline the offer 'til he caught a glimpse of Vitray out of the corner of his eye.

Sighing, he accepted as the other did as well.

The clatter of tableware and chatter of valets, couriers and kitchen staff filled the air with a subtle under current of concern for the king.

"You dolt!", Someone screeched, "Pick it up..Oh no, you can not serve it like that!" Prompted the voice that was unfamiliar to them.

"They will never know the difference." Came a meek reply.

"Alas, I will know the difference!" Was the retorted reply.

Porthos scowled and said nothing.

A door was heard to open and shut and muffled sounds of shuffling of chairs.

"Aye your Majesty." Was heard.

Bompar made his appearance and announced, "His Majesty has requested your presence to join him at breakfast. If you will, follow me."

The men regained their feet and followed the kings' favored valet to the next room.

The king sat in the middle of a large round table and the men one by one sat themselves in no particular order other than De Treville being to his right.

Vitray had been standing behind the vacant one to the left, which was a clue that Athos truly had hoped he mis-read.

He had not mis-read the clue, fore the door opened and closed once again, this time allowing the admittance of Cardinal Richelieu, who promptly occupied the empty seat next to the king.

The king himself, looked pale and drawn and sat upon an overstuffed bolster.

"Does his Majesty request Monsieur le Heroard?" Queried Bompar, with *sotto voc* in the kings' ear.

The king had been toying with a fork, set it across his plate and replied, "At present ne'. I will have possibly another decision to be made at the conclusion of this counsel. As for now, serve what we have, allow Richelieu his moment of glory and send my well wishes to the queen."

When the meal was adequately on their plates and more wine had been poured, Louis glanced in the direction of Richelieu who then regained his feet, looked about, clasped his hands in front of him and bowed his head.

The small assemblage followed his example.

"Oh heaven Father, we humbly come afore you to request your blessings upon our weary sinful souls, we request a blessing over our bountiful meal.

We seek guidance and protection from all evil, be spiritual, physical or mental.

Grant us peace oh merciful one in our trouble times. Amen."

Murmurs of, "Amen" were heard from around the table

Louis then proceeded to pick up a spoon and dipped into the consommé then to his mouth.

He grimaced for which Bompar observed.

"Your Majesty?"

"'Tis bland."

"Shall I send it back to the kitchen?"

"Ne'. There is plenty to eat besides this. There is the cored apple with brandied raisins, the poached pear that I would assume that if made the way I prefer has that new spice that was just acquired, sprinkled on it as well as sugar."

"There is also the mirepoix." Suggested Bompar.

"Perchance I should add that to the consommé." Mused Louis, "Certainly would add and not detract from its integrity being something consumable. Oh bother!, just leave it be."

"As you wish your majesty.", Replied Bompar he retreated a pace or two behind his master and stood silently.

The young king who was seated upon an overstuffed bolster, glanced about to see who was in attendance, his countenance was pale and drawn.

Seemingly pleased it was his favored three with their captain, he sighed with relief that it was not a formal counsel with foreign dignitaries, for that always caused undue grief due to arguing over their policies of unwavering stances concerning their boundaries and alliances with each other and neighboring countries and at times unresolvable issues. Thus more conflicts arose, more policies and sanctions imposed by the host country that beheld their ambassadors and with the contentions, a siege was a certainty.

"Now, if you please, who is responsible for relaying the forth coming information?" He queried, glancing about.

"Your Majesty," Replied De Treville, who was well acquainted with the valets as they often accompanied their Masters on many occasions, political or otherwise, "Messieurs Porthos and Aramis sent forth their valet to secure information concerning the movements of Rohan, in an attempt of apprehending him and defuse the Huguenot strategies."

Louis glanced in the direction of the valets.

"Who is who? I for I am well acquainted with the likes of Messieurs: Porthos, Athos and Aramis."

The three respectfully rose and bowed.

"By the bye," the newly produced tabards look splendid. Again, who is who?" Queried Louis.

"I...I...am Mousequeton." Answered the valet as he regained his feet and bowed reverently in the kings direction.

"Who is your Master?" Queried Louis, as he was assisted in plating a piece of roast quail, with a generous helping of the suggested mirepoix.

"Monsieur Porthos."

"I understand there were two of you?"

"Indeed, Sire." Replied Aramis as he too regained his feet.

The young king arched his brow and slightly inclined his head.

"'Tis none other than my own valet, Bazin."

Bazin slowly rose.

"I assure you gentlemen, I may appear timid, but I promise you that I am anything but. Laying a siege to benefit and further the state of France, is what I do best therefore delay me not in the pursuit of victory." Said Louis, smiling.

"I am, you Majesty the second of the inquery." Replied Bazin.

"Then I query of you, where or whom did you acquire your information from?" Queried the king as he gestured for them to reseat themselves.

"Take ease, I anticipated that your soliloquy might be lengthy."

"Our first encounter with him," Began Bazin, "was in Castres, we gained his confidence and led him to believe that in short of treason, we opposed the crown."

The king furrowed his brow.

"My apologies your Majesty, it was only to gain his confessions and trust, not to mislead us to commit treason. The consequences would have been too dire."

Louis inclined his head again and prompted, "….And?"

"He has a munitions depot at Malamort. It is an extensive cavern filled to capacity with diverted munitions. From there he divides them out to where he deems is most needed. We do know La Rochelle is being fortified as well as cities and towns in the south."

"Are you aware of which order is his intent?"

Bazin shook his head.

"Beg your pardon, your Majesty, I know not."

"How long ago did you part company with your master?"

"Approximately two and half fortnights prior.

The king glanced towards the ornately decorated paneled ceiling, and sighed.

"That gives him a seventeen day advantage." He quietly mused, then added, knowingly the abilities of a horse under the directions of a chevalier, "A horse can easily accomplish twenty leagues in a given day. Bompar! Send for the most recent chart."

Bompar silently withdrew to do as he was bid.

"A lot can happen in seventeen days." Commented De Treville.

"Um hmm." Agreed the king, "…And a lot of retaliation from both oppositions trying to prove who has the upper hand, thus a lot of destruction in their wake. Are you aware of exactly what areas he had on his roster?"

"He disclosed some. The roster is incomplete and now it is left to pure speculation as to what and where he will be known." Replied Bazin, now more at ease in speaking with the king, in spite of what he had heard.

"Did he suspect you were of a greater power?" Inquired Richelieu, who had been sitting silently, observing forming his own conclusions.

"I doubt it." Answered Mousequeton.

The Cardinal leaned forward and tented his fingers.

"Then why did he not disclose the remains of his roster?"

Mousequeton shifted about uneasily in his chair.

"Your Eminence, that I can not tell you. Perchance he become preoccupied with other aspects of his self proclaimed campaign."

"Humph!" Interjected the Cardinal.

"Take ease Richelieu, let them relate what they know. They would have to have had to be perched on a shoulder of his to make sense of the whole scheme." Said Louis, calmly almost sounding condescending.

The Cardinal, growing impatient, let his ire get the best of him and in a raised voice, "Then gentlemen, what was the purpose of your excursion if you can not adequately provide us with enough information to put an end all this Huguenot nonsense?"

"Richelieu! You are far too old for tantrums." Smiled the young king, wryly.

"May I contribute something?" Inquired the Cardinal.

"No." Muttered Athos, as the king echoed his thought.

"Ne' Richelieu, for I know you will want to differ and dicker and try to make it more of an issue than it already is."

Athos managed to hide his countenance behind his freshly replumed cap as he chuckled lightly.

The three covertly suppressed laughing aloud at the kings' comment to his advisor.

Bompar allowed himself the liberty of addressing the king upon his return.

"Your Majesty."

"Let us see what we can surmise from this if anything." Murmured the king, who momentarily pushed his plate and implements aside in order to make room for the chart.

The King silently immersed himself in his reveries as he made calculations, estimates and postulations of possibilities as to the whereabouts of his cousin, Duke Henri le Rohan.

"If he truly is heading south as projected, there is a few possible key areas if he were, that would be to his advantage. Given the seventeen day lead, he might try and take Toulouse and or make a push to Bordeaux. Bordeaux is approximately two hundred sixty five leagues from where I govern."

De Treville took a sip of his wine.

"What is it your Majesty suggests should be our counter strategies?"

"May I add something?" Queried Mousequeton.

"Surely." Replied the king, without glancing up.

"He did comment that he wants to organize a regiment or two of support from each area he conquers. Strength in numbers."

"Confiscate surrendered armaments and use them in his refortifications." Added Bazin.

"As we have mentioned, afore he is refortifying Montebaun, Nimes and Uzes." Concurred Porthos.

The kings' countenance immediately went red with ire.

"So, he has total disregard for the treaty he signed then."

"Must not forget La Rochelle. His belief is if he adds that and uses that as part of his defense, and defeats you there, you will relish all your holds on the Huguenots." Said Aramis.

"My suggestion then, take a day and make haste in assembling five regiments, and you as well gain further munitions, armaments and regiments as you progress south. Follow him. Forsooth, he probably has left a trail easily followed. Keep moving, overtake him. You must prevent him from doing further irreparable damage! At La Rochelle, firmly entrench yourselves. Place yourselves betwixt the sea and them, for then they can not plead with England for assistance, then betwixt them and the state. Surround them. Subdue the heathens. Put the fear of God in them."

"They believe they already have the fear of God." Said Aramis, in *sotto voc.*

"How can they?" Queried Richelieu, quite loudly, "For they are not Catholic!", pounding his fist upon the table for reiteration of his statement.

"Captain! Send regiments and armaments towards La Rochelle, you three take regiments and armaments, run south. Richelieu! Be at ease! Send couriers to the Catholic south. Relay to them to take heed of impending harm and their structural integrity of ways and means could be jeopardized. To the Huguenots' south, send couriers to warn them I will not tolerate their insubordination and retaliation is futile." Said Louis, loudly and with much conviction.

The musketeers whole heartedly approved of the kings' strategy and was eager to set it in motion.

Seeing the young king regain his feet, they as well did too out of reverence to their sovereign.

The king clearly agitated from his own doing, became even more pallid, drained his goblet and requested to adjourn the counsel and with assistance from Bompar, returned to his bed chamber and Monsieur Heroard being summoned.

When the adjacent chambers' door closed, Cardinal Richelieu hastily departed, saying as he went, "Gentlemen, you know the way, see yourselves to the gate."

De Treville re-seated himself and gestured for the others to do the same.

As they complied, an unopened wine bottle was opened hastily and neatly without loosing even a drop of it contents, by Athos.

It made its rounds to all, including the valets for they were the reason they were there, fore they had the necessary information the king sought and utilized.

Even when Richelieu had grave concerns the given information was inadequate, the king, to his merit could and would extrapolate more information and relay it to the necessary office, De Treville.

"Gentlemen, I commend you on the task you have completed and I might add, to the kings' delight."

"Richelieu was not satisfied. Appears that he thought there was more to it than we let on." Added Porthos.

"Peste!" thundered Porthos, "Is that man never happy?"

"One has to wonder." Replied Aramis.

"What say you?" Queried De Treville, "Opinions?"

"If I may?" Began Aramis, "I am almost certain my companions would agree that any and all attempts we try in apprehending him, will be futile."

"...And why do you proclaim thus?"

"We are delayed another day for preparation. Summoning men to assemble, form regiments, gathering the munitions and armaments, lay in supplies for when we are not billeted, and seek current charts."

"My good Aramis, these on going sieges that Rohan lays, if anything has left us prepared. Various areas have already been established and well equipped and by sending additional supplies just reinforces it."

"Montpellier was to be recovered and deactivated, dismantled, if you will, he has chose other."

"I assure you it has not been overlooked."

"Perchance not, but surely to go through such efforts to dismantle once then having to do it again, it is taxing."

"True, but the king will see to it his orders stand." Replied De Treville, eating the remains of a roasted goose.

"My point being good captain, is that since we are delayed a day, we might loose track of him, he could have veered off trek. If he passes through Calais and into England, we will not be able to apprehend him, he will have gained asylum with Buckingham. This is one of the few time England actually finds us tolerable."

"We have to make the effort my dear companion." Said Porthos.

"I agree, alas I do not want to see our effort be all for naught." Added Athos.

"We have to at least make an attempt at his apprehension. Perchance the fates will smile on us and we will be able to catch up to him." Replied De Treville, optimistically.

"It will be a matter of which way the wind blows." Commented Aramis, "The fates are fickle at best."

As they were finishing off the remains of the platters, plates and tureen, loud clatterings, various other sounds of commotions, along with musket shots, and shouts made their way to the chamber in which they sat.

"By Jove!" Exclaimed Porthos as he struggled to swallow a bite of cheese, followed by wine, "It sounds as if the siege has begun here in the city without us."

They all hastily regained their feet and made way to the large expansive courtyard where the preparations were taking place.

"WHAT GIVES?" Shouted De Treville over the din, hoping to catch someone's, anyones' attention.

His first sub-captain approached with a horse by the reins.

"Monsieur le Captain," He Began, "Within the last hour Richelieu sent word to the barracks we were to get organized to march. Alas, chaos ensued for we do not know where we are to march to and why."

"The why is not important at this point. The where is and it is Dijon. We are to pick up the trail that Rohan has left. Hopefully it is clear and concise and the way passable where we can over take him afore too much more damage has been done and apprehend him." Replied De Treville, "Retrieve the armaments and munitions.", then to the three, "Gentlemen, if you please, I see not your horses, get them and return your newly acquired tabards to your apartments, then back here. Have your valets prepare what they can for your departure and rejoin me. Afore you inquire, yes your valets are allowed to joins us, for the two of them know what land marks to go by."

"I heard you say, "Dijon." Why not Malamort and his cavern of munitions and have a regiment dismantle that and disperse it to our favored sights?" Queried Porthos.

The captain pondered a moment then sighed as he replied, "My dear Porthos, although that makes perfect sense the kings' thoughts are to attack his hindmost and flanks if we can and work our way forward. Granted it is not my first choice in maneuvers. I would go directly west 'neath Calais and wait. Alas, can not go against Louis, he would deem it pure treason even it meant a favorable outcome. Then you will know my permanent address and I will more than like be playing chess with Pasquel and Tomas."

Porthos laughed, "You will have to teach them how to play respectfully for they know not. It would take a bit of time."

"Alas, dear Porthos, that is all they have." Chuckled Athos at the image he conjured of them playing chess.

"Apparently Richelieu could not wait and clear Louis' last sentiments afore he ordered this chaos." Muttered Athos, "This is so like him."

"GENTLEMEN!" De Treville called out, the assemblage quieted at his gestures and turned the attentions towards him. He then stood on an elevated edge of a fountain to gain a vantage point over the assembled men.

"I realize this is such a short notice that we gather, alas we need to make the most of it. We will be heading south to Dijon and further. We will be acquiring more munitions and regiments and leaving a partial regiment in place in case he back tracks we will not be caught totally unaware. Granted it will be a arduous trek, we HAVE to apprehend him. The Huguenots are a restless lot and so are we. We need things settled so that we may have peace. Go forth, gather men and armaments, make haste."

The crowd quickly dispersed to go and recruit additional men and armaments to form the needed regiments.

"Captain?" Queried Porthos, as he assisted the captain from his small perch.

"Aye." He replied.

"Would the king be opposed to the idea of splitting the regiments. Part would follow his trail as dictated, bearing south and the other, try and intercept him afore Calais, bear east, north?"

Captain De Treville paused.

"That might be feasible. While they are assembling, you take care of your needs and I will go silently to obtain a short counsel with his and get his opinion. I shall make haste for I know he has fallen ill."

De Treville was able to navigate the multitude and could make his way to the kings' private chambers with minimal effort, for being easily recognized had its merits.

The three parted company momentarily so that their valets could gather what they needed and to leave their new tabards behind unscathed.

"Master?"

"Mousequeton?"

"Would you care for your musket?"

"That cumbersome cannon? I should say not. It is difficult enough to manipulate it while on foot but even more so on horse back. Do need my harquebus and munitions to go with it, ponaird, and tinder box. Oh! My blade, sheath and baldric. The harquebus is much easier to use in tight places and it is more accurate than that cannon they call a musket. What was that man thinking when he constructed the first one, let alone the subsequent ones there after?"

As Porthos was closing his apartments' door behind him, he turned to his valet, "If you please, go to the stables and get my horse and ready her for the trek. Forget not the blacksmith, have him check her shoes. She mimics a mime in an inebriated state. Quite an amusing antic, I admit, alas I am not that gullible."

"Aye, Master." Replied Mousequeton as he hurried off in the direction of the musketeers' stable.

The sun too was making haste, alas for another more beneficial cause.

With a few minutes left afore the brazier keep began his rounds, De Treville reappeared and took his place on his perch once more.

"Gentlemen," he began, "I have just come from the king and he has granted that we split the regiments. Part will go with me to the south to Dijon and continue and the others will bear east to the coast and up the coast in an effort to set up a blockade to cut off Calais. Dig trenches, wide enough and deep enough to drop a horse at full gallop. A lea That ought to put a stop to a good share of his regiments."

He then summoned four of his sub-captains that he considered to be almost as good as his three.

Once they gathered around him as the chaos slowly and methodically turned into order amoung the ranks, he gave his instructions.

"With the utmost discretions, I want you four to head up two regiments a piece, stay to the rear, you will not be readily missed, once you reach Toulouse, break off and aim for Pontivy. That will put you above him and prevent him from reaching La Rochelle. This part will be left up to two regiments, the other two regiments will place themselves betwixt Rouen and Calais, if perchance he slips by them at Pontivy. Spare part of a regiment and draw in behind La Rochelle, cut of access to the sea. Rumour has it, he wants to make a run for England and seek asylum from Buckingham."

"Captain?"

"Monsieur Aramis?" Replied the Captain, with a smile.

"What of us?" He queried in reference to himself and his companions.

"What else? You are coming with me. I need the best defense there is."

XIII

"Monsieur Rohan, we are approximately thirty leagues from Bordeaux, and eve is setting in hastily. The sentries reports that Bordeaux and their activity does not indicate that they are concerned. Indeed they are fortified, but with a little persuasion from a volley or two of cannon shot they will agree to be dismantled and refortified by our standards' coat of arms and not Louis'.

"Ride through and divide out the regiments. Tell the south side, stay and prepare themselves in case we have been followed, although I doubt we are. For we would have been overtaken if we had. The north side will continue with me to La Rochelle, there we will send for reinforcements from Nantes and Angers. Send word on to Calais to receive us, it is there I will cross over the channel to England and seek Monsieur Villiers."

"Is he expecting you?"

"Unfortunately not for everything I have sent a courier out, he never returns and with that it is my assumption that he was apprehended afore he even got through the gates."

"One way t'other, we will get word to him that you are requesting his assistance, for they understand the Huguenots cause for more than the king does." Assured his captain.

"It is Madame de Medicis' doing. She is Catholic and for those that are not, suffer the dire consequences in the name of the church. Henri, Louis' father was originally a Huguenot, 'til it was arranged that he marry Marie, then to appease all, he became Catholic and wrote the Edict of Nantes, which gave tolerances and concessions on our behalf.

That was all fine and good 'til he was assassinated by Ravilliac, an fanatic." Rohan sighed, he too was fatigued by the strife, alas refused to surrender for he was firmly ensconced in his belief and want for freedom.

His captain turned his horse about and was ready to set spurs to its haunches when Rohan said, "Tell the men as they ready for the eve and set up wares for supper, keep the flames in their pits low, so they can not be seen from a distance. The cover of the night will cover the sight of smoke but not the smell of it. Be ever mindful and alert, take rest in shifts. We do not need to be caught unawares."

"Aye, Monsieur, all will not be for naught." He replied as he departed.

Rohan in the twilight, gestured for his officials and sub-captains to follow him, along with a multitude of brave couriers, who to their benefit was naïve about the risks they were to undertake in relaying their missives to other parts of the regiments, and valets who were employed to prepare his meals and take care of his vestments and his belongings.

His intent was to settle his spurs for the night approximately a half a league ahead acting as a vanguard, to gain a vantage point and knowledge of what lay ahead so that he could adequately prepare himself and his regiments.

As dawn approached, he rose early, tended to his horse himself and rode silently along a flank and a bit beyond in the rear to make sure the regiments were safe and he had not been followed.

Although he did besiege Dijon, Lyons, and refortified Montpellier and Nimes again he readily guessed by now, the king had heard somehow of the exploits and set his regiments in pursuit.

Not seeing nor hearing of any evidence of approaching adversaries, he released his tight grip on his horses' flanks with his thighs, for they ached with the arduous preparations of possible sieges and his need to stay upright in his saddle.

Glancing towards the east, very slight slivers of the sun, began to herald the morn, but looked a bit bit odd to Rohan.

He then realized that those kind of indications normally a storm would blow in at some point and at this point seeking shelter in an establishment was something he could not provide his regiments with, for they were at least thirty leagues away from any town or city. "Perchance", he silently reasoned, "there is a peasant about with a stable, but that would not accommodate the whole of us."

He turned to come up the the other flank when he saw one of his men, huddled close to the fire, knees drawn close to his chest and a harcabus aside him.

At first glance, he thought the man to be resting, alas as he drew closer he could hear him weeping.

Removing himself from his saddle, he cautiously came upon him.

The man instinctively reached hastily for his harcabus, and clumsily fumbled with the flintlock with one hand and his tinder box with the other.

"Stop, or I will set the fuse." He said.

"Take ease, take ease, I mean you no harm I assure you, for I am Rohan. May I inquire what causes you such grief?"

The man, as more light illuminated them with the morn, it became more evident he was a mere boy.

"I..I..I do not want to die this way." He replied, trying in vain to control his sobs.

"What way?" Queried Rohan.

"In a siege."

"We are not in a siege."

"Not yet."

"If you felt this way, then why did you join one of my regiments?"

"Mother thought this was a way to bring honor to our family."

"There are other ways to obtain honor."

"Alas Mother thinks the very best way is defending our belief in the Huguenot cause."

"Do you want to return to your family?" Quietly queried Rohan as he crouched next to the boy, "I will not think any less of you if you did."

"Mother will. I will be disgraced."

"There are far worse things then being considered a disgrace."

The young man turned to face Rohan, searching for a more complete answer to the statement.

Rohan took a deep breath and said, "To be part of court, the kings' most favored, nothing could harm you, the king protected your every movement and every word. You could do no wrong."

"What happened to that?" Inquired the young man, with a keen interest in the outcome.

"Too many advisors had access to call counsel, once in counsel, they proceeded to fill his heart and mind with poison to the point he turned deaf and blind to his favored and one way t'other they either went away on their own accord or was escorted by new favored. Either way, pure disgrace, never to be trusted again. That is why I so can not swear my whole alliance to the king nor to our cause for they still in part are very dear to me and I do not want to deny either, or."

The young man wiped his cheeks with the back of a dirty hand for the trek towards Calais was unaccommodating and demanding both physically and mentally.

"There was a man named Concini, it was Her Majestys' Madame de Medicis' favorite, too many people had access as I mentioned and as a result saw to it that he was eliminated and he Louis, exiled his own mother. Court favor indeed! 'Tis a disgrace being queen mother and exiled by your minor child the king." Rohan halted abruptly and changed the subject to lighten the somberness of the conversation.

"Would you like to join me at the front?"

"With all due respect Monsieur, I decline. Others are probably far more worthy of that station than I."

"So be it." Replied Rohan as he stood, then regained his saddle and continued up the flank.

As he did so, the young man contemplated which direction his life should take.

Follow Rohan, which could ultimately result in death and gain the honor his mother so desperately wanted for her family so that they might be recognized, again, possibly follow Rohan to victory and surely he would gain the honor he desired, fall back and take a detour home with the assumption he had his moment of glory and honor AND he might add, still alive, unscathed.

Satisfied that repercussions from his last siege against Lyon and his continued efforts to refortify Montpellier were not forth coming, he decided to give his regiments a slight reprieve and lay over 'til the next eve and under the cover of eve they would continue onto Bordeaux.

As he entered his tented shelter, it shuddered with the breeze that had increased with the impending storm.

He sheltered his eyes from the bright sunlight and scanned the east horizon.

He just barely was able to glimpse the dark clouds that were gathering and pushing their ways towards himself and his regiments.

He instructed his valets to hastily assemble his breakfast for knowing with the rain it will soak everything and make it nigh impossible to set a fire.

Others in his encampment perceived the same situation and proceeded to follow their leaders example and they too hastily laid fires and on to breakfast.

The best they could do was pray the storm would move on around them. If not they unfortunately they too would be soaked and to their disadvantage, it still was early spring and although the sun would be welcome, it would not radiate enough heat as the summer would, to dry them and their vestments in a short length of time.

Knowing this, he already had to acknowledge that sickness would follow. He said a silent prayer in hopes it would not run rampant through his regiments and reduce their numbers.

In his time, he had seen various sicknesses carry off whole towns, regiments and a share of court, he suddenly shuddered.

Physicians with limited knowledge concerning such could do little to prevent or cure for that matter what ailed a denizen.

Many sought herbal remedies with limited degree of success, blood letting was a method of choice for many ailments, while other other methods were considered impractical and were used as a last resource.

As he finished his breakfast, he heard the distant rumblings of thunder.

He then preoccupied his time perusing his charts in preparation of taking Bordeaux.

Situated on the Gironde River, it could be used a line of defense and let him enter the city undetected til it was too late to raise arms and munition in opposition.

On its banks, sat castles and fortresses of old and thus he assumed their structural integrity would be compromised through age and neglect.

He thought it best since he had adequate numbers, they would take rue by rue. A direct assault on older structures still amused him and watching them crumble under his pressure delighted him and he knew it would infuriate his cousin and thus a new treaty would be drawn in his favor.

Hefting the armaments into position would be daunting, alas done with precision would mean an assured victory.

He had instructed his regiments prior, to spare no one, for the king had not spared any of his fellow Huguenots.

He so wanted Louis to agree to his opinion that any and all should have the freedom to worship as they chose as his father had acknowledged, so why would he not also follow what what set afore.

Louis had the freedom to pick and choose his path, including his religion, but all too often his advisors counsel led him into false securities that jeopardized the value of France, and his popularity with the denizens faltered 'til the next volley of debates, then why is it the common denizen had not the same consideration and that of choice.

As he paused in his ponderings, the storm blew in with ferocity of a cleric exorcising a demon from the processed.

The thunder sounded as cannons and munitions in a siege of an unfortunate city as the lightening lit the heavens with streaks of hazy illuminations, creating silhouettes of uncertainties.

His tenting wavered in the gales as he sat at his small secretary and his valet paced nervously in the small confines and chaffed his hands as he did so.

"If you will, Monsieur, please sit aside me and take ease. Your pacing is creating havoc within my soul."

The young man sat momentarily, but all too soon regained his feet and resumed his pacing.

Rohan took a deep breath and held it momentarily and slowly released it.

"Young man, I suggest you sit. Pacing will not lessen nor increase the volume of the storm. It will abate I assure you, therefore be it at ease. Set your ponderings in another direction, and erstwhile what say you peruse these charts with me and offer suggestions as you have so often afore. Your promptings are sound."

The young man sat next to Rohan and ran his fingers over the chart as he followed the contours of the river.

"Here Monsieur Rohan, around this bend, the quays are far in betwixt and the banks are steep, t'would be best to enter the city here." He said as he pointed to a small indentation in the river, then continued, "here it is quite shallow which will make it easy to disembark the small vessels that we can commandeer from our standings."

He chaffed his hands roughly as a crashed of thunder sounded very nigh.

"As you want my suggestions,". He stammered with fear, "I suggest that you send the heavy munitions ahead to set the way and their aim has to bear height to gain distance, alas low enough to cause structural integrity that would cause grave concern to the occupants."

"What say you of the chevaliers?" Queried Rohan.

"Flank the city and come in from behind and set the archers informations to move forward afront of the chevaliers then have them step aside. Grenadiers lob what they have towards the arrow slits of the garrisons. The ones with muskets and harquebuses will follow them for they need the protection from the horses fore being of foot borne."

"Every so often move the cannons forward to gain additional vantage points and never loose sight of the adversaries." Suggested Rohan.

"Precisely." Replied the young man.

"If I did not know any different, I would think you were an appointed a captain a sub- captain at the very least."

The young mans' countenance reddened with embarrassment at the compliment.

"How is it you know these things?" Queried Rohan.

"Begging your pardon Monsieur, a lot of listening. I was considered a mute as a child, chose not to speak and when I did, I was told it was either irrelevant and out of context. Always being told that by those about me, did little to persuade me to be ambitious, so I chose to listen and observe things out of the ordinary."

"You have observed things very well."

The young man bowed slightly.

Once again, thunder sounded. This time from a distance. Indicating the storm was hastily moving away, alas the fact remained, a good share of his regiment would be soaked and the best they could do is build up their fires and cope with the risks involved.

As the storm abated, Rohans' sub-captains filtered in to seek his advice as to how he chose to proceed.

"As I take it," He began, "the men are probably very wet and irritated, so under the circumstances, have them build up their fires..."

"What of the smoke? Do you not think it will be a beckoning? The wind is not in our favor", Queried one officer, quite taken aback by the mere suggestion of possible disclosure.

Rohan chose to ignore the inquiries and continued.

"Have them stand close to the warmth and occasionally turn about in the attempt at drying their vestments and themselves. Hopefully this will deter any sickness that threatens a cold and wet regiment. Ne' I think not it will be a beckoning."

"One column of smoke surely could be considered a hunter or a lonely chateau, alas there is a multitude that could very well indicate to an experienced sentry that they belong to regiments."

Rohan shook his head.

"Those are risk we will have to take. It is dinner time, thus while they re drying off, they can prepare what they have or pilfer the forest for a hare or two. Make haste, lest you waste."

He then relayed the strategies his young valet had. No murmurs of discontent were heard, Rohan then deducted they were all in agreement.

Most time a few of the sub-captains would disagree and try and persuade Rohan to see their perspective and they would have the regiment follow their orders in retaliation when he refused thus chaos would erupt and they would be worse off if they had heed his words.

The sub-captains dispersed to spread the instructions and have them prepare themselves for a cool if not a cold eve.

Numerous men, quickly made for the forest to collect up wood while others went in search of their dinner and supper.

A small stream coincidently ran through the wooded canopy, thus provided relief from their thirst, filled the kettles to prepare whatever they managed to garner from the abundantly supplied forest.

The archers were selected to silently search for deer and use their bows for the crack from a harquebus would frightened what was there and they would flee, making dinner and supper a memory past.

Others still tried to dry and warm themselves from what was left of their fires, 'til more wood was added.

As the sub-captains rode through the regiments they relayed the strategies that were formulated and were to be enforced as soon as the conditions were right.

Each of the regiments had specialties, be it grenadiers, archers with long bows, archers with short bows, men with swords for when it became face to face, more of a duel rather than combat, men with crossbows for more precision and force, men who used harquebuses, heavier artillery as with cannons and catapults, poniards and pistols and even the inaccurate, cumbersome muskets.

Many queried when they would be on the move again and the reply came, "As soon as Rohan deems it so."

As darkness enfolded them, still huddled around their fires, began coughing with the hopes of it being nothing serious.

Most knew if the cough lasted more than three days, it stood a good chance of settling in their lungs and causing pleurisy a post effect of pneumonia.

The ones who had severe coughs would have to take refuge by returning to either Castes or Montpellier to find rest and relief from the ailment.

The sub-captains made their last appearance and inquired if there was any additional information forthcoming.

"Just that, I want a pause afore we proceed. That will be on the morrows' eve when the moon is low with horizon. I want to catch them totally unaware and not give them a chance to strategize and out maneuver us. By delaying, it will prove out if anyone has fallen with sickness. Never does any good to be damp and cold. Not a healthy combination, I dare say. I know, some have counterpanes, alas they are probably threadbare by now due to the numerous campaigns they have endured, and those that do not have counterpanes, have heavy woolen mantles made for campaigns and such. It may not be much, but it something. Surely there needs to be a better way to equip our regiments and not be overly burdened with unnecessary implements and thus having to forsake their armaments." He shook his head, "The life of a soldier is never easy. Have away with you, let them know of the intent of the morrows eve. As for now, *bon soir.*"

Various murmured responses were heard as they receded into the darkness that once again enfolded them.

The Huguenot leader found himself awake while the sun still slumbered as he imagined he would like to be as well.

Out of a pure repetitious habit, he dressed in the darkness, not needing a cheval nor valet, he was able to get all the ties, bows and hooks in the right spot.

His young valet heard his stirrings and hastily rose.

"Would Monsieur Rohan care for breakfast?

"I would indeed. Alas first I would like my horse taken care of and brought to me. Tacked. When I return, breakfast. Have you anything to prepare?"

"Forsooth Monsieur. A couple of men were fortunate enough to bring down a nice sized buck last eve, and shared what they had and with the some of the root vegetables that were stowed, I was able to assemble a stew. That Monsieur is what you dined on last eve. There were remains and what was your supper *voila* it is now your breakfast."

Rohan smiled slightly.

Although the meal was tasty, it would have been more palatable if it was not repeated so soon.

Alas, he was hungry, he conceded.

While waiting for his valet attend to his horse then bring him, he stood in front of his canopy, straining his eyes to see how his regiments were faring.

From what he could see were bumps on the ground that resembled fallen timbers strewn about by a force of nature, dotted by smoldering hot embers from spent fires.

His young valet brought him his horse, and with little effort, seated himself in the saddle.

Abruptly turning the horse about, he lightly touched the horses haunches with his spurs and the horse obeyed by gently and rhythmically cantering.

The smell of wood burning greeted him as well as various spitted spoils of a hunt the day afore.

The men shared and traded what they had to help it be more appeasing, alas their thoughts invariably turned towards their homes and what was familiar.

The fires were being urged to renew the little life they had into something more glorious than almost stagnant embers.

The men still huddled close to their fires and each other for warmth for the morn brought a renewed hope and unfortunately, dampness and cold.

It saddened Rohan upon hearing the coughs the damp and cold had caused. He knew when he addressed his sub-captains, he would require of them to assemble those that had fallen ill, be recruited and return them to Montpellier, for he decided it was closer than Castres.

The sentries he came upon, reported the night was calm and heard nothing but a screech owl once or twice, alas nothing that would cause concern.

At the outer perimeter of the encampment he found his sub-captains rallying the regiments and manipulating the heavier armaments, thus assembled readied to be moved forward and put in place.

"How did your men of armaments fare the storm and subsequent cold?" Queried Rohan, who was a generous man and had genuine concern for his mens' well being.

"At first they were miserable fore the cold was taken to their cores, alas once their fires had flared and emitted the warmth they were seeking, they dried out and warmed up, then with a hearty meal they created last eve and this morn, they have been restored."

"Splendid! Give them the benefit of an hour to gather up and proceed towards Bordeaux, when you get within a third of a league, arm and dress the cannons and ready the catapults to aim at the towers. Give the cannons enough of an adjustment to hit the lowers side of a wall. Enough to create a weak spots. It will be dawn in a couple of hours and by the time daylight arrives, we should be ready to take aim on the morrow after dark. Just pray no one happens by to convey our presence to someone of worth."

"Very well, Monsieur."

"I tell you this now, so I will not have to repeat myself on the morrow and we can keep moving forward."

"Yes, Monsieur Rohan."

Rohan again turned his horse and cantered towards another regiments to convey the formations he wanted them to utilize and then moved on to the other regiments. He additionally informed them to organize a regiment of the sick and decide amongst themselves as sub-captains which two will lead them in returning to Montpellier

As he moved closer to his canopy, he heard the creaking of the wheels that bore the heavy weight of the cannons and catapults, as they began to move forward afront of all regiments, to be strategically placed behind the city of Bordeaux as it populated the rivers' edge at a comfortable distance.

The distance the cannons and catapults could still keep the necessary gap that would allow them to close it under the cover of eve the following day, which was still many hours away. Then the following hours would allow the regiments to add and make preparations for the impending assault.

Rohan unseated himself and stood glancing about all again and sighed.

He too agreed that all sieges even if they were waged to prove out an opinion, it was still a waste.

His young valet appeared and took his horses' reins and led him to a small but adequate tree and tethered him, and allowed him enough length to graze if he chose.

The horse chose an option of his own and dozed.

Rohan followed the valet into the canopy and was grateful breakfast had been prepared for he was quite hungry at the early hour and sat down.

He noticed other places had been set and inquired after them and his valet simply replied, "Your sub-captains come and go, and the ones that come, no doubt are hungry as well, therefore a well fed officer will make sound decisions."

True to his word, sub-captains came and went and those that lingered longer were invited to sit and eat and discuss the matters at hand.

He also sent out sentries to act as sojourners to frequent the city to get a feel of it and observe the current activities and pay close mind for any underlying currents if there were any. If so, where did they begin and where did they end.

One young sub-captain with a fit of nervous anxiety shook so bad, he found difficulty in eating or drinking an Rohan commenting, "I did not think stewed apples could be made into a fashion statement, alas I admit, I was mistaken. Ah! Alas, be it at ease. When everyone follows my instructions, everything will fall into place and it will well over afore it even begins." Rohan smiled, "It will be nothing but a small skirmish."

"What happens if the wind blows the other way and takes our favor with it?" Queried the nervous young man, as his sheathed swords, rhythmically hit his spurs and jingled lightly.

"I will see to it that it blows constantly in our favor." Rohan replied, smiling.

The young man was so nervous that he had difficulty conveying his thoughts and queries to Rohan.

"Take ease. All will be well."

The young man regained his feet, bowed reverently to his superior officer, touched the brim of his cap and retreated.

As the day progressed, more sub-captains and other other officers filtered in and sat awhile as well. The last two sub-captains that made their appearance were the ones that it was decided it would be they who were to lead the newly formed regiment of the sick back to Montpellier

At one point, Rohan regained his feet and went out of his canopy to lean against a tree that was just beginning to get its seasonal foliage.

A sub-captain of heft galloped up hard and fast and halted so abruptly that it stirred up the dry dust afore Rohan, that encased him, causing him to cough and sputter as he tried to wave it away.

"Is there many fallen ill?" Queried Rohan.

"Regrettably Monsieur, yes."

Rohan clenched his jowls and fists, then queried, "How many?"

"Approximately twelve dozen, too may." Came the reply.

"Are they able to go on their own accord?"

"I do believe so. Their cough is not debilitating. Although there are some that unfortunately will not see the morns' light. The regiments' surgeons' resources are limited if not useless in this matter."

"How many are that ill?"

"Approximately three dozens."

"Would they last long enough to see the end of the siege and aid for what ails them?"

"The cold has settled deep in their chest and as painful and frequent as their coughs are, it is all for naught. Some have developed a paroxysm of ague. Yes we tried to keep them warm to fend off the chill. Futile, simply futile." The Chevalier said, shaking his head in disbelief. "No disrespect Monsieur, but there is no telling how long the siege will be."

"True enough." Then added, "Are they ready to depart?" Queried Rohan.

"I do believe so."

Rohan shielded his eyes and glanced toward the sun to get his bearings and see if there were any tell tale signs of what the elements beheld.

"You still have at least six hours of daylight, so I suggest that you make the most of it."

"Aye, Monsieur." He replied as he suddenly turned the horse so hard that it nearly sat on its haunches, as he took off in full gallop.

"What a sure way to degrade a good horse." Thought Rohan, shaking his head sadly, for he had a deep affection, appreciation and knowledge of horses.

As if the mere mention of movement, the carts of cannon shot began creakily rolling by as well as carts of kegged power and other armaments.

When he deducted it was nearing the hour of one, smoke from their fires had increased as an indicator his men thought the same as it was dinner time.

His valet managed to slip by him, renewed their fire and began his preparations for with their dinner and those that might happen by.

As he sat down with a goblet of mulled wine, a sentry from the vanguard enter and requested permission to speak.

"Granted." Replied Rohan, who gestured impatiently, for he wanted to begin eating the small hare someone had procured.

"The city is at ease, seems they do not fear either faction, Huguenot nor Catholic, although they do abide by the kings issued edicts. They have garrisons on both sides of the Gironde River. The citadel with its turrets mainly face the river, it is what they consider their weak spot. Their quays and piers are active with trade and fear little. There walls do not have the height nor thickness as Montpellier and Montebaun. Breech-able? With persistence, yes. The outer parameters of the city are dotted with cannons, that are well stocked, alas unmanned. every fifty paces or so. Little evidence of formed regiments. The Cailhau Gate, if stormed simultaneously with the quays and the parameters of the city and move inward and cut off their means of escape, both ends of the river, they will have no choice but to surrender."

Rohan nodded as he listened to the narrative.

"Then we will stay to our first strategy. Under the cover of darkness, no torches included, we will move into place. As of now, the heavier artillery is afore us, getting within reach and when eves' darkness encloses all, they will move into place, save the quays. Just afore dawn then the quays will be included. The regiments will have already fallen into place and wait for their given instructions." Added Rohan, sipping his wine and jabbed at a piece of vegetable with his fork. It rolled away. "Corbleu!" He muttered. His second attempt was successful as he put it in his mouth.

"Return to your regiment, obtain dinner and be at ease til this eve, it is then we will move forward."

"Do you not fear for the well being of the horses?" Queried the sentry, with his brow furrowed in distress.

"This road appears well travelled and there will be moonlight, all will be right. We just need to be within range by daylight. Do they too have sentries?"

"They do indeed. Alas they do not see a need to send them out beyond a league. They do not feel threatened. They believe God will have mercy on them and be spared any strife."

Rohan chuckled, "They do not know what strife is. Strife comes with a name and that is Duc Henri de Rohan."

Within the hour, as the sun was hovering over the horizon, some of the men went back into the wooded area to find means of filling their kettles.

With a periodic crack of a harquebus, or the swoosh of a cross bows' arrow, hopefully meant success.

The dormant fires were brought back to life as kettles were filled and began to cook its contents.

Some of the men who were considered experts, were able to add a couple of quail, partridge, and or pheasant to the kettle, thus adding a variety rather than the norm of heavily salted preservation of the meats of pork, beef and fish with an occasional lamb.

The vegetables were from seasons' end the year afore, somewhat shriveled but still edible, were added to their boiled concoctions.

The men were permitted to choose a handful of various ones from a cart that followed the regiments encampments, thus allowing the men something to eat. How they were prepared, was at their own discretion.

"Anything is better than nothing. There is no telling when or if their next meal would be forthcoming or no, better make the best of what we have now.", was their theory, thus what ever they had available, they added.

Bread and cheese were omitted, for stale bread would not be tolerated nor eaten and would be tossed by the wayside, thus benefitting no one.

As for the cheese, what good is the cheese without the bread?

After they were encapsulated by the darkness, Rohan had his young valet, who seemed quite versed in many attributes use his astronomical nocturnal calculating instruments to give the approximately time.

"Monsieur Rohan?"

Rohan glanced towards the young man.

"It is approximately nine o'clock."

"Splendid. That will give me time to ride through the regiments and formations and inform them we will be on the move within the hour. If you please, tack and bring me my horse and a torch to light my way so as not to tread on anyone. A hoof mark is not considered a fashion statement."

Once in the saddle and received a torch, he set the horse to a gated trot and set out to inform his troops that they need to begin preparing to be on the move.

When he reached the rear of the encampment, he cautiously approached the sentries.

The last thing he needed, he pondered was not to feel the sting of a musket ball as it hit betwixt his eyes.

"Salut gentlemen!" He said as he hailed them.

"Put your pistol aside," He heard someone say, "It is Monsieur Rohan, he means you no harm."

Rohan decided to stay in his saddle, in spite of his horses' nervous fidgeting and not standing still.

"I am here to inform you, to gather your things, extinguish your fires, and be on the ready. By the by, what say you? Have you observed anything approaching? Corbleu! Stand still, will you? You are making things rather difficult." He said to the horse, as it continued its movements. "You must be sensing something I am not. Alas, allow these men to answer my query, have you observed anything approaching or anything out of the ordinary?" He queried again.

"Monsieur, we ride out two leagues daily in all directions. At this time we have observed nothing out of the ordinary. No smoke from fires, no sounds out of the ordinary, only birds calling out to one another and their creative responses."

Rohan sighed.

"Monsieur?"

"Just relieved to know I wont have to divide my forces. All can be devoted to the frontal assault. Division of forces causes a weakness and I can not afford to loose men. Lost enough in their return to Montpellier with sickness."

"Aye Monsieur." Replied the sentry, "I will get them moving."

"Splendid! We should all be in place by morn, wait for to put on the eves' mantle of darkness and move everyone and everything within range, then afore the sun makes its appearance, we will have made ours."

By the time Rohan returned to his encampment, his valet had disassembled his canopy and stowed it with other implements that accompanied it. The fire had been extinguished and was now nothing more then a smoldering pile of ash and he was ready to begin moving forward.

The men seeing the torch Rohan carried raised higher and moving away was their indication to begin the trek.

Rohan forbade anyone other than himself to carry a torch for he did not want to cause excessive concern with the common man along the way and they in turn would alert Bordeaux and the out lying communities of the impending danger.

If the men were allowed to carry such, their position as well as an estimate of their numbered regiments could be surmised and create chaos.

The less seen the better.

The regiments were making attempts at being light hearted alas it was not easy for the trek ahead was arduous.

As Rohan had projected, they were covertly within reach of their target the following eve.

He instructed them not to start any fires, for they would easily be detected since they were so close. He apologized for they had to endure a cold meal, a least favored task, alas soon enough things would return to what was familiar, have patience, perfection could not be obtained in haste.

They silently crept forward til' they saw the tops of the turrets standards, to give their cannons and catapults more of an advantage of a more accurate strike.

Rohan, who was refilling his goblet from the remainders of a bottle when a couriers' arrival was announced by his now indispensable young valet.

The courier, bowed low, as he did so, he rested his hands on his knees afore he straightened his posture.

"Monsieur?"

The courier straightened as he retrieved a sealed missive from with his tightly fitted doublet and handed it to the Duc.

Rohan immediately recognized the seal as his brothers' and hastily relieved the seal of his hold with his ponaird, and read:

"My dear brother and brother of arms, I fear by the time

This reaches you, you will either have struck your intentions,

Or about to. Either way, I have been severely delayed and Will not reach you in time to do you any benefit.

Betwixt and Pontivy and La Rochelle is heavily patrolled as they wait for your anticipated arrival.

I look forward to our rendezvous in Calais.

I shall not dictate a set date for this rendezvous for fear of being intercepted by Louis, for he has taken an active interest in our activities and would like nothing better than to put a halt to them.

In closing, keep your flanks tight and your rear guards even Tighter. Fan out your vanguard.

Best regards, your brother,
Benjamin de Rohan
Seigneur de Soubise.

The Duc drained his goblet and turned to the courier.

"No reply, except "Calais it is.""

Rohan clenched his fist and in so doing, crumpled the missive, that was written on fragile piece of parchment.

"We will just have to make the best of it." Then to his valet, "Have the officers representing the cannons and catapults continue forward, 'til they can see the more of the turrets and the tops of the nearest wall. I will set off a cannon as a means of commencing our little skirmish."

"Is there not Huguenots within the walls?" Queried the young valet.

"That maybe so, but enough Catholics also pass through there to justify our means." Rohan shrugged.

"I would think the sentries gave them ample notice of our impending intent. We have a by word to acknowledge our faith and thus when spoken, I hope they would flee to escape harm. Now if you will, my horse."

Rohan hastily took to his saddle and made haste to the formatted cannon line.

"Line them up and load them." he yelled, then "Set the fuses."

A cannon master, with his tinder box, lit a torch for Rohan and handed it to him.

"READY? AIM! FIRE!" He yelled as he touched the fuse and as the spark disappeared, a loud thunderous boom was heard, followed by the other cannons.

Men poured forth with grappling hooks and within a short time the cannon shots were answered by their adversaries cannon in return volley.

The walls of the citadel were breached and massive holes caused by catapults and cannon alike, allowed more men with muskets, pistols and harquebuses followed by the archers to enter the city and begin their own agenda.

The piers and quays were blocked and allowed no one to pass and at the same time as part of the scheme, Cailhau Gate was stormed and opened, save if you were an acknowledged Huguenot you were spared.

The archers began their assault with accuracy, but to Rohan's dismay, Bordeaux's archers were perched along a high wall where their arrows found their mark skillfully placed.

Even when the air filled with smoke, cannon and catapult shot, raining arrows and musket shot, Rohan still took to his horse to ride up and down the line occasionally halting to observe the activity through his newly acquired spyglass.

As the Duc rode up and down his lines of formation, musket balls, with a dull thud hit the hard ground around him narrowly missing his horses' feet, causing the animal to shy one way t'other in avoidance of being struck.

Amoung the thunderous response from the volleying cannons, screaming muskets, were shrieking horses, who were in pain from shattered knees and haunches, as a marksman tried to unseat its rider to make their confrontation with their adversary less complicated.

For better part of the week he watched his men proceed and make progress only to on the following day sag, lag and fall back.

"I thought my sentries said they were at ease and unsuspecting." He complained to his valet, who remained silent.

As the siege wore on, the battle field became littered with corpses, those that had been mortally wounded and those that still needed a camp surgeons attention. Quite a few were confused and witless, those lying prone with fatigue and sadly, many horses whose only fault, they carried a rider into the siege.

A fortnight ended as it found Rohan pale and drawn, thoroughly fatigued and vexed.

In the few times he had to draw his blade in defense, he was the victor and could rest for a short time afore he was summoned to another sector.

Sitting his canopy, during the third fortnight, a courier was announced and was allowed admittance.

The fairly stout soldier, quite disheveled, stood afore him.

The Duc glanced up at him as he set his fork and spoon across his plate.

"My captain, has sent me to request a cease fire in observance of the many fallen. By his estimations you now lack the force to continue and if you do continue, you surely will be annihilated and your return to whence you came will be minimal. By surrendering, Louis will see to it you are treated with fairness and kindness."

"I would expect that of a cousin, yes. Alas I will not commit to surrender. If anything, your attempts to subdue us will prove all for naught. My response, many more of yours will fall as we shall be the victors. Go now as I spare you afore I have the chance to unsheathe my blade."

The soldier, turned and hastily withdrew.

Late one eve or early morn, depends on who you spoke to, Rohan slouched in an uncomfortable chair, with his grizzled unshaven chin, resting on his heaving chest, opened his eyes and glanced about.

His canopy was engulfed in total darkness, for the lantroon had long spent its wick and what little oil it had, a few hours back, he listened.

There was total silence. Not even the usual night sounds one would hear in the spring on warm gentle nights.

As he hefted himself out of his chair, he knocked over his goblet.

"Corbleu, I so hope there was nothing in it. What a waste if t'were not."

He stepped into the cool air as a slight breeze toyed with his wilted plumes.

He glanced towards the heavens as the unassuming heavenly bodies seen to glimmer like diamonds set in a tiara.

He looked for the moon so as to have some light to see by.

It was bright and full and just clearing the tops of the trees when he, himself as fatigued as he was, went to get his horse.

When he reached out to the horse to untether him, he flinched and shied away.

"Easy old man, 'tis just I. You know I mean you no harm. Come with me for a little jaunt." As he checked the cinch and other straps and buckles that may have loosened, he patted the horses' neck as he rested his brow against the horses' unkempt shoulder.

This time acquiring his saddle was a little bit of a struggle for he thought himself well beyond fatigued if indeed there were such a state.

It saddened him deeply as he rode for he heard many screams and cries for assistance, water and mercy as he approached.

The camps surgeons were working as hastily as they possibly could to provide comfort to those in need.

Little was said as he picked his way cautiously back to his canopy to make use of his bed.

Once there, he re-tethered his horse and loosened the cinch as to afford some comfort for his equally fatigued horse.

He chose not to locate and utilize his valet for the poor boy was a battle worn as the survivors and needed rest.

He seemed unflappable, but as the siege wore on, he performed given tasks as requested, alas he lacked the enthusiasm he once had and with much gratitude towards the Duc, he continued to endure all.

He glanced towards' Bordeaux, realizing the city was more intact than he was hoping for, even in the darkness, he realized it was formidable and he out of concern for what few men he had left, refused to sacrifice them for the inevitable defeat if he continued and knowing too, he might be amoung the sacrificed as well.

From a distance, observed many torches being carried about, appearing and disappearing, Rohan deducted it was Bordeauxs' regiments inspecting damage that had been done to their fair city and if possible to shore up everything that could be in prevention of any more of his men pilfering the city further.

Rohan was standing in front of his canopy when a slight man approached.

He was dusty and pallid, alas he sought the Huguenots' audacious leader with caution, not know what to expect from the silence.

"Monsieur le Rohan?"

Rohan turned to face him.

"I am a courier from Bordeaux and my master request a response."

"How am I to respond to such, when I know not what I am responding to." Queried Rohan, impatiently.

"He wants you to acknowledge defeat and remove your regiments, if you choose not to capitulate, he will be forced to take what men of yours he has captured inside our citys' walls, and lodge them in the nearest chateaux' cellars that will act as a dungeon til further arrangement can be made."

"Since there is this annoying silence, I would imagine that it is a cease-fire." Observed Rohan.

"Indeed."

Rohan heaved a sigh, "Tell him, I concede."

"I shall indeed tell him. Therefore, I shall return with a treaty in hand for you to sign and uphold, henceforth."

It was apparent the courier was unaware of the fact, as many times the Duc was offered a treaty, yes he would sign it alas it was only a matter of time afore he would walk through it and it would go unheeded.

"May I inquire as to how long that is?"

"Monsieur, I assure you not long. My master is quite elegant with words and with little or no effort, he has a document drawn and ready. The part that takes the longest if finding the right person to sign it, which is you, use your recognizable official seal, return it to my master for his signature and seal it and deliver it to the king for his authorization. In closing, I implore you not to leave the consequences would be dire."

"I have no desire to leave at this point. I need to be assured though that my men that have survived shall not be harmed or harassed 'til I have a proper procedure in place."

"I can see to that. I request reciprocation of the request in return. Yes Bordeaux has suffered damage and casualties, alas let us not harass one another. Further actions from either side will only complicate matters. Now if I might…". He turned to take his leave.

When the light of dawn was hovering over the horizon, a couple of sub-captains approached Rohan.

"Monsieur, what is it we are waiting for? We need to proceed if we are going to make any difference in this campaign."

"I had to admit defeat. Bordeaux was more than I had anticipated, alas if we turned and sweep back to the south from Calais, we might have a chance of capturing the city, for they will not expect it. That will be the difference. For now, find your spades and bury our dead and tally the remainder so that I may get a glimpse of what the future may hold."

The sub-captains bowed and withdrew and as they did so, his young dutiful valet came to stand next to him.

"It is quiet." He commented.

"Too quiet and I so dislike that I assure you." Fore from where he was standing he could not hear the imploring pleas of the unfortunate casualties of the siege, for most of them were upon and around a small knoll ahead of him, approximately a half a league.

Some made it as far as the river and across it to breech the walls, but did not make a return.

"Are you going to present arms and continue the siege?" He queried.

Again, Rohan sighed.

"Ne', I have already admitted defeat to a young courier from Bordeaux and he will be returning in time with a treaty."

"What do you think it will say?"

"I can just imagine!" Scoffed Rohan, quite wryly.

"Will you let it stand?"

"Of course not!"

"Breakfast then?"

"Yes breakfast, for that is one pleasantry that I would not forsake. Now that I can see better by the light of day, I will now see what is behind us, for truly I do hope a sufficient number so that we can get to Pontivy and La Rochelle. The forthcoming treaty, if they know what is best for them, should state that we will be allowed to pass without prejudice, harassment or retaliation."

Rohan returned to his horse, untethered him and regained his saddle.

He carefully picked his way through his fallen regiments and as many times as he has seen a siege and been apart of one, the devastation it caused always saddened him.

As he neared the rear guard, a ever so slight movement caught his attention.

He found the young with whom thought it necessary to be part of a siege in order to gain honor.

As he knelt by the young man, he heard him repeat how cold he felt and lamented how lonely he was.

Rohan removed his mantle and laid it over him and took his fragile hand in his, and whispered, "You are not alone, for the Lord is with you."

The young man turned toward Rohan, "Mother? Are you here?"

Rohan was horrified at the appearance of the young man.

His countenance was quite disfigured caused by a concussion of a blast from a hand held device, as he had lain there, his life force ebbing, stealing his earthly existence little by little and in doing so, it was turning his fair hair, to a darker shade.

Rohan swallowed hard and replied, "No, *mon fil,* she is not."

"Then how will she know if I had obtained the honor she so wanted me to, who will tell her?

In *sotto voc*, Rohan answered, "I will. I will tell her."

The young man turned his head again, away from Rohan and let out long, loud sough as if he were mimicking a tree in a breeze and as he released his grip on Rohans' hand it went limp and he expired.

Rohan retrieved his mantle, found the young mans' plumeless cap and covered his now lifeless face with it and he reluctantly regained his saddle.

"Now young man, all honor is yours." He said as he turned his horse to return to his canopy and breakfast.

XIV

He had hopes of making use of his bed afore the young courier returned with the promised document for once it was signed his intent was to regroup his regiments and set forth to Pontivy and La Rochelle.

Once those were secure and had the promise of forwarding munitions to their locations, he would covertly meet his brother in Calais and seek refuge in England and sanctuary from Buckingham.

He did realize, however, that afore he set out for Calais, he still had many leagues that he had to cover and towns to either, support and gain additional regiments and munitions from, or find that they were adversaries that needed to be dealt with in short order and pray-fully it would not be as devastating as Bordeaux or as costly in men and munitions.

Upon reaching his canopy, he saw the beginning of the remainder of his regiments start reassembling and reassessing what that had and what they needed to secure.

Smoldering embers were forced back to life with proddings of a stick or heavy boot and thus feeding the multitude a warm breakfast would be welcomed and provide a new source of untapped strength to continue.

He could not help but a-liken the situation to the Greek mythical creature, the Phoenix.

Regenerated and arising out of ashes, to be reborn to continue and persevere and thus he too was determined to persevere.

Once inside his canopy, he sat on the edge of the trundle bed that was stowed just for him to afford him some comfort from his exhaustive efforts with the Huguenots, removed his heavy boots.

His intent was to sit silently with his ponderings to collect his wits, for they had been scattered for the last couple of days because of all the activities from and with the siege.

Alas, he inadvertently leaned to one side and although his ponderings argued with reason that it would be more beneficial if he righted himself and formulate more strategic maneuvers, alas he allowed himself to lean so far as to lie down and he succumbing to fatigue, fell asleep.

In a matter of a relatively short period of time, his valet tried to roust him for the courier re-appeared with the document in his hand that needed his signature to indicate he had seen the document and acknowledged its contents and let the truce begin.

Even with several attempts to roust him were unsuccessful, the young valet invited the courier to sit awhile and enjoin him in a goblet of wine and afford his protectant some peace, for he was thoroughly exhausted.

Repose had been only a word, not often implemented in the past fortnight, alas as the sieges' intensity slackened, he was able to make use of his bed. Alas not for a long period of time.

Once, twice even thrice the valet attended to the contents of the kettle that was gently simmering over the hot embers in the fire pit.

He knew Rohan was fond of fine food and when prepared properly, he as was the French custom, would often take hours to eat and when in the company of fellow regimental officers, or common companions, would take even longer that the next meal would have been prepared and served without rising from the table.

He too detested cold food, alas would eat it if there was no other means of satiating his current state of being hungry.

From a distance the young valet heard the tolling of a bell tower and glanced towards the courier, whom only shrugged. For neither were educated in figures or words.

Therefore the hour of three came and went unheeded.

As the hour of five rapidly approached, Rohan finally stirred and awoke.

Laying in his bed and glancing towards the top of his canopy, he took notice of an insect crawling hastily towards the opened flaps and light of day.

"I would make haste too if I could and by pass the current situation, alas must persevere and secure what we have afore us in the name of being a Hugeunot."

The young valet, who had been sitting by the fire, heard Rohan, excused himself and went to seek the Duc.

"Monsieur, the courier has returned and has requested to seek counsel with you."

"How long has he been here?" Queried Rohan.

"Quite some time, Monsieur."

"Why did you not awaken me?"

"I tried. The only response I received was a snore, then silence. I thus afforded you some peace, that you so needed. Now that you have decided that you have had plenty of repose, near as I can tell, you can attend to the business at hand while I prepare you your dinner."

Rohan inclined his head in acknowledgement of his valets' intent.

The Duc followed the valet, who had a small table and couple of chairs set about, sat in a chair closet to the fire, for he felt a slight chill even as the elements were fair and accommodating.

The young valet ladled out two bowls of the make shift stew, poured the remainders of a bottle of wine into small goblets and withdrew.

"My apologize Monsieur le Duc, for any inconvenience that I may have caused…."

"Where is the document?" Queried Rohan, trying in vain to subdue a yawn.

The courier gave the folded sealed document to Rohan, who did not recognize the seal.

"How do I know this document is not forged by some witless jester?" Inquire Rohan, wryly accepting it.

"You have my word, 'tis not."

"What is your word actually worth? Just the same, you are an adversary."

Rohan broke the seal and read all the provision allowed and prohibitations set forth on that day.

'What is this gibberish, that we are not allowed within the perimeter of city to establish a synod or anything resembling such in accordance to the edict or admittance into the city without permission from its governing seat?"

The courier, unsure how to adequately respond, stood silent.

Rohan read the remainder of the document afore setting it aside momentarily as he picked up a spoon and his shallow bowl and began eating it.

He slid the second bowl toward the the young courier.

"You may be an adversary, alas adversaries become hungry too." He said, sympathetically.

The young courier, gratefully sat again and ate the proffered stew.

The valet, without being summoned appeared and proceeded to refill the bowls and retreated.

When Rohan had finished his third bowl and declined a fourth, he re-read the document afore requesting his quill, ink and blotter.

"If I did not know the difference, I would say your officials do not like us very well." Commented Rohan, with a mocking smile.

"My captain has requested that when you are to disassemble your regiments and disperse and need to cross the river, he will have escorts awaiting you."

"I will assemble them to inform them that when we are on the other side of your river and a league beyond, we will accept your escort to that point, disassemble there and retreat." Equivocated Rohan, for he had no intentions of collectively or singularly disassembling.

"Let them think that, alas, we will reassemble and when we get within cannon shot of Pontivy, we will then be a force to be reckoned with for my family seat will accompany me and understand my intent. Thus continue our campaign. Dolts if they think I believe this is all for naught." He thought silently to himself.

Hastily Rohan signed his name and affixed his seal.

With the seal cooled and solidified, he refolded the document and handed it to the courier, who had silently admired Rohan for his courage to pursue what he deemed was right, bowed slightly then returned to his officials within the walls of Bordeaux.

The Duc just shook his head, "How young and gullible."

Rohans' young valet once again appeared.

"Monsieur?"

"I would like to ride through my remaining regiments to have them ready at the light of dawn on the morrow, to cross the river. Let Bordeaux observe us going on about our separate ways as they think we will, only to reassemble just below Pontivy. Pontivy will welcome us and will be accommodating."

"Do the Catholics honestly think that you will cease all your endeavors?"

"It is their choice to believe or no. For they, for the moment, believe. As I believe it is worth fighting for what we as Huguenots believe. We had an edict issued in our behalf but when Henri died so I'd our hope of ever having that freedom again, 'till now. For as long as I have breath, I will continue."

"Old habits die hard?" Queried the young valet.

"You can say that." Replied Rohan, as he returned again to his horse.

The sun was just below the horizon when he returned to his canopy to find his valet adjusting his pillow and counterpanes.

"What I would not give to have a long hot bath." He commented, as he once again, removed his boots while sitting on the edge of his bed.

"Would Monsieur like some mulled wine? I took the liberty of preparing some while you were instructing your regiments."

Rohan gratefully accepted the goblet, holding it with both hands in the attempt at warming his hands and fingers. Fore with the disappearance of the sun from the heavens taking the warmth with it, the darkness brought in cooler elements.

"Everything ready?"

Rohan nodded as he swallowed the warming wine and handed back the goblet.

Just afore the break of dawn, the young valet had gotten up to replenish the nigh empty kettle and restore the fire.

He reminded himself he needed to attend to Rohans' tinder box as well as his own, although the pistol of choice was rather small and hid snuggly in the top of his boot, it was sufficient of doing damage to an adversary if the need ever arose and he reasoned he had to be on the ready.

As Rohan was getting himself ready for the trek over the river, various sub-captain sought him for any last minute counsel.

"...And then be on the ready, the heavier armaments left already and half are going to Pontivy and the other half to La Rochelle. Our acquired victories will not be short lived and only when Louis concedes and reinstates the documented edict his father issued in our behalf, is when I will step away, thus knowing our freedom is no something in the past but something that will endure and transcend time."

With their dead buried and a short service commemorating their passage and heroic actions, they began the trek towards the river and utilizing the ferries and wherries.

Taking better part of the day was spent in all the regiments moving forward under the supervision of Bordeaux's officers.

Many denizens lined the rues and avenues leading out of the city to witness what they thought was an exodus of the Huguenots and that was the last of their insurrections thereof.

As planned, after they had crossed the river, and out of view from Bordeaux, they reassembled just afore they reached Pontivy so that they could collectively make use of his family seat.

Once, there he and his officers made use of his chateau that overlooked the *River Blavet* and most of the sub-captains were billeted at *Maison de trois piliers*.

As he had stated, the little town was accepting and accommodating, thus their clothes mended, their stomachs filled and warm fires during the cool eves and Rohan himself was able to take a long hot bath as he had been wanting for quite some time.

"Do you not fear for your safety, Monsieur Le Rohan?" A sub-captain once queried of him.

"Ne'. Should I?" He queried in return, "I am quite certain Bordeaux has sent couriers to the far reaches of our fair state and relayed our dismantlement. Thus it is safe to say, we shall finish our trek and when we come back upon Calais, it will be then time to re-strategize and reorganize our thoughts and actions."

Little did anyone, save his trustworthy young valet, know of his intent, when returning to Calais, of seeking asylum in England.

With his visit to Pontivy, he secured additional regiments and munitions and a promise more if needed, of each.

When it came time to continue, the caring denizens, provided additional provisions, fresh horses and lifted spirits.

As he was within reach of La Rochelle, realizing that many sentries from the opposition would be constantly surveying the area in search of him and other Huguenots. He believed if they filtered through in part at a time and caused no commotion, they will be overlooked and safe.

Alas the sentries that he had sent out prior, were beginning to return.

Two sentries who took on the vestments of the neighboring arrondissement of La Rochelle for it was a sea-faring port and of Nantes.

Their vestments were constrictive and structured more so as that of Paris and other fashion minded noble denizens who lived in and around the king and court.

Working on the piers and quays with non-constrictive vestments were more than a bothersome annoyance, they could become a hazard to those that earned their wage from harvestings of the seas by being ensnared or become entangled in ropes and nets and not be as forgiving as a tighter version of.

Breathless from assertions, the hastily approached Rohan.

"Monsieur?"

"Hold good man," he instructed, "Catch your breath, then tell me. It will keep, whatever it is, 'til you are able to speak evenly."

The two bent forward, hands steadying their knees, shook their heads.

"Yes, I assure you it can keep. Steady on."

The first sentry, straightened, removed his cap and clutched it against his still heaving chest.

"Monsieur," he stammered with frustration, "The rear guards have detected we are being pursued."

"By whom? Surely it can not be from Bordeaux. Too soon for that." He reasoned, "How far back?" He queried, turning about, raised his spyglass to his eye and peered through it, scanning the distant horizon.

The second sentry straightened his posture as well.

"We ride the distance a horse can comfortably accomplish without effort and return, which is approximately twenty leagues. At the fifteen league mark, we observed smoke rising in the distance."

"Are you sure the smoke is ones that oppose us and not a single chateau set apart from a community of its own accord? Beyond the fifteen mark, how far and from what direction?"

"It was like ours 'til we heeded what you instructed, quite thick and dark, nearly blotted out the sun."

"Another twenty-five leagues and from the east." Replied the first.

"Do not forget that there is a sliver of smoke arising from the south as well." Prompted the second.

"Anything from the north?" Rohan inquired.

"Not to our knowledge. Our sectors were south and we happened upon the east."

"Then, allow me some time to address this situation at La Rochelle and assure them that their stronghold will be even stronger, stronger to the point of infallible. Then, while I am doing that, find my sub-captains and relay what you just said. Omit nothing! Have them assembled and begin for Angers and Calais."

"Aye, Monsieur!" They replied in unison, turned and withdrew to find their horses and do as they were bid.

Without fail, his young valet appeared, startling Rohan.

"How is it you know precisely when you are to be summoned and yet I do not have to utter a word?"

"Just a matter of judging the circumstances." He replied with a knowing smile.

Rohan had another query for the young man, but chose to remain silent.

"Monsieur?"

"Nothing." Replied Rohan, with a gesture.

"I shall summon your courier. Do you need him presently?"

Rohan shook his head, vexed.

"Monsieur?"

"Amazing. Simply amazing." He muttered, then, "Yes, by all means, summon my courier. The sooner the better."

His valet poured some wine for Rohan set it afore him along with the remainder of the bottle, then withdrew silently, leaving Rohan to contemplate what he will write in his missive and hastily attend to the kettle and its contents, added a log or two and seek the courier Rohan had desired.

Rohan had removed his cap and ran his fingers through his tangled locks and sighed.

He so wanted to culminate this insurrection. He was fatigued and wanted to rest and regain his stamina and renew his keen sense of stability he possessed when balancing the ratio of men and munitions.

"There will be a day soon," He theorized, being a seasoned soldier and was very familiar with the art of a siege,"and Louis cousin or no, will concede. If not we will long persist and exhaust his resources and cause collapse. We can last long if not longer that he, no matter what his advisor relay to him."

As he awaited for his courier to draw up his horse and respond to his summon, another three sentries arrived, seeking him.

"'Tis I you seek?"

"Monsieur la Rohan?"

"Indeed !"

The sentry who allowed his facial hair overtake his countenance and conceal everything but his eyes, unseated himself from his saddle and stood respectfully in front of Rohan.

"Speak man, what gives?"

"You had sent us north and east to find evidence of any adverse conditions and we happened upon in the north, evidence of large regiments being conveyed from one location to the next."

"What of Castres and Malamort?"

"Castres has suffered casualties and Malamort has been fired upon." Reported the sentry.

"Is the cache of munitions intact?" Queried Rohan, gravely concerned over the mass accumulation of armaments to be used in the Huguenots defense of freedom.

"Unfortunately, the entrance to the valley appears to have been kegged and barricaded. We could not get within range to scrutinize the state of the caves and caverns containing your cache of such."

Rohan paced nervously, chaffing his hands as he did so.

"I have to know what state the cache is in." He muttered to himself, "Alas, I shall assume the worse which will make my plea to Buckingham more plausible. Is it feasible for you get a better observation of such and reply to me in Calais in two days time?" He queried, trying desperately not to allow them to know how crucial it was to have the whole cache intact. It could mean the difference betwixt victory and defeat.

"Only if you want to be held accountable for two dead horses, for surely their passing would be due to exhaustion."

"I for one do not want to be on one that keels over in mid stride and be pitched as a stone across the river. It could end badly."

"If I do not know for sure, it could end badly just the same." Added Rohan, still muttering. Then aloud, "Go then to Malamort, gain entry to the valley, survey the circumstances and meet me in Calais. I will be there in two days time. Use post horses along the way. Surely then those will not pass from under you."

He took a couple of paces towards a small group of his officers, then turned.

"Get rid of this." He said to the one with facial hair, giving the long chin whiskers a tug, "It looks like your goatee has gone astray."

As the two pivoted about, the first with a *sotto voc* said, "Does he not realize it will take time to infiltrate the guards in gaining their trust then be rostered in?"

The second likewise replied, "Indeed. It will take better part of a fortnight. Might as well be at ease. We need not break our necks or any horses' for that matter. Two days? It can not be done safely and I can not speak for you, alas, I for one want to live yet another day."

As they reached their horses, softly chuckling, they gained their saddles and hastily made their way towards Malamort, only for appearance sake.

His courier appeared upon his horse, alas as he near the Duc, he unseated himself to regain his feet and cautiously approached, leading his horse.

"Is he well rested?" Queried Rohan in reference to the horse.

"Indeed Monsieur. He was dozing as I untethered him."

"Does his cinch strap need adjusted?"

"Done. As well as the other buckles, hasps, clasps and straps you can think of.

Rohan appreciated the young mans' enthusiasm and his attention to detail.

"Tether him once more follow me."

The young man complied and followed Rohan, who had seated himself at a small in front of an officers' canopy.

He unstopped the bottle of ink and dipped the tip of the quill in.

Observing the fact the quill now held its share of ink, he flicked it off to the side towards the ground, this he once explained would prevent the ink from puddling on the parchment, thus inducing him to begin anew.

Setting the quill to the parchment he wrote,

"Benjamin, two days, Calais, Buckingham. Henri."

He blotted it, folded it and sealed it and handed to his courier, who tucked it snuggly within his double.

Normally he would have put and missive he received in his cap, alas being this close to the sea and strong breezes created by such, had convinced him he would loose his cap and it would be irretrievable and the missive would be lost and so would any trust that officials had in him to successfully convey their correspondences to and fro.

He patted his side and said, "Monsieur?"

"Ah yes!," He replied, "In Calais seek Soubise and give him that. He will understand. Prayfully no-one else shall. God speed."

The courier hastily turned about, lightly touched his horses' flanks with his spurs and the two left nothing but dust in their wake.

"Gentlemen,". Began Rohan addressing his sub captains and other officers, "It has come to my attention that the cache in Malamort might be a thing of the past."

Murmurs of disbelief and discontentment rippled through the small congregation of men.

"All we can do, now that we are again together is continue to La Rochelle and assist in any possible way then, on to Nantes and Angers."

"Have you considered recruiting Buckingham in our continued efforts of resistance?" Queried someone quite loudly.

"At this point in time, ne'." He equivocated again. "Alas, I shall put forth the idea and implement a plan. By the time we reach Calais, turn and re-sweep from whence we came, I shall have an adequate reply."

"By re-sweeping, would that not be in violation of the treaty Louis has set forth? Queried another.

"Since when did any treaty prevent us from accomplishing our goals?"

His multitude chuckled lightly.

"What of Malamort?"

"At present, I have re-sent sentries there to verify once and for all the state it is in, whether disrepair or withstanding the oppositions."

He paused as if to ponder further, their turned once again to face his regiments.

"What say you, consider dividing the regiments, take half and take to Malamort, if it is indeed kegged and barricaded, storm it and re-take it in the name of freedom. Send word to La Rochelle that you need additional regiments, at the same, La Rochelle will make a plea with Castres? Yes it sounds like a lot of movement of regiments and armaments forsooth it is, but what greater way to accommodate the situation than to have the closer ones, move closer than those that are at a distance and disadvantage. For it would take them longer to reach the designated area and they would be so fatigued they would not be able to aim their Harquebuses or muskets accurately."

"As if they were accurate to ever begin with." Commented a soldier.

Those around him, hearing the utterance, laughed loudly for they knew the comment to be true, thus their weapon of choice, being shorter and easier to both manipulate and aim with more accuracy, was their muskets.

Rohan, with a slight wry smile toying about his pursed lips, just shook his head.

"Then looking about, he said, "At the moment, I and some sub-captains will continue on to La Rochelle to verify or nullify their needs and wants. The remainder shall be given over to the remaining sub-captains to divide and be on your way specified by them. Those remain from that, prepare to lay over til I return. I guarantee you, I will not be long for Nantes and Angers still await as well."

Rohan with a half of a dozen of his most trusted sub-captains, regained their saddles and set off for La Rochelle.

By the time he had reached La Rochelle, it was dusk and the guards had just began closing the gates and the brazier-keep was just beginning his rounds.

"Hold Monsieur, I beseech you, hold!"

"…And may I inquire as to who you are?" Inquired the Guard, keeper of the gate.

"Monsieur le Duc Le Rohan."

"Who is it you seek?"

"Soubise."

"Ne' Monsieur le Duc, he is not here."

"Was he?"

"Not recently. At least a fortnight."

"Then, if I may request admission to speak to your captain in charge of this campaign."

"It is an ongoing campaign and we occasionally have lost our captain in charge, thus a freshly procured one is summoned and given the position that was unduly vacated."

Rohan gestured with annoyance.

"No matter. I, we need to speak to the captain and or the master of the citadel."

"Take pause. I shall return. For all concerns, allow me to shut the gate."

"I promise no harm will come if I am allowed admittance."

The guard eyed him, said nothing, shut the gate with a loud thud, regained his saddle and went in the direction of the barracks to seek a hasty counsel with their newly appointed captain.

"Just what we need is inexperience during a troublesome time. One that will not be able to cope when the need arises." Muttered Rohan, to no one in particular.

Rohan had began to pace anxiously afore the gate with his sub-captains chaffing their hands.

The soldier returned with a torch in one hand and his horses' reins in the other.

"He was just sitting down to supper with his own officers and has extended an invitation for you to join him, there is plenty. La Rochelle will be accommodating and offer supper and shelter for the eve."

"Graciously I shall accept your offer, alas we can not stay the eve, for we must see what lies within at Nantes and Angers. Unfortunately, not only is the crown against us, so is time."

The soldier gestured to companions to raise the gate and allow them entrance.

The gate was wide enough to allow a small riot to enter, although they were not a small riot they still made use of the opened gate.

The soldier walked in front of them rather than regaining his saddle. His intent was to allow a stable to care for the weary animal, who was readily accepted as they arrived.

As he handed the reins to the stable lackey, he gently stroked the thick fur that had began to seasonally thin out as it did as the elements began to more or less be more agreeable to those that tilled fields in an effort to supply denizens with the necessary grains they so often sought.

The soldier had them follow him to the barracks to where the officers gathered to take their meals.

Rohan, although grateful for the chance to eat something other than cellar root vegetables and salt preserved meat, he was disappointed in that it was not the grand hall in the citadel where a warming fire in the hearth would have been light to chase the eve's chill from the air about them, away.

He silently ached from the long arduous trek and would seek willow when allowed.

Alas, he was seated next to a colonel who chattered incessantly of the the needs and wants of the city.

Rohan allowed him to drone on, occasionally nodding his head in an convincing assenting manner.

He did fully grasp the concept that they needed additional armaments and regiments and he reassured the colonel all would be forth coming and they will be well prepared if and when the crown tried to assault them.

The colonel suddenly slammed his fist upon the table, totally catching Rohan and his sub-captains unawares.

"Now!" He exclaimed, "What is it we can do for you? Here, you let me prattle on and give you a chance to state your position."

Rohan set his goblet down as he speared a piece of a roasted hare and a vegetable, laid it across his plate, then with a fork, removed them and cut them into smaller pieces.

Then toyed with a piece of bread, afore his shoved it aside, only to have it lay in a shallow puddle of an unfamiliar sauce.

"We are being pursued, I have a thought as to whom it may be, alas, no matter, we need them to be delayed, waylaid even better, we will take what you have to offer. In return I will arrange to have additional armaments and regiments sent."

"If it t'were that easy." Sighed the Colonel.

"Why say you, that?" Queried Rohan.

"It seems that the cause is a loosing battle. Not many are in support of that."

"Ne', tis not the case. Yes you are here enclosed within the walls of La Rochelle. Yes the cause has been exhausting of resources, both of regiments and armaments and if we let the crown pervade, we will not be able to persevere. It will all be for naught. We will see our efforts til the end. All our endeavors will not go unnoticed."

"I shall make the necessary strategic arrangements around the parameter and even some facing the sea lest they try from that aspect. They will not be able to breech that front, even if they swam." Laughed the Colonel as he envisioned a whole regiment attempting to swim ashore with the proper armaments for a confrontation.

"May I make a request for accompaniments 'til Angers? I do not fear an ambush betwixt there and Calais, alas there is no harm in having a multitude of force to ward off anything that is unexpected. One thing is for certain and that is that things constantly change and shift. The king is a good example of saying something one hour and the next hour when the hour glass has been inverted, he says another. Alas along the coast, here and beyond we have Huguenot sympathizers with smatterings of Catholics to keep things interesting."

"We certainly do not need to have you caught unawares and thus scatter as chickens would with a fox about."

Rohan chuckled, "Certainly not."

The colonel summoned two seasoned captains and four equally seasoned majors and relayed his desire to hastily assemble six basic regiments with little refinements for he did not think there would be so much as a *sotto voc* retaliation with their movements north.

If their adversaries were able to track them, he felt they were far enough ahead so he and his brother, Benjamin, could slip through any blockade and make England afore the eve set in late and heavy.

Although Rohan was still awaiting word from sentries that were still up the coast, he decided to hastily proceed as he imagined that there had a blockade in place in an attempted effort to maintain and contain him within the state and true as it may be, there would be nothing to prevent him and his brother from obtaining asylum and assistance from Buckingham.

La Rochelle was their stronghold and was a symbol of all they had strived for and they were not ready to surrender it to the likes of Louis nor Richelieu and thus the sieges wore on.

As The citadels' bell tower announced one, Rohan was once again on the opposite side of a closed gate, but this time he was greeted by assembled regiments of his own and the ones the colonel had promised him. A freshly procured horse was brought to him and although he was more familiar with his own, he readily accepted the more vivacious and attentive one.

With Rohan in the lead, followed by and on the outer flanks of his regiments were his officers, all striving to reach Nantes, Angers, Rouen and finally Calais.

The Duc consistently and constantly sent forth sentries to relay and receive information as to the whereabouts of any adversaries to be on the ready if the occasion arose.

When they were within a days ride of Rouen, sentries returned with information of the north and as he had foreseen, his adversaries were instilling a blockade at the port and entrance into the city.

He shook his head in amusement, for he knew he could and would formulate a plan to be able to slip through unnoticed and thus when all was said and done it will have appeared he had just vanished and thus the court officials would have to explain to Louis their ineptness and their lacking ability to identify fugitives of justice. *"Bon chance."* He thought, smiling wring.

"Any indication of additional regiments being added to what is already there as they may appear to ready themselves for a small siege or skirmish?" He inquired.

"Ne'." Came their replies.

As Rouen finally came into view, he had them pause and gave instructions as to not light fires for he did not want their smoke to cause the denizens to panic and have them take up arms in defense and fire upon them when they were for they were of the same thoughts concerning their beliefs, thus they would accidentally reduce their numbers because of a case of mistaken identify and misinformation and thus run the risk of being short handed when a true situation arose.

He fed the colonels' men with his own, then had them return to the colonel and La Rochelle for he sensed nothing out of the ordinary.

As it dawned the following day, Rohan had his men gather and let it be known his desire to have a few men at a time filter through Rouens' gates. His reason for the few, was as to again, not incite the denizens into a frenzied fit of anxiety into thinking they were being besieged and thus taking up a means of defending themselves against intruders. They were then to assemble within cannon shot of Calais and await his arrival, then when all things were considered, they would either progress forward or take pause 'til all ponderings were established.

When most of the regiment was on the move towards the city, he summoned his young valet, who promptly appeared.

"Yes, Monsieur?"

"I need you to find Mademoiselle Lizbett Fle'champ and covertly tell her, "Freedom Rings quite loudly." Then return hence. She is located near Quai de Paris."

The young man curtly bowed reverently, and hastily departed.

In his valets' absence, he perused his charts, seeking alternative ways of securing opposing cities and towns.

"Cannon fire and a hail of arrows and musket balls are not enough of a persuasive measure." He mused, "Surely as we try to flank them, we will be seen and a volley of chaos will ensue. There has to be a better way. Strength in numbers is a fine standard to live by and so if this is the better way, then so be it. With additional regiments, naturally comes armaments." He weakly smiled, for he was most fatigued.

In reality, he had not the fore thoughts that wanting and declaring a need for religious freedom would cost as much as it did. He could not understand why the edict was reversed and set against him. He knew Louis had many advisors relaying one thing or another alas the most influential advisor he heeded on too many occasions was his own mother, Marie de Medici. He hoped as his cousin grew to the age of majority he would rely more on himself and those that had compassion for the populace and their well being.

The Huguenots only error was to take up arms to prove their seriousness and Louis, feeling threatened, retaliated the only way he saw fit, take up arms as well.

Picking up his goblet, to drain the contents, that he had inadvertently set on the corner of the chart left an indelible stain on the parchment.

Out of curiosity, he peered at what the stain had encompassed and to his amusement, not only Calais but Dover and the outer fringes of London.

Rohan had just picked up a bottle to pour the remains into his goblet, alas all he was able to get was a couple of drops, when his valet returned.

"Monsieur?"

Rohan turned and inclined his head slightly.

"Were you successful?" He queried.

The young man reddened and replied, "Indeed, I do believe I did. She replied, "Let it ring for the sake of the Huguenots."

Rohans' smile engulfed his face as he comprehended what his valet relayed.

"She also said supper is promptly at seven."

"What time is it now?"

"As I was leaving, the bell tower rang out five."

"Then I suggest to go and untether our horses and bring them around, for we have a supper engagement."

As the light of day faded, Rohan observed that the encampment was nigh vacant thus most all had complied and would be awaiting him to join them just outside of Calais and the few that remained were on the move.

The Duc, knowing where he was going did not have the need to reaffirm the location and was able to navigate the avenues and rues that led to the familiar establishment of a compatriot with the intentions of soliciting her assistance.

"She has many grand ideas on assisting our gentlemen of common interests and now let us see what she can think of now when we are pressed for time."

Even though she lived near the Seine, it was a quiet and somewhat secluded and when the eves settled in, the tranquility was mesmerizing causing any sojourner, great pause.

As the came into the courtyard of the grand establishment, a valet greeted them and accepted the reins and another valet escorted them to the door, knocked twice and when it was opened to allow them admittance, he stepped back and another valet allowed them to follow him to the drawing room where Mademoiselle Lizbett sat on a bolstered and richly upholstered chair with a half dozen companions in attendance.

"Monsieur Rohan, how magnificent it is to see you again." She said as she smiled behind a fan she fluttered about her countenance.

"Mademoiselle." Replied Rohan as he caressed her extended hand and he and his valet bowed, respectfully afore her.

"How kind of you to accept my invitation to supper."

"How can one refuse such charm and wit?"

Her countenance reddened coquettishly.

"Do tell, how are the Huguenots faring?" She queried, "Fear not, these denizens are compatriots and sympathizers. Dear me,". She said, "I should think that is one and the same."

"If it t'were not for Louis having a difference of an opinion, we certainly would have had our freedom long ago as we did with the edict. Alas, Marie had other ideas of how this state should be. She forgets, this is not Italy from whence she came. True, she had to learn the French way, but she still is an Italian at heart and always will be. We have had our share of victories and advancements and unfortunately set backs and defeats."

"Then, other than my company what is it you request of me?" She queried.

"I shall tell you at supper." He smiled wryly. Then queried, "Do you think the denizens of Rouen would be sympathetic enough to add additional regiments and armaments to our existing inventory?"

"Depends on the time of day. In the morn, not likely, by dinner time they are more compliment and yet at supper time they are arguementive and what better time to query of them something they so often argue about, our freedom?"

One of the gentlemen inquired, "How soon do you need such?"

"How soon can they be assembled?"

"I shall put it forth in the morn."

Lizbett leaned forward and said in *sotto voc,* "He is the head master at the citadel."

He again inclined his head in acceptance of the circumstance and replied, "Splendid."

As the conversation continued. A stout valet appeared and announced supper was served.

The little entourage allowed Mademoiselle Lizbett to precede them and allowed her to be seated at the head of the table with back to a warming hearth.

One of the gentlemen attempted to sit next to her right but was removed and then replaced by Rohan and his young valet.

Mademoiselle Lizbett Fle'champ, a woman of ample mind and body. She was well versed in the arts and educated in reading, scribing and numbers. She was fluent in dialects of, Latin, English, Greek and Italian, which was convenient as to when a document had been issued from another adversary or of France itself, she was able to understand its full content and translate it so the denizens around her knew if it was a threat or request for peace.

She had many ardent suitors, alas not one was what she considered her equal in thoughts and deeds, thus never consented to marry.

Duc Henri de Rohan was totally dedicated to his wife he sought Lizbett on the occasion she would have the resources and means toward the Huguenots' cause and now was one of those times.

Their conversations were light and were noncommittal to current affairs, for they left the states affairs to the state, the eve was meant to alleviate the bothersome burden of strategizing defenses of La Rochelle and along the coast to and through Rouen to Calais.

Rohan unaware of the fact the supper was just that, had decided not to speak of his need to exit the state through Calais and needed a means to do so, undetected. The less denizens knew of his intent the better.

As the eve waned toward early morns' hours, her guests begged their leave to seek the comforts of their own beds, which left Rohan to make his request.

They again found themselves in her drawing room with the comforts of a glowing fire in the hearth.

"Mademoiselle,". He sighed, "I have come to request your assistance."

She, not thinking, tittered coquettishly.

"I knew you had an ulterior motive." She said as she smiled.

"You did, did you?"

"Indeed." She gestured, "What is it you request?"

"Can your valets and lackeys be trusted?" He queried in *sotto voc.*

"I should say so, for if they were not, I would have long released them from their service."

He paused then said, "I need a means of exiting Calais without being detected."

She did not reply but let him continue.

"My intent is pure and simple. I want to seek Buckingham and implore him to assist us with refortifying La Rochelle and other coastal strongholds and make a strong push toward inland and Paris. This is one of the few time that England actually likes us and we are not dickering over our differences. What a difference a little bit of water makes."

"You mean a concealment of self?"

"Yes. Benjamin is rendezvousing in Calais and then we will continue."

"Does he need concealment as well?"

"I do not believe so. The state is not fully aware of his motives as they are of mine."

"What of your young man there?" She queried, nodding in the direction of the young man.

"Ne' they know not know him or his associations."

She pondered a moment.

"What say you, the state is seeking you, a gentleman, correct?"

Rohan nodded as he sipped some wine from an etched glass goblet.

She again tittered.

"What say you?" Inquired Rohan.

"I say, give the appearance of woman of means and go about your way."

"Use the vestments of a woman?" Gasped Rohan, taken quite aback at the mere suggestion.

"You do not want to be detected do you?" She queried.

Rohan slowly shook his head.

"Then, follow me." She instructed as she rose from her chair and with the early light of dawn filtering through the shutters, she was able make her way unattended, to her boudoir, for she had dismissed her attendants after the last of the meal was served and the last of the wine poured and there was not a need for a lit taper.

She went to her armoire and took out a petticoat, ladened with multiple layers of imported lace, a corset, held together with gold fasteners and fine plaited leather, shoes rather than slippers to accommodate his feet in rougher terrain and more concealing, a bolster to add beneath and around the waist, to the bottom half of the frock so as to not let it lay flat against his legs as fashion had dictated, giving a more fuller appearance, the frock had a frill around the neck, contributing to more concealment of his gender.

"Here, step behind this." She said, indicating a foldable, four paneled partition.

Rohan complied as his valet sat silently on a settee near the shuttered window.

When she had seen his linen shirt and pantaloons draped from the top, she tossed him the petticoat.

"Umph!" He groaned, "How do you ever manage?"

"With the assistance of my chamber maid, alas I thought I would save you from dying."

"Dying? From what?" He queried almost shrieking.

"From humiliation." She chuckled so softly he could not hear her.

"Tie in the front, then, here catch this." She said as she tossed over the bolster.

He tied the petticoat in place then the bolster.

"What next?" He queried.

"Come around." She suggested.

"A query." He said, as he came from behind the partition.

"...And that is?"

"Does this bolster make me look fat?"

She laughed, "Of course it does, but that is the least of your worries. Here." She added as she held the corset.

He groaned again, "How do you expect me to wear that?" He queried.

"Very carefully." She smiled, "Alas, here use this."

She had a much thinner, refined bolster she tied around his chest.

"This will give the illusion you have an ample bosom and this corset will keep it in place."

He held the corset to his chest as she began to secure it up the back. When she reached the top, below his shoulder blades, she began again at the bottom to pull the plaited bindings more taught.

She repeated the process thrice in order to close the gap betwixt the components made of whale bone.

"How do you breathe with this thing?" He managed to inquire.

"Short shallow breaths."

She then beckoned Rohans' valet.

"Assist me with this." She said as the both managed to slip the frock in place and began fastening the closures.

Once complete, she had him turn about and when he did, she gasped.

"What do you find amiss?" He queried, anxiously.

"Oh!" She exclaimed, "This will not do. It so will not do."

"Do tell, what will not do?"

"This!" She replied as she chaffed a cheek, heavy with neglected facial hair.

"What? Does it not add?" He jested.

"I should say not." She retorted as she failed to see the levity of his comment.

"Here, sit!" She instructed, "It shall be taken care of."

She then poured water from her pitcher to the shallow basin and allowed his valet to proceed with what had been a daily ritual if they were not involved in sieges.

When he had completed the task, Rohan was offered a linen clothe to pat dry his countenance.

Although it had reddened with the procedure, he now could have the necessary applications of paint to enhance his features.

Lizbett stepped back to assess his new appearance and to self critique her given task.

"Perchance this rouge will enhance what God has given you. Although, I may need a lot more than what I have available." She tittered,

"Then again, I shall send it along with you, it might be premature to apply it now. You still have at least a days ride ahead of you."

"Am I going to even be able to stride a horse in this?" He queried.

"Hmm, I think not. If you are to pass for a woman, you will need a carriage and this." She replied as she handed him a lace fan.

"Use it often."

As he regained his feet, he caught sight of himself in a cheval.

He slightly raised his voice to resemble that of a woman and said, "If I truly were in need of a man, I would not look twice in this direction for consolation."

She tittered, "Now if you will..be on your way. We have victories awaiting. One last thing," She added as she handed him a cap, "Tuck all your hair under this."

As he was about to depart, her chamber maid appeared and queried if she would like to readied for the day.

"Ne'. On the contrary. I need rest and lots of it. As for now, have the stable lackey ready a small carriage and bring it to the front."

The chamber maid bowed and departed.

"How can I repay such kindness and assistance?" He queried.

"I will take your two horses in exchange."

Rohan inclined his head in agreement.

"We do indeed."

The chamber maid reappeared, as Lizbett said, "Please allow Madame Henrietta to buy her leave and I will need your assistance." She tried in vain to conceal a yawn.

Rohan smiled, he understood, bowed and departed.

XV

Once out of doors, the stable lackey held the door to the carriage open and Rohan was able to somewhat convey the gracefulness of the fairer gender as sat upon some bolsters and with the closing of the door, he immediately slumped against other bolsters.

As they began, the gently rhythmic swaying of the carriage, persuaded him to close his eyes and mind to his surroundings as he gratefully agreed.

His valet gained the seat and picked up the reins and with a short whistle and a tap from the whip on their haunches, they set out for the last stretch of their trek, Calais.

When they arrived at Calais' gates, to their benefit it again was dusk.

As his valet drew up the reins, he awoke somewhat startled as he glanced about.

His valet opened the door and heartily greeted him.

"I take it, we are in Calais."

"Indeed Monsieur. Is there some specific location we need to obtain?"

"Knowing we spent our two day notice to Benjamin, I suggest we go to the nearest quai and secure passage across the channel to Dover. Then we shall find a hearty supper and Benjamin and depart."

"Do you still fear that you are being pursued?"

"Ne'. We have reached our destination and if we truly are, it matters not, for there is still plenty of rear guards to preoccupy them if that be the case in fact. The others are here and will make use of their time and reassemble. Afore we embark, I will send word to my sub-captains to inform them thus of my intent. Now if you will, I do believe I see the ferry that will traverse over the channel. Take this doubloon and secure passage for three. See if you can gain four, Benjamin may have a valet with him as well."

"Am to go with you?" the young valet inquired enthusiastically.

"Why would you not? You have come this far and far be it to omit a value when I see it it. Mind you, you have value, yourself have proved that on your own merit. You have what it takes my good man. Your casual observations have paid off as you have used it to the benefit of all. A dolt for being mute? Bah! They know not what they have lost, alas I have gained. When you return, we will seek Benjamin and then you can sell the horses and this petit carriage."

The valet shut the door and strode towards the quai.

Rohan gazed towards the quai, observing the caravels bobbing lightly on the gentle waves from the channels' current.

He knew, at times the crossing could be rough and hazardous, alas, he was not going to allow himself to feel dread, regret nor fear. He was hoping the crossing would be swift and uneventful.

In time, his young valet returned.

"Ah splendid! Now let us choose a hostler and make use of it, then seek my brother. It should not be hard to recognize him, for he carries a heavy resemblance of a younger me."

"A younger you? How conventional." Smiled the young valet, "By the by, the ferry departs at three."

The valet reseated himself and they began for the nearest hostler.

The quais were congested still with denizens though the hour was late.

Men coming in from the sea to sell their catch to mongers and ferries coming from and going to England and Caravels departing for parts unknown, for the boon of exploration was on the rise and many wanted to partake in the adventure and the possibility of staking a claim in a far off land in the name of France.

The young valet halted the carriage in front of a hostler that was alive with activity which suited Rohan. For if it were subdued, he reasoned it would be more likely someone would pause just long enough to recognize him in spite of his current alterations.

For appearance sake, he accepted the arm of his young valet and was escorted to the door and allowed to pass afore his valet.

Once inside, a maritime theme prevailed as seamen relayed tales of woe to those that embellished their tales of how much they were going to be compensated for their latest haul from the see that they obtained.

An a loud argument or two that was just shy of fisticuffs, erupted as denizens challenged one another with the art of gambling and bottomless goblets of wine.

Rohan just shook his head as he hid behind the fan Lizbett had lent him, "It should be one or t'other. The two activities do not go well together."

The Duc tugged lightly on his valets' sleeve and nodded to a corner that was nigh vacant.

Once seated, they were hastily approached by the inn keep who inquired what was the wine of choice as well, did they prefer a stew that the sea freshly provided the kettles' contents or would they prefer, something his huntsmen procured earlier in the day.

Rohan having had a wide diversity of regional dishes choose the kettle that beheld what the seamen had procured and his valet being very skeptical of what the sea can possible produce, choose a spitted goose and mirepoix.

"Would your mother like some cheese, wine and bread as well?"

A curt nod of his head and the inn keep went to assembled the requested meal.

Rohan chuckled lightly, "Mother indeed!"

From behind his fan, he surveyed the current activities and the denizens that were preoccupied with such, 'til he caught sight of slight movement from a couple of denizens to their right, who were in return observing them.

"If you will, extend an invitation to those two, to join us so that will have no need to observe us from afar." Suggested Rohan as he nodded covertly in their direction.

His valet arose, smiled, "Yes mother.", he said, bowed slightly and respectfully, then went to do as he was bid.

To his delight, the two followed his young valet as he returned to the table they were sitting.

As one sat down in across from him, he knew immediately who it was.

The stranger leaned forward, "Do I not know you Madame?" He queried, with a mischievous twinkle in his eye.

"…And I you?" Rohan queried in return, coquettishly as possible.

The gentleman's valet sat very perplexed over the circumstances, not knowing if he should inquire of his master what the significance of this rendezvous was or was it truly by coincidence that they just happened to find themselves in need of conversation with others and the two amply provided that.

"My, my, my Madame, such a grand transformation since the last time I saw you."

"Is that a good thing or a bad thing?" Rohan queried, with an arched brow, in mock seriousness.

Then the gentleman leaned even closer still and in a *sotto voc* said, "Being a woman does not wear well with you."

"Nor you, if you ever be so inclined." Replied Rohan with a wry crooked smile, then added, "Oh Monsieur if only you knew."

"Alas, "Madame", I do know."

They all laughed heartily, save the gentleman's valet, for he still did not comprehend the given circumstances.

Still with *sotto voc*, "How is it you came to this?" Queried the gentleman.

Afore the Duc could answer, the inn keep followed by attendants, brought the supper and laid it afore them as well as their tableware.

Rohan hastily hid behind the extended fan.

"Anything else Madame?" He queried.

"Ne', this will do." Replied the gentleman, gesturing, then added, as the inn keep departed, "As you were saying, "Madame"?

"I know our cousin Louis has a different opinion than that of the Huguenots, and the only error we have made, a mortal one at that, is arms were taken up against him and thus, although he has offered treaties in the past in which I have signed, seriously they are not worth the parchment they are printed on if they are not upheld. Now, the edict his father issued was a masterpiece. Translated our needs and wants in terms the common man would comprehend. Alas, he is seeking me as we speak and I for one do not want to see the likes of the Bastille from the inside, looking out provided I would get the chance to look out. I so would rather see it from the outside and to prevent capture, I needed a disguise, an altered appearance if you will and thus this is the handiwork of Mademoiselle Lizbett Fle'champ."

"Henri…"

"Pardon Monsieur, Henrietta.." Replied Rohan, smiling with a *falsetto voc.*

"Henrietta, what is to become of our rendezvous?"

"Benjamin, dear brother, it has been arranged that the four of us will seek asylum in England under the Duke of Buckingham. They are looking for Henri, not Henrietta."

Benjamins' valet smiled.

"He is a bit thick at times, alas he is loyal." Replied Benjamin.

"'Tis a good thing to have a loyal, trustworthy valet that has many talents in assisting in your daily existence."

His own valet reddened at the compliment.

"When are we to depart for England?" Queried Benjamin, as he cut off a chunk of roasted fowl, rolled it in his piece of bread, then dipped it in his wine and began to eat it.

Rohan swallowed what he was eating and said, "At three. By the time we reach Dover, the sun will have illuminated the new day and we can see clearly enough to seek London."

"Is Buckingham expecting you?"

"Ne', but he will when we seek his counsel and implore him to assist us in our cause."

"Toy with his sympathies?"

"If the need arises, yes."

"By the by dear brother, why is the valise accompanying you?"

"'Tis my vestments."

"Why bother, you can frequent a tailor and have him prepare proper vestments to befit that of a gentleman. No need to add."

"Good Benjamin, I do not wish to have the appearance of an Englishman, even though that is what in reality we should." He tugged lightly at the tight ruff about his neck. "I find this quite annoying, yet I know we should have the appearance of such. We do have a problem though."

"….And that is? Queried Benjamin.

"We may speak their dialect, but we do not have the proper accent to allow them forgive that we are from across the channel."

"It truly is only necessary to communicate with Monsieur Villiers, for he will convey our necessities to members of the court."

"How long do we intend to stay?" Queried Benjamin.

"As long as it takes to convince Buckingham that his assistance is vital to the success of the Huguenots."

"Do you speculate that it will be a lengthy endeavor?"

"I can not hazard to even try to guess. The English are so fickle."

Benjamin drained the contains of his goblet as a distance bell tower announced the hour of two.

"They, no doubt say the same of us."

They both chuckled.

"Let them." Smiled Rohan.

Benjamin began to regain his feet when a denizen approached, clearly inebriated.

"Monsieur, I approach and claim at the stake of my reputation, Madame."

Benjamin determined to be as somber as possible and refrain from even the slightest chuckled for fear of infuriating the gentleman.

Being inebriated and full of ire was not a good combination in any circumstances.

"How say you thus, when it is obvious she is in the company of myself and our valets?"

"Father, Mother has had no other intentions other than that of your welfare." Smiled Rohan's young valet, "I assure you, although she mistakenly wears her heart on her sleeve, she does not leave it in the company of any other than you."

The gentleman wavered as he stood.

"What? Is she not worth a duel?"

"There is an edict in place that forbids as such and since we are abiding denizens, I choose not to jeopardize my freedom for something as trivial as a duel. Indeed she is a jewel of choice, alas not to be tarnished by the likes of you."

Rohan in a *sotto voc* to his valet, "Make haste, bring up a chair behind him. Try not to make a sound."

The young valet raised an inquiring brow, in which Rohan gestured, "Just observe."

He then did as Rohan instructed. He brought a chair up as close as he could without the gentleman being aware of the activity.

Benjamin was able to regain his feet and said, "Being a gentleman as I am, allow me to offer you a goblet of wine in good faith."

The gentleman accepted the goblet as he attempted to drain its contents, Benjamin gave a rough nudge to the mans' slight chest.

As anticipated, he fell backwards and ended up sitting in the chair instead upon the hard planking.

He struggled to regain his feet and as he did so, Benjamin had his hands upon the gentleman shoulders, preventing him standing.

"What gives?" He queried as he hic-coughed and let the goblet clatter to the floor.

"If I were you, I would let this matter go by the way-side and do not attempt to sway the situation for I assure you, you will not like the outcome. I could enlist your services with one of the caravels and list you as part of their manifest. Annoy me not further."

The other regained their feet as well and as they strode toward the door, the gentleman called out, "Madame, my heart. It is yours."

As Benjamin settled their debt, Rohan said, "Save it for someone who cares, for I do not."

The four then disappeared into the darkness of the eve and sought the ferry as their conveyance across the channel.

"Madame, indeed." Said Benjamin, "It is certain he was not able to see to clearly."

"Even if he had, he would have been disappointed."

They all laughed aloud.

When they reached the gangplank, a hasty flash of lightening in the distance, momentarily illuminated the thick dark clouds, followed by a low rumbling of thunder.

"I do so hope that is not meant for us." Said Rohan.

"Allow me, Madame." Said one of the deckhands as he escorted them and directed the four and were shown their quarters below deck and as the settled in for the remainder of the eve, the increase of the wind caused the masts to flap frantically.

Shouted orders were heard as the ferry lurched into motion as they set out for England.

XVI

"Mousequeton, my powder horn." Requested Porthos as he slung it across his massive wide chest, adjusting the brass buckle.

"Tinder box. Sash. Harquebus."

Porthos stomped his heavy booted foot.

"Master?"

"Mousequeton?"

"Would you care to bring along your Musket?"

Porthos arched a brow in a silent inquery.

"I take that as a, ne' I think not." Chuckled the valet, "Even though it has been stowed along with other implements."

"Then leave it. The first chance I get I too will leave it somewhere appropriate for a cumbersome, useless cannon." He sighed, "All this for preparation for departure, alas I must begin again." Replied Porthos as he removed the implements.

"Now…baldric and sheath, blade. Now my powder horn." He again slung it across his chest, "tinder box and Harquebus. Sash."

After tying his sash in place he requested the little purse that contained a rather large measure of wick, the satchel that beheld his freshly procured musket balls, would be arranged as the trestle would, upon his horse.

"Master?"

Porthos turned to find Mousequeton holding out his ponaird.

"I do believe you will be needing this."

The musketeer softly chuckled as he accepted it and tucked it into the top of a boot as he so often did.

As he was tying his mantle in place, a light rap was bestowed upon his door, Porthos nodded and Mousequeton opened it only to be greeted by his masters' companions and their valets.

He had just stepped aside to allow them admittance when a young courier appeared in front of them.

"What gives?" Queried Porthos, astonished, "Who is this that accompanies you?"

"We know not, for he did not accompany us. He was a pace or two ahead of us and that is how he was able to proceed slightly afore us."

Porthos bent at the waist be eye to eye with the young courier.

The young courier took a pace backwards and tilted his head back to be able to see the glint of mischievousness in Porthos' eyes.

"Do not let him frighten you. He may seem imposing but truly he is quite harmless." Said Aramis.

"Unless you anger him." Muttered Athos, and that did not go unnoticed by youngster.

"Does he anger easily?" He queried, swallowing hard.

"I can not say, for I have not been the cause." Replied Athos.

"What brings you?" Queried Porthos.

"The Cardinal wishes your presence within the hour."

"Whatever for, does he not know we are in the midst of preparing for departure?" Queried Athos, clearly annoyed by the inconvenience the Cardinal just imposed.

"I know not. He just said he wants you in his chambers within the hour. *Av Revoir.*"

Said the young man as he pirouetted on his toes and hastily strode away only to disappear into a crowd of denizens.

"What could he possibly want with us?" Queried Porthos, straightening his posture. Then queried, "Athos, my good man, you have not antagonized Jussac have you?"

"Why is it, the moment we are summoned to the King or the cardinal, it is assumed I have antagonized the wrong person?" He queried in return.

"Given the chance you would, would you not?" Smiled Porthos.

"Of course, especially Jussac."

"Well?" Queried Aramis.

"This is one of those rare occasions that I have not. I have not had the opportunity."

"Then you are in accordance with the edict." Added Aramis.

"What edict?" Queried Athos, mischievous as well.

The six men, gathered the remainder of their implements and began walking towards the *Palais Royals,* and the musketeers' stables.

They took a hasty pause at the stables and gave instructions to have their favored horse be ready for a lengthy sojourn and have a thorough scrutinization. From the tips of their ears to the tip of their hooves.

"Leave nothing amiss. If you please, be meticulous of where their saddles rests upon them. Make certain nothing can or will chaff them. It will be a long ride and nothing is as uncomfortable than an irritable horse. It makes it a rough go." Instructed Porthos.

The stable lackeys then took it upon themselves to see that the horses were properly prepared as the musketeers had instructed.

The musketeers left their implements with the lackeys to let them adjust them accordingly on their horse so it would be as comfortable as possible for the horse as the rider.

"I just hope we do not over burden the poor beasts. The can be so fragile." Said Aramis, concerned for their well being.

"They have been with us afore." Reminded Athos.

"Indeed they have, alas every new trek forward is taxing."

"The lackeys are seeing to it that they are properly fitted with a saddle and shoes." Reminded Athos.

"That is more than I can say for myself." Said Porthos, with a slight smile.

Aramis turned and queried, "You mean to tell me, after all that bleating about your boots over the last week, you had not replaced them as you were."

"I did not have the means." Replied Porthos, lightly equivocating.

Aramis raised his brow, but said nothing.

"That is true." Added Athos, "Our coffers have not been refilled since our return. The Cardinal nor the king have offered to compensate us for doing our stately duty."

Porthos nodded.

"Then we will have to remind them and rectify the situation." Said Aramis, quite sternly.

As they approached the courtyard, a rather large mass of denizens had gathered.

Porthos' furrowed his brow and queried of a denizen closest to him, "What gives?"

"Every capable gentleman is to assemble and be on the ready to depart." Replied the denizen.

"Depart? For where?"

"I know not."

"Whom did the summoning?" Queried Porthos.

The denizen shrugged, then said, "I do believe it was the king."

"It really matters not. For I know who summons us and in turn will find out the cause of this chaos." Replied Porthos.

The six men, jostled by the crowd was still able to make it to the side door they so often used when seeking the king or Cardinal.

When they topped the grand marble stairs, they were amazed of how much chaos was with in as well.

Beginning down the wide corridor toward Richelieu's chambers, a small group of his guards were loitering about.

"Give way." Said Porthos, in a most authoritative voice as he could rally from within.

"What say you?" Inquired an inauspicious looking gentleman, for his countenance did not coincide with his vestments of choice.

The three stood aside one another, with Porthos in the middle.

"Give way." Repeated Aramis, "We have a directive from the Cardinal."

"Why would he summon the kings men and not his own, perchance he is short handed?" Inquired another.

"Ne' we just think he is desperate for adequate protection." Replied Athos.

"From whom?" Scowled another.

"You." Returned Athos, as the three brushed pass them and found the Cardinals' chamber door and rapped hastily upon it.

Vitray grimaced as he glanced Athos as he stepped aside to allow them admittance.

He led them through the anti-chamber and offered them comfortable chairs in which to sit and a goblet of wine.

Aramis and Porthos declined the wine, citing they needed to stay in the saddle and they were in for a long trek.

Athos, on the other hand readily accepted, if not so much as to numb his mind, alas his derrière.

Somewhere, in one of the chambers a clocks' ticking echoed, reminding them of the time passing.

As Vitray offered to refill their goblets, the tapestry on the wall was shoved hastily aside and the cardinal stepped into the chamber.

His silhouette casted by the mid day sun, resembled an aged, stooped elder, a poor representation of the Cardinal himself, to alleviate this, he persuaded his frame to stand taller and straighter, even though he was not that old.

As he whisked past his desk, he took up a piece of parchment that had some writing upon it, and he sat heavily in a chair in front of the musketeers and they, forming a half circle about him.

"I know you are wondering why you have been summoned," He began.

"That thought did not take much to cross our mind." Said Athos.

The cardinal chose to ignore the comment and continued, "I have had sentries report from the south, and east that Rohan has frequented there. To have a certainty, I have summoned any and all able bodied gentlemen to form regiments and march forth. Beginning in Montpelier and then head to Montauban. Forget not, Nimes. Truly if has been there then there should be clear evidence of such. Granted, he has a spanse betwixt us, we have to close it, make haste. Take the men form regiment and begin."

"For the love of God, we are so aware to that fact. In fact, that is what we were in the process of doing." Blurted out Athos, by now, slumped in his chair, eye closed.

"Forsooth, young man, I know God loves me." Replied the Cardinal, calmly, refusing to engage the musketeer.

"As you should think" interjected Athos, with his eyes still shut, giving the illusion he was not as coherent as his companion would like to have had him.

"You do realize do you not I can rescind your *Carte Blanche?*"

Athos raised his brow, "I think not. Your name maybe many things, but Louis is certainly not one of them."

The Cardinals' countenance reddened, alas he chose to again ignore the comment.

"Are you ready to lead them south then?" Inquired Richelieu, in reference to the regiments.

"We should think so." Replied Porthos.

"May I inquire why south? We heard he was aiming to exit France through Calais, cross over to England to seek Buckinghams' assistance. Why not make haste directly to Calais and cut off his access to the channel?"

"Monsieur Aramis, your key word is, "heard". We do not know this with absolute certainty. We have to make sure he is not loitering around Montauban or Montpellier we need a trustworthy source. Too, if he got wind of that plan, he might draw up earlier than Calais and use La Rochelle as an exit point, or earlier still. In fact he may have already done so." He laid the parchment across his lap and tented his fingers. "Fair warning, he may have set up rear guards. He is quite siege minded and intelligent. So, be awares."

Suddenly they heard musket fire.

Caught unawares, Porthos muttered mild oaths as Athos smiled.

"They are beginning the siege without us." He suggested and shrugged.

"Let them." Added Aramis, somberly, "Less blood shed."

"Good gentlemen, it is a signal to indicate all is in place and it is time to proceed. Godspeed."

Aramis accepted the Cardinals words, regained his feet, bowed, kissed the Cardinals' signet ring and slightly inclined his head.

Athos opened his eyes and regained his feet, waiting for Porthos to do the same.

Porthos bowed slightly and strode towards the door, Aramis following closely and Athos once again taking up the decanter as he sauntered by the small cart.

"You can have it back when it is empty." He called over his shoulder as he closed the door.

Once out of doors, having drained the decanter, he turned and much to the chagrin of Vitray, who had tried to follow covertly close, Athos gave the decorative piece of glass to the him.

"Now you can tell him, 'tis empty."

Athos paused and glanced at the *Palais*.

"What gives?" Queried Aramis as he gained his saddle.

"Do you realize, do you not, we have not requested to have our coffers refilled."

Aramis began to unseat himself as Athos said, "Fear not *mon mi*, I will address the matter."

"Indeed. We know just how tactful you can be, especially when it comes to the Cardinal." Porthos said, as he and Aramis chuckled.

"I shall not be gone long enough to have my absence felt."

Athos with a hasty gate made for the side door again, up the narrow, down the dimly lit passageway, up the grand marble staircase and once again down the wide passageway to the Cardinals' chamber door.

Athos took it upon himself to allow himself in unannounced, less chance for the cardinal to refuse if caught un awares.

The Cardinal was standing afore a wider than a normal cheval, turning this way and that and speaking to it as if he were to a rather large multitude.

The musketeer paused in the door way and said with a wry very lopsided grin, "What have we here, an audience of one?"

"What is it you want?" Turning at the sounds of a muffled chuckle, With reddened countenance, due to extreme embarrassment, queried the Cardinal, curtly.

"A request to have our coffers refilled."

The Cardinal gave a hasty, hearty tug on a lengthy sash that hung from the ceiling.

Immediately, from the far end of the chamber, a door opened and closed.

"Your Eminence?" Inquired Vitray.

"Seek my large coffer and withdraw sixty Louis d'ors and bring them hence. Inscribe in the ledger, 'payment for absence.'"

The time they spent with the cardinal and seemed minimal, yet in fact it was close to two hours and in that time, the men had assembled and loosely formed five regiments.

Knowing the heavy artillery had long departed, the three gained their saddles and took the lead, smiling, and knowing they had means to accommodate their needs while the were once again, away from Paris.

Their captain, Captain De Treville would not being going with them for he had been sent on a diplomatic mission of empathy, to a neighboring country.

Afore he left, he had appointed adequate sub-captains and requested his musketeers to accompany and assist them.

Their first destination was Dijon to look for indications of Rohan.

"I know not why we can not take aim at Calais. If he truly is going the way our valets observed, then he should be there." Suggested Porthos.

"Granted that sounds very implementable, alas Richelieu is directing this adventure. We need to abide. If he thinks for brief minute that we did not abide by his word, he could withhold future funds."

"Alas, my good man, we have De Treville and Louis." Reasoned Porthos.

"Do remember, he has control over the coffers. Even though Schomberg is the man behind the means, do not pause for one minute to think Richelieu does not have a say." Returned Aramis.

"Do you remember do you not, one of our schemes was to divert the munitions and re-direct them?" Queried Porthos.

"Ah, so correct." Replied Athos, "Alas at times some of the best schemes go awry as new thoughts and schemes are implemented in the stead. We have this one and as it even goes against what we believe, we must abide."

"Did I hear you correctly, you are in agreement with Richelieu?" Jested Porthos.

"Consider it a brief lapse in my judgements."

The three turned their horses about as Athos unsheathed his blade and raised it over his head and waved it as he would a standard, to signify they were to begin to move forward towards the gate and on to Dijon.

Mid day came and went as the sun was making its final bid on the day, they decided to layover for the night.

Disappointed that there was not any evidence of Rohan, they had their valet build and maintain a fire and had them prepare what the could.

Some of the men were equipped with canopies which they were able to erect and make use and the three were amoung the fortunate to possess one large enough the three of them.

"Must remember to inquire if sentries need to sent forth." Mumbled Porthos as he began to softly snore and drifted off to sleep.

Their valets had been given an adequate sized tarpaulin and was able to use a very low hanging branch and create a shelter for themselves, though the elements had not forewarned them of inclemency.

The morn was heralded by a light warm rain that a good shaking or a warm fire would not take care of and had the assistance of a warm breeze from the south as well.

The valet collectively prepared their masters' breakfast with what they had available which to Porthos' delight was quite adequate.

As Porthos sipped his mulled wine, he posed the query to his companions, "Do you not think it best if we sent our valets ahead again to find any residual evidence of Rohan? I still maintain that it would be best if our aim was truly Calais and forgo all this unnecessary frivolous traipsing about."

Aramis shook his head, "Ne', t'would be a waste of what precious time we have. Granted he may have already slipped away, alas, Richelieu want to make sure he is not loitering about Montauban or Montpellier.

Yes he was refortifying them, and can give directives from afar, alas if he t'were in custody his correspondences would be censored, thus curtail any prospective progress."

Athos at the moment was enacting tilting with his blade as he speared a piece of bread and as he brought it towards him he said, "I agree, but the time they observe or do not observe evidence and return hence, he will still be advancing toward his goal. They would only have to do that a half a dozen times and by the time they would be completing their seventh endeavor, he will have succeeded and be gone."

"True enough." Agreed Porthos, "I truly can not say, I care to follow him into England for I am not familiar with the likes of them or their ways. They have a peculiar dialect, incomprehensible."

"They say the same of us." Smiled Aramis, "Alas my good man, I do understand some of what they say. Their words are similar to ours, if you look at the them they originate from Latin as well as Italian and Spanish."

Porthos rolled his eyes, "Indeed. It all begins with the church and having to know that."

"Amoung other things."

The giant began to laugh.

"May I inquire as to what you find so amusing?" Queried Aramis, with a serious manner.

"By Jove! You can be our mouth piece if we so choose or be chosen to go across that mere riverlet. Alas in all seriousness, it t'would be best if we collectively pursued them and not send our valets out again as sentries."

Aramis nodded as he swallowed his wine.

Athos speared another piece of bread and instead of eating it, he thrusted in Aramis direction, in which without even flinching the young prelate successfully parried it.

"Really?" Queried Aramis, "Tis a poor substitute for buttoning your blade. Tsk, Tsk, Tsk."

Aramis flicked his wrist and blade abruptly upward and caught the ties to Athos' mantle and neatly sliced through it without leaving a mark on Athos or his linen shirt.

"*Mon Dieu!* Now that means I have to wear that ugly cloak pin that Madame de Medici gave me even though I declined her overtures." Smirked Athos.

"Was that afore Henri's assassination or after?" Queried Porthos, with a wry grin.

"Like it matters." Replied Athos, sternly, as he removed the piece of bread, resheathed his blade, dipped his piece of bread in the remains of a marmalade, then began eating it.

As the sun had cleared the tops of the nearby trees, a couple of sub-captains approached and slightly bowed.

"Messieurs?"

Porthos arched an brow and slightly leaned forward.

"Is it your intent to proceed?" Inquired one.

"Indeed. The whole intent is to be beyond Dijon and put us within a cannon toss of Lyon." Replied Porthos.

"In all reality, we no doubt will be in the saddle til the eve settles in and can see no further. I will not deny it will be arduous, alas it is a necessity that can not be allowed to fall by the wayside." Added Aramis, as he finished off a poached apple that had been sprinkled with the new spice, cinnamon.

Aramis gestured for the valets to begin readying themselves and the musketeers belonging so as to continue their trek towards Calais.

It seemed the rest of the encampment followed the example and they too began their preparations as well.

Fires had been extinguished, remains of kettles where either eaten or disposed of, the horses were thoroughly scrutinized again for any chaffing or maladies and their cinch straps tightened as needed.

The musketeers were a bit apprehensive as their heavy artillery were proceeding them and in the same thought relieved that if there were any obstacles, or being a rough way to go, it would be cleared away afore they came along.

They knew if they feared much, it would be a hinderance to their humour, thus they always knew and felt they needed to be courageous in presence of eminent danger or at the very least give the indifferent appearance.

A large wooded area ahead could pose a threat for they knew not lie within and it could cause a delay, for which they could nor afford if they were going to successfully capture Rohan and anyone else responsible for the Huguenots' insurrections.

The men took to their horses, with humour light and jovial.

As they entered the woods, they slowed so as to listened for anything out of the ordinary and be observant.

Porthos noticed that his horses' ears twitched anxiously rapid. An indication that a dangerous situation could arise.

He silently gestured to his companions to observe their horses for they too were becoming agitated.

Aramis indicated that they should regain their feet and carefully proceed.

Athos, understanding the intent, gestured for the regiments to continue, for if indeed their movements were being observed, surely they knew not how many men there were to begin with and certainly would not phantom three had regained their footing to cautiously proceed.

With the regiment continuing forward, muffled the musketeers stealth movements.

Pausing, behind large girthed trees, they glanced about and listened intently.

The hefty giant, indicated they should form a line across and proceed, alas pause briefly often for observations of visual and audible afore continuing.

A snap of a twig, caused Porthos to ready his harquebus, save the fuse, as he paused aside a rather large oak.

He suddenly heard movement above his head.

He gestured for his companions to stay silent and do not move and pointed upward.

Without glancing up, silently as he could, he cocked the trigger, he heard the clicking of a cross-bows mechanism.

He lit the fuse, held the harquebus over his head and pulled the trigger.

A loud shriek, followed by strong oaths of discontent and sounds of breaking boughs, followed by a loud thud.

To their utter amazement, an injured man fell from the ground.

As he lie upon the ground, writhing with pain and holding his hip, he screamed, "You shot me!"

"Better you than me." Commented Porthos, as he tucked his harquebus into his sash.

The others had gathered around in an attempt to identify the denizen.

"Are you Huguenot?" Queried Aramis.

"What difference would that have made?" The denizen replied.

"Whether you live or die." Added Athos, with a hand casually resting on his pummel.

"Or be free or be incarcerated." Suggested Porthos, with a shrug as he leaned forward.

"What if I choose not to say?"

"Then it will be assumed you are a Huguenot and be dealt with accordingly. Your silence will indicate, Huguenot." Said Athos, then added, "Can you stand?"

The denizen moaned, "I think not."

"Why can you not? 'Tis a mere flesh wound." Replied Athos as he adjusted a cuff on one of his gauntlets.

Porthos stooped further to get a hold of the back of the denizens' simple linen shirt, a very worn doublet that should have been turned and mantle, collectively and with a hasty movement, the denizen was brought to his feet.

"I forewarn you, do not crumble for if indeed I have to repeat myself, you will not like the consequences for I have no patience for dolts."

Athos nudged him, "Begin walking. We are in need of regaining our regiments."

Aramis inspected the denizens' wound.

"'Tis not as damaging as it appears. Granted he will see the surgeon, alas 'til then, we need to hasten our pace. 'Tis unfortunate that we are delayed, alas we will more than make up for it when we reach Calais."

"'Tis too late." The denizen mumbled, unheard.

"Mousequeton and Grimaud, assist keeping him upright." Suggested Aramis.

"...And moving.", added Porthos.

The men began making haste to close the gap betwixt them and their regiment.

By early eve, without pause, they were finally in contact with their rear guards of the regiments as they were within a league of Dijon.

When they were finally able to afford a pause, Porthos queried, "Again, we inquire are you a Huguenot or a Catholic?"

"Must I be either, or?" He queried in return.

They all nodded in unison.

"Upon all that is holy, be truthful." Aramis said as he folded his arms a crossed his chest, trying to strike an opposing pose.

The denizen paused.

"It is a simple response, either you are for the crown or find adversity with it." Said Athos, impatiently, reiterating, "Staying silent will only conform our thoughts of your opposition."

"What say you, for the sake of your soul, be converted to Catholic? Either way, if you are Catholic, it will only strengthen and reconfirm your faith, it will cause no harm, and if you are a Huguenot, converting will save your life." Queried Aramis.

"...And if I decline?...". He queried.

"Then I will be forced to persuade you." Replied Porthos as he withdrew his blade from its protective sheath and with the tip tapping the mans' chest, "Now do you get my point?"

Mousequeton chuckled, "My master and his point of persuasion, never fails."

"I admit...I am a Catholic."

XVII

A young sub-captain that was part of the rear guard and being vigilant in his observations, acknowledged the small group of men.

In a hasty decision, he brought the musketeers' and valets horses to them, for they chose to send them with the progressing regiments, in order to maintain the current situation for which in their uncertainty of the outcome, would preserve their horses well being.

"No time like the present." Commented Porthos, "I maintain, upon our return to Paris, I will most definitely seek the services of a cobbler."

In the dimness of twilight, a second sub-captain approached, cap in hand and bowed respectfully to the three and in acknowledgment, they in turn, bowed.

"What is my good man?" Queried Porthos.

"Actually, it is a couple of points to be made."

"Like?" Queried Athos.

"We are within a league of Dijon, and there still is no indication that Rohan passed through." Informed the young captain.

"Are there any hoof impressions? For the sod is quite soft." Observed Aramis, proving his point by picking up a foot that indeed left an impression of his foot and spur that was missing a tine that Aramis somehow conveniently forgets needing to be repaired or replaced.

"Perchance, when he passed through, it was drier and the wind to our disadvantage and Rohan advantage has swept away what evidence was here priorly." Yawned Porthos.

"You have another point?" Queried Aramis.

"Indeed. It is getting rather on the waning side of the eve, the regiments are fatigued and hungry. To their credit, we have made great progress."

"We are not as thick as Rohan, I assure you. Therefore, I understand what you are saying." Replied Aramis, sympathetically, "Allow them a lay over and if some of them have made it into the city, tell them if they desire to be billeted, they are to tell the occupants of the establishments it is in the name of the king that they are seeking shelter for the eve."

"…And for the remainders, we will make due here. Now if you will, take this gentleman with you and see to it the surgeon has a look at his needs and address it accordingly." Instructed Athos, as he shuffled his feet in annoyance, for he as with the others was quite fatigued.

During the conversations with the sub-captains, the valets had set about constructing a fire and began preparing a meal for their masters.

When the contents of the kettle were gently simmering, the valets then set about erecting the canopy for their much fatigued masters and their own tarpaulin.

In spite of the familiar night sounds, the camp was eerily silent, which sent a haunting apprehension throughout.

Porthos sitting upon the ground, propped against a tree, took great efforts to maintain his composure, for his large fatigue body and soul sagged with the weight of the eve.

Through half shut eyelids, Porthos could see his companions already at repose within the canopy using their mantles as a counterpane.

He tried to crawl the short distance for he thought it would offer a sense of security against the elements and to know if danger loomed over them, they would confront it as a unified force.

Mousequeton hastened to his masters' assistance in which Porthos declined and once inside the canopy collapsed mumbling to his valet they needed to be awaken at dawn.

The conscientious valet adjusted his masters' mantle to cover what he could of the giant. He was most grateful that he had not been given the task of removing his masters' boots, for he found that most daunting, and having the boots left on, meant the mantle could conceal areas that were more apt to get chilled first and keep his master warm and comfortable.

Just as the first rays of the morns' sun peeped above the horizon, Mousequeton and his fellow valets set about creating a fire and rousting their masters.

Soon, thin wisps of smoke arose from various areas, an indication that others had the same intent, and they were beginning to prepare for the day.

As Porthos regained his feet, a young sub-captain with whom he had spoken to recently approached.

"Monsieur?"

Porthos turned as Athos joined him.

"What gives?" Queried Athos.

"I know not." Replied Porthos, "Give him your time as well, and rest assured he will be most willing to share his ponderings."

"Indeed I shall." Replied the young man, smiling.

Afore the young man proceeded, Porthos queried, "What of Aramis?"

"What of him?" Queried Aramis, in reference to himself as he joined his companions.

"The young man was just going to say something, were you not?" Inquired Athos.

The young man slightly nodded his head.

"A sentry," he began, "has just returned from Lyon stating there still is no solid evidence of Rohan actually traversing through."

"Did they inquire anything of the denizens?" Queried Athos, skeptically.

"Yes Messieurs, some indicated a rather large regiment passed through almost two fortnights ago. Since no conflicts arose from that, they reasoned they were of the king."

Porthos had removed his cap to run his hand through his hair, which he did often when he was disheartened by unfavorable information. Athos chaffed a rough cheek and Aramis pinched an earlobe as they received the information, they too disheartened.

"Is there no impression there either?, Man? Horse? Armaments?" Queried Aramis, thoroughly vexed over the lack of evidence of man or beast.

"There is plenty of imprints of boots, but the denizens maintain, it is them in their daily struggles to survive."

"Is it plausible they are in favor of Rohans' motives are not disclosing all that they are aware of?" Queried Athos, as he adjusted his gauntlets.

"Of course it is plausible. We just need proof that this is the way he went so as to able to overtake him and let him have a conversation with Louis." Replied Aramis.

"Indeed Louis desires a conversation with him as I am certain the cardinal as well." Added Porthos.

Mousequeton silently offered his master a deep bowl of mirepoix and a bottle of wine.

Porthos glanced at it and inclined his head.

With that, Mousequeton knew that his master was inquiring after a spoon, in which the valet them began rummaging through a satchel that contain small, looseable incidentals that included eating utensils such as spoon and a newly introduced utensil from Italy, a fork. He offered both.

Accepting Mousequetons' gesture, he found a fallen tree, straddled Ashe would his horse, set the bottle down by his foot, poked and prodded at the mirepoix 'til he found something to his liking, with the thoughts of medieval tilting, he speared it and ate it.

The others grimaced at eating the mirepoix, for they had eaten it three times a day for week.

Athos commented that if he never saw mirepoix again, it would far be too soon, then thought it would be better than nothing. At least it was plentiful even though it was end of seasons' vegetables.

The three musketeers systematically returned their wares to their valets and regained their saddles.

"Lyon is ahead and hopefully the fates will smile and bestow us a favor and find what we seek." Said Porthos.

"Either that or laugh hysterically fore we are truly on a knights' errand that will come to naught." Added Athos.

With their implements gathered and stowed, saddles regained, reins and gauntlets adjusted, they hastily began for Lyon.

Even with the clouds hovering above the western horizon, it did not deter their light humour.

Each reasoned with each passing league it was closing the gap on their adversary and his apprehension was an almost a certainty.

With Lyon coming into view, a senior sub-captain went through the regiments to assess their stamina and queried if they had what it would take to by-pass Lyon and push for Montpellier.

A general consensus was taken and revealed, yes they had what it would take, but in order to go further, they need to lay over at Montpellier or make haste just shy of Nimes.

Although time was against them, they knew they had to give it their all, for failure was not part of their vocabulary, De Treville had once told them, and if by chance they did fail, it could not be said they did not try.

Rest was an indeed an option, even if it only meant a couple of hours at a time.

The leagues silently slipped away 'til Nimes arrived in the distance.

At one point a sentry returned and said they had seen evidence of a large multitude of denizens had gone through the area and requested to have the impressions inspected to garner what information they could.

The three were well versed in observations of this sort and hastily followed the sentry to the area that was believed to be remnants of Rohan.

Upon arriving, another sentry, with the appearance of a genuflecting monk, was already present and he was inspecting the imprints.

"There you have it my good gentlemen." He stated as all of the men alighted from their saddles.

"Have what?" Queried Athos, as he pulled off his gauntlets and gave them to Grimaud to maintain.

Glancing in three's direction, replied, "They were just through here. Here is the evidence you so desperately sought."

"I beg to differ." Interjected Porthos, he leaned forward, then decided to kneel as the sentry regained his stature.

The sentry furrowed his brow, "Why say you that?"

"First observations is the imprints you are are observing are truly a multitude and more than likely was, Rohan, alas they are scattered and not in a formation as a marching regiment would be…"

"…And," Added Aramis who joined his companion in kneeling, "They are were not, "just through here" as you seem to think."

"Praytell, why say you, not?"

"The grass is not level nor matted by heavy travel, it had time to recover it's original state and that being upright. If they had been here the day afore this day or so, they would be prone and given the amount of the activity upon, it would still have the appearance of being at rest."

"True, they are heading in the directions we desire, alas we can not ascertain 'tis who we seek." Said Athos.

"Is there any way to prove one way or t'other if it is Rohan?" Queried the sentry, with agitation.

"Afore I make my reply," Replied Porthos, "I sense you are agitated. What gives?"

The sentry shuffled his feet slightly.

"Messieurs, we might as well have been chasing the wind. We know not where it originates nor where it culminates. At times we can observe where it has been, alas know not which direction it is aiming for. For all we know, the cardinal has sent us on a knights' errand. Time wasted. I should think if we had a definitive answer to our quest we would have the end justify our means. Be useful and meaning, not stagnant. If we did as we originally had thoughts towards, cross the state and go directly to Calais, he would already be in custody and having his conversations with the Cardinal and the king to explain his stance."

Porthos inclined his head slightly.

"Quite right my good man. We understand your frustration and if it t'were not for the fact Richelieu quietly holds our coffers hostage, we have to abide by what he says even though we are the kings' musketeers. He turns the key. As for proof, we just have to persevere. To have definitive proof, in short of actually having him in custody, it will be difficult to prove. He may have used an alternate route and used aliases and all, what we have to do is follow this route and not deviate, this will ensure we are consist with his intent and if the fates have found favor, he will have slackened his pace for the sake of and not realize we are directly behind him and then when he least expects it, apprehend him."

The young sentry shuffled his feet again.

"You have something to add?" Queried Aramis, with an arched brow.

With curt nod he replied, "I just hope our efforts are not in vain."

"So do we all." Commented Athos, "As for now, what say you, we continue so as to close the gap?"

They all again regained their saddles and again began to follow the impressions leading south.

Once outside of Nimes city's gates they assembled for instructions to go forth seek shelter in the name of the king and take rest and a hearty meal.

"If you choose to imbibe, be easy and do not deplete your hosts' cellar for that would cause you not to be welcome on our trek back to Paris."

"What says we have to return the same from whence we came?" Queried a member of the regiment.

A subdued chuckled from all rippled through the regiment.

"Alas, we need not dull our wits with our favored drink of choice." A sub-captain instructed.

"If some of us would have enough wits to even dull in the first place." Commented a young regimental officer, newly appointed to his post.

"Just the same be complimentary, you represent the monarchy. See to it you take care. One last thing, converge a league beyond the city's walls just as soon as the clears the tops of the trees and the roosters have crowed. Which means gentlemen, rise, abide by what daily routine you have established for yourself, have had breakfast, make haste and then we must continue."

"As for now, you are on your own, do as you would do as if you were still in Paris. 'Til the morrow, God speed."

Porthos tried to subdue a chuckle as Aramis understood.

"He must not know you too well." Porthos said to Athos.

"Apparently not." Wryly smiled Aramis.

"I am not that difficult to get to know." Said Athos, jestingly.

"That is not what I heard." Added Porthos as he could not laugh, but heartily.

The three lightly touched their horses' flanks with their spurs and their horses, with a sudden lunge, sprinted for the city's gate with valets somewhat lagging behind.

Porthos let out a laugh that cleared a nearby bush of it bird occupants as he reached the gate ahead of his two companions.

"What do you find so amusing." Queried Athos.

"Reminds me of a race a brother and I undertook and he ended up on his arse in a riverlet that ran through the domains of our fathers' estate."

The weary horses began to tug on their reins as if they knew it was time to rest and was anxious to do so.

"Halt!" Porthos instructed his horse, "I assure you, you will find rest as we shall."

"No rest for the weary." Sadly smiled Athos, as he slowly shook his head

"True enough, for they are the ones that are more fatigue than us for they are the ones that are in constant motion." Added Aramis in reference to the horses.

As they were passing through the gates, other members of the regiments were funneling through as well.

The three decided to be billeted together to save themselves from having to misuse time seeking one another in the morn.

The towns' brazier-keep was setting flame a lantroon as they rode up and halted.

Gathering around him, still in the saddle, Aramis queried, "What say you, as a recommendation for accommodations on this eve?"

The man scowled.

"I have nothing to say nor add. Except this Huguenot sedition is a squanderance of time on the side of the Catholics."

"Why say you, that?" Queried Aramis.

"I say this, no matter how much cardinal what is-his name tries to eradicate France with what he calls vermIn, they will survive and continue and transcend time. A man should have ample opportunity to express his choice in matters, including religion. God is God, only difference how you worship Him is a matter of different words."

Aramis chose to remain silent, for there really was nothing he nor his companions could say for the denizen summed the situation in so very few words it left no room for an additional explanation.

The denizen took a step forward and took Mousequetons' horses' bridle and moved the animals' head cautiously aside and the animal compliantly stepped aside, allowing him to pass.

Porthos shrugged as he turned about, his companions flanked and followed him up the rue in search of shelter and supper.

Athos paused in front of a hostler and glanced about.

His companions, noticing his absence turned about to rejoin him.

"What gives?" Queried Aramis.

"Aside from being hungry, I am parched." He replied.

"You had drink afore we continued this morn." Reminded Porthos.

Athos arched a row as Aramis laughed softly.

"It has been a fortnight or longer. I remember not what it tastes like, for it has been awhile and I have thus lost the continuity of time."

"Such reasoning in an effort to preserve oneself as his companions remember him for." Smiled Aramis.

"It is as good as an excuse can get." Added Porthos.

"Like he needs an excuse." Commented Aramis.

Athos began to remove himself from his saddle to stand next to his horse.

"Besides, my good companions, I am hungry as well and since we have the opportunity to forgo mirepoix, I have chosen to seize that opportunity afore it disappears."

Porthos and Aramis alighted from their horses as well, they glanced back to see their valets as well were doing the same.

Using the tethering rings, they paused. The rues were nigh vacant in spite of the vast amount of regimental personal that filtered through the gates.

"Do we use this hostler and hope for the best or do we seek our chances of being fairly billeted from the private sector?" Queried Porthos, with one booted foot on a step to the establishment.

"It does not appear to be very welcoming." Suggested Bazin, apprehensively.

"Indeed it does not." Agreed Mousequeton.

"Suggestion my good gentlemen, if we choose to relocate, we may not be as fortunate and there will be no vacancy and we will be forced to tolerate what the kettles presently contains and may I remind you, the ground upon which we lie does not do us any favors." Said Aramis, as Athos coughed lightly and grimaced at the thought of eating mirepoix once again.

"I agree." Said Porthos, "For we know not what lies ahead and we not give the fates further reason to jest with us."

"Athos?"

"Aramis?"

"Takes little to persuade me." Replied Athos, shrugging.

"Lead the way." Suggested Aramis.

They collectively entered the establishment.

"Peste!" Exclaimed Porthos.

"Why you say that?" Queried Athos.

"Appearances are deceptive. There are more denizens here than in the rues."

"Does it matter?" Queried Aramis.

"Not really. Ah perchance it does, for what if the kettles are empty?"

"Fret not my good man." Reassured Aramis, "They will have to improvise."

The musketeers with valets, made their way to the back of the establishment.

Porthos pulled his cap to conceal his countenance.

Once seated, Athos roughly nudged him.

"What gives?" He queried.

"Do you not recognize those two?" Replied Porthos, as he nodded in the direction of two denizens, who were sitting aside the deep, large hearth, rather subdued, unconcerned.

"No. Should I?" Replied Athos.

"Indeed you should."

Both Aramis and Athos glanced in the indicated direction.

With Aramis shrugging and Aramis shaking his head.

"Think back." Prompted Porthos.

"It is a blur." Wryly smiled Athos, "As if looking through the bottom of a glass goblet, with contents.

Porthos furrowed his brow and replied, "We engaged them in a game of *lansquenet.*"

"Surely they will recognize us not." Replied Athos.

"If someone played me for a dolt, I assure you I would remember who they were." Commented Porthos.

Aramis and Athos chuckled at the thoughts of Porthos occasionally being the brunt of a caper gone awry.

"In addition, they looks as they have had a bottle or two and are obviously ignorant of their surroundings." Observed Aramis.

"I would not be so sure that they know not what is occurring, they no doubt do, alas they care not, unless it is to benefit them." Replied Athos.

As he said that, the two glanced in their direction and nodded.

"Peste! I do believe we have been recognized." Said Porthos as he tried to conceal his stature by slouching in his chair but to know avail.

One hastily regained his feet and swayed to and fro as he made his way towards the musketeers.

"I told my companion there," He began, pointing to his companion, whose cheek was resting upon the table top, "that I knew you. For it was you who conveniently and systematically emptied my purse." He hic-coughed.

"My good man, we did not leave you sou-less, we spared you some coinage so that you would not appear to be a well dressed pauper and you could procure a meal or two 'til you were able to secure your next payment from your benefactor."

"...Or Benefactress." Mumbled Aramis, in which Porthos heard and sternly glanced at him.

"Upon my faith as gentleman," He said beginning to unsheathe his blade, "I dare you to say correctly how you were able to do that with such minimal effort. It is apparent now, that something was amiss."

"It is our game of choice." Equivocated Porthos, lightly.

"'Tis more to it than that, I assure you." He replied, as his blade wavered in front of the portly musketeers' countenance.

"I would not do that if I were you." Cautioned Aramis.

"Praytell, why say you such? It is not like he will able to defend his nor your honor as gentlemen."

"If I t'were you and thankfully I am not, I would retract what you just uttered. For he does not take jesting very well, sitting down." Added Athos as he tried to in vain to conceal a derisive chuckle.

"You obviously know him not and what he is capable of." Added Aramis.

Porthos pushed himself away from the table in order to regain his feet more easily.

He withdrew his ponaird from his boot after he unsheathed his blade.

"You have erred me for someone that gives a care. As for errors, you have already committed a few. I SHAll defend their honor for they ARE gentlemen and I shall see to it their honor is left intact after this encounter, to accuse me of something amiss with the game, it is a game of chance. I, we have played it often enough to be able to verify the cards. Alas there is always a chance I will bet too much and loose. Unlikely. Alas, it is what it is. May I inquire why say you feel something was amiss?"

"It was quite obvious." Replied the denizen, as he suddenly lunged at Porthos, who on the ready, side-stepped and deflected the thrust and in turn parried.

"I play as I normally do. Nothing amiss." Porthos, in turn stomped his heavy foot and lunged forward.

The denizen thought he had seen something upon the toe of his boot and stooped to brush it off.

"I dare say, that may have well been a mouse." He hic-coughed, as his stance wavered as his blade did as well.

Porthos lunged again, this time catching the excess material of the mantle on the shoulder and piercing it.

The denizen shuttered as he came in contact with the musketeers' broad heaving chest, he attempted to take a step back and as he did Porthos did the same.

With his back against the wall, he shrieked, "Again this is unjust!"

Porthos raised an inquiring brow and queried, "How so?"

"'Tis three against two. I am out numbered."

"My companions, I have not beckoned them forth to assist me nor you of yours. You must not know how to calculate the circumstances correctly."

"Indeed I do. One is your sword as well as one for me, two is you as for me and your advantage, three is your ponaird."

Porthos shook his head.

"You dolt!" He said, then added, chuckling more to himself, than to the others "Then allow one of my companions keep you in fellowship til we are gone on the morrow. Then on the morrow you will be released on your own recognizance into your own custody with the cautionary words, do no attempt to follow."

He the withdrew the blade of his sword then replaced it his ponaird and struck the mantle so hard and fast, the denizen would need assistance from more than just his companion to release him and since the hostler was full of many regimental personal and the common denizens, mingling and carrying on as if a cease-fire had been implemented, it would be thus difficult to request additional assistance from someone that was sober enough to pry him loose.

Muttering mild oaths of revenge, he succumbed to the effects of too much wine as his companion had already preceded him in doing so.

Finally an inn-keep or someone representing him approached and inquired what it was they sought.

"Whatever your kettles contain, be it regional or traditional, we do believe it matters not and somewhere to lay silently down for the remainder of the eve." Replied Porthos.

"Just bring it. Must not forget the wine." Added Athos, attempting to sound stern and authoritative.

"Porthos, you just waylaid our chance of amusement." Commented Aramis.

Porthos inclined his head slightly.

"Perchance I have, but I would rather have done that, than get poked through with unnecessary holes. I surely would leak more than just wine. I do believe that he does not hold a blade well. Do we dare try the fates with other unsuspecting dolts?" He queried.

"Must not tempt the fates to often, for they might favor adding weights to their side of the scales." Replied Aramis, "By the by, our coffers were recently refilled, we are not in want."

"Mousequeton my good valet, where is that satchel of mine that has a fine selection of trinkets and incidentals?" Queried Porthos.

The valet took it upon himself to rummage through it to search for either the dice or the worn deck of cards.

He was able to locate three dice and a better share of a very worn deck and readily handed them to Porthos.

"What do you propose we do with these?" Queried Athos.

"Improvise. It is obvious that the whole deck is not available, so my dear Mousequeton, dig further to see if the others can be accounted for. If so, I have a thought of a game."

The valet began taking the objects out of the satchel a handful at a time and as the mound grew the absent cards began to appear.

Porthos reached across the table to gather up the cards, sorted through them to retrieved the queens. He then placed those in front of each of his companions, including Mousequeton as he explained, they needed four to play, then thoroughly shuffled the remaining and dealt his companions, and Mousequeton five cards each.

The remaining pile he laid in the center of the table.

"The object is complete the column descending order. Play from your hand, as many as you can, if you can not, take one from the middle. When those are gone, if it is your turn and if you can not go forward, pass one of your choice to your companion on your left."

"….And what do you call this pastime?" Queried Athos.

"Deception." Smiled Porthos with an arched brow, "By the by, to make in more interesting, toss in a few sous and the one who completes his column, can claim the wagers."

"At first glance, looks easy enough." Added Aramis, "Who goes first?"

"Toss a die, lowest goes first."

They each gave a light toss and Mousequeton was able to go first.

He was able to place down the knave and the ten spot.

Athos not able to play from his hand, drew one, same as Aramis.

With enough turns, the center pile was soon depleted where then they had to rely on each other for completion of their columns.

Porthos had completed his column to the point of three, he had begun to think he might be the one who would be claiming the wagers, alas his valet had other thoughts, for he was able to culminate his column with the card that Athos had passed him.

"What are you waiting for?" Queried Aramis, "The sous are yours."

Mousequeton chuckled as he claimed the small pile.

"I can now see why you call it, "Deception.", Said Aramis, smiling wryly, as he tossed his cards towards Porthos, with the others doing so as well, for their long awaited meal arrived.

"When you have finished," began the inn-keep, "at the very end of the passageway, the chamber to the left, with the door ajar, is the one set aside for you."

As they began to devour their meal, they had not realized the once noisy hostler was beginning to quietly slip towards the morns' hours.

The regiments sought billeted comfort and the common denizen sought their chateaux.

When they had finished, they had regained their feet and began for the passageway and as the did so, they passed by Porthos' conquest.

Porthos stooped to pick up the cap from the planking and afore he placed it upon the denizens' head, he lifted it.

"Hold!" Exclaimed Aramis.

"Why, what gives?" Queried Porthos', vexed.

"Being somewhat cultured, what is the byway of some artists that paint images of inanimate objects?"

"You dolt," Added Athos, "'Tis a still life."

"*Voila*! Now you have a masterpiece from Porthos. How appropriate, he even took time to hang his piece on the wall, thus saving a curator a might of time." Said Aramis.

They all laughed til their sides ached.

Upon hearing light snoring, he let the denizens' chin rest again against the chest, replaced the cap then followed his companions to the assigned chamber.

Afore much else could be said, Porthos who had been sitting on the side of the unadorned, simple bed, that was lacking a counterpane as well as other bedclothes, had silently fell backwards and he too began to snore softly.

Mousequeton beckoned to his fellow valets to assist him in getting his masters' boots off and get his entire body upon the bed.

With much effort, the three valets managed and with one hefty nudge they were able to roll Porthos to his side and his snoring ceased.

Athos, not being very selective, slouched in a chair, pulled his cap over his eyes as Grimaud used his masters' mantle as a counterpane, and covered him.

Aramis, erstwhile gently laid his fatigued self next to his companion and he too promptly fell asleep.

When morn arrived, the suns rays illuminated the small dismal chamber, they hastily shut their eyes to avoid its brightness.

Although it provided a temporary relief, it was time to move on as they realized it was still a half of a fortnight to reach Bordeaux.

The valets dutifully rousted their masters and assisted them in their daily preparations.

Athos had regained his feet, only to lie on the planking and sighed.

Porthos stooped over him and queried, "My good Athos, what gives, are you not right?"

"I am quite right, with the exception of being quite parched. I was not able to suppress my want last eve and by the looks of things, I will not be able to do much about it 'til we have a celebratory bottles of wine when we finally are able to lay our hands on Rohan and his co-conspirators." Replied Athos.

"That does not explain why you are upon the planking in such a manner."

"You would be too, if you felt you were out of alignment after finding repose in an uncomfortable chair. Aside from that, it adds to have a new perspective of things."

"How so?" Queried Aramis, "What is your new perspective?"

Squinting, he could see small fissures in the plaster.

"When one only sees what is afore him, he continues as such. Given the chance see things from a different viewpoint, he might see the flaws and make corrections to avoid a catastrophe or if he has a devil may care attitude, he will go blindly forth and let fate take utter and complete control."

"Controlled chaos?" Queried Aramis.

Athos nodded.

"Do you need assistance?" Queried the gentle giant, "The offer is valid momentarily." He added smiling wryly.

Athos accepted the extended hand and regained his feet.

When they all had gathered their belongings, they sought the grand hall, in reality it was rather *petit*, given the circumstances, so as to seek out breakfast and gather beyond as instructions had been dictated.

As they entered the hall, the denizen was still adhered to the wall with the assistance of Porthos' ponaird and his companion, still sitting, pitched forward where he was left the eve afore.

"Must be they like your masterpiece Porthos for the curator has let it still hang where you left it." Said Aramis.

Finding breakfast rather on the lean side, they made the best of it with reasoning perchance the inn-keep had not employed the right denizen for not knowing how to sufficiently prepare enough food for a multitude rather than a small establishment. Then their thoughts turned, that too many denizens already preceded them in their quest for a meal as well. Then again, perchance Louis' regiments t'were not the only regiments to have been billeted and other regiments had thus depleted his reserves.

"No matter," thought the Musketeers, "As we come across another hostler, tavern, inn whatever the case may be or what it was called, we will make use of its services."

As the exited the establishment, it occurred to them that they were beginning to see the regiments gathering and moving towards their designation rendezvous point.

They too realized it was left up to them to retrieve their own horses and secure their possessions.

When they thought they had everything its place and began to lead their horses into the courtyard in order to settle their incurred debt, although the were billeted, the inn keep scoffed at the mere thought of billeting anyone, though it was court mandated, he believe he would not recoup a single sou and thus sustain a loss over the ordeal, they inadvertently left a few things upon the ground.

"They all had proper places when we began." Lamented Porthos, "I for one, do not want to leave anything behind. It is all beneficial."

"I suggest you tuck a few things in your satchel and a few things under your horses' saddle. Mind you things that will not impede his movements or irritate him." Suggested Aramis.

"Your valet knows what is what." Commented Athos, "They have all learned how to cope with things like this in the relative short time we have had their services."

Aramis inclined his head in agreement.

"True enough." Said Porthos, then, "Mousequeton, my good man. See what you can do to finish this task, I am going to settle our debt. Then we ought to continue."

The musketeer then handed his reins to his valet and re-entered the tavern, to seek the inn-keep.

As Porthos returned, Aramis nudged Athos.

"Something is amiss." He said with a *sotto voc.*

"Why say you?" Inquired Athos, vexed.

"That dolt wanted two doubloons." Said Porthos, quite piqued at the mere thought of parting with that much.

"Why say he, so much?" Queried Aramis.

"He claims we emptied his wine vault and nigh depleted his pantry." Said Porthos, disdainfully, "We could not have emptied his wine vault. For Athos was still upright."

"….And?" Prompted Aramis, trying not to laugh aloud.

"And, nothing. Although I wanted to pummel him, I settled our debt. Let us continue afore I change my thoughts!"

The six men took up the reins to their horses and began for the gate, the rue that would lead the to Bordeaux and beyond to Calais.

Upon reuniting with their regiments at their destination rendezvous, many personal were gathered and glancing towards the ground as if observing something out of the ordinary.

The three joined the others to assist in the assessment.

A sub-captain righted himself as the three approached.

"What gives?" Queried Aramis.

"We have the evidence we have so long sought."

"How so?" Inquired Porthos.

"A denizen plying his trade, observed a rather large multitude of regiments, armaments and munitions passed by this way about a fortnight ago. The evidence of such is the deep ruts created by the heavy cumbersome cannons, many imprints from man and beast. When the denizen queried if they were friend or foe, the reply was, "Some deem us friend and some deems us foe."

"That is quite a vague reply and circumstances." Added Athos, brushing a plume away from his brow.

"Ah my good man, that is where you are in error."

Athos furrowed his brow.

"How so?" He queried.

"A very over zealous cadet voluntarily surrendered information concerning their identity." Replied the sub-captain.

"Then, what said?"

"We stand for the unification of all Huguenots."

"Being identified as Huguenot is all well and good, alas, was Rohan leading them? He may have had a different agenda." Suggested Aramis.

"Nothing was said to indicate one way or t'other."

"Is it then decided to continue in the direction of these imprints?" Queried Porthos.

"Given they lead to Bordeaux." Replied the sub-captain, as himself regained his saddle and turned his horse about.

Others, following his example, regained their saddles and began making their way to Bordeaux.

From somewhere in the regiment, someone queried how far was Bordeaux a reply came back as about a week of steady riding.

Four sub-captains in front went through the regiments getting them to fall into formation, being fatigued as they were, they begrudgingly complied.

The terrain was uneven and hazardous as the elements had taken its toll on the older trees and they had begun to decay where they were fallen.

The larger ones impeded progress of the procession, with many left wondering if the Huguenots dared to truly be adventurous enough and had gone this way.

Resting when they could find accommodations, at time meager and left a lot to be desired, they took advantage of whatever was offered.

As Bordeaux arrived on the horizon, gull appeared as small dots against the azure heavens, the whisky clouds with assistance of a strong breeze, pushing them hastily towards an unknown destination, the smell of the sea greeted them as the descended down a rather steep knoll.

Finally a wide swath, worn away by the many sojourner over the years, seeking refuge, finished leading them to the city's massive iron gates, to their delight were opened but no doubt would close as dusk settled in.

Again the regiments were instructed to seek being billeted and a warm supper.

By now, many of their horses were as fatigued as their riders, for their heads hung low as they walked and their gaits were out of rhythm.

As the last rays from the descending sun were being extinguished, they all found the relief that they so sought.

When morn arrived, too soon many proclaimed, as they collected their wits and their belongs, they went to seek their horses to ready them.

Many retaliated when they were approached by personal holding a bridal or saddle.

Many of the officers opted to obtain a new horse thus close the gap more hastily than maintain one that threatened to drop in its imprints if it took one more step.

With their keen ears laid back, head lowered and threatening to either buck or kick, they were let be 'til the end of the task, then with a kind but a manipulative way, success.

After a hasty breakfast and then when all the tack was in the proper place, and the regiments regained their saddles and continued.

With the bright sunlight, came the gulls, screeching loudly above, as if demanding the sea faring vessels feed them, caravels were being loaded, while anchored ones in the harbor bobbed reluctantly on the waves, waiting to make port and be relieved of their burdens that they had acquired from far off lands, the heavens were cloudless and bright and no indications of inclement elements.

Armed with the information that the Huguenots indeed did pass through there and they were on the right trail, it lifted their sullen humour to a more hopeful one.

When they were within a two days' ride of La Rochelle, the sub-captains requested a counsel with all of the officers and the three musketeers to orchestrate their tactics for the next few days in the event they were to have an encounter with the Huguenots.

One sub-captain, whom De Treville trusted, went by the name of Marcel du Champs. He readily and hastily accepted factual information and was able to formulate successful strategies against any given adversaries.

"Approximately a league from La Rochelle our byway here narrows considerably, it could be used to our disadvantage. Rohans' may have instructed a regiment or two remain behind and be used as an obstruction in any pursuing regiments. We need to be alert and aware of our surroundings and at any slight movement, take notice, react accordingly, be ever cautious. Some of the armaments have been in place afore La Rochelle and have been trying to breech their walls and gain entrance into the city. The last word I have received, they have hope but alas, their efforts thus far is are vain."

He then instructed the particular regiments as to where to place themselves in revalence to the city's south and east wall. The west wall faced the sea with its many well guarded piers and well equipped caravels patrolling the harbor. The north wall had been reinforced over the years to prevent marauding adversaries from overtaking the citadel and control of the city.

They again would move into place when the eve had firmly settled in and even if they were on the ready, Marcel reasoned they would not be expecting a regiment of grapplers.

When the way had began to narrow as Marcel had predicted, a sudden explosion was heard on their left.

As Porthos exclaimed, "Peste! What was that?", a cannon ball hit hard, displaced a large amount if earth, momentarily creating a cloud of dust.

His horse reared and unconventionally unseated him, causing unceremoniously a pratfall.

"Someone is firing upon us, you dolt!" Replied Athos quite sternly, "Seek cover, seek cover!" He yelled as men scrambled from their horses to use nearby trees as shields against the barrage of musket balls that began screaming passed them in a frantic effort to find its mark.

More loud thunderous explosions were heard, followed by trees falling and men shouting, "It is an ambush! Seek cover!"

The musketeers managed to load their harquebuses and set the fuse.

A musketeer ball suddenly hit above Porthos' head, causing the sapling to shatter and send out splinters in all directions.

"They must be using muskets." He thought as he chuckled to himself.

Much to their dismay, arrows began raining in upon them causing even more confusion.

Someone fell behind Athos.

The musketeer turned to see what was occurring and upon seeing a fallen companion, he knelt beside him.

"Are you hit or did you stumble?" He queried as he saw a small fallen tree.

"Feels like both." Came the reply.

"Where?"

The young man rolled to his back, then sat up and held a knee.

"Leave go." Instructed Athos pried the young mans' fingers away from the indicated spot, which had been initially covered by a boot.

Athos sighed.

"Indeed you have been hit." He said.

The young man glanced heavenward and mumbled an imploring prayer.

"Alas, my good man, your boot has prevented contact with your knee, for if it had, it no doubt would have been shattered and we would be having quite a different conversation with others than ourselves."

"Musket balls, need musket balls here." Someone yelled as Mousequeton recognized that voice and it belong to Aramis.

"Master? Monsieur Aramis, there!" Mousequeton said, pointing to a large tree that was well concealing his companion.

Porthos began to search his satchel for a small weighted wrapped parcel that contained spare musket balls.

The hail storm of munitions continued as Porthos, gave a handful of musket balls to Mousequeton and instructions to keep low and unseen and fire only when necessary.

The musketeer was able to nimbly bound from one tree to the next, unscathed.

Upon reaching his companion, he found Bazin desperately attempting to set a fuse.

"Take ease my good man. Here, use these as well." Said Porthos as he handed the valet a measure of wick and a large handful of munition.

Aramis deftly reloaded his harquebus with the munitions that his companion had provided, set the fuse, aimed and fired it.

They collectively heard a shriek, unsure if it t'were from man or beast, they continue to fire off volleys til it became silent and the rapid responses that had been occurring, had slowed then became nigh non-existent, only an infrequent sounding from a musket or harquebus gave indications that the little skirmish had ended.

As the darkness of the eve began to enfold them, sub-captains began to make their way through the well concealed regiments beckoning them to reassemble in the nearby the small well secluded clearing it would be there they could collectively take ease, have some supper and get some rest if they could and they again decide if they had enough stamina to try for La Rochelle.

Once they had reassembled, the sub-captain assessed any losses they incurred.

"By the grace of God," One was heard to say, "The loss we sustained is less than one hundred men. How unfortunate for the loss, alas the odds were not in our favor considering we were ambushed, it truly is minimal and a miracle that we did not loose more than we had."

"Indeed" Said a second.

The regiments, very fatigued found their way to the specified clearing.

When the fires had been lit and kettles filled to capacity and beginning to simmer its contents, the sub-captain called for a counsel.

"We still can either by pass La Rochelle, and let them think have a victory over us, or assist them in self destruction of their own citadel. If it is chosen to keg the citadel, that would mean they would have to deplete their inventory at Cre'teil. Both would be at our mercy and then Louis would have the opportunity to present them with an appropriate treaty of peace." Said one of the sub-captain as he tried to discreetly get a companions' attention to assist in the explanation of legging La Rochelle with little or no effort.

The sub-captain and his assistant who was tying his mantle in place, explained one of the munition cart contained small easily portable kegs that could easily be concealed with a mantle.

After the mantle was tied in place, he lifted the corner of his mantle and exposed the small keg.

"It's weight is minimal and will not impede the grapplers. The wick you set should be your arms' length betwixt the kegs and that should give you adequately enough time to make haste to and through the gate. By a report of a sentry, they close their gates at the stroke of twelve. By our calculations it is just after ten."

"Prescisely, where is the citadel in relation to the sea?" Queried an officer.

"Half a league through the main gate, then a third league to the west. It is guarded well, so that means some of you can ascend the wall behind it and some will ride through the gate and be wayward sojourners in search of a hostler. The sentry also located the citadel one hundred fifty paces behind, "The Black Swan."

"Do we use a torch or lantroon to light our way?" Queried a young stout officer, "for the moon is none more that a waning sliver."

"Neither." Replied the sub-captain in charge, "They need not see us coming. Do watch your step, there is a lot of fallen timber about and do not go charging ahead like a raging bull. That surely would forewarn them. Porthos, if you will, go through the main gate as Athos and Aramis, will help the grapplers get in place and set the fuses and lit them unitedly then without causing suspicion, yes Athos you may have "a" goblet of wine."

"That will cause suspicion in its self." Smiled Athos, weakly.

"How so?" Queried the sub-captain with an arched brow of curiosity.

"He drinks far more than "a" goblet of wine in one sitting." Said Aramis as he tried not to chuckle too loudly.

The sub-captain sighed, "You needs your wits about you, one goblet and return with the others."

"Far be it for me to to disobey an order." He replied.

"My good man, you know as well as I do, it depends on who did the instructing." Said Porthos, shaking his head.

The hefty musketeer then checked the contents of his powder horn, the measure of wick to be used as a fuse and the count of musket ball.

He then readied a pistol and harquebus without setting the fuse.

The grapplers gathered about Athos and Aramis and the munitions cart to prepare themselves with the small kegs.

The ones following Porthos slung the small kegs from their shoulders using the measure of wick as a strap.

They concealed the kegs by using their dark colored mantles, another measure of wick was metered out, and they also readied a small pistol tucked neatly in the sashes about their waists.

If all went well, there would be no need to draw their sheathed blades that hung conveniently at their sides, by their unadorned baldrics.

"Monsieur Porthos, if you please, escort these twelve and begin." Suggested the young sub-captain as he tapped the twelve chosen fledglings on the shoulder and indicated they needed follow Porthos, "They will help assist in the placements of the small kegs and if needed they can curtail any delays caused by interferences."

Athos and Aramis assisted their eighteen fledglings too, affixing the small kegs to the small of their backs, so that they could be easily concealed by their mantles as well.

"When you accomplish your set task, you need not locate one another. Alas make haste back here and once all in one place, we will continue for Angers. That *mon amis* is a three days ride."

As Porthos was about to begin his trek towards La Rochelles' main gate, Aramis called out to him.

"Porthos my good man, hold!"

"What gives?" Queried Porthos.

"Turn your mantle."

"Why for?"

"You have the kings' favored color exposed. Many will recognize you as for the king. Turn it, the inner color will suffice."

"Alas in midst of the eve, one color closely resembles the other and will not be detected even by one of high ranking."

"We can not chance it." Reasoned Aramis.

Porthos hastily and nimble removed the mantles' decorative brooch, and turned the mantle inside out and as he was about tie the mantle in place and fasten the brooch, Aramis covered his hand.

"Do not use that either."

"Why for not?" Inquire Porthos, quite vexed.

"It resembled the kings' coat of arms, thus it would be a dead give away if you t'were to use it. Put it in your purse and tie it tight."

"'Tis not his coat of arms, I assure you. T'was a gift."

Aramis inclined his head slightly and said, with a *sotto voc*, "I know."

Porthos then tied it in place and placed his valued brooch in his purse and securely tied it closed.

The two groups of men departed and began for La Rochelle.

When they began to see torch lights emanating from the keep and turrets of the citadel, Porthos indicated for them to part and have them continue and to come up behind the structure, once there, stay in the silhouettes of the structures and his companions will indicate where to set the little kegs so they will create the most disruption.

The three knew that the citadels' arsenal was the main structure that needed their immediate attention as well as the ones within close proximity. In this case, it was the barracks of the regiments as well as a common storage area of dried and preserved foods, mainly fish.

As Porthos approached the main gate, he let his shoulders sag as if he was on an extensive, exhaustive sojourn. His fledglings did the same.

"Hold Monsieur! Are you right?" Queried a sentry at the gate.

"To be perfectly honest, some say I am a little off center." Smiled Porthos, "Alas, we are in need of supper, late as the hour is, it matters not."

"There is a very well worn path leading east towards the sea, it is the one upon which you presently stand, follow it 'til another crosses it and becomes four corners, use the left side, it will led you to the "Black Swan." It should be nigh empty at this time and all will be well." Instructed the sentry.

As Porthos inclined his head in acknowledgment, a bell began to toll.

"I am curious as to why such a bell would should at this hour. Is something amiss?"

The sentry laughed at Porthos ignorance and replied, "Ne' my good man. It is tolling to announce another arrival of munitions and it is summoning all available men to assist in its storage."

"I would not think twice, for I could be of assistance for I truly am able to carry fifteen stone easy."

Again the sentry laugh.

"Indeed. It then should make the process a rather short one and then they can all rest for the remainder of the eve. For in the morn, when it dawns, new strategies will be implanted for our safety and security. Louis knows not what he is up against for he certainly would tread a whole lot more lightly if he only knew."

Porthos smiled and said nothing as he beckoned his small regiment to follow.

"Why Monsieur did you say you will assist when we have other intentions?" Queried one.

"Just observe." Replied Porthos as they turned left as instructed.

As they did so, a cart with a stack of barrels, precariously placed, appeared and continued towards the citadel in slow procession, obviously being cargo from a moored caravel.

It halted in front of a rather large well guarded structure. Two men carefully removed the barrels one at a time and laid it on its side so it could be easily rolled into place.

"Where do you want this?" Queried Porthos, who had picked it up and placed it on his shoulder.

"Hold my good man. Take caution and do not jostle them about in a careless manner.", Warned a denizen.

Porthos knew the difference but said nothing in reply.

"In here, against the wall. There is fifteen in all that have to be stowed away neatly so that other arriving munitions can can be stowed as well."

Porthos gestured for his men to cautiously roll some in his direction as well so he could place them inside.

Other men arrived and proceeded to assist as well.

Porthos retrieved the last one and as he entered the structure, he deliberately dropped it, thus loosened the top enough, spilling some of the contents.

"OH! Monsieur. Take ease, 'tis not something that needs to be jostled about." Cautioned another of the men.

"Right end it and some how manage to get it back whence it came." Instructed another, as he and his companions returned to their previous activities, calling out as they departed, "Appreciate your assistance good gentlemen. *Bon Soir.*"

The musketeer immediately recognized it as gun powder and instructed his regiment to scoop it up an follow him in which they did and as he was about to close the door, he heard a small thud above his head.

"They are here." He said smiling, indicating the grappler and his companions were about to come over the wall behind them.

He began to make a fine line with his gun powder leading towards the wall and as his hands were emptied another man stepped forward and continued 'til they had all used what the had collected.

As they reached the wall, he recognized his two companions.

"Here is where I left off, set the wicks collectively with the one end to follow forth the other wicks lead off your little kegs that will be place about the given structures. Have the available end be over the wall at a distance afore you set them. Although a goblet of wine sounds rather tempting at the moment, I would not want to be in the vicinity when these structures go heavenward." Again the musketeer smiled as he raised a brow.

Athos and Aramis curtly nodded and they and the armed grapplers slipped silently and hastily amoung the structures silhouettes to lay and prepare the small kegs for detonation.

The clock within the citadel announced the hour of eleven just as Porthos arrived at the gate.

"What? Leaving so soon Monsieur?" Queried the sentry.

"We have reached our limits and now it is time to press on. So many leagues, so little time." Lamented Porthos, as his little regiment grumbled, feigning discontentment.

Porthos turned to his regiment and said, "Enough! 'Tis a task we must bear and no amount of discontentment will alter the fact that we have been summoned to Calais to prevent the overture of the kings' current intent."

The sentry slightly inclined his head, said nothing further and stepped aside to let them pass.

"Monsieur, what is the kings' current intent?" Queried a member of his regiment, when they were an adequate distance away from La Rochelle.

Porthos shrugged, "I know not, it just sounded well to utter such. Apparently the young sentry is not current with the kings' utterances."

Once they reached the clearing where they all originally congregated, the musketeer relayed the current events and added, "At any moment we should see fireworks that will far out distance the kings' celebrated marriage to Anne or his coronation and then be joined by my companions."

Just as he yawned a loud explosion was heard.

"....And so the display has commenced, now to await for Athos and Aramis."

322 KATHLEEN CLARE

They all converged to the edge of the clearing to observe the display of their handiwork.

In rapid succession, explosions were heard as the brightness from the flashes were seen and forms mens running hastily towards them.

Athos and Aramis nearly knocked into Porthos as they hastened by, completely breathless, turned and fell to the ground at the giants feet.

The sub-captains in charge approached Porthos and patiently waited for the running figures to halt and hoping it was Porthos' his companions.

To their delight it was, then to patiently await them to steady their breaths so they could relate what was accomplished.

Porthos lent his companions a hand to assist them in regaining their feet.

As they did so, they began laughing.

"Inform us as to what you find so amusing so that we join you in its levity." Said one of the sub-captains, sternly.

"Ah Messieurs, scaling the wall was accomplished with little effort," Began Aramis, "Once over that obstacle, if you so choose to call it that, there was Porthos and his *petit* regiment. He had laid a small line of powder towards the rear of the establishment, for he claims is well stocked with armaments and numerous large kegs of powder. He even assisted in storing powder." Aramis laughed again.

"Indeed," Added Athos, "His original scheme was to assist them in kegging their own fort, and he did just that."

"We then set the small kegs, pried to tops just enough for spillage and laid wicks long enough and had them converge at the wall. Thankfully we did not encounter any opposition, and thus we reclaimed the wall and I set the wick and as the sparks indicated it was aiming for the first little keg, I made haste."

"Forsooth, you did indeed." Smiled a sub-captain.

"Rohan has a false sense of security. Alas, that pride and downfall is to our benefit." Said another.

"I can just imagine the chaos it has created." Chuckled Porthos.

"Is there any chance of a pursuit?" Inquired a sub-captain, cautiously, afore he could hear a reply, more of the grapplers were running towards them, stumbling through the dark.

"Ne, I think not for they would not know; whom, nor what nor where to which direction in order to begin. If sent out in all directions, they would leave themselves vulnerable, "Aside, they shall be well preoccupied with the circumstances and they thus will be easily defeated. I do believe they would not want to risk such." Said Aramis.

"In any event, we realize we are all experiencing fatigue and there is a great need for rest, in which we will comply. Alas, it will be a rather brief layover. For we still need to reach Calais."

"Were you able to surmise if Rohan was here or had been here?" Queried a Sub-captain.

Aramis, who was removing debris from his knees, replied, "Ne'. All was silent and calm. 'Til now." He smiled, mischievously. "I would imagine if he were present he would have gathered up a regiment or two and celebrate previous victories in the name of the Huguenots and do some carousing."

"Ah, but if he t'were there, we provided the fireworks as the king would, provided he t'were in favor of the king rather than oppose him." Added Porthos, "Ah but we did some celebrating of our own."

A sub-captain inquired of Aramis, "Pardon Monsieur, what are you about?"

"In haste, in my levity, I stumbled numerous times over fallen timber. Without a torch to light our way, we managed the best we could. I am just removing the debris. Bother! Not even a sliver of the moon to guide us."

The sub-captain then returned his attention back to the matter at hand.

"Then by the sounds of things, you have created a means of accessing the city by the way of a rather large gaping whitlow in the wall and the arsenal."

"*Oui* Monsieur and no matter if a tourniquet is applied it will not stem the flow of defeat." Commented Athos.

The sub-captains chuckled at the metaphor.

They then turned about to observe whether they could actually hear anything or see anything of worth.

They were able to perceive a convergence of numerous pin pricks of flickering light, in which they imagined it to be torches, in a certain area in which their display of firework originated from. They took as an indication that the damage was being assessed and calculations being made as to its mending.

"Looks as we have success in the name of Louis. It will take them a bit to repair your little breech you created and thus as they commence their repairs, more regiments will accost them from another section. It will continue 'til they submit voluntarily or forced, no matter. It will get costly both monetarily and physically. A man and structure can endure just so much afore a white flag goes upon a standard. Rest awhile gentlemen, as much as we need to continue towards Angers and Nantes', many of you will not be able to make the trek lest we get some much needed rest. Since they truly know not we are here, a lay over is needed. Mind you not a prolonged one for we can not afford to have Rohan slip away. It would not set well with me if he did." Suggested one of the sub-captains.

"Many of you have your valets accompanying you, seek them. Have them feed you, make you comfortable as possible under the circumstances, and get your much needed rest." Added another.

"Monsieur, may we have the comforts of a fire? It would certainly add." Commented a musketeer.

"Aside from the fact we have to be able restore our tinder boxes." Someone else added.

"Indeed. If you can dig out a small trenches and do not let the flames be as obvious, then, so be it. In the light of day, have your valets set snares and not use anything such as your harquebuses to create unwarrented attention."

"What if they do not know how to set a snare?" Came a query.

"Then they had better have hasty instructions so that they as well as the rest of us will not go hungry. Our provisions can last just so long."

"We commend your efforts this eve gentlemen, do as you need. *Bon soir.*" Added a third sub-captain.

The sub-captains sought each other to form their own *petit* encampment.

Each of the regimental personnel were able to locate their prospective valet and made adequate use of the remainder of the pre-dawn hours.

Just as the sun was going to make its daily debut, Porthos was roughly nudged repeatedly 'til he opened an eye to get a glimpse of the one responsible for such insolence at such an early hour.

"What gives?" He queried as he rolled to his back.

"Tis I Master, Mousequeton." Came the replied, quite urgently.

"I only had one valet and if memory serves, his name was Mousequeton."

"Oh! Master do not say, "was"." He implored, "Hear me, then decide if I am to be a 'was'".

"Hmmm." Mumbled the musketeer.

"We have problems."

"What sort of problems are you referring to?"

"There are regiments in the wooded area betwixt here and La Rochelle."

"How is it you came to know this?" Queried Porthos as he sat himself up and leaned back against an adequate sized tree.

"I was summoned." Replied the valet, who was thoroughly embarrassed and not ready to admit the cause of his absence.

Porthos immediately understood and said, "We all need to at one point or t'other. Now, why are you saying there are regiments amoung the trees."

The valet had an anxious look in his eyes and clearly agitated and replied, "Master the trees Monsieur Aramis stumbled over in the dark were not fallen timber, they pose no threat."

"How is it you know this?"

Mousequetons' eyes widened as if struck by fear, "They" he stammered, "They, the regiments. They are dead."

"Peste!" Muttered Porthos, "Just when we thought we were making progress. I shall wake my companions and inform them as you their valets. We then will go inform the sub-captains. Erstwhile, set some snare about with caution then prepare breakfast. With the fates smiling in our favor, your snares will prove worthy, our kettle filled then ourselves and yes, try and make sense whose responsible for this melee."

Porthos regained his feet, then strode over to Aramis and lightly kicked the bottom his booted foot.

Aramis, who was laying on his side facing the small nigh lifeless fire, mumbled something incomprehensible.

"Aramis! Rise! There is something amiss about."

Sitting up, he pushed his cap away from his eyes and as he was gathering his wits about him, Porthos rousted Athos as well.

"What gives?" Queried Athos, crossly.

"Mousequeton claims there are fallen regiments amoung the wooded area betwixt here and La Rochelle. Those fallen timber you stumbled over, t'was not timber but are a deceased regiments."

Aramis scowled.

Athos, still heavy lidded for the want of sleep, struggled to regain his feet, surrendered to fatigue and sat silently upon his mantle on the dampen ground.

"It can mean only one thing, actually two." Said Porthos, pausing.

"Well ?...", Queried Aramis, attempting in vain to conceal a yawn.

"The regiments we requested of Louis afore, managed to be here, alas Rohan had out maneuvered them and readily laid waste to them."

"Or ?....", Prompted Athos, finally regaining his feet, assisted by Porthos' extended hand.

"They are causalities of Rohans' who were caught unawares. Upon hearing an unfamiliar sound, they chose to investigate and *voila,* they were greeted by a regiment or two of Louis'."

"Unfamiliar sound?", Scoffed Athos, "The sound of cannon fire should be quite familiar to them by now. Something so repetitive becomes familiar."

"What would they expect? A welcoming committee on behalf of Louis and Richelieu? I think not." Added Aramis, wryly.

"Either way we look at it, the captains need to be informed of the situation." Concluded Porthos.

"Do you realize, *mon amis* that during this little adventure of Louis', we know not the names of our fearless leaders?" Observed Athos.

"Forsooth, you are correct. Des Essarts, is not amoung these, for he is elsewhere." Added Aramis.

Mousequeton and the two other valets appeared behind Aramis, startling all, as he was carrying a half dozen or so hares, and his companions found some wild but edible vegetation.

"By Jove Mousequeton, it surely looks as if your snares were successfully utilized." Complimented Porthos.

"...And since we have the light of day on our side, I would think laying a fire will not be as obvious and bring unwarranted attention to our current activities. Therefore, do what you must and we shall return momentarily." Added Aramis.

The three then went to seek their leaders and relay the information they had thus garnered from a valet.

XVIII

"How do we know this to be true?" Queried one of the sub-captains.

"Pardon Monsieur, afore we go further with this conversation, may I inquire as to whom I am speaking?" Queried Porthos, as politely as possible.

The young sub-captain who was approximately the same age as the inquiring musketeer, replied, "It really matters not. I do not readily stand on formalities."

"Then may I inquire how you should be addressed?" He inquired.

"Monsieur, is most befitting, all things considered."

"Monsieur, What say you, appoint a partial regiment to inspect the circumstances and form a postulation on the current situation and to assess how viable it is ?"

The young sub-captain turned to glance towards La Rochelle as if he was expecting repercussions from Rohan who always reacted impetuously, seldom rethinking or regretting his actions.

Another young captain stepped forward and roughly nudged his companion.

"Your musings is costly. Time wasted is never regained."

"Oh! Pardon!" The first sub-captain exclaimed.

Then turning about he said, "Take Antoine and Joel and these three and have a look ahead." He said as he pointed to areas he wanted scrutinized. "I will appoint others for other sections to be inspected. Be wary."

The six men cautiously and silently as possible, crept forward.

Although they were an adequate distance from La Rochelle, it was thought there still might be a soldier or two malingering about and would, though not wanting to be put in the line of fire, hastily report their presence.

Aramis upon seeing what he perceived as a fallen soldier, became rigid, silently made the sign of the cross and muttered, "Lord, lead him to heaven through your divine mercy. Amen."

Then realizing it was fallen timber, he sighed heavily with relief and continued forward.

The surrounding air still had the lingering scent of gunpowder, smouldering embers and unfortunately death and destruction.

"Hold!" Porthos heard one of the other two shout and he hastened his pace to scrutinize the situation.

As he crashed through the under brush, causing chaos amoungst the inhabitants of the forest, to scatter in all directions, he found the soldier standing over someone lying on the ground.

Porthos followed his fellow guards' gaze to the one lying supine and as he did so, he heard something unnerving, a gasp and a long hollow sigh.

The man drew his last breath as he was released from his earthly physical ties.

"Perchance he finally found the peace and freedom he has so vainly sought." Said Porthos, half aloud.

Erstwhile, while the others drew silently closer to the fort, they began to encounter more deceased soldiers.

Identifying them as if they were for Rohan or Louis was not only difficult, but nigh impossible, for neither possessed standard issued uniforms as of yet, with the three and their newly procured tabards was a pace or two in the right direction.

When the six were within sight of La Rochelle, they could not subdue adequately their chuckling, in spite of the dire surroundings.

"My dear companions, it is better than I had hoped for." Said Porthos as he observed the large aperture in the once formidable wall, "It will take a small efficient maintenance troupe to do the repairs and by the looks of it, it could take a couple of fortnights at best."

"I so hope my dear Porthos, you have no intentions of frequenting any of the establishments therein, do you?" Inquired Aramis.

"Ne', good Aramis, I shall not risk being remembered. Even a village sot remembers the uncommon when prompted properly."

"Now for the current affairs. What are we observing ?" Queried Athos, brow furrowed.

"There was obviously a siege with plenty of casualties. The query is, who belongs to whom? Yes we mentioned to Louis to send a regiment or two to block Rohan progression to Calais. Alas, we know not if they are for the crowns' defenses or Rohans."

They suddenly heard a low moan from behind a large fallen timber, startling them all.

"The timber speaks." Said Athos, with a large jesting smile, resheathing his blade.

They sought the source and found a mortally wounded soldier, somewhat propped against the timber with another close by.

"My good man, here." Said Aramis as he offered the man a bit of wine from his own reserves.

The man sputtered as he accepted the gracious offer.

"May we offer you our assistance?" Queried Joel.

As they gathered about sitting on other fallen timbers, sitting close enough to hear what words were exchanged betwixt the young prelate and the soldier, they barely heard him reply, "I am well beyond that point. A point well beyond any valid assistance."

"Monsieur, may we inquire who it is that you represent?" Queried Aramis, as he dampened his kerchief to dab at the mans' sweat ladened brow.

"So much confusion and disarrayment." Commented the man.

"Are you aware of Duc de Rohan?" Inquired Porthos.

The soldier managed to nod slightly in acknowledgment.

"Was he the cause of this?" Queried Athos.

He again slightly nodded, then said, "Men within the fort caused a minor mutiny, for they felt the Duc was in error."

Aramis offered him a little more wine and queried, "How was it thought that he t'was in error?"

"He wanted to keep the kings' meant arms' length and to persuade Louis to concede, he was going to agree to open the gates and welcome the king and entourage. His men felt that would have been the wrong thing to do." The man paused and closed his eyes.

The three looked at each other, Aramis who was sitting the closest to him, placed his hand on his chest and sighed.

As he removed his hand, the soldiers' eyes fluttered open again.

The soldier drew a deep breath and moan, his grievous wound caused him unbearable discomfort, Aramis again offered him wine.

"We were fired upon and our response was swift and what we thought was efficient, like ants vacating their hill as if engulfed in flame. Only as we were to defend dear La Rochelle, a gaping hole was breeched in a wall allowing them to swarm in. It was a grand combination of Louis' soldiers as well as Richelieus' and indeed the Ducs' in defense. We fought till it was once again quiet, nothing stirred. We could not differentiate who was who. We know not which direction they came from. Mass confusion."

"When did all this occur, in order of events. Think if you will, when did all this transpire? If it becomes to taxing, accept my apologies now, but it is vital you recall." Encouraged Porthos.

"As the eve afore settled in," he began, "We heard cannon fire and grenades exploding. Monsieur le Duc insisted we greet them in a timely productive manner. As ordered, we did. Then when we thought we had accomplished success over our foes there were three rather large explosions within the walls. A captain considered it to be the munitions were stowed away wrong within the arsenal. In the confusion, he failed to realize there were multiple smaller explosions. A store house took on heavy damage and as that was contained an explosion loud and large enough to cause the bell to toll unattended, occurred and locating the source it was a wall with a large aperture betwixt two *faux* turrets."

Aramis again offered him wine.

"...And that Messieurs, is Gil'ber. He passed attempting to preserve me. As you can plainly see, his efforts are in vain. For naught."

"Would you care to have last rites?" Queried Aramis.

"That means you are Catholic."

"A Jesuit by trade." Smiled the young prelate, "Alas in the eyes of God, it does not matter what you label your physical being, it is what the soul acknowledges."

"One more query and I shall say no more." Said Athos.

The man slowly and cautiously turned his head towards the musketeer.

"Is Monsieur le Duc still present?"

The dying man, let his head drop to his heaving chest for he was having difficulty in something simple as breathing.

With a *sotto voc,* he mumbled, "Ne'. He fled after the wall was ruptured and our security became debatable."

"Is he alone?" Queried Porthos.

"Ne', one other."

Aramis solemnly preformed the last rites ritual and prayed that his soul be mercifully lead to heaven, for peace, and sanctuary.

As Aramis said, "Amen" and made the sign of the the cross over him, he sighed loudly and his head rolled slowly to the side away from them.

The musketeer once again placed his hand on the mans' chest and waited for what seemed like an eternity.

Taking his hand back, he retrieved his kerchief from within his doublet and wiped his hand clean, then pulled the mans' cap over his vacant now lifeless eyes.

He slowly shook his head.

They regained their feet and silently returned to the clearing and inform the sub-captains of their findings.

"Then there is absolutely no reason to pursue him, provided it is just him and the one other. Did he say who the one other is?" Queried the sub-captain.

The musketeers shook their heads.

"By the appearance of things, La Rochelle will not be causing us any grief any time soon." Said Aramis, "Therefore, all the regiments will not be needed in Rohans apprehension."

"Can you three make the best of it and retrieve him?"

"Is the Cardinal Richelieu Louis' mouthpiece?" Queried Athos, with a raised brow.

Porthos glanced about to find Mousequeton and the other valets.

He caught sight of them approaching after departing from a small group of valets.

"What gives?" Queried Porthos.

"We, collectively were curious as to the outcome of your intensive scrutinizations. Forsooth, we are not in the habit of hallucinating. Especially the likes of an aftermath of a siege." Equivocated Mousequeton.

The small group disbanded as they sought their prospected masters and finish off breakfast and as they did so the sub-captains beckons the soldiers to come forth and hear the current instructions.

"Hear us all!" Shouted a sub-captain, "There has been a siege. A siege that we are not responsible. La Rochelle is in desperate need of repair and they will be too preoccupied with that rather than replenishing their munitions and armaments. La Duc de Rohan is not present. Our presence is not warranted therefore, take ease, finish what you have begun, your breakfast. Fret not good gentlemen, he will still be sought and if fates are on our side, he will be soon apprehended as we will all rendezvous in Paris under the direction of the king. A small posse comitatus, will continue."

"What say you if he has a regiment about him, will that not impede progression?" Queried a young soldier.

"Ne' it will not impede progress. For we have information that we just received is that he is alone, save one individual. Although we know not who that is, it will become apparent soon enough. The selected men will continue and the remains will return to Paris. We ought to stay in formation least we encounter repercussions from any remnants of resistance."

"They are a stubborn lot." Commented another young soldier.

"It is what they believe to be a worthy cause." Said Aramis, in *sotto voc.*

Regiment after regiment finished their breakfast, broke down their encampments and stowed their wares, returned to formation and began for Paris.

"My feet ache just thinking about the trek back to Paris." Lamented Porthos.

"We still have a bit to go afore we reach Nantes." Commented Athos.

Porthos as well as his companions, making use of their time, as they watched the clearing become vacant of regiments and accruements, they began to eat their breakfast.

At the urging of some of the sub-captains, they were encouraged not to loiter, for they still had Rohan to apprehend and there was still a chance that they would succeed.

Each valet served their masters respectfully and carefully seeing to it that their needs were met afore they themselves sat down to consume their roasted meal of hare and various wild edible root vegetables.

As Porthos was cinching up his horses' saddle, the valets commenced in breaking down their encampment as well and began stowing their wares.

The musketeers did not wait for their valets to care for their every want or need and took it upon themselves to ready their own horses and when they had completed that, they assisted they valets with theirs.

"By all things evident, the time is nighly four." Commented Athos as he shielded his eyes as a knights' visor would, as he glanced about, seeking a sapling that would emulate the likes of an of a sundials' gnomon. "Indeed it is." He exclaimed, as he stuck his ponaird fast into the ground in the stead of a sapling and allowing the sun to use it as the gnomon and cast an appropriate shadow.

Aramis, Porthos and the valets had gained their saddled as Athos retrieved his ponaird, wipes its blade across his pantaloons and replaced it in the top of a boot and with minimal effort he too regained his saddle.

"I dare say, we still need to keep our distance from La Rochelle." Said Aramis as they all turned and touched the flanks of their horses to encouraged them to begin their trek towards Nantes.

"Why say you? Do you not want to assist them in the reconstruction of their wall that we so kindly assisted in causing a breach in one of their well fortified walls?" Jested Porthos, "It is the least we can do."

"Must not have been all that fortified if were able to breach it." Smiled Athos.

Not much of a conversation was held for they were still fatigued and longed for a bed in which to lie themselves down and have a quiet devil may care attitude towards the culmination of the day as it quietly slipped into the eve.

Nantes was still a days' ride away when the silhouettes from the low hanging moons' light, caused them danced about as the night sounds serenely serenaded them, with an occasional shriek from an owl piercing the darkness, letting them know they were not alone.

By the time the moon had reached its zenith, their horses heads had lowered and their pace had slackened, for they too were fatigued.

The well travelled path that lead through the wooded area had to lead somewhere of worth, they collectively thought.

Some how the fatigued horses were able to avoid stumbling and shying away from things that during the light of day would frightened them senseless, such as low hanging boughs resembling a serpent or a oddly shaped fallen timber resembling a crouching soldier with a readied harquebus, or worse, small wind twisted boughs resembling a falcon readying for a strike on an unsuspecting shrew.

Porthos who was riding betwixt his companions, he abruptly pulled up his reins causing his horse to almost sit on its haunches.

"What gives?" Queried Aramis, as he yawned.

"Ahead." Replied Porthos.

"Ahead? Where, what?" queried Athos.

"There! Betwixt the two trees, ahead, there is a slight glimmer of light." Vainly pointing in his desire for them to observe what he was observing.

"Lead the way my good man, for I see not what you are making references to and since you seem to think there is something of worth for us to see, them by all means, show us so that we may share in its discovery." Said Aramis.

"By all means, my good companion." Added Athos.

Porthos had thus allowed his horse to regain his composure as he touched its flanks with his spurs, he began for the flicker of light that he silently prayed was a hostler or inn.

The well worn path widened enough to allow carriage to pass as well as other sojourners seeking shelter or a meal, alas in this case both.

At approximately one hundred paces from the source of light, Porthos again pulled his reins taught.

His horse retaliated by sharply bobbing and tossing his head in an attempt to get the hefty musketeer to loosen his grip on the reins and causing discomfort about his mouth.

"By Jove!" Exclaimed Athos, "It looks like there is something of worth here."

"Indeed. That is quite a way of summoning sojourners in search of accommodations." Observed Aramis.

The beckoning light they saw, was emanated from a rather large brazier in the courtyard of a small hostler.

As they briefly sat silently in their saddles, a small band of men stepped out from the tree line and into the courtyard, only to be readily greeted by a stable lackey.

Another lackey, with a piece of wood in each hand, tossed them into the brazier, then hastily departed.

The three, through gestures, decided to join the small band and try to be as inconspicuous as possible.

Athos encouraged his fatigued horse to proceed forward as the others followed closely and within a matter of a few minutes they had handed stable lackeys the reins to their weary horses and joined the others to what appeared to be an weak attempt at a grand hall.

The hall, lacking décor, save a painted portrait or two of what was thought to be predecessors of the tavern, became a center of activity as valets, servants and lackey prepared the hearth with spits and kettles, lit sconces and chandeliers.

"Gratefully we left our newly acquired tabards behind, for we do not need to be known that we are in association with Louis. If it be know, it would jeopardize our chances of apprehending Rohan." Said Porthos with a *sotto voc* to his companion, Aramis, who nodded his reply.

"I had to remind you to turn your mantle." Smiled Aramis.

"Indeed." Replied Porthos as the three ingratiated themselves into the small band, they decidedly would be best if they sat a part from one another so as to try and obtain further information.

The din was bothersome to their fatigued ears, but bore it well.

As bits and pieces of conversations were heard, it became apparent that the men were of a rogue regiment belonging to Rohan, struggling in vain to regain their absent leader.

A soldier close to the hearth, regained his feet, faltered as he held up a bottle and shouted, "Marchel, Marchel!"

"Here, Ma'Meau! What is it?" He too regained his feet, so that his companion could see him and address him.

"Is Monsieur Le Rohan with you, here?" He queried as he hic -coughed and attempted to fill his goblet, as some ended up on the table top and not in the goblet.

Athos cringed.

"What is it my good companion?" Queried Aramis, who by now was standing next to him and touched his elbow.

"I can not bear to observe such lack of respect." He replied.

"To whom,? Queried Aramis furrowing his brow, "For he did not utter insults to anyone in particular."

"It is not a matter of whom, rather what." Sighed Athos.

"I do not understand what you are making references to." Said Aramis, thoroughly perplexed at his companions words.

Athos sat himself down heavily in a chair. Then glanced at Aramis, and said, "Monsieur Companion, it is the wine. He has let perfectly good wine go by the wayside."

"I do not understand."

"Why should you? Your sacrificial wine satisfies no one save a distraught soul or two."

"Ne Ma'Meau. I have not seen him, for if he is not with you or present than he made good with his word and began for and will end in Calais."

Returning their to the situation at hand, they heard, "Hold!" Someone shouted from a far corner as the chamber went silent and turned their attentions there.

"I do believe my good man, I shall be making your purse a bit lighter and mine dear fellow a bit more heavier as you have seen to it that I am no longer in want."

Laughter irrupted from the corner as a chair toppled loudly to the floor.

Aramis caught a quick glance from Athos, who just shrugged in response.

With closer scrutinizations, they realized it was Porthos at the core of the disturbance.

"Care to lay another wager?" They heard him say.

The small crowd dispersed as Aramis and Athos moved closer.

Porthos had a roasted fowl upon his blade and and the stopper to a bottle of wine on the tip of his ponaird.

When the men dissolved and turned into silhouettes, Aramis queried skeptically, "Do I dare inquire what you are about?"

"I wanted to prove a point and I did so with this roasted goose and the ponaird was a splendidly used tool in removing the wines' stopper and I may add, not one drop was wasted."

"You certainly can not prove your point with it buttoned." Weakly smiled Athos. "Alas a man after my own heart, provided Monsieur, I was a woman." Sighed Athos, feigning infatuation

XIX

Their meal was served and then proceeded to be devoured with minimal effort.

The three, with their valets managed to slip silently from the chamber and secure private lodgings for the remainder of the eve.

Athos, being the last to cross the threshold of the adequate sized bed chamber, closed the small, unadorned door, then leaned heavily against it and hung his head.

Porthos who managed to find a chair close to the lifeless hearth, sat down, stretched out his legs and said, "My dear Athos, my sentiments exactly."

Aramis chuckled softly as the valet, without directions from their masters, began readying the chamber for the comforts of their masters.

Although the chamber beheld the basics necessities, they were able to make it appear and be more accommodating much to the delight of the travel worn musketeers.

"Master?"

Bazin?"

"Care to have a fire laid?"

Aramis glanced from one companion to the next, both curtly shook their head in response to the silent inquiry.

"I think not." Replied the young prelate, "For it would mean that it would have to be attended to throughout and being as fatigued as we are, it would cease no matter how attentive we would have striven to be."

With great effort, Porthos removed himself from the chair and made his way to the bed to lie down.

Mousequeton silently hastened to his master to assist him in removing his boots.

When the hefty musketeer laid down, his feet over hung the end of the bed.

"Peste!" He thundered, "I dare say, this was constructed with a child sized imp in mind."

Aramis shrugged at the comment then said, "Surely, for they had not seen the likes of you to have someone of your stature truly exist, for only in someone's vivid imagination giants exist."

"I can vouch only for myself and no more, for I have not had even one come close to my stature. I hazard to say, verily there must be one elsewhere."

"Perchance. As for now, consider yourself unique and nothing can compare nor compete with you in any aspects of what we call life." Commented Athos.

"Who betwixt us has enough courage to share with Porthos?" Queried Athos, wryly.

Aramis inclined his head slightly and arched a brow.

"I shall forfeit my comfort in order to get some rest and not dicker over the triviality of it for we still have quite a bit to do afore we reach Calais and apprehend Rohan." Said Athos.

"Indeed. We need our wits about us and be clear witted as well, so that we do not apprehend the wrong adversary." Agreed Aramis, "What say you Porthos?"

The portly musketeer softly snoring, did not answer.

In the pre-dawn hours of the morn, Mousequeton stirred and sat up.

All was silent and unfamiliar.

He nudged a companion that was closest to him, it was Grimaud.

"I would imagine our masters would no doubt like to rousted so that we may continue. I also would imagine they would like to continue with their reposing, alas with that it would prolong the culmination of justice." Said Porthos' valet with a *sotto voc*.

Grimaud replied, "Stop procrastinating."

Mousequeton regained his feet, then sought his master.

Porthos' suddenly gasped and startled Mousequeton.

Trembling, the valet nudged his master. As Porthos stirred slightly as Mousequeton nudged him again.

"I understand dear Master that it is too early to consider rising, but you must if you and the others are to fulfill your promised obligations to the king." Gently reminded Mousequeton.

Aramis, at the sounds of the valet trying to roust his master, awoke and cautiously sat up.

"What gives?" He queried.

"Trying to be the dutiful valet Monsieur Porthos perceives me to be, I took it upon myself to roust him and in turn your valets so that you will not full short of the trust the king has instilled in all of you."

Aramis ran his hand through his disheveled hair, then queried, "Is Monsieur Athos about?"

"Ne'."

Porthos mumbled something incoherent as he opened his eyes and allowed them to adjust to the dimness of the chamber.

"By Jove!" Exclaimed Athos, "My wine has spilt."

Porthos chuckled, "He is delirious."

"Do you not think that we ought to be up and about?" Queried Aramis.

"I should think so. The longer we loiter about, the distance betwixt us and Rohan grows greater."

"My dear gentlemen, let us not let any more time go by the wayside. Somewhere, breakfast awaits."

Grimaud then proceeded to roust his master in the customary silent manner as his daily ritual dictated.

There was not a lot to gather that morn, for most of their wares were stowed with their horses in the staples.

As they made their way through the grand hall, they had to step over and around the causalities of imbibing too much.

Emptied bottles along with tableware strewn about, littered the tabletops and floors, making it difficult to depart silently.

As they entered the nigh vacant courtyard, they paused as if to catch their following a race. In an essence it truly was a race, a race against time.

Knowing, one can never regain lost time, they needed to make the most of what they have been allotted.

Upon entering the stables, they caught the stable lackey unaware.

"Steady on old man, we mean no harm. We are here to collect our belongings and our horses." Said Porthos.

The young man fumbled nervously with a bridle.

The horse he attempted to utilize it on, abruptly swung his head away then back again.

On the back swing, the horse managed to knock the lackey off center, causing him a pratfall.

Aramis stepped forward, "The bridle you have, does not fit this one. His is on the peg by his head. This one is for the one on the end. Here." Instructed Aramis as he held out his hand to accept the bridle lying next to lackey, then handed to his own valet to be put on the proper horse.

Without prompting, the valets assisted in readying the little entourage for their continuation, but paused as Porthos began challenging his horse as to who was the authoritative.

Porthos horse in particular did not want to participate in the preparation as he kept his head lowered and inaccessible.

"I", He corrected himself, "we do not have the humour nor the time to tolerate such nonsense from a noncompliant horse. I assure you, when this trek is completed, I personally will see to it you will not be bothered with, save to feed you." Coaxed Porthos.

"Hold!" Exclaimed Aramis, "We need not dawdle and observe Porthos' horse toy with him. We need to make haste!" Instructed the prelate, always impatient when delayed by inconsequential things.

"Mousequeton, if you please."

Porthos gestured for his valet to stand on the other side of his horses' head.

The horse tried to turn away, alas the valet caught his gaze and held it, thus the horse turned his head in the musketeers' direction.

The hefty musketeer was than able to fit the bridle securely on his horses' white blazoned head.

"Now! Was that so bad?" Queried Porthos of the horse.

In response the horse snorted and whinnied.

The other horses were readily equipped and readied, then lead out to the courtyard as the first rays of sunlight appeared on the horizon.

Porthos retrieved his purse from deep within his tight fitting doublet.

Untying it, he offered the stable lackey two Louis d'ors in an effort to settle their debt.

As they alighted into their saddles as nimbly and hastily as possible, the lackey glared at the small entourage and cleared his throat.

"My good man, I dare say, the services rendered were minimal and the consumption of your kettles and spits were the remains from the regiment. By our accounts your payment is well sufficient of what we utilized. Nothing was begged, borrowed or stolen to warrant additional coinage. Make due."

"Problem Monsieur Porthos?" Queried Aramis.

Porthos glanced at the lackey who with *voix tremblante* replied, "Ne'. Nary a problem."

The musketeer slightly and curtly inclined his head as they all turned about and began for Nantes.

"Do you presume a possibility that Rohan is somewhere betwixt here and Calais awaiting his wayward regiment?" Queried Porthos, to no one in particular, hoping to break the somber silence that befell them.

"It is a possibility. He is intelligent and cunning." Replied Aramis.

"Mind you he too is deceptive." Reminded Athos, "Forsooth, that poor regimental dolts, they seem to think he is about."

"Do you, do you not?" Inquired Aramis of Athos.

"I am not a soothsayer, but if I had to speculate, I would say, ne'. Alas, I could be in error and I pray this time, I am."

Athos glanced off in the distance in order to gain possible knowledge of what was expected of the elements that the day beheld.

As he did so, a cloud passed over the sun, causing a sudden dimness to their surroundings.

"It appears that dark clouds are once again on the horizon." Athos observed.

"In which way are they drifting?" Queried Aramis

"They seem to be coming in from the sea side." Replied Porthos.

"Then it certainly something to take notice of and see how far it progresses. Hopefully it will bypass our intended path. Last thing I want in this lifetime is again be thoroughly drenched and left to dry." Commented Porthos.

"Ah, *mon ami* it is well afore eve, therefore if that should happen, your misery will be short lived fore you will have been dry afore the sun has slipped below the horizon and the coolness of the eve has a chance to set in." Replied Aramis.

"Which reminds my good gentlemen, we left in such haste, our valets had not the chance to prepare breakfast, from my guess it is well nigh approaching dinner." Commented Porthos.

"There is a consulated thought." Suggested Athos.

Porthos arched a brow in inquery.

"Indeed, when we reach Nantes', provided we did not by pass it by accident,". Jested Athos, "We can afford to linger a bit afore we continue."

Porthos scowled at the thoughts of having to accidentally by passing Nantes'. If that were the case, then surely they would have to go without til they reached Angers, which was eaten further, yet closer to Calais.

"In all seriousness, how do we honestly know if we have closed the gap and are closer to apprehending Rohan?" Queried Aramis.

"We do not. We have to have faith, all will be well." Replied Porthos.

"Hate to be a bearer of bad news…", began Athos.

"You do remember, do you not, what happens to messengers that bear bad news?", queried Porthos, smiling sardonically.

"That was from days of yore. Jesting aside, mind you, he had a seventeen day advance on us."

"Ah, alas days of yore are not that far gone. It is truly, it is speculation." Reminded Aramis.

"The fates has smiled on us in the past." Said Porthos.

"Yes, and they have also frowned." Added Athos.

Time moved forward as they did and it was not long afore they happened upon a small riverlet that flowed to a tributary then to the sea.

It was there they decided to pause.

They loosened the cinches on the saddles and tethered them to nearby trees, allowing them to loiter.

As they sat lounged about, Athos again scanned the horizon to see what the elements had in store for them.

The dark clouds that formally sat on the horizon at a comfortable distance had grown and darkened as they approached as a slight breeze began toying with the plumes in their caps.

"What say you?" Queried Aramis.

"I am inclined to think we still have adequate time to reach Nantes' afore the inclement elements reach us as to cause us distress. I too perceive that it lacks ambition."

"Why you say that?" Inquired Porthos.

"I took notice of the plumes in your cap. They are not dancing like a mad man, with hasty and erratic movements. They are more alike the kings' favorite ballet. Slow, fluent and with intent."

Athos nodded at Grimaud, who then regained his feet and went to attend his masters' horse.

The two other valet followed his example and attended their masters' horses as well.

After the three were in their prospective saddles, the valets regained theirs, turned about, strode through the little riverlet and continued towards Nantes.

"...And aside from that, the birds are still about and have not sought shelter." Added Athos, "As they would with inclement elements."

As the silhouettes began to grow long, and the screeching calls from the birds of the sea, Nantes' finally came into view.

"Apparently we did not bypass our intent." Observed the partly musketeer, as he inclined his head and smiled.

"Which by the by, our desired destination is not that far and as much as we want to reach it, alas we not risk what we have gained or will gain by the lack of some rest and a good meal." Suggested Aramis, thinking logically.

Athos' horse stumbled slightly.

"Our horses are in desperate need of a good rest as well. Yours dear Porthos certainly knows how to prove that."

They all laughed at the recollected thoughts from the morn.

"Are you sure we did not just go in one big circle?" Queried Aramis, suspiciously.

"Why did you inquire such?" Queried Athos.

"This has the resemblance of La Rochelle." He replied, as he observed the establishments and quais in relation to the sea.

As they entered the fair city of Nantes', they observed a small entourage, including a carriage with a faded coat of arms painted on a side, in front of an adequate sized establishment.

"Hold!" Exclaimed Athos.

"Why say you with such apprehension?" Queried Porthos, as he came along the side of his companion.

"Is that not Richelieus' coat of arms?" Athos queried, anxious, then allowed his ire to rise.

"Why would he be here?" Inquired Porthos.

"Rest easy." Replied Aramis, "'Tis not Richelieu, I assure you, forsooth, observe. The shield has a tower centered, and upon Richelieus' there are mantles on either side. A cap atop. A thought, he is the minister of finance as well as the minister of war and he has the capacity to wander as from the *Palais* as he desires. By the by, let him bother you not, for we and he have other things to preoccupy himself and ourselves with than with the likes of Richelieu."

"Far be it from me to utter his importance." Muttered Athos.

"The sun shall, with no excuses, will be slipping below the horizon shortly and regrettably, it has been almost a day without a meal." Observed Porthos.

"True enough." Agree Athos.

"Alas, my good gentlemen, sitting here as we are, dickering over a coat of arms, the availability of a meal is within and not without." Laughed Aramis.

At that they all alighted from their horses and as they did so they were greeted abruptly by stable lackeys who readily accepted the reins of the weary animals and lead them away.

Sounds of thunder in the distance, rumbled.

As the clopping footfalls of the horses faded, they entered the establishment.

To their fatigued delight, the hostler were nigh vacant, in spite of the activities at the quais and adjoining rues and avenues.

The six men meandered to the rear of the establishment as was their peculiar habit dictated and sat in the silhouette of a rather large sculpture.

Although it was draped with a toga, it was headless and missing an arm and the remaining arm beheld a sagging sword as if it were from a defeated soldier of old, making it difficult to identify of whom it was depicting or who the sculptor was as well.

The hostler keep appeared and inquired of them of what their desires were.

"Anything and everything." Replied Porthos, genuinely smiling, with Athos and Aramis chuckling in agreement.

"Forget not the wine, bread or cheese." Reminded Porthos as the hostler keep went to find his attending lackeys.

As a young valet strode by, Athos was able to make a purchase on his sleeve.

"Hold! What gives?" Queried the young valet, taken quite unaware, trying to free himself from Athos' sudden grasp.

"Who is here?" Queried the suspicious musketeer with a *sotto voc.*

"What or who are you making references too?" Inquired the valet.

"The carriage out of doors. To whom does it belong?"

The valet glanced about then nodded in the direction of a small collection of men on the side of the hearth that were in the midst of their abundant meal.

Following the valets' gaze, Athos gasped.

Porthos furrowed his brow as he observed his companions' present concern.

"It belongs to a Monsieur Jussac." Replied the valet, then inquired, "Is there something amiss with that?"

"Ne'." Replied Athos.

"He is a well of many attributes.", Added the valet, smiling.

"That well has been well tapped and thus has run dry." Replied Athos, quite sarcastically.

"Then how is it a man of his shallow means is able to acquire such a carriage? The well is obviously deeper than one seems to think."

"He has found a new one, per say, well."

"Ne'. It is quite a bit older." Replied Athos, with a raised brow, "his name is Richelieu."

The young valet, visibly annoyed at Athos' brash statement, hastened away.

They all laughed at the comment as wine, bread and cheese was brought to them.

As they began to parcel out the bead and cheese amongst themselves and their valets, a brawl irrupted.

Porthos began to regain his feet.

"If you will, stay. It concerns you not." Reminded Aramis.

Porthos sighed and reseated himself and as he did so, other parts of their meal was set about them.

"Master?"

"Mousequeton?"

"May I inquire as to are we going to lay over?"

Porthos then glanced at each of his companions respectively.

Each in turn, slightly nodded their affirmation.

"I concur. Indeed my dear valet. I fear if we were to continue on, we would not be able to stay in the saddle for very long. Fatigue has a way of making an example of you when you least expect." He replied.

The sounds of the wooden tables and chairs being splintered, bottles broken by either being thrown and striking a wall or falling to the planking, men occasionally landing on the well worn planking or they intentionally striking a wall, while strong oaths loudly uttered, all continuous and they not committing themselves to either for the or against the fray.

"'Tis all for the benefit of our purses if we do not participate." Added Aramis, "Rest assured dear Porthos, there will be plenty of opportunities for you as more worthy causes arise. Fret not."

The scuffling disgruntled men, being in the proximity of a swords' length, Athos causally said, "If you by chance see one of them loose their footing and threaten to fall upon the table, save the wine."

Just soon as he uttered the words, someone fell upon the table as if to prove a point and emphasize what was said.

Each respecting their companions' words, they were quick enough to save the bottles of wine and to their advantage, the meal was nigh complete afore disaster struck.

The hostler keep tried in vain to convince them it was not in their best to continue their discussions.

One disgruntled combative denizen had cornered a diminutive valet and offered him a position at court.

"Leave me be!", growled the valet.

"Matherine would consider you quite quaint and find you useful."

Then a query from the valet was heard, "…pardon my ignorance, who praytell is Matherine?"

Porthos chuckled softly at recollected thoughts.

"She *mon ami* is the court jestress. For what ever his reasons are, the king and his mother find her quite amusing."

"Louis must find her amusing because he has kept her at court and has not exiled her." Said Porthos in a *sotto voc.*

As the inn-keep happened by, shaking his head in dismay, Aramis lightly touched his shoulder.

Startled the inn-keep hastily turned about.

"What is it Monsieur?" He queried, "I need to address this situation so that my establishment is not totally destroyed. Besieged by inebriated dolts…" He did not finished his thought as his voice faltered.

"We need to sublet a chamber for the eve." Replied Aramis as Porthos tried to stifle a yawn.

"Down the corridor, choose. They are all vacant but I would image not much longer."

He replied as he hastened to remove two combative denizens from his establishment that had fallen at his feet as they had begun a fisticuff.

They scanned the establishment, searching for the corridor the inn-keep mentioned.

Grimaud lightly touched his masters' elbow and pointed.

Athos' gazed was drawn towards two lit sconces that indicated the presence of something significant.

He gestured for his companions to follow him as they dodged bottles and bodies amongst the melee of what appeared to be a free for all.

The corridor was dimly lit, alas they managed to find their way.

"It is so apparent that this hostler has been bypassed many times over." Commented Athos.

"…And you can tell, how?" Queried Porthos.

"There is that redolence of dankness and darkness.", he replied, then queried, "Which chamber or chambers do you request?"

"We always use one for one is sufficient and less of a burden on the purse." Replied Porthos.

Aramis inclined his head slightly as he took the initiative and lifted the latch to a door that was directly beside him and peered into the dimness.

Thunder rumbled again, followed by a hasty flash of lightening.

As Athos had predicted, it had not been used in quite sometime.

"If I t'were not so fatigued, I would bypass this hostler altogether." Commented Aramis.

The others with muffled chuckles, entered the chamber.

"Master?"

"Mousequeton?"

"T'was not I, Monsieur." Came a reply.

"T'was I, Bazin."

"Pardon. Aramis?"

"What is it Bazin?" Queried Aramis of his valet.

"I realize we will not be able to identify all in the dimness of, alas in my observations, I do not observe the likeness of a taper or lantroon."

In the dimness of the chamber, the contoured outlines of objects appeared as silhouettes for the lack of light prevented their definition as to what it truly was.

Although they found the bed, the valets were able turned down the counterpane for they knew whichever of their masters decided to make use of it, they would not like the oder of stale linen about them.

"Do I dare inquire if there is a hearth?" Queried Mousequeton.

"Inquire if you will, alas I can not guarantee the reply you get will be as accurate." Replied Porthos, who was by, now sitting on the side of the bed.

Within a short length of time, their eyes had grown accustomed to their surroundings and was able to identity the scant accommodations.

Thankfully, there were two chairs arranged in front of the silent, cold hearth and one had been shoved aside and into a corner.

Athos found one of the chairs and sat down heavily and allowed himself to sink into it as much as it would allow, pulled his cap over his eyes and his mantle more tightly about him.

Aramis chose the other chair and did the same.

Mousequeton took the liberty and laid himself down next to his master who was already lightly snoring.

Grimaud and Bazin used their mantles as counterpanes, and a bent, folded arm as a bolster, upon the planking in front of the silent hearth.

As Bazin drifted off to sleep, the light snorings reminded him of a chorus of crickets in the mildness of elements as the heavenly bodies twinkled and a light draught rustled the surrounding foliage.

Smiling fondly at the memory, he fell asleep.

If the elements were to throw a tantrum, it would matter not.

Somewhere in the midst of time afore the morn a loud thud sounded outside their door which jolted Porthos and Athos awake.

"What gives?" Queried Porthos as he hastily sat up, swinging his legs to the side.

Athos had already regained his feet.

Both waited to see if the sound was repeated.

Porthos moved closer to the door as Athos was directly behind him.

They both listened intently.

There was the sounds of shuffling, something being dragged, in the corridor to which Porthos suddenly flung the door open.

As the two musketeers peered down the corridor, a denizen was dragging another and was just rounding the corner out of sight.

By that time, the others were huddled behind Porthos.

"What was that?" Inquired Aramis.

"I know not, nor do I wish to." Replied the hefty musketeer.

Athos concurred.

"I fear if we become involved with that little escapade, we may become a part of it and there will be a point that we may not be able to return."

"Were they recognizable?" Queried Aramis, yawning.

"Alas, ne'."

In their moment of silent contemplation, a rooster crowed in the distance.

"There was nothing familiar about them. Their movements, their vestments, nothing." Observed Porthos.

"Therefore, you were unable to assess if the one was an inebriated sot or other?" Queried Aramis.

Porthos slowly shook his head.

"Since we are all awake now, do we make an attempt to find breakfast or continue on our way?" Queried Athos.

"What say you?" Queried Porthos to Aramis.

Aramis shrugged.

"Breakfast is a splendid thought. Let us find the inn-keep and have him put his kettles and spit to use as well as that argumentative diminutive valet." Aramis suggested.

The small entourage filled the corridor and silently re-entered the grand hall.

It was quiet and lifeless.

The debris and denizens imbibing from the eve afore lie about, littering the planking.

"It does not seem to our advantage. I know not where to seek the inn-keep or anyone of worth to express our desires and intents." Said Aramis.

Porthos sighed.

"Then the only thing we can truly do, is continue." Said Athos.

"If it t'were not for the fact my stomach is protesting this current dilemma, I would tend to agree." Added Porthos.

"Then it is all well and good we go round up our horses and be on our way. Considering Angers is only a days worth of riding away.", Said Athos, ignoring his companions' comment.

"Only! Peste, it might as well as be a life time!" Scoffed Porthos.

Entering the stable, it was just as dim as the establishment with the exception of being greeted by a lackey bearing a lit lantroon, taking the men completely unaware.

Porthos grasped his chest in mock seriousness.

"My good man, do you always do that?" He queried.

The young lackey inclined his head.

"Do what?"

"Take denizens unaware, causing health issues?"

"No, not intentionally."

Porthos sighed as the others tried not to laugh.

The young lackey cleared his throat, then queried, "Is there something I can assist you with?"

"Yes. We need to have our horses readied so that we may continue our trek." Replied Athos.

As the lackey turned and began for the first horse, the valets were again instructed to give assistance so they can hastily be able to continue.

The lackey then readied additional lantroon and handed each valet one.

From somewhere in the depth of the stable a valet called to his master.

"Master, here."

The three glanced upon one another.

"'Tis Grimaud." Said Athos, "What is it he is about?" He grumbled.

They then cautiously picked their way through the fodder, ordure, and fowls that noisily scattered in every direction to avoid being stepped on or being caught and spitted.

Locating the valet was no easy task, alas when they did happen upon him, he was kneeling next to one of the horses' and holding its lifeless head upon his knees.

"Peste!" Thundered Porthos, startling everything that breathed, in the stable.

The lackey nervously said, "He t'was quite right when I last saw him."

"…And when was that?" Queried Athos, realizing the horse was his.

"Shortly after the storm abated and when one of the denizens wanted to depart."

"May we inquire as to who and what time was that? Inquired Aramis.

"It was after the main clock struck two, all was silent. The little skirmish ended about the half way mark."

"Then who was it that departed?" Queried Athos, a second time.

"I do believe his name was Monsieur Jussac."

"Leave it to him to leave just when it was beginning to get interesting." Smiled Porthos.

"Indeed." Added Aramis, "Begins grief, inflicts pain, then departs so as to not see the after effects."

"Just like Richelieu." Grumbled Athos, then aloud, "What praytell happened here?"

"Difficult to say, Monsieur. For truly if it t'were by the light of day, we could see much better than we can. Near as I figure, t'was age."

"Age! By Jove the scoundrel that I purchased him from testified that he had him since a colt and was coming into his own at six. He caused me turn my purse inside out, leaving in desperate want. "Two meager months wage, I dare say."

"Sorry Monsieur that you lost out."

Athos sighed heavily, then turned about abruptly, nearly knocking into Aramis.

"It just occurred to me.'

'What did?" Queried Porthos.

"That little dolt that I challenged and he never showed. He was present when I purchased the horse and the denizen called him, "son". The boy was going to say something concerning the horse and he was commanded not to say anything. Thus stayed silent and departed. Thinking not past the purchase, I proceeded and here we are."

"Do you have any horses to lease?" Inquired Aramis, in hopes of easing the pressure the situation was causing.

"Do you not mean, purchase?" Curtly inquired Athos, "Forsooth, we shall not pass this way again."

"I will sell you my horse." The lackey said, "He is sure and steady on his feet. He will get you to where you are going. I might add, he was reshod the week afore."

"To what extent do I have to empty my purse?" Inquired Athos.

"Four Louis d'ors." Came the reply.

"Three and consider it sold. Alas afore I totally agree, I would like to assess his attributes."

"Certainly Monsieur."

As they withdrew from the confines of the *petit* stall, slivers of daylight began to infiltrate the stable as a whole and began to illuminate and define the common contrivances.

Tethered by the door was the animal that the stable lackey mentioned.

"'Od's Bodikin, What is the meaning of this? 'Tis no horse, 'tis nothing but a beast of burden." He scoffed.

The young lackey chuckled.

"I know not what you find so amusing, alas I assure you, I do not take this matter lightly, for we have an obligation from the king to fulfill and although he may be sure footed, et all alas he will not be able to keep stride with the others. I refuse to stay simply because of an inadequate animal."

"Monsieur all jesting aside, the one I am making references to, stands close to the shuttered window. There." He replied, pointing towards a dosing horse.

"Easy my good man, easy." Said the valet, reaching to smooth, the firm barreled horses' mane.

As the animal was touched, he swished his neatly manicured tail in the direction of.

"His chest looks firm and wide observed.", Athos

Athos then ran his hands over each leg, feeling for any abnormalities or afflictions.

Finding none, he came back around to the head of the animal, who now was pulling hay out of a corner rack.

"He is not broken nor sway back. Alas, I can assure you, my tack will not fit the likes of this one. Care to trade, you ill still have tack and so will I?"

The young lackey replied, "Fair enough. Although he is worth more than what you are offering, I am will to sacrifice my purse in the name of the state. God Speed."

It was then, all the lackeys set about readying all the horses with their implements and possessions so as to continue on til Angers and finally Calais.

The young valet tightened the cinch and other straps to insure no slippage or mishap would befall the musketeer.

One by one the horses were lead and tethered in the courtyard of the hostler.

Porthos had given his companion the coinage to conclude the transaction so as to continue on.

Athos retreated to the back of the stable where his lifeless horse lie.

"*Au Revoir,* old man." He said as he touch the brim of his cap.

As he entered the courtyard, the others had already gained the saddles, save Grimaud who was holding his masters' new acquisition by the reins.

Seeing the horse in more light of day convinced him that this horse will serve him well, for he appeared quite sound and capable.

Athos attempted to his place his spurred foot in the stirrup as the horse shied, sideward moving away from the musketeer.

"By Jove! Does he not let anyone upon him?" Queried Athos of the lackey.

"He does if he knows you. Alas, you are unfamiliar to him, but given, he will accept the fact and let be that.", He replied as he stood on the other side and held the bridle.

The horse, silently submitted to the fact that he had someone other than the young lackey was going to take up his reins and govern his demeanor and paces.

XX

Once in the saddle, the horse slightly faltered.

Athos, glanced hastily at the young lackey, who was was trying in vain to conceal his amusements.

"What gives?" Inquired Athos, quite sternly, "This certainly must not mean I overlooked something and he is truly lame."

The young lackey cleared his throat.

"Ne' Monsieur, it just means he is not accustomed to the added stones. As you can plainly see, I am of a slight frame and truly you Monsieur are a man of means."

Once His master was firmly in the saddle, Grimaud too gained his saddle.

"One more thing." Said Aramis.

"Monsieur?"

"Has a man, named Henri Rohan, been here in the last two fortnights?"

The young lackey paused, then said, "I have no recollected thoughts of such. In truth a mans' identity is truly his own. Names are inconsequential."

"*Adieu.*" They turned, then called in unison as they departed and began for Angers.

They all glanced towards the sun and tried to get a purchase on the day.

"I dare say, it is well past two. Better part of the day is gone by the wayside." Commented Porthos.

"By the by, I have lost count, does anyone know what day it is?", queried Athos.

"By my accounts it is a Sunday." Sighed Aramis, "Another devotion missed."

"You will have plenty of time to catch up on all the devotions you desire once we return to Paris." Smiled Athos.

The path they chose that would lead them directly to Angers gates, was well trod and debris free, thus making the conveyance swift and uncomplicated.

Athos' new horse tried to out pace the rest, but was hastily retained.

"If only all of you could have such an ambitious animal. We certainly would have reached Calais by now, perchance when we refill our coffers at journeys' end, you will be able to." Smiled Athos.

"They are a rarity. For most are used for trade." Sighed Porthos, "Alas,". He added hopefully, "The king has plied a new trade to list amoung the gilds and that is of being a musketeer. So, dear companions, it is likely we shall be able to acquire such."

"Our coffers will not offer such." Said Aramis.

"Ah, but Louis' will."

They all laughed and smiled at the thoughts of bettering their lots.

"Do you think you shall come across that young dolt that took advantage of you, Athos, concerning your horse?" Queried Porthos.

"All I can reply to that is, I had better not. I can assure you the consequences will not befit him well. He obviously knew something was amiss, but said nothing. Now, at that expense, my purse has grown leaner."

Afore their conversations could continue, a small inn came into view.

Porthos held up his hand and gestured for all them to gather around.

"Observe." He said as he pointed to it.

"That is a welcomed sight." Said Athos.

"Indeed it is, alas the time that was let by wayside can not be recovered, I propose that as much as my stomach will protest, I urge us to continue. Allow the horses to refresh themselves and then let us continue. If we can reach Angers afore the eve sets in, all will be good.

We can all rest for the eve. For we still have at least a weeks' worth of riding afore we even will get a hopeful glimpse of Calais."

"He is correct." Concurred Athos, "For on the other side of Angers is Rouen and that is a good four days off, lest we hasten their pace and our stamina, we could make it in three."

Aramis murmured, *"Mon Dieu."*

"Angers surely can not be that far into the distance." Encouraged Porthos.

Aramis then touched his horse with his spurred heels and the horse lunged abruptly forward, with the others following close behind.

In front of the small in was a trough that beheld water, next to a well that appeared in need of repair.

"Salut!" Thundered Porthos, hopeful someone would greet them accordingly.

To their dismay, silence.

"Might as well consider this a lost effort." Said Porthos, as he slid out of his saddle to regain his feet.

The valets then assisted their masters with their horses as Bazin took it upon himself to make use of the bucket to fill the nigh empty trough.

"Afore you allow them to have their fill, walk all of them around what appears to be a spent courtyard five times. Give them a minute to catch their breath. They and we do not need them to be seized with pangs of discomfort. That would delay us even more. Prevent what we can.", Said Athos, knowingly.

Each valet took two horses each, and began walking.

An occasional call from a bird sounded, breaking the silence.

"Do you think something is amiss?" Queried Aramis.

"Why query such?" Inquired Athos.

"It is far too silent.""

"Ne'." Replied Athos, "Consider the time of day."

Aramis glanced about and nodded in acknowledgment of his companions' comment.

As the horses finished off the trough, the men cupped their hands and they too drank their fill.

"It is too bad we can not linger about Angers." Said Athos.

"...And why is that?" Queried Porthos.

"Do you not know, it seats Anjou and our drink of choice hails from here." He replied smiling, "I have nearly forgotten what it tastes like since it has been a time since we last had a full bottle."

"You, forget what Anjou tastes like? Truly, never!" Laughed Porthos.

The valets then assisted their masters in regaining their saddles as they, their own.

Angers eventually became apparent as the moon began its accent into the heavens, casting rather dim silhouettes that became more discernible with the assistance of the brazier-keep as he began his rounds.

"Do take a choice of what hostler. There are many. Far be it for me say, I will agree to almost anything, far too exhausted to even suggest." Commented Porthos as his companions concurred.

They came upon, "The Green Sow.", which caused them to laugh til tears rolling down their cheeks had to be wiped away with their rough gloved hands.

"What a name of an establishment. I certainly hope that does not reflect what they have in their kettles." Remarked Porthos.

"Then just query after a couple of spitted fowls." Suggested Aramis.

As they regained their feet, they were readily greeted by a stable lackey.

"Will you be wanting to spend a couple of hours or the eve with my master?" He queried.

"The eve. Here if you will." Replied Porthos as he handed the young lackey his reins and headed for the establishments' door.

The others did the same and followed the hefty musketeer indoors.

They were hastily greeted and shown a small secluded chamber in which they could take their meal in peace and finally sleep.

As they sat themselves around the table, reminiscent of their time spent with their young sovereign, they found to their utter delight, silence.

The chamber had more accommodations then previous hostlers, for there were four rolled pallets against a wall for sleeping, an oversized bed with a multitude of bolsters and an oversized bolster upon which to lay, a small table beholding an unlit taper.

A large hearth in which the making of a fire, had been laid and all it needed was proper encouragement from someone's tinder box.

Aside a shuttered window, was a highly polished looking glass with a pitcher of water and basin below, upon a small stand, with linen kerchiefs folded neatly aside.

Their supper was served, the wine poured then left to their own devices.

"With this kind of hospitality, I certainly hope it will not make us turn our purses inside out to scrape out the remains." Said Porthos, quite concerned.

"Fear not my good man, it will be all well if we arise afore the light of day, leave a doubloon or two, finish off if there are any remains of this, find and tack our horses and we will proceed. My this Anjou is so pleasing to my parched palate." Commented Athos, draining his goblet.

"God in His infinite mercy, will see that we are provided for." Said Aramis, crossing himself after a brief utterance of thankfulness.

Their conversation lacked for they silently thought if they were not so exhausted, they would be more animated and engaging themselves in the games of chance that were occurring in the grand hall.

Alas, it was their choice to abstain in the name of self preservation.

As was decided the eve afore, they rose afore the light of day had a chance to perforate the confines of their chamber.

Indeed the meal from the eve was clearly abundant and they were able to obtain an adequate breakfast afore they began again for their destination of Calais.

Porthos wiped his ponaird's blade across a sleeve and replaced it in top of a boot, then regained his feet.

He retrieved his purse from inside his doublet, untied it and sought two doubloons and laid them upon the table.

"If only all that we had come across had been this accommodating." Sadly Smiled Porthos.

"True enough, alas it is the life chosen for us by Louis in becoming his musketeers. Abide by what is available and make do as meager as it may sometimes get." Said Aramis.

"Sounds more like a monk than a musketeer.", Commented Athos, with an inclined head and a wry smile toying about his countenance.

Once out of doors, they glanced towards the sea in an effort to observe any and all elements.

The draught was coming from the west, thus indicating the day would be cloudless and uneventful.

Porthos and Aramis were going to request different horses, fearing their current ones were nigh spent, alas they could not locate a lackey.

The stable was silent as the occupants dosed comfortably within the confines of the darkness.

Therefore, they all set about re-tacking their animals.

They all had their prospective horse and lead them as silently as they could to the rue that lead towards Rouen.

The rue that ran without constraint, aside the river, led them out of the city.

Indeed the elements held and posed no real threat as they progressed forward and the leagues slipped away into the distance and their past.

When then they were eventually within a days' ride of Calais, on the other side of Rouen, they paused at a small tavern is were they were finally able to get the idea Rohan had actually passed through.

The tavern-keep was jesting with a lackey.

"My, how you were smitten with that Mademoiselle, that passed through a bit ago."

"That was not a "Madamoiselle", t'was a Monsieur, I assure you." The lackey scowled.

"He certainly was hard on the eyes.", laughed the inn-keep.

"Praytell, what did denizens' appearance behold?" Queried Porthos, causally interfering.

"When he stood, it was about to here." Rising his hand to the musketeers' mid-broad chest.

"Needed desperately to seek a barber.", Added the lackey.

The inn-keep shook his head, "Certainly did. His hands were in desperate need of a manicure as well."

"The perfume that was used, smelt as a foregone stable."

They all laughed.

"Such a weak attempt at the concealing the obvious of such."

"The *voc* oh the *voc,* so forced, so unnatural." Added the lackey, "I would be hard pressed to be smitten with that."

"His gait had the appearance of being in the saddle far too long." Concluded the inn-keep, "As his countenance had no favors bestowed upon it and being summoned to court would be unheard of."

"Was his name uttered?" Queried Aramis, hopeful of confirmation.

"When he did speak, he referred to his companion as, Benjamin."

"That is Henri's brother, Duc de Guise." Said Athos, with a *sotto voc.*

"By the by, he was referenced to as Henrietta."

They all laughed.

"How long ago was that?" Queried Athos.

"I remember not. All my days run together and I pay no mind to the days for they are so repetitious. I go about my days with the certainty that nothing will deviate. Left is left and right is right. Now is there something I can do for you?"

Athos stepped forward.

"A chamber of means, the likes of a good supper and a comforts of a stable for the horses."

The inn-keep gestured to three lackeys to take cake of the horses and the lackey he was jesting with, instructed him to provide a chamber for them, then return to the kitchen.

Once settled in their chamber, Porthos with the assistance of his valet, removed his boots and stretched out on the bed.

"Knowingly the minute I dose off, supper will arrived." Commented Porthos.

"Does it not always happen that way?" Queried Athos, unshuttering the window to glance towards the rue, congested with denizens of trade and those seeking the market and other establishments.

Supper, unceremoniously was served and the lackey withdrew to continue his duties elsewhere.

"Do you now think this has been a knights' errand?" Queried Porthos, to no one in particular.

"I am inclined to agree." Said Athos, "Alas, we must continue on to Calais and confirm our suspicions once and for all. The king would never accept an response based on suspicion. Facts I all he cares about."

"We should be in Calais when the sun has reached its zenith on the morrow and we can inquire about and perchance come across Henri." Said Aramis.

"Do you not mean, Henrietta?" Queried Athos, as they all laughed at the thoughts of their adversary, attempting to conceal his identity under a woman's frock.

"If he truly is in London, maybe ol' George Villiers will take a liking to her." Commented Aramis.

Athos inclined his head in inquery.

"The Duke of Buckingham."

"Oh." Replied Athos.

"Only 'til he realizes, Henrietta is a Henri." Said Porthos.

"All that remains to be seen." Said Athos as he drained his goblet.

With their supper eaten, and chosen spots in which they wanted to sleep, they all drifted peacefully off.

Since Athos forgot to shutter the window, the sun took the liberty to fully illuminate the chamber afore the men could protest its presence.

There was light raps upon the door in which Bazin opened it to find a lackey with a small conveying cart laden with breakfast.

"Compliments of my master for he is most ambitious when it comes to supporting the king and his endeavors."

"Who said we are for the king?" Queried Porthos, suspiciously, with an arched brow.

"You had not need too say much. As I could ascertain the difference in that little dolt, I certainly can conclude by conversation what you are about. No references needed." He replied, smiling.

"An attribute?" Queried Athos.

"Most assuredly." The lackey winked, bowed and departed.

They then helped themselves to an abundance sausages, two large geese roasted, brioche breads, cheese, dried dates and poached apples, grapes and pears, wading in a honey laced pool, adorned with cinnamon.

"I say..", began Porthos, even though he had a mouthful of roast goose, "No matter when we arrive in Calais, when find a hostler, secure a chamber, take on a meal, then each with our prospective valet begin to search the city for Rohan."

"Even though our chances of finding him is rather beyond lean." Commented Athos, filling his and his companions' goblets.

"Even so. We have to prove that."

"We forgot to request our horses." Suggested Aramis.

"No matter. Haste is just a word now. When we have finished, we can request them then set out."

XXI

When they had entered the establishments grand hall, the inn-keep readily and enthusiastically greeted the.

"Ah, Messieurs, I trust you enjoyed your meal that I provided."

"Indeed. It was most delectable and appreciated." Replied Porthos.

"What is it request, another day of leisure?" He queried.

"As much as that would be welcomed, alas ne'. We have to continue and are requesting our horses." Interjected Athos.

The inn-keep beckoned his lackey once more and instructed him to ready the horses and so as to not detain them, make haste.

It was not long afore the horses were brought to them and the reins given.

Once in the saddle, Porthos offered to settle the debt they had incurred, alas the inn-refused and simply said, "God speed."

As they turned about, they touched the brims of their caps afore they lightly touched the flanks of their horses to set them in motion.

Their predictions were spot on.

They reached Calais as clocks about the city from various towers peeled the hour of twelve.

"What a welcoming." Smiled Porthos as the sea birds noisily besieged incoming vessels, be it the ferry or one leased by a monger, no matter for they knew not the difference, the quais, were actively receiving and sending goods, the common denizens seeking the markets and establishments and denizens plying their trade to those seeking their assistance, be it an apothecary or lawyer.

"What say you, the first hostler we happen on, we take on a chamber?" Queried Athos.

"I would agree to that. What say you Aramis?" Replied Porthos.

Aramis nodded.

A rather small secluded establishment caught their immediate attention for they did not want the presence to cause concern amoung the denizens.

As the stable lackey received the reins, they were greeted by a slight tavern-keep.

"It really matters not what your kettles behold, bring a fair share of all." Instructed Porthos.

"You certainly care not what a kettle beholds as long as it contains something of substantial worth.", Jested Athos.

Porthos laughed.

"When you are hungry, even your gauntlets have a certain appeal to them."

At that particular time that they were able to sit on something other than their saddles was to their advantage, for it was betwixt dinner and supper. Thus the establishment was nigh empty.

When their meal was served, they inquired after a chamber for the eve, and as for now attend to their horses, alas have them readied for they were going about the city.

"By the By," Inquired Athos, with a newly acquired implement from Italy that had made its debut a month prior and that was a fork.

Although the fork fist made its appearance in Italy in 1608, it took sometime afore its migration brought it to France and beyond as blacksmiths and silversmiths eventually took to the novel idea that there was something more than a knife, ladle and spoon.

"Has a man,". Athos cleared his throat, "A woman, accompanied by two gentlemen, pass through this hostler, making their way to possibly England?"

The inn-keep shook his head.

"Can not recall anyone specific. Many come and go."

"Indeed." Replied Aramis.

The inn-keep retreated to the kitchen to oversee the musketeers' meal preparation.

"Do you trust him?" Queried Porthos, to Athos.

"Why would I not?" Athos replied.

"He is quite slight. I fear his kettle will be in as much want as he is."

"That remains to be seen." Added Aramis.

The valets were quietly conversing as the meal as served and consumed.

As Aramis poured the remains of a bottle into his goblet, the innkeep reappeared.

"I trust everything was to your satisfaction."

They all nodded.

"Are you in need of your horses now?"

Again, they nodded.

"We shall return." They said unison as they went to acquire their horses. "What say you Athos, you begin on the north end then rendezvous at the city' bell tower in the center, I will take the center and the quais." Said Porthos, "…And Aramis the south end."

"Agreed." Replied Athos and Aramis.

"In all reality it would have served us better if we searched all the hostlers as we entered the city, rather double trek." Observed Aramis.

"True enough. Alas we have to be certain. I fear we would have been to hasty, for we were hungry." Said Porthos.

They chuckled realizing the truth in their companions comment.

Porthos and Mousequeton set off behind the hostler as Bazin and Aramis retreated to the south end erstwhile Athos and Grimaud to the north and then rendezvous at the clock

Yes Calais has its share of hostlers and inns, but with the three dividing the set task it did not as long.

As Athos and Grimaud rounded a corner, Grimaud so abruptly brought his horse to a halt, that Athos nearly collided with his master.

'What gives?" Queried Athos sternly.

Grimaud pointed in the direction of a richly decorated carriage in which Athos recognized immediately belonging to none other than the Cardinal.

"By Jove! Why is he here?" He muttered. "Only one way to find out. Confront the man. As for now, if Rohan is here he clearly will have nothing to do with Richelieu for he represents the king. Most of the time, except when he has a selfish tantrum and only thinks of himself. I therefore doubt seriously that Rohan is here." He continued.

Porthos and Mousequeton after they had finished their surveyance of their given sector, they say on the edge of a fountain close by.

Without warning, Mousequeton roughly nudged his master.

In so doing, he nearly knock Porthos off center and cause him to fall backwards into the fountain.

"What gives?" Queried Porthos.

"I do believe I saw MonsieurJussac."

"Again, what does he have to do with the pursuit of Rohan? The king enlisted our assistance since we are his musketeers. Not Jussac and his hoard of careless men."

As the clock struck the hour of six, Aramis made is appearance and with Bazins' assistance he was able to regain his feet, then strode over and sat next to his hefty companion.

"I have nothing to relay except that Mousequeton thinks he saw Jussac."

Aramis laughed.

"He turns up at the oddest times and places."

"That he does. Now, if he only t'were worth what his wage dictates."

As the days' light began to fade, Athos and Grimaud arrived.

"Ah my dear companions, there is a mystery about." He said.

"Why say you such?" Inquired Porthos.

"North, near a quai mooring a caravel, a discreet *petit* hostler, and Richelieu's carriage."

Porthos glanced at his valet and shrugged and said, "Perchance you did see Jussac."

"Why would he be here? Certainly leaves a lot to be desired.", Mumbled Athos.

"What do you suggest we do?" Queried Aramis.

"For the moment, nothing. In the morn, we shall seek counsel with him and see if and how we are to proceed. No doubt Louis has instructions he wants us to adhere to." Suggested Porthos, "I will send Mousequeton first thing requesting such."

As the continued to converse, the eve befell them and the brazier-keep began his rounds.

In the coolness of the sea air, they chose to amble towards the hostler.

They then again left their horses in care of the stable lackey.

"Gentlemen, we have forgotten the outcome of the rumour that he has passed into England.", Suggested Porthos.

"The quais is a rather short distance from here, we can go and inquire and thus if anyone should inquire we will have a reply ready."

They turned about and headed for the quai that moored the ferries.

At the quai, the master of the ferry was perusing the manifest and seeking his passengers amoung the stacked barrels and crates.

"Monsieur, are you the master of the ferry?", Queried Porthos.

"Indeed. What is it you are inquiring?" He inquired in return.

"To be perfectly honest, I know not when precisely, alas approximately a fortnight or so ago, three denizens possibly passed through here wanting to go to England. One is extremely unlikely to being a true woman."

The ferry master, pondered for a brief moment then said, "Ah, indeed there have many that have passed through." He paused again, then said, "There was in fact one with a truly suspicious nature. Did not have the attributions of a woman. She or he, or whatever, was very hard on the eyes and soul."

"Did they cross?"

"I believe they did."

"Did they return?"

The ferry master slowly shook his head.

"Did any call out a name?" Queried Athos, trying desperately not to yawn.

"As they walked the gangplank to board, the wind picked up, a storm was hastily approaching as they so often do. We blame England for the ill humoured elements. Have to blame them for something, do we not?" Inquired the ferry master, with a lop sided grin.

"Not unless you want them to pick an uneven skirmish.", Replied Athos.

"Name?", Prompted Porthos.

"Ah yes, one beckoned another as, "Henrietta." Her reply, she was an agreeement with a, "Benjamin.""

All three simultaneously sighed they realized their adversary had been able to slip through the fissures of society and no doubt while in England convince Buckingham, it would be in Englands' best interest to assist in the reconstruction of La Rochelle and aid in the re-arming it with munitions as well.

"Merci Monsieur, adieu"

XXII

The inn-keeps preferred lackey met them in the foyer and escorted them to the chosen chamber.

The fire in the hearth had been started to dry out the dampness the sea created and warm their weary souls.

"Will you see to it a couple of bottles of wine, some cheese and some bread?" Queried Porthos, "Oh, and a couple of dice."

The lackey bowed slightly and departed.

"Do we dare pursue him?" Queried Porthos.

"Only if we want a dousing. I do know, the channel and its waters are totally unpredictable, even on the stillness of days.", Replied Athos.

They then arranged themselves in from of the warming flames, chaffing their hands.

"How peculiar is it that Richelieu happens to be here as well.", Observed Aramis.

"Indeed. Perchance he got word that Rohan is here and he wants to take recognition for his apprehension." Theorized Porthos.

"I would not doubt that is what he is doing. An attention grabbing reprobate.", Muttered Athos.

"It truly makes me wonder what he is about?" Sighed Aramis.

Porthos was about to comment, when a rap came upon there chamber door.

They glanced at each other.

"Mousequeton, if you will. Do not keep whoever it is, waiting. It is rather inconsiderate."

Mousequeton opened the door to find a page in court attire, waiting to hand him a folded piece of parchment, sealed with the cardinals' insignia.

Mousequeton then gave it to Porthos, who scrutinized it and as he turned it over to get thoughts as to who sent it, he gasped.

"What gives?" Queried Aramis.

"Just how does he know we are here when we have not seen the likes him?", Queried the portly musketeer, "That is uncanny."

"If you do not break the seal and open it to read its contents, we will never know what his demands are." Commented Athos.

Porthos then broke the seal and read the contents.

"In short, he knows we are here and is requesting a counsel at six in the morn."

"So much for leisure.", commented Athos.

"How about a game of *des,* and enjoy the wine?" Porthos queried.

"I would enjoy it better if it were present." Said Athos.

As Aramis regained his feet to add a log to the heath, another rap was bestowed upon the door.

"Ask and you shall receive." Smiled Aramis.

The lackey was carrying a tray laden with the request.

He set it down upon a small table and as he was departing, "We are requesting to be awaken by five and the half way mark." Requested Aramis.

The lackey bowed curtly and departed.

They chose to forego gaming, have some wine, then seek sleep for the early morn was never that far off.

In the morn as they were awaken by the valet, they had a bit of difficulty getting their boots on for their feet having been freed from the constrictions of the boot they tried to refuse re-admittance to the confines.

"Not too much to persuade you with.", chided Porthos, in addressing his feet.

Frustrating as it was, they all succeeded in getting their feet in their boots.

Their horses were ready when they were and then set off for the given establishment that accommodated the Cardinal.

"He had better be a gracious host and offer breakfast.", Grumbled Athos.

Entering the hostler, all was still, save two guards in front of a corridor.

"Apparently this where he and his entourage is. A point we can not return from.", Commented Porthos.

"Yes we could for he knows not that we arrived.", Said Athos.

"He knows everything." Sighed Aramis.

"I do not see Jussac." Observed Porthos.

"Fortunate you.", Wryly smiled Athos.

A guard stepped forward and said, "He is expecting you."

"I am sure he is.", Added Athos.

The guard opened the door and allowed them admittance then stepped aside.

The Cardinal was gazing out the glass doors of the balcony that gave a panoramic view of the sea, hands clasped behind his back.

As he turned about he gestured for them to help themselves to breakfast that he was providing.

"Good to see you gentlemen, breakfast awaits you." He said as he picked up his goblet of wine with Vitray at his elbow offering him a small plate of grapes and dates.

As he sat down, the others accepted their given seats and sat down on the worn upholstered chairs.

A blessing was was offered, followed by a chorus of, "Amens".

"Tell me your Eminence, how is it you are here as well?" Queried Aramis, taking a sip of the gold colored wine.

"I was given knowledge that this is where he is and I came to make him an offer if he ceased his activities."

"Unfortunately, we inquired after him within all the hostler, taverns and inns, alas to no avail." Informed Porthos.

"Rumour has it, he was going to cross the channel into England to solicit the assistance of Buckingham.", Said Aramis.

"Did you go to the quais and the ferries and inquire after him?"

The three toyed with the poached grapes upon their plates.

"Indeed we did." Hesitated Porthos.

"…And the results are?...."

"He managed to cross over to England.", Said Aramis.

"There is not a whole lot to say concerning this, except we tried.", Sighed Porthos

The Cardinal regained his feet and strode over to the doors once again, glanced to the open sea and paused.

"I know. You are expecting retribution, a barrage of harsh words, and a tirade. Alas what good would that do? What is done, is done.", The Cardinal said as he returned to the table and re-seated himself.

"You have not failed. It was a hardy attempt at an impossible situation. Let the king hear me not that I uttered such.", Chuckled the Cardinal. "Alas you have done what the king requested. It was nigh impossible from the beginning to apprehend him, considering he had almost a fortnight and a half advance. The king is short sighted whereas he expects to have reliable accurate results when he gives instructions even if there is not adequate allowed time to accomplish his requests."

The small band of men silently finished their meal and regained their feet as well as the Cardinal once again.

"Gather your belongings and go home, to Paris. I will follow shortly and hold counsel with the king and no doubt he will want to hold counsel with all of you as well."

Without being too obvious as the others made their way to the door, Athos grabbed the Cardinals' palm and as he pressed it, he drew the Cardinal close and with a *sotto voc* said, "God be with you."

Printed in the United States
By Bookmasters